Robert Elegant

The Seeking

Penguin Books

Penguin Books Ltd, Harmondsworth, Middlesex, England
Penguin Books, 625 Madison Avenue, New York, New York 10022, U.S.A.
Penguin Books Australia Ltd, Ringwood, Victoria, Australia
Penguin Books Canada Ltd, 2801 John Street, Markham, Ontario, Canada L3R 1B4
Penguin Books (N.Z.) Ltd, 182–190 Wairau Road, Auckland 10, New Zealand

First published in the U.S.A. by Funk & Wagnalls 1969
Published in Penguin Books 1982

Filmset, printed and bound in Great Britain by
Hazell Watson & Viney Ltd, Aylesbury, Bucks
Set in VIP Times Roman

For L. E. (1898–1965)

Forenote

The white spire of the Bodinath stupa strives Heavenward above a medieval maze where dingy houses of wood and stone lean wearily toward each other and cast everlasting twilight on the narrow street below. Bewildered on the slime-coated cobblestones of the maze, the pilgrim loses all sight of his goal: the soaring shrine beneath which lie a few hairs from the head of the Gautama Buddha who attained Nirvana almost two and a half millennia ago. The faith that sustained the pilgrim during his arduous journey south through the mountains to Kathmandu, the navel of the holy land of Nepal, wavers in the fetid gloom, although the Tantric Buddhism he professes springs from the perpetual conflict between light and darkness. But his faith leaps up strong when he emerges from the artificial twilight and once again beholds the Bodinath, dazzling in a broad circle of sunlight.

Although I had not come as a pilgrim and I had flown north above the mountains in the relative comfort of a venerable Dakota of the Indian Airways Corporation, I too felt the hand of awe upon my shoulder when I first saw the Bodinath close on a spring morning in 1956. The great eyes painted on the faces of the massive obelisk stared unwinking into the white glare of the sun's rays cast back by the snow-draped flanks of the Himalayas. An iridescent fringe of light – red, yellow, and blue – shimmered upward from the low wall that surrounded the stupa. The curtain of color rose from the restless play of the sunlight upon the semiprecious stones studding the heavy gilt-and-ivory prayer wheels set at close intervals atop the wall. Walking briskly around the shrine, the pilgrims spun the prayer wheels with the flat of their hands to send their automatic prayers soaring toward Heaven on shafts of light as a small boy draws a stick along a picket fence to call forth the clatter that exalts his soul. For a few enraptured minutes the Buddhist ideal of enlightenment was a visible reality of freshness and brilliance and pellucid color.

I returned to the reality of my own purpose when I stooped through a low, narrow doorway into the smoke-laden dusk of the pilgrims' inn, which lay just outside the great circle of light. For a moment I stood blind in the darkness, my stomach rising at the stench of bodies unwashed for years, all clothed in half-cured sheepskins steeped in human sweat and rancid butter since they were first put on. The smell of Tibetans is unique and quite unmistakable. I knew that I had come to the place appointed for my rendezvous with a group of Tibetan refugees from Chinese Communist rule of their homeland. The meeting had been arranged for a small fee by the monk who presided over the shrine. The Nepalis called him the Chini Lama, meaning the Chinese Monk, though I thought of him as the American Lama because of his brisk, businesslike ways and the zippered pockets in his traditional crimson robes. Sight returning slowly, I saw five Tibetan men squatting around a small fire, roasting chunks of lamb. One spoke in broken Chinese, and I knew he was the interpreter the Chini Lama had promised.

We talked for hours that day, although my head ached from the stench and the pots of chang – beer almost as strong as spirits – I bought our company from the inn-keeper, an evil-visaged Tibetan, who was squat and smoke-begrimed as one of the devils of his own dark pantheon. I learned much of the manner of the Chinese 'liberators' in Tibet and of the fierce – if futile – resistance offered by the Tibetans under the leadership of a Buddhist church which, having its origins in a movement of social protest and political reform, had through the centuries become the master and the champion of a fossilized social order whose ritualized injustice was nonetheless benign in comparison with the violent changes the Chinese wrought. All I learned that day is now a matter of public knowledge. Indeed, the early contention between Tibetans and Chinese today appears pallid compared to the ferocity of their later strife.

When I was about to leave, the interpreter pulled a small packet of papers from the pouched breast of his sheepskin robe.

'What are these worth to you?' he asked hopefully.

Shuffling the documents, I saw a few single sheets in Tibetan. 'Broadsides of the Resistance Movement,' he explained.

A tattered booklet, I later learned, was a modern reproduction of one of the *Sutras*, and I recognized an issue of the Chinese-language *Tibetan Liberation Daily*, as well as a few administrative orders in Chinese. A booklet in Chinese, called *Ku-tai Ku-shih* (*Tales of Antiquity*), seemed of no particular interest, though it was thrown in for the equivalent in Nepali rupees of ten dollars I finally paid for the lot. It may have been our imperfect communication or the working of the chang, but I felt that the Tibetan was being deliberately vague as to where he had acquired the cache. Finally gaining the impression that the documents had come from a lamasery destroyed by the Chinese, I asked no more.

The modern documents were immediately useful, and the others I put aside. I had forgotten about the *Tales of Antiquity* until I sorted my papers after moving from New Delhi to Hong Kong in the autumn of 1957. I put the booklet between the bookends on my desk, but it was not until the middle of 1958 that I finally examined it at leisure.

It was not at all what I had expected from its outward appearance. It was not a printed work, but a manuscript, the Chinese characters brushed so meticulously they seemed printed. It was not a retelling of familiar stories from Chinese mythology or ancient history, but an account of a specific episode, which at first I found almost impossible to extract from the highly elided classical Chinese.

The manuscript, written on remarkably thin and strong paper, was much longer than it had first appeared, and it was studded with transliterations of proper names and terms from other languages. It took some time to grasp the gist of the manuscript, which was torn or defaced in a number of places. The miracle, of course, was that it had been preserved at all, despite the arid climate and the ritual care given all printed matter in Tibet.

Finding assistance in Hong Kong, I was finally able to decipher the document. Further examination by specialists elsewhere might have amplified the meaning, but unfortunately a fire in my home in late 1959 destroyed the original manuscript, leaving only my voluminous and detailed notes. It was determined before the manuscript's destruction that it dated from about 1500, and that it had apparently been copied from an older Chinese manuscript. The account translated into Chinese had, it appeared, originally been written in a mixture of Sanskrit and Turkyi, with some Greek words interlarded. I believe the first version was translated from a much older original manuscript by order of some Chinese official who was deeply concerned with Central Asia, perhaps during the splendid Tang Dynasty, which ruled China from A.D. 618 to 907 and greatly extended the frontiers of the Empire.

The manuscript that came into my hands was undoubtedly corrupt, for it showed traces of Moslem and other influences that could obviously not have been present at the time with which it dealt. I have, however, followed the manuscript – or, more correctly, my notes – as closely as possible, eliminating only the most glaring anachronisms. Proper names I have reproduced as best I could, following the transliterations. Since I am not a specialist in either the period or the area, errors have undoubtedly persisted. I felt, however, that it was better to convey the spirit of the original without striving for absolute historical accuracy, which is, in any event, unattainable since our information on Central Asia at the presumed time of the events is fragmentary.

The manuscript was the record of an expedition that rode across the heart of Central Asia about 100 B.C., if my dating is correct. The small state of Kamardol, a kingdom lying to the north and west of present-day Kashmir, was impelled by great pride and by internal intrigue to revive the Quest of the Sanctified Horse, which I have called the Seeking. That practice, already half-forgotten at the time of the tale, was a vestige of Vedic days when the Aryans came to India. Though all its records but this one have vanished, Kamardol appears to have been an Aryan kingdom with strong Greek and Central Asian strains in its blood and culture. The men who rode behind the Sanctified Horse were themselves the products of a confluence of races. Because great historical forces were meeting in Central Asia at the time, the expedition encountered representatives of a number of major civilizations, themselves all in flux, either creative or decadent.

The reader may be surprised, as I have been, by the incongruous elements that appear in the account. Naïveté that is quite extraordinary, though perhaps to be anticipated, stands beside a total cynicism that is astonishing to modern minds. The extent and accuracy of psychological, geographical, and medical knowledge is particularly startling and originally aroused my fears that the account had been much altered in transmission. I have, however, been assured that the Aryan culture of the time had in truth attained a remarkably high standard of knowledge in such matters. I have employed modern terms and thus, perhaps, rendered some concepts with more precision than they originally possessed. Since modern English is a more flexible means of expression than was either the original bastard Sanskrit or classical Chinese, some distortion was unavoidable. There are, however, today – as there were then – men who believe that they are charged with portentous missions, either by divine command or by the immutable logic of progress, whether they call themselves the scourges of God or the locomotives of history. It is hard to say that they are either wholly right or utterly mistaken.

It seems to me vain to dwell on either the similarities or the discrepancies between the last Seeking of Kamardol and events in our own time. The adventures of the warriors of Kamardol seeking a greater place in the world and the favor of their Gods for their realm are no more than a glimpse of an epoch that has almost totally vanished from recorded history. Their quest into the unknown, though perhaps foolhardy, was one of the last trumpet blasts of the springtime of the world. Superstitious, cruel, and bloody, it rings with the raw vigor of youth all mankind knew before mankind grew old.

Book One

One

We rode two hours beyond the crest of night before we crossed
the first stream in thaw. The Horse, still coltlike, half at war with
his own tendons, stumbled against the slick boulders when the
torrent from the glaciers caught his ankles. But my pony and
Harrap's closed in unbidden on either side, as if already sworn to
the mission, and we came into Kamardol, the New Land, three
abreast and all erect.

I heard Harrap speak across the night and glanced at his
ravaged profile, a black and secret silhouette against the dim
radiance cast upward by the snow. A net of stars spanned the
dome of night, hanging in sky-sweeping folds from the cold, new
moon.

'If we could only lay a thong across this Godlet's neck,' Harrap
rumbled, 'the road would be smoother – and faster, too.'

'And the journey, perhaps, ended before it was begun,' I
replied, my voice rising over the rasping of the tired horses'
hooves on the crust of the snow. I was but half aware that my
words carried behind us, where I heard the priest moving up. He
gasped like a heavy-burdened porter toiling through the throngs
of the bazaar at the dry peak of summer, though we three were
all alone in the white wind.

Harrap fell silent, plaiting his rawhide reins around his broad
knuckles. But I knew the priest had marked his complaint,
comprehended if only from my own piping reply. I was afraid
then for Harrap, with his pride of place so fierce it would burst
his heart if he were set down. I was afraid for myself, who loved
Harrap well, but myself so much more, and him best when he
was defeated. I feared that I might someday seek to strike him
down so that I could give him succor.

The priest offered us no words when he came up to us, where

we had halted obedient to an unspoken command to make the last descent to home all together. He sat silent in his saddle, peering down into the valley as though his eyes could pierce the night and the clouds that lay over the City.

'This is not the time,' he had told me, even before we set out, 'for seeking to plumb the will of the Gods so that we may serve Them better. This is only our time for moving before Their will as weathers float on the winds.'

Mocking his silent rapture, the priest's breath surged through his mouth in harsh gasps. The rasping rhythm was broken by a sharp outrush of air when pain twisted its hooks in his bowels. The Gods had wreaked Their will upon him during the three months since we rode out from Kamardol, which the men of our race have called the New Land for generations beyond my counting. I wondered again whether he had sought with herbs to alter Their decree for him of unremitting dysentery, but once again I did not dare to ask.

'The night breaks early here, as if to lead us on!' The priest's deep, prophetic tones were the voice of the night, and the sweep of his bony hand encompassed the dim horizon. He gazed toward the valley, his hooded eyes searching through the clinging darkness and the mist, avid for half-melted patches where moss might show dark through the shallow snow. Those patches would offer green promise of the warmth his racked body craved, though his spirit, I sometimes feared, could ride on forever.

Across the broad river basin, which was a monstrous trough heaped with clouds, we saw the first light caress the far rim of mountains a hundred miles to the east. As we cantered toward the oncoming sun, the pale ribbon of luminescence lying on the peaks unfolded into a broad crimson sash encrusted with shining gold and the brilliance of rubies. Drinking strength from the imminent dawn, the priest gave up his silence. He spoke, perforce, of kings and empires and doctrines, not of his pain-knifed bowels.

'We have, after much hardship,' he declaimed to the cold hills, his sonority marred equally by the rasping of pain and the throbbing of joy, 'come again to the Valley of Pragpati, where we shall begin.'

Harrap swung startled in his saddle, then shrugged his shoulders in irritable understanding and turned to the east again.

'We have come twice ten thousand leagues over the ice-white teeth of the world, moving lightly across glaciers and through mountain forests like feathers borne forward by His . . . by Their favor. We have been preserved from the ferocity of savages and from the soft corruption of the wicked cities set amid the sands. We have been drawn on by the will of the Gods incarnate in this horse-like creature that is Their vehicle, that is the animate expression of Their will and Himself a God – all the Gods – as well. We shall do great deeds in Their name, slaying multitudes and bringing our armored hosts to glory beyond any the world has seen. We have come again to the Valley of Pragpati, which is our beginning.'

Harrap's shoulders twitched in anger, the gesture so fleeting even I was almost deceived into believing it no more than a suppressed shiver. It was hardly time to glory in the final grand assaults when we had not yet mounted the first, nor even received the golden threads dedicating us to the Seeking. It was likely that we should be chosen, but it was by no means certain. Musing unfettered, I loosed all the fears I had so long held in check. I would not rejoice until I had heard from Tamar what intrigue had coursed through palace and temple since our departure. Nor could we hope for an armored host, but no more than a thousand archers in padded-leather coats, if fortune cast for us.

Once more the priest raised his arm against the empty dawn, as if to invoke in that instant an army all in steel. But his mood altered in the instant before he spoke, and he relaxed the prophetic posture that woke such silent fury in my Harrap.

'When shall we arrive?' he asked, an old man longing for rest. 'What lies before us?'

'It still lacks three hours of full dawn,' answered Harrap, speaking for the first time since I had chided him beside the stream. 'From here, if I remember right, it is but two hours to the ford, where we could camp for the morning and rest the beasts. From the ford, perhaps three hours to the Towers . . . but we have been riding all night.'

'Not to the ford,' the priest commanded. 'Not to the ford, where men would see us and carry the word . . .'

'And where we might hear some word of what has passed in our absence,' I interrupted.

The priest's dark glare reproached me for my eagerness and for the worldliness his persistent counsel had still not suppressed.

'Not to the ford,' he repeated. 'We will camp just below the snow line, where no men stray. We shall ride through the night tomorrow, coming upon the Towers and the City with the next dawn.'

'And keep ourselves so much longer from news of the City,' I objected, 'and from learning whether the Old King still lives and our journey has been in vain.'

'By Vishnu's bones,' Harrap's words overtook my own to taunt the priest, 'it is simple foolishness to keep the beasts from their stables another night. And it is wanton cruelty to keep us from the curry kettles and the wine goblets, and someone's soft bed and softer arms.'

'What is ordained will be,' the priest reminded me, strangely gentle. Staring with remote distaste at Harrap, he said, 'It were best if you waited forever, but it will be that much better if you wait another day before sotting your flesh. And my own so worn I can barely ride, but still I will wait upon His . . . upon Their will.'

'I am appointed chief of the march,' Harrap said, 'and I . . .'

But the priest's voice was already cutting across my own. I could tell from his shallow breathing that the pain was once more within him. His tone half querulous and half portentous, he said, 'And I am appointed to heed Their will. The Horse shall decide.'

I unlocked my own eyes from their angry eyes. His tail switching gently, the Horse grazed where a few spears of grass stood green below the snow line.

'His will is Theirs,' the priest intoned. 'We shall come upon the City tomorrow, riding to the Towers out of the morning clouds.'

Two

For all his hungry words, Harrap slept long before the priest and I found rest or the horses gave up their quest for fresh grass. His weary breathing soughed like the wind among the dunes of the desert. I plucked my lute within my nest of cloaks, and the soft chords glowed with the warmth of home. Harrap and I lay beside each other with the priest, as always, a dozen paces away. Even in sleep he kept his distinction from the soldier and the scribe. Between his racking breaths he crooned a Veda too low for me to make out the words.

When the priest's prayers at length ceased, I lay awake alone, watching the dawn besiege our coign between two great rocks. The horses were humped hillocks in the haze, our three mounts and the pack beast hobbled. The Colt circled the stolid four uneasily, His bright flanks and ice-white mane a crystal of pure light flickering through the gray dawn.

With his grumbling consent to the delay, Harrap had put forward his accustomed argument, more it seemed from habit than conviction – or any hope of convincing.

'Why not,' he had asked, 'lace a hobble round the Godlet's forelegs and save ourselves a search tomorrow?'

'Would you dare,' the priest's habitual reply had come, 'to hobble the will of the Gods? Would a thousand hobbles, each a thousand tempered links, hold this One if He would stray?'

'We are not yet dedicated,' Harrap snapped, though repetition had rubbed all meaning from his words. 'The Spirit has not yet entered. He is but a candidate, still a horse that can wear a hobble and save our steps.'

Then the familiar climax of our nightly litany, the priest's indignation still searing as it had at the start: 'But He will be chosen, for I can read the signs your head, thickened by the helmet's weight, cannot comprehend. I break the grains of truth between my molars and place them in your mouth as a mother softens the wheat for her baby, but still you cannot taste the truth. This Seeking will be perfect. Only a fool would now mar perfection out of laziness.'

'He will not stray this night in the wilderness, but will stay with His companions,' I had offered, weary of the flow of empty words.

As I spoke I heard Harrap, abashed once more, mutter the Soldier's Prayer and begin to snore. Harrap, who had so much more to gain than we two men of words, would not desecrate his own fate. Yet, I recalled, the priest had himself tied the hobble during the first week, when we rode on the edges of the Colt's familiar grazing grounds. Once again I wondered for what stakes the priest played. Chewing the well-worn puzzle, I fell into sleep, my fingers still on the strings of my lute.

I woke at noon. The priest was already trudging up the slope to the stream, where he would wash and pray. The bent back had hardly hobbled out of hearing when Harrap's plaint burst forth again. Though he lay among his cloaks on the soft moss, a grin of ease upon his fleshy lips, his voice was fierce – when it was not bewildered.

'Read me, Yakir,' he asked, 'the riddle of this mad priest. A man faster to force an omen I have never seen, but he will not let me hobble this Godlet of his. We have lost weeks through his stubbornness, perhaps forfeiting our chance.'

'Many weeks – and twenty good men,' I reminded him.

'Yes, the men too,' he agreed sadly, 'whom we could hardly spare. And why? Just the fantasies of one mad priest, who would, in the beginning, have bound the Colt in a web of ropes and hurled Him on His back rather than He should flee back to His herd.'

'Be patient still, Harrap,' I counseled. 'We shall yet have need of the priest in the City. We cannot yet cut the thongs that bind our fates.'

'Perhaps,' he conceded. 'But where lies his holiness that mocks the true path of sacrifice? A white stallion, the Brahmayanas declare, born in the King's own herds within the King's own fields. But we have journeyed to Ferghana – and beyond – to find a colt of an alien strain. What virtue lies in this – and what advancement?'

'You know we could find no horse within the King's domains, when the Old King loves only his own ease. The priest has promised that our Seeking shall be the mightiest of all, because the Horse was sought afar and not merely given.'

'I know his promises,' Harrap grumbled. 'But I do not see the sense. A hobble is a small thing that cannot strain the great chain. Fate can work through men's own hands. But an alien Horse, that is a big thing.'

'I cannot read the riddle – yet,' I answered softly, for the priest's stooped figure was a black shepherd's crook wavering toward us across the white snow.

We talked little that afternoon. The priest lay apart, gazing at the purple and white peaks we had crossed, as if to read the future from the past. But his silent presence, though a hundred paces distant, hobbled Harrap's tongue as his sour reproaches had not. My friend – this prince of the third order whom a scribe might call friend – was stung by fear of what we might find when we came to the City. For myself, I was content with the delay, the moment suspended between two strophes of violent action. When we came to the City, I should probably cry hardest after news, but the forced repose left my mind as well as my body at rest.

All that afternoon and evening I lay among my cloaks, strumming my lute and mouthing the love songs of the City, which lay just beyond the verge of sight. The sun, storming out of the east, had harried the mist ghosts from the slopes, but a froth of clouds still roofed the chasmed valley. For all the eye could see we still lay in the wilderness, remote alike from the sorrows and the splendors of the cities of men. For a time my despairing spirit sank into a vision of the Horse, the priest, and myself driven forever across the high, frozen mountains and through the endless, molten days of the broad deserts. Harrap was strangely absent from the vision.

As the afternoon shadows spilled into lakes of blackness

between the crags, I knew that Harrap was right and the priest indeed mad. I saw our quest spoiled before its start by his desecration of the plain decree of the Brahmayanas. I was bidding farewell to Tamar and the City, my hand uninstructed plucking a dirge from my lute, when the evening wind cleft the clouds and, for the space of two heartbeats, the red-sandstone Towers rose ponderous above the wheat-feathered fields. Beyond the Towers the City's iridescent glory was bound by chains of gold. I knew then that triumph would crown our quest.

Yet I was oddly reluctant to unwind my cocoon of cloaks and mount when the sun swept westward toward the wild lands where we had found the Horse. When Harrap mounted, I would have held off this first test if I could. I would have been content to ride weeks longer through the unsettled wastes, troubled only by the squabbles between Harrap and the priest.

The glittering points of the stars still lay in their sheaths, and the night was black as we picked our way down the slope, almost losing the trail where the stunted pines began. But Harrap's remarkable sense of the right road quickened as the air became warmer, and we came to the river within the two hours he had promised.

Our way dipped abruptly to the broad and shallow ford. The placid summer pool we had left behind us months earlier was vanished. Speckled and brown trout jumped among the rocks, and the white water, fresh from mountain streams, stung like hail pellets when the horses splashed. Though we curled our legs around our pommels, a thousand claws of ice seeped through the felt we had bound around our legs against the winds of the high plateaux. The Horse hung back, perhaps scenting His fate. Harrap and I rode wide circles around Him, urging Him onward with shouts, but never touching Him. The priest was silent.

I heard myself humming and let the words roll out. Harrap joined in the braggart chant of 'The Warriors' Return':

> We have drawn a curtain of fears
> Between this bright City and the foes of the King.
> We have borne the magic power of his ring
> To the skybound cave, where the years

22

Lie sleeping till the earth, their dam,
Wakes each – to rule and to die.

We have affrighted the big-horned ram,
Hurtling down on his peak from the sky.
Ten thousand times ten thousand leagues away,
The blue-veined glaciers echo still
The awesome clatter of the red-blood-flowing
    fray,
That broke the savage tribes to our Lord's will.

Oh, you maidens of Kamardol,
The warriors return from the kill!
Hear, you slow townsmen's wives,
The warriors return from the kill!
Bearing, empouched, ten thousand foemen's lives
To lay between your soft thighs,
And breed up more warriors still!
The warriors return from the kill!

Our last glad shout shattered against the silent stars, and the priest complained behind us, 'Enough, you young asses. Would you alarm the ferryman?'

Eager for a greeting, longing even for the welcome a villein could give us in our own tongue, we would indeed have awakened the ferryman. But when we came to the far bank and rose dripping from the dark water, the cleft of his cave gaped black. The straw mat that served him as a door lay on the dew-rimed earth, and no fire glowed within.

'No matter,' Harrap laughed, 'the kerl has crept away from his post this night. We will soon come upon the Guardians of the Ford, and all this creeping secrecy will be done.'

'Then watch your tongues,' the priest charged us.

'Be easy, old man, we speak as we agreed,' Harrap answered, grave for an instant.

We followed the path for half an hour, avid for the sounds of men. But the night was silent around us, even when we came to the highroad laid with irregularly hewn blocks of pink stone. It was named the Chandrarajpath to commemorate the founder of the Dynasty. But the children called it Alexander's Road, after the Great Conqueror who had taken that straight course like a spear shaft to the Indus.

My hand strayed of its own will to the leather pouch at my belt. I remembered my ayah threatening that Alexander – Iskandar, she called him – would gallop again down that road, his blond footmen following at the trot, to snatch me away if I did not drink my milk. I had always wanted to throw my cup from me to invoke his presence, but I had never dared. My blind fingers searched the pouch and closed on the rough-hammered silver of the coin. They traced the imprint of the Conqueror's head, unhelmed and lifted to the sky, the fleshy column of his throat rising from the neckpiece of his armor. I had found the coin myself when I was just ten and my father, being on a survey, had taken me with him to the hillock overlooking the village still called Alexander's Rest. It was my first treasure – and still my most prized.

Against clouds streaked white by the new moon, the hillock rose again before my eyes and, to the right, the cubelike houses of Alexander's Rest, the unchanging baked clay and pink stone. Harrap looked at me in puzzled silence. We should long since have been challenged by the patrols of the Guardians of the Ford. But soldiers had slept on guard before. We forgot our care when the horses began to trot toward the scent of the places of men – and the memory of warm stables with abundant fodder. The Colt hung back a moment before tossing His heels and chasing after His fellows. I heard the barking of dogs, and lean black shapes drifted out of the village to lope baying alongside the road just beyond the cast of stones.

The breeze was burdened with the scent of pepper, coriander, mustard, and new-baked bread. We let the eager horses gallop; we were ourselves more eager than the beasts, yearning to see the faces of men of our own race and to hear the singing syllables of our own tongue. Even the priest forgot his pain and gave his mare her head. We came to the first huts at a mad gallop, a squadron of cavalry in full charge with penhons streaming, our valor heralded only by the dogs.

No lanterns flared, and no pillow-tousled heads popped through the narrow clefts in the thick walls. I thought I saw a bent crone disappear around a corner, but it may have been a trick of the moonlight. Alexander's Rest lay in the pale light, silent and empty as if the villagers had risen from their unfinished meal to flee before an invader. Harrap rattled his sword against his pommel, and I dismounted to thrust a door open with the haft of my javelin. There was no one within, though the ashes in the clay hearth were still warm.

'Our humble thanks, O Mighty Ones, for this sign of grace!' The priest's whisper rang in our bewildered silence.

'More like a catastrophe,' Harrap snorted. 'Let us ride. The Towers lie near by, and the Towers *must* be manned.'

The dogs saw us out of the village, the boldest yapping at the horses' hooves while the rest sang of their triumph until Harrap, exasperated, spitted a rough-haired hound on his javelin. The chorus scampered from their comrade's wail of anguish as he was hurled beneath the horses' hooves. We heard the dogs baying their way back to the village, where no human ear heard their proud report of yet another invader repelled. I shivered and drew my cloak around my shoulders and throat. Though the night air, even at the beginning of the valley, was warmer than we had known for months, the chill of the mountains lingered in my veins.

The crescent moon, a sliver thicker than the night before, shone clear of the mist and cloud that had been drawn away in the wake of the departing sun. The starlight was bright and hard. We swept between fields of amber wheat, the bearded shafts rising higher than our heads and sculpted like cameos by the light of the mock day. Broad white faces hung over hedges and mild eyes peered at us as the curious bullocks stirred in their wallows. Though we slowed to a steady canter, villages rose before us and receded ever faster, flawed pearls strung ever closer upon the strand of Alexander's Road. Each village turned out its guard of curs to curse us on our way. We heard no human voice and we saw no cooking fires.

The land embraced us with its abundance of grain and fruit and beasts, but it was barren of men. Each crazy pavingstone and each time-twisted dwelling was woven into the fabric of our lives. This fair valley of Kamardol was the goal toward which we had yearned through the slow, cruel months. And we found it as empty as if eighteen Hells had cast their devils into Kamardol to harry men and women and children before their flaming lances like bullocks to the knackers.

The priest chanted a hollow prayer of propitiation. Yet Harrap grinned at me, his teeth flashing beneath his shattered nose, and shouted with stubborn good cheer, 'We are almost upon the Towers. And the Towers must be manned.'

Our horses' pace slackened to mount a sharp incline, and the Towers stood before us. They rose in an instant out of the rolling countryside, a paling of brown fangs stretching to the horizon on either side to guard the soft delights of the City. Raj Chandra, the first builder, had cunningly traced the undulations of the land and set the Towers so that they would spring up from the empty fields to awe the City's returning sons and affright its enemies. He had raveled the highroad into a web of narrow paths that coiled through the hillocks so that all travelers rode in single file under the eyes of the Guardians of the Towers before they finally came to the weathered foundations.

Prudently I struck up 'The Wayfarers' Return,' striking my lute hard. Even the priest joined in the chorus of the pacific song, so different from 'The Warriors' Return':

> We have come from afar,
> Longing for our native lands,
> With love in our glad hearts,
> And tribute in our obedient hands.

Hinges creaked beneath the crenelated cap of the Tower, a hundred feet above us. Faint light flickered through the opened port, spilling around the black mass of a domed helmet and casting an unreal green glow through a feathered crest.

'Stand, strangers!' shouted the hoarse voice of a man-at-arms. I felt my eyelids prickle at last to hear the tongue of Kamardol, broad and countrified though the soldier's accents were.

We waited while the ready squad debouched from the great double doors in the Tower's base. Eight men-at-arms rode toward us, caution manifest in the drawn swords that shone in their torches' flare. Their leader wore the white sash of a sub-lieutenant.

Harrap chortled and whispered in delight, 'I told you the Towers would be manned – and the drill kept: "No group of arrivals, however small, is harmless; all sallies shall be under the command of at least a sub-lieutenant, who shall challenge . . ." '

The lieutenant's voice, young but assured, continued the passage from the manual, as if he had heard Harrap's whisper: ' "Who affronts the peace of Kamardol by night?" '

My friend's slow answer rumbled forth, 'Harrap, a prince of Kamardol, together with a scribe and a priest.'

'And the white colt?'

'For my stables, for the racecourse,' Harrap gave the answer we had contrived. 'From Ferghana, where they breed the fastest horses in all the world.'

'Advance, Prince Harrap – but slowly.'

The horses walked forward till we stood almost breastplate to breastplate with the guard.

'You speak the tongue,' said the lieutenant, who was young even for his small rank, 'though I do not recognize you. You say you are Harrap, a prince of the land?'

'That I have said, and that I am,' answered Harrap. I heard puzzlement in his voice because he did not know the lieutenant – and hurt because he was not known to the lieutenant.

The lieutenant laid his sword across his pommel, and the men-at-arms split into two columns, forming two half-circles around us.

'What greeting is this?' demanded Harrap.

'Such are my orders,' answered the lieutenant, quite unmoved by my Harrap, a prince of the blood and the Army's pride. 'No prince rides abroad tonight without an escort and a guard. Such you should know, for it is the custom of Kamardol. And no strangers ride free to the city on this night.'

'Why this night?' asked Harrap. 'Why are the villages deserted and the Guardians of the Fords absent from their posts?'

'How long have you been away?' The lieutenant gave back a question to Harrap's question.

'Three months or more,' replied Harrap, his voice rising in anger. 'But answer my questions, man.'

'Otherwise you would know. No prince rides abroad for fear of the mischief he might do. The village folk are all drawn into the City, and the Guardians of the Fords dispatched to keep the peace in the swollen streets. Tonight the Great King enters the gateway to Nirvana.'

I should normally have been startled at discovering an avowed Buddhist in the officer corps. But I was so fascinated by the meaning of the lieutenant's words that their manner passed me by.

My heart started with joy, the blood tumbling swift and imperious as the mountain torrents we had crossed. The priest muttered a prayer of thanksgiving, and I knew that his prophetic gift was true. We had won the first case. Harrap sat stolid, his eyes cast down, for his father lay dying.

Three

The lieutenant was courteous, but guarded. He seemed more diplomat than soldier, for he was quite unmoved by my friend's name.

'I am sorry, Prince Harrap,' he said, granting the title lest he offend, but withholding the style Highness, which may on pain of mutilation be rendered only to a prince of the blood. 'I am sorry that I do not recognize your features, though I know the name. I am but new in this service. It pains me that you may not, in any case, ride unescorted to the City.'

'What choice do you offer me, Lieutenant?' asked Harrap sharply.

'You may spend the night here in the Tower. Or you may ride, under guard, directly to the Great Palace.'

'To the Palace, swiftly as we can,' I whispered urgently.

'We shall ride to the Palace, Lieutenant,' said Harrap.

'As you wish, Prince Harrap. Sergeant, take the full patrol and escort these gentlemen to the South Portico of the Great Palace. They are not to stop on the way, and they are to talk with no one – not even yourself.'

As we cantered away, four soldiers before us and four behind, the lieutenant raised his sword in salute.

'Good night, Prince Harrap. A pleasant ride,' he said.

Harrap returned the salute cursorily. He muttered, 'A cool one, that lieutenant. Not so much as a goblet of wine to break our journey. We shall see about him.'

But he was mollified when the sergeant drew up beside us in spear-stiff salute, his sword's point quivering the breadth of a gnat's hair from the tip of his sweeping black cavalryman's mustache.

'Profound apologies, Highness,' he boomed. 'Orders are most

definite tonight. But if you will share a flask with an old sergeant, as you did when we rode together against the Jats . . .'

'Of course,' Harrap grinned, taking the leather flask. 'Of course, I should have remembered had I seen your face clear before this moment. Your name . . . your name . . . there is something about water. Yes . . . Jorat . . .'

'Jorat of the River,' the sergeant answered pluming himself. 'Not three years ago we crossed the Indus together.'

'The battle in the defile,' Harrap laughed, delighting alike in the soldier's talk and his quick identification of the sergeant. 'Your squad was beside me for nearly an hour, was it not?'

'Yes, Highness. And all the Army waits but to ride with you again,' answered the sergeant, by this time so engorged with pride he swelled like a rutting peacock.

Jorat sat suspended in full-blown euphoria while Harrap passed the flask to me. But he shrank a little when Harrap asked, 'What has happened since my departure, Jorat? What in the Palace? Why didn't you tell your lieutenant you knew me?'

'I am sorry, Highness,' Jorat replied, his face all at once shriveled and pale. 'That one speaks, but he does not hear. I may say no more, though these good fellows of mine would never. . . But you heard my orders.'

'Quite right, Jorat, you must – as long as you are under your lieutenant's orders – keep discipline.'

'Thank you, Highness!' the old sergeant whispered his relief. 'And, Highness, the Army lives only to ride behind you again . . . against the Jats, against the Kushans, even to the Mountains of Heaven – or beyond to Loyang to sack the treasury of the Great Emperor himself.'

'You may soon, Jorat, my friend.'

'Thank you, Highness, thank you,' Jorat repeated, once more swollen with pride. He essayed a bow in the saddle, almost losing his helmet as his crest scraped his horse's neck. He slapped his sword into his sheath and turned his horse's head. A moment later, I heard him shouting at the escort, 'Straighten up, you boneless bullocks' things. Ride with pride. You escort the great general, Prince Harrap himself.'

Harrap's black anger had been transmuted to crystalline joy.

He laughed, forgetting alike his father's fate and the cruel, silken web toward which we rode. The Great Palace would be aquiver with vicious intrigue, all the perfumed spiders greedily watching each other and marking the fattest flies while they waited for the Great King to die.

'Yakir, my friend,' Harrap bellowed, 'give me ten thousand men like that one, true and disciplined, and I'll sweep the world. Even that young lieutenant, at least he knows his orders . . .'

'Oh, Great Prince,' I interrupted, though I knew him impervious to sarcasm, 'before we storm the pinnacles of Heaven, there are a few matters here on earth . . . here in Kamardol . . . we must deal with. Perhaps, we should be thinking of them?'

The priest, closing up, whispered sibilantly, 'Perhaps, my noble friends, we should *all* be quiet till we see where the wind is blowing us? There is much work before us tonight. If the Great King is indeed passing away, who will succeed him? Have you thought of that small problem?'

I remembered to whisper in my anger, 'Would you deny your own omens? You have assured us that all will be well.'

'And so it will. But we must be ready . . . alert to work with the will of the Gods. Now, silence, for Their sake.'

Harrap pricked his mount to a trot, his silence seeming sullen. But his lips twisted in his secret smile, and his eyes glittered when he swung his head to survey the cavalrymen. I could never understand his delight in gossiping with low soldiers, the stench of the dung campfires, and the rough wine, hardly better than tinted vinegar, gulped from hairy leather flasks. He wondered at my joy in the conversation of scholars and the care I gave my lute. But each workman loves the tools of his craft, and men in armor were Harrap's tools. He would, I feared, have need of them.

The Colt, frightened by the soldiers, trotted beside the priest's familiar mare. In the darkness no one could mark His lack of a bridle. Indeed, the strongest portent of hope was that He came so eagerly to the City. But the priest cast a loop of rope around His neck, and the Colt, astonished, made no move to shake it off. Though a skittish racehorse would be brought into the City with a rope around his neck, I wondered again at this show of the priest's disregard for his own laws. I nudged Harrap and pointed, but he only motioned me to be quiet.

The villages marched in ever closer procession as we mounted the last hill before the City. From time to time we overtook a bullock-cart toiling upward with an entire family from nodding grandparents to fat babies at the breast jammed into the truncated angle formed by its sloping rope sides. For the most part, though, the road was empty, and the only noise we heard was the clashing of our escort's armor.

Just beneath the crest of the hill, I heard a thousand hives of wild bees buzzing their mad rage in harsh, ululating chant. Then Kamardol lay before us on the plain, the pale-red walls glowing in the glare of ten times ten thousand torches. Slender, rounded towers overtopped the squat city wall like a race of giants, the fluted balconies girding their temples crowned by billowing cupolas, great turbans alight with gold and silver and copper. The wrathful buzzing resolved into its parts: the shrill defiance of trumpets and the clanging of brazen cymbals rising above the gleeful sighing of violins; choruses of thousands of concerted voices hymning their joy through the roar of the million-tongued rabble; and, above all, hoarse cries wrenched from aching throats. The sweet stench of incense mingling with the slick scent of melted butter rose in a palpable cloud, enveloping us even at a distance so that the horses snorted and laid their ears back in disgust.

We had come home to glory, though the jubilation was not for us. For an instant, I dreamt that the Quest lay behind us and we rode back in triumph, the music and the cheering all for us and our battle-winnowed host. But this night our purpose was simply a quiet – with the Gods' grant, a secret – passage through the tumult of the streets. Before we came to the drawbridge in the City wall, I pulled my cloak around my head as if still suffering the cold. Harrap, too, hid the features so well known to the rabble. The priest had retreated into the hood that capped his cloak, and his pale features were shadowed, though they gleamed skull-like when I looked directly at him.

The soldier at the head of the bridge, a cavalryman by his

accoutrement, barred our path with his pike. 'The password, Jorat,' he demanded.

'Nirvana – and the night is cold,' the sergeant replied.

'The Wheel – and the day will be warm,' answered the sentry, porting his pike.

I marveled at the curious juxtaposition of the familiar forms and the Buddhist cant, for the first time in my knowledge used in the password. But the next instant overwhelmed my wonder. The City engulfed us, and the implacable din beat like sword strokes upon us who had so long known only the frozen stillness of the high plateaux. Stolid in command, Jorat of the River ordered his troopers into the lancehead formation to force a way through the massed throngs.

He did not call out the ringing summons 'Make way for the Prince!' Even in that crush the fearful command might have eased our progress, but he refrained. Two troopers rode behind to keep us from straying, though Jorat might have spared himself even that token precaution. A man on horseback could only go forward, following the flashing of the reversed lances that prodded a path through the mass.

I had forgotten how to be a townsman. The noise and the light cast off by the boiling rabble drugged all my senses. I was hardly aware of which streets we took and was certainly incapable of escape, if that had been my desire. I saw only briefly flashing images amid the wind-whipped fronds of waving arms and the gargoyle faces with shrieking mouths. An oily merchant, paunch distended beneath violet silk, was jammed helpless against a red-brick wall by the weight of the crowd. A slim upper-servant in a nobleman's livery held his small son above the swaying heads so that the boy, at least, might see more than his neighbor's sweat-stained back. A royal messenger tinkled his bells in unheard appeal as he fought to move through the throng with the violent, vain strokes of a swimmer in a storm-lashed sea.

We hurtled like a bolt from a catapult out of the narrow street into the broad bazaar, and the pressure eased for an instant. The soldiers wheeled, skirting a beggar who sat cross-legged on a low stool, a magic circle of space drawn around him by the flat pallor of his eroded features and the leprous stumps that were his arms.

A child in the coarse brown tunic of the poor lay on its back, arms clenched around its throat. Girl or boy I could not tell, for the head was crushed into a pulp of white bone, gray brains, crimson flesh, and yellow hair. The elephants, I saw, had been in the streets, gorgeous in their diamond-and-ruby caparison, their trunks striped yellow and red beneath their broad purple foreheads.

But they had been withdrawn, for I saw not one royal beast, even when we came to the South Portico of the Great Palace. Squat footmen of the Royal Guards barred our way, their flat features and slitted eyes rigid under their archaic blue helmets. Their sergeant lisped the response in his barbaric mountain way when Jorat gave the password. One stocky guardsman nudged his neighbor, and fleeting smiles touched their flat lips when Harrap dropped his cloak from his face and stretched his arms wide.

We had still to wait in the gateway, the guardsmen's ponderous pikes a fence before our horses' legs, until the Duty Captain came to the shouted summons. It was old Ranbir Bahadur, who had taught us both the use of the sword and had been at Harrap's side through his first campaign. He came on unhurried, rolling on his short mountaineer's legs. When the guards raised the torch to our faces, Ranbir's brown lips curved, and his eyes sank into their padded pouches. He whipped to the salute, shouting, 'Hail, Highness! Welcome home, Yakir my son. You are well come this night.'

'Hail, Father Ranbir!' we answered together. The guards stood straighter when they heard that salutation from Harrap's tongue.

As we led our horses down the long passageway, I pressed close to Ranbir and asked low, 'Is the Great King already dead?'

'Dead?' His voice was puzzled. 'The Great King is not dying.'

'But the lieutenant at the Tower,' Harrap broke in, 'said the Great King, my father, was passing the gateway to Nirvana. Why else the feasting in the city?'

'And so he does – or so they say,' answered Ranbir. 'Tonight he leaves the Throne forever, entering the Monastery of Ghok-rao.'

'And the succession?' demanded the priest.

'Why, the Sub-King becomes Great King, but not for two weeks, not until the first mourning is passed.'

'And who . . . who . . .' I drew the question out, fearful of the answer, 'who is appointed Sub-King?'

Ranbir's face set in the impassivity of surprise. He answered slowly, dragging his syllables in compassion, 'You boys have been away a while, haven't you? I am sorry, Highness! The Sub-King is Chandra.'

My spirit shriveled at the word.

If the Great King had indeed been dying, Gupta might have snatched the Crown in the turmoil that followed the death. But the Great King had, as ever, been too cunning. After delaying for years, he had appointed a Sub-King and himself withdrawn – all in the course of a few months. He knew well that the common people tasted truth unsauced when they said, 'Princes, like crabs, eat their fathers!' He had for years goaded Gupta, the elder, and Chandra, the younger, into bitter rivalry so that they might not join and rend him. Then he had in an instant designated his successor and withdrawn to sanctuary, forever safe from his sons' malice behind monastery walls. The City would be serene, the succession unbreakable.

A veil had fallen over our hopes, silken and slight as an old man's whim, yet solid and impassable as a wall of granite. Gupta could never reverse the ordered pomp of an antehumous succession. The Throne was lost to him forever. Chandra would be Great King, Chandra with his pale-whey face and pious words, his love of cant and fear of deeds, Chandra, the royal monk.

No tongue of our three had words as we entered the first courtyard. It was hung with purple, and it was dark and hushed after the tumult and light without. I longed only for a quiet corner, where I could sleep and forget the Quest that would never flame across the world.

Four

The Horse entered His stall freely, even eagerly when He sniffed the fresh oats laid up in Harrap's stables.

The priest stared long at Ranbir in puzzlement. This barbarian, who was obviously tamed, but as clearly outside our religion, was also outside his experience. He said deliberately, 'Highness, perhaps it would be well to caution the captain that the Colt has never known coercion, nor even felt the weight of bonds? We would not touch His spirit and destroy His value on the track after He has come so far.'

Ranbir's gaze lingered as long on the priest, his face closed to keep his thoughts prisoner. Finally he drawled, his mountaineer's lisp exaggerated, 'O Holy One, I see that you are as well versed in the government of horses as you are in your divine books. Be assured we shall not so much as breathe upon this colt's spirit. I too would see him outrace the wind for Prince Harrap – and perhaps win a few pence for me.'

That assurance ingested, the priest excluded Ranbir from his sight as if the captain no longer existed, indeed, had never existed. His sallow features and hooded eyes were set in a complacent mask expressing the stern ecstasy known only to him who serves the Gods selflessly despite Their unfeeling caprice and his own great pain. The priest hastened away on his own errands. He might well uncover that which was hidden from us, for he could seek knowledge at levels so far from Harrap's or my own that we were but half aware of their existence – and quite blind to their nature.

Harrap had been wholly silent since the single word, Chandra, spoken low, shattered the blade of our purpose. But the commander's instinct for his men's welfare was still strong in defeat.

'Go, Yakir, go,' he said. 'I do not need you tonight. Ranbir and I can manage the horses. There is, it seems, little else for me to do here. It was a good ride. Come to me in the morning.'

I drew my cloak about me, as much to hide my face as for protection from the dank cold that wept from the rough-hewn sandstone blocks, and threaded the maze of passageways toward my father's apartment on the far side of the Palace. Not trusting the cloak's concealment, I turned my face into the shadows when I passed groups of courtiers. They walked with eyes cast down, and their garments of coarse cotton were rent and smeared with dung as if the Great King were in truth dying. Greed for fresh spoils clamored and squealed, thrusting snout-hard behind the too seemly lineaments of sorrow the courtiers displayed. I could see, too, chop-licking lust for the revenge so often imagined in vicious reveries, revenge for humiliations so long and so bitterly accepted. Only the face of joy was banished from the Great Palace of Kamardol.

Fear lay behind the ritual grief, for no man or woman in the Great Palace was secure in his place or his life. Each, I knew, was examining his past deeds and past promises, testing in his mind the web of alliances, antipathies, and obligations in which he was suspended in his due place. Those who were more courageous – or perhaps merely more intelligent – would finally cast up their balances and force themselves to sleep, realizing that action must wait upon events. A few would sleep well, believing themselves wholly secure by their possession of such talents as neither the Palace nor City could live without. But even to them fear would come in the night, trailing her clammy fingers across their bare backs till the short hairs rose in silent defense. Chandra would be King – Chandra, whose deeds no man could predict because no man knew him, except, perhaps, the Buddhist monks.

Since I knew I could not find Tamar, who would be attending the Queen, I went directly to the Chronicler's apartment. My father, unhurried as ever, rolled up the scroll that lay before him and pushed the butter lamp toward the wall before rising. His beard scratched my ear when he embraced me, but not so stiffly as at my departure. It had, I saw, grown finer and whiter during the three months of my absence.

'Aminsa, Yarie is here,' my father called and pushed me gently down on a cushion. He studied my face for half a minute and then, apparently content, began to question me about the customs, the books, and the governments of the nations I had seen. I had hardly begun to answer when my mother, tying her skirt about her broad hips, billowed into the chamber.

She enclosed me in that soft, voluminous embrace so well remembered, and the mingled odors of jasmine, garlic, and mace, all dusted with the dry fragrance of fine flour, bore me backward through the years. She could no more keep herself from directing her maids in the kitchen than I could keep my hands from my lute.

'Yarie, my Yarie!' she cried. 'You are well? Of course you are. Never have I seen you look so fit and hard. But you are too thin. I can feel that. Look at your arms. I must . . .'

She raised her hands to summon a serving maid by clapping. But the gesture stopped in midair, and she mused, 'No, I'll do it myself. There's a pot of mutton broth that just needs heating up. That's the best thing for you after all the strange foods you must have eaten.'

'Your mother, Yarie,' my father smiled, 'still thinks mutton broth the sovereign panacea for all the body's ills – and the spirit's as well. Now tell me . . .'

'Leave the boy alone,' my mother scolded. 'Can't you see he's exhausted and hungry. All he wants is to forget about all those strange places for a while, but you . . .'

I stretched full length on the cushions, lapped by my parents' familiar squabbling. They were soon so immersed that they forgot the original cause, for they turned casually to me from time to time to invoke my support: 'Am I not right, Yarie? . . . Is that not so, my son?'

I did not answer, nor did they expect me to. I must have fallen asleep reassured by their quarrel and reflecting that all was well with them. My father had followed custom and taken concubines as he grew older. But it was my mother, his first wife, he had chosen to keep by him during the tremulous days of the transition of kings when he had to leave our walled villa on the hill overlooking the City for his cramped apartment in the Great Palace.

The priest never did tell me where he went that night, nor with whom he talked. But the entire Court knew that Harrap was not allowed to bathe or even change his traveling clothes. He was summoned by the Great King even before our horses were groomed. Harrap himself described the audience when we took counsel together the next day. What he forgot – or would not relate – I heard from Ranbir, who was commanded to attend the Great King and the Prince while they said their farewells. Neither Ranbir nor Harrap could say whether the captain was present because the Great King, knowing Ranbir's love for his son, wished to show the pair special favor or because he did not wholly trust his son.

The Great King received Harrap in his private apartments, not in the Great Hall, where just before dawn, he would sit for the last time on the Emerald Throne, his scarlet and yellow robes of ibex fleece glowing with great gems and trimmed with shining marten's fur. Only two tall lamps burned in the far corners, their refined butter heavy with musk. The outlines of the room wavered under the ponderous scent's assault on the mind, and heat waves shimmered upward from twenty charcoal braziers that were glowing islands on the lotus-patterned Bokhara carpet. Other carpets hung on the stone walls, for the Great King had felt aching cold in his ancient bones for many years. He had already lived almost seventy-one years.

Harrap spoke with his father for the last time in that sealed chamber, steaming like the streets at high noon in August. Tempered to the arid cold of the high plateaux, his thoughts teetered amid the fumes of charcoal, musk, and butter. The heat wrung finger-thin freshets from the walls behind the hangings, and they puddled along the carpet's edge.

Through the hangings Harrap heard the shrill wailing of the Great King's women. Some, Tamar later told me, wept in boundless sorrow, for the Great King would be borne from their sight forever, as if he had in truth died. Those who felt the purest grief were, curiously, the younger women. Their older sisters wept in fear of the days ahead, though they knew the Great King had charged his heir to care for his women. Only the Queen, barely ten years younger than her lord, sat silent, beyond sorrow and fear alike. She had been denied suttee by Buddhists and Brahmans both, the first because their law proscribed the deed, the second because the Great King was not truly dead. I should have found the women's sorrow an awesome spectacle, but Tamar giggled when she told me that they looked like bewildered, unwilling ghosts, their faces and breasts blanched with the paste of wheat flour and cow's urine that signified their mourning.

The Great King was gay with Harrap, almost sportive. Like a man who lays down a great burden, he had, at last, time and breath for laughter and frivolity. His lean body wrapped in a simple yellow robe of wool, he half reclined on the brilliant silk cushions strewn upon his dais. He wore no headdress, and his narrow skull shone pink through his wispy white hair. His lips, strawberry red, twisted and sank over his toothless gums as he spoke, but his blue eyes, though rheumy, were bright sentinels beside his long, thin nose that the common people said was the organ of his cunning.

Despite his gaiety, it must have been a hard parting for the Great King. Harrap was the favorite son of his age; barely twenty-five, he had been born when his father was already forty-six. He was the youngest – and most unruly – of the thirty-seven legitimate princes who still lived. Harrap sat on a cushion at his father's feet. He stank of horses. The journey's filth on his heavy crimson tunic and his tight horseman's trousers of faded green stained the fine silk. In his haste he had forgotten to put aside his sword, but the Great King did not reprove him.

After the ceremonial greetings, they sat silent gazing at each other. The Great King had been honed by the years to the frail bone. The skin of his face was dry and crumbling, fragile as autumn's fallen leaves. He was all but drained of the elixir of life. The young prince sat dark and stocky, his green eyes turned up slightly at the outer corners. The Fifth Queen, his mother, was a mountain princess, and he bore the mark of her blood. His nose jutted in the true fashion of the princes of Kamardol, though it had been broader than his brothers' even before the backhanded blow of a Jat axeshaft pulped it. The surgeons had cut away the shattered bone, leaving a flat, white scar where the bridge had been. Harrap had thanked them gaily, laughing, 'Better half a nose than half a head!' He sometimes joked to me of his sinister aspect, swearing that it frightened his enemies more than did his past victories. But I could not forgive the malice of fate that compelled such abundant generosity and kindness to dwell behind the mask of a warrior-devil from the Eighth Hell.

When the Great King spoke, his voice was again the brazen trumpet that had rallied armies in his youth. But he paused often for breath.

'Hari, my son,' he said, 'I am glad of this night. It was my hope that you would return, so that I might speak with you once more before I went behind the curtain.'

'My father! My father!' Harrap answered, the plump tears glistening on his cheeks. 'I rejoice to see you so well. When I came to the Towers they told me you were dying.'

'Nothing quite so drastic, Hari,' the Old King smiled. 'But it is good to see you this last time.'

'Why do you say the last time, Father? I shall certainly come and visit you as often as you permit.'

'That I cannot permit – even once,' answered the Great King. 'Had you come even a few hours later, we would not have spoken again.'

'But why, Father? Why am I banished from your sight? What is my crime that I must bid you farewell forever this night?'

'No crime, Hari. But the rules of the order of Ghokrao are not to be bent. Besides, I do not leave the world in order to invite the world to come to me.'

'Not even your sons, Father, not even me?'

'Not your brothers and, above all, not you, Hari!'

'Why, Father, why?' Harrap demanded again, his broken hopes forgotten in his bewilderment.

'Because all men know that you are my best-beloved, the darling of the Army, and the joy of our people . . . because our enemies know that you are the bright sword of Kamardol. For these reasons, I may never see you again.'

'I begin to understand, Father,' answered Harrap. 'But might I not come in secret sometimes?'

'Hari,' said the Great King, impatience edging his voice, 'you should know better than to ask. Are there any secrets for such as us? Can you imagine, let us say, in three months' time, when your brother Chandra has been King for a brief time, and Gupta has been Viceroy . . .'

Harrap stiffened at the name Chandra like a mastiff of the gates spying a strange cur sniffing at his doorway, nor did he rejoice at hearing that Gupta was to be Viceroy. Though it was largely ceremonial and rarely filled, that second office of the realm would engage Gupta's energies and defer him from plotting to seize the Throne for himself. The Great King had foreseen much, and he had provided as well as any man could against the rapacity of all his jealous sons.

'. . . can you imagine,' the old man continued, 'what would happen when it became known that you had come to see me at Ghokrao? The least would be an avalanche of rumor: I was dissatisfied with the ruling of the City; I had called you for counsel and to alter the succession. Such would be the least that might happen, a sapping of the foundation of the Throne. The worst would be a full-fledged rebellion before Chandra began to press twin grooves upon the throne to fit his fat buttocks.'

The Great King stretched out his hand, and Harrap bent his head to kiss the swollen knuckles. He was overcome by the brown blotches on the thickened, chalky skin, so shrunken around the broad fingerbones that had once wielded the heaviest and longest lance through full days of battle.

'I understand, Father,' he whispered.

'Not yet, Hari, not yet do you understand all. I have long planned for this day – and for its aftermath. I would not have the peace of Kamardol shattered because I yearned to see my scapegrace son again. Nor would I have my remaining days ended betimes by the stroke of a dagger on your brother's orders.'

'But why, Father, why Chandra?'

42

'You would have liked it yourself, boy, wouldn't you?' the Great King laughed. 'But you know that is impossible. The people love you as their general of hosts, but not as Great King. They would always fear that you would call your mother's people in. You would be a King in fetters of suspicion. Whatever you did would breed distrust. Better that you remain the bright sword of Kamardol, our realm's defense.'

'I understand, Father,' Harrap said again, bowing his head in submission.

'Not yet, Hari, not yet is your understanding complete. You might still have prevailed over all distrust. The people love you even better than they loved me in my youth, and the people will permit their beloved much. But I myself would not see you Great King.'

Harrap released his father's hand, and the Great King drew back, tucking his hand into his sash for warmth. Harrap rose, tugged his tunic into place, and formally declared, 'I now understand completely, Your Majesty. I beg your leave to depart, now that all has been said.'

'Sit down, Hari! Sit down!' The command cracked, though the Great King did not raise his voice. 'You have not yet begun to understand. For that too I did not choose you, that swift anger always at tension, ready to fly like an arrow from a bow ever taut. But that is not the chief reason.'

'May I ask the chief reason, Majesty?' asked Harrap, kneeling stiff upon his cushion.

'I will tell you, if you will bear with an old man, Hari.'

'I am sorry, Father.'

'You are not old, Hari, but you are a man of the past, not the present. You are better made for the times of my great-great-grandfather than my own. You have, it is true, almost finished the work I have begun. The name of Kamardol is feared by our foes and our friends. Our frontiers are secure. Around us lies a ring of subordinate states that pay us grudging fealty and, more important, guard us by their existence against attack.

'If you were Great King, the trumpets would sound and the banners would whip in the wind. You would lead our Armies forth to new conquests in an unending and sterile quest for glory.

'But there is a new spirit in the land, and we have made that spirit, though you know it not. Now is a time for peace, for building upon the firm foundations you and I have laid. The land must flower, and men's minds must soar . . . but the arrows must not fly.'

The Great King's parchment eyelids flickered. He fumbled in the jeweled casket beside him for a brown pellet of opium. When it lay under his tongue, he wearily took up his argument.

'That much have we done – and many of the great deeds were yours, Hari.'

'My Father,' answered Harrap in his bitterness, 'you have won glory for yourself and for our name. I do understand now, fully. Those of us who come after you are to build within the circle you have drawn. We may not seek your own glory through our own deeds.'

'It is the times, Hari,' said the old man. 'Look you, we are hemmed in, but secure. There is nowhere to go, except north to the empty plateaux. Any other move would break the ring of grumbling vassals we have built and would open Kamardol to disaster. There is even greater glory to be found in exalting the spirit of our people, but you are not the man to do it. Better, as I have said, that you should remain the bright sword and shield of Kamardol and let your brother build the new City.'

'I shall endeavor to obey you, Father,' said Harrap, adding almost inaudibly, 'if I can.'

'See that you do, Hari,' the old King adjured him. 'That colt of yours must find his own glory on the racecourse and later at stud. He will certainly enjoy that better than the fate you have planned for him.'

Hardly surprised that the Great King knew our plan for the Horse, Harrap did not plead innocence. He asked in despair, 'Why Chandra, Father? Why not Gupta, who is at least a man – for all his deceit. Why a mock monk who wears a title of prince like a player acting a part he hates?'

'Chandra will be Great King, Hari, because Chandra – of all my sons – Chandra is the only one whose mind is not mired in the furrows of the tiltyard or, like Gupta, so mesmerized by the exercise of power that he does not understand why men rule other men. I would have my own monument! I would *not* have Kamardol a remount station for wild cavalry, a base for mad adventure, nor yet a buzzing hive of intrigue – of poisoning and stiletto play and torture.

'Either your way or Gupta's could bring our house down, for these republics' – the Great King spat out the word – 'to the south become ever stronger. Never fear, Hari, there will be work for your sword still.'

'That I never doubted, Father. Your new world is not yet made.'

'No, Hari, not yet,' answered the Great King, his voice gentle again. 'Nor will it come in the few years remaining to me. But I have provided as best I could that the Crown pass on without bloodshed. I have done all I could to give the new age a fair beginning. And you, Hari, must not seek to break my plans.'

'No, Father.'

'I do not know what shape it will take. But there are so many shapes as yet unshaped. We must seek to know our world – and ourselves – better, wielding our minds and not always our swords. All men must walk in Kamardol as men – not as chattels, lower than the beasts, condemned to live amid filth of the body and the spirit. We must seek to know the will – and the purpose – of the Gods that made us. There is glory to be won in realms that exist, though we know not of their existence – and cannot imagine where they lie. First we must make Kamardol a new realm for all men – and even women. Then the world will lie before us . . . before our eyes and our questing minds, but not before our spears or beneath the hooves of our chargers.'

'All this from your Buddhists, Father?'

'Yes, Hari, in part. That is what the Buddhists say. And they are not wrong. We must seek a new kind of glory . . . but the old world is still with us, and you must be still the shield of Kamardol, as Generalissimo of the Armies.'

Harrap's spirits did not rise to the promise of the great office, though they would have soared to it only a few hours earlier. Silent, he bowed his head.

'But now, my son, I am tired. We shall behold each other once again at the Disenthronement. I shall pray for you.'

Harrap bowed himself out of the room. When his hand lay on the doorknob, the Great King grinned, and his mouth was for an instant the twin of Harrap's.

'And, Hari,' he said, 'I have found that bran is best for racehorses. It gives them much speed, though it may cut their endurance. Feed your colt bran, not grass!'

Five

The Seeking was forbidden. Expectation had died upon the instant Ranbir reluctantly spoke Chandra's name, but not hope. Now hope too was dead, for the Great King had forbidden Harrap to hope.

Harrap was to be Generalissimo of the Armies of Kamardol, the title toward which he had longed since he first felt the grip of his miniature lance rough against his boy's palm. But he was to command an army of defense, his chief arm the molelike infantry, their palms calloused not by the sword's hilt, but by the pick and the spade. He would be a grand clerk in armor, siting fortifications and provisioning them; his subtlest strategy would be to hold a line; his boldest campaign the brief sweep of a squadron of light cavalry on close reconnaissance.

'Though I cannot, I feel that I should give up, Yakir. I should go into the monastery beside my father – or rip my heart with my sword's point,' he told me just before the dawn, when we entered the Great Hall for the lugubrious Rites of Disenthronement.

The Great King sat, as he had by right for fifty years, upon the broad platform of silver. Like an altar figure, he was set off on either side and at his back by the hemispherical sweep of arching screens of golden filigree entwined with gems. The half-light of butter lamps, which flickered like his shallow breath, glinted on the hammered gold crown, which was twined with rubies in the shape of ivy leaves. He did not seem a human being, a creature subject to the fears and desires the Gods put upon us all. His shrunken features were shadowed by the searing brilliance of the great sunburst of emeralds on the soaring mandala behind him. His body was but an inadequate armature for the ponderous folds of his scarlet and yellow robes, their bulk swollen by flowing masses of gray and white fur.

The Royal Princes said their formal farewells, each alone. Chandra first moved ponderously forward, his eyes downcast and sunken in his bulbous cheeks. Tall Gupta was burnt lean by ambition, his stealthy stride arrogant as that of a black leopard that has not killed for weeks. Harrap's stocky grace was all flown, and his gestures were like a child's disjointed toy. Some thirty or more Princes followed, some quick and lithe, others heavy and slothful. All wore faces of sorrow, some unquestionably feigned, others certainly responsive to the heart. The procession spun its slow length out of the throng massed in the rear of the cold, echoing hall and, returning, was swallowed again in the throng.

After the Princes the Queens came, attended by their ladies. Their hair was disordered and torn and matted with the same paste of wheat flour and cow's urine that caked their faces and bared breasts. Their legs, hips, and the dark triangles of their sex winked through the tatters of their skirts. The great officers of state followed the Queens, my father among them. Then came the rest of us, the minor officers, the supernumeraries, and the hangers-on. Among those last, I was drawing near the Great King with bowed head, when a beam of light transfixed the eastern port and the butter lamps guttered out. Raising my head, I saw that the Emerald Throne was empty. The Great King had passed from us.

We bowed once more to the vacant throne, our foreheads resting on the gritty sandstone floor, before the Court began to disperse in solemn haste. We were close-faced, like men awakened from a shameful dream or conspirators who, having done some great crime together, wish only to part without meeting each other's eyes. Among the sagging bodies pressing silently toward the doors, I squirmed close to Tamar and took her hand. She looked up, her surprise turning to a fleeting smile, and nodded when I whispered, 'This afternoon, when the shadows begin to lengthen.' Then she was gone, following the Old Queen.

The Great Palace slept that day, except for the servants, the guards, and the priest of our Quest. Ranbir later complained to me, 'That priest of yours kept popping in and out like a shuttle. I had no orders to hold him, but would have kept him from returning, except that I thought the Prince might want him. And

I was loath to add to Harrap's grief. If he could take consolation from that wild priest, I would not stand in his way.'

Tamar came to me late that afternoon, when I had finally abandoned my pallet, my nerves engorged with too much sleep too often interrupted. The clotted flour still clung to her arms and shoulders, but she had changed her torn skirt for a simple length of fine pink cotton such as the daughter of a country landlord would wear. After twining many times around her legs and waist, the long end-piece was drawn across her shoulders and over her head, falling loosely across her breasts after covering the lustrous fall of her amber hair.

When we lay together in the tower room above my father's apartment, her body was as silken and vibrant as I remembered, though it may have been haste that made her less skillful in her movements. I myself offered no proud display of the teachings of the sage of love, Vatsyayana. Of their own our eager bodies scorned the prescribed arts after our long deprivation of each other.

When we lay together exhausted, I lingeringly drew my forefinger from the silken stubble the razor had left on the hillock that capped her thighs' joining to the brown tower that guarded the summit of her left breast.

'One would think,' I smiled, 'that you had lain with no man during all the three months I was gone.'

'Yakir,' she answered, only half laughing, 'I know you will not believe it, but it is true.'

I drew a face of mock astonishment, eyebrows raised and lips curled down. Her throat and breasts flushed red, and she added shyly, 'It is almost impossible to believe . . . even for me. But, truly, I did not want a man until you returned. The girls thought I must be ill, but you see, it is not that.' After a moment's silence, she said, 'But tell me of the strange women you have met and how they made love.'

I began to tell her, remembering with wonder the curious practices of the unshaven women of Ferghana and the cold nights in the yurts of the Uighur when a dozen men and women would lie all together for warmth. She interrupted from time to time, demanding that I explain in detail all of the odd customs I had met.

We could have lain together all afternoon talking half in words and half between those words as lovers do. But time present and the world beyond came between us, and I forced myself to ask, 'Tell me what has happened in our absence. With what stealth did Chandra creep upon the Emerald Throne? And he that was the Great King, how did he come to enter the monastery of Ghokrao? What of Gupta and . . .'

Laying her almond-scented palm across my lips, she admonished, 'Ask one question at a time, my Yarie!'

Then, solemn in an instant, she recalled the gossip of the women's quarters and the talk of her father, the Colonel-in-Chief of the Palace Guard. Her gray eyes caught the afternoon sunlight that cast a glowing net through the grilled port across the silken cushions and our entwined bodies. Her cheeks were golden and plump as new-mown wheat, and her throat was curved and round as a dove's. But her features' full image conveyed determination rather than feminine complaisance. Perhaps it was the short column of her nose, springing straight from her eyebrows, like Alexander's on my coin, that surprised me again with the realization that her soft contours were laid over an unbending spirit. She spoke rapidly, though pausing often to kiss my face and shoulders and belly, and once, when my hand trailed down her buttocks to stroke the secret opening below, we did not speak at all for a time. But her account was ordered and succinct.

Almost at the moment Harrap, the priest, and I rode out with my prince's own guard, speculation had begun to buzz through the Court. (She recalled.) Everyone knew Harrap's love of the racecourse, but few believed that he had left Kamardol merely to find a new stallion just when the succession must soon be fixed. Curiously, our friends were most skeptical, for they contended that Harrap sought an alliance with his mother's people to bring him to the Throne. Our jealous enemies maintained – in numbers greater than we had reckoned them – that he had been forced to withdraw, either in obedience to Gupta or in fear of Chandra's wiles. No one of them all had spoken of a Seeking. That rite lay buried so deep under half-forgotten events of the past that only a few scholars carried the memory in the waking parts of their minds – and they knew that the Horse must be born into the Great King's own herds within his own fields. Since no one of the Court knew that the priest had ridden out with us, no one held the key that might have opened the secret of our Quest. Harrap's departure, nonetheless, precipitated the issue of the succession.

It began when the Great King confided to the Queen that he had dreamed a vision of all the order he had made dissolved in the blood of his contending sons; his monuments shattered by flailing pikes, crushed by the weight of war elephants, and scattered by the frenzied hooves of cavalry chargers. After this vision and during all the time of the Great King's anguish, the Chief Monk of the Buddhist Sangha became a familiar of the corridors of the Great Palace. The Great King had, before his vision, tolerated the Buddhists because they did not attack his own power, but indirectly made his rule smoother by harrying the arrogant Brahmans' hold on the people and also because they had become too strong to destroy without provoking civil war. But he had held them in contempt and had never patronized them.

Sensing his father's distress, Chandra suggested that he talk with the Chief Monk. From their first formal meeting, the monk's slyly cast bait caught the Great King's mind. He had carved his life with the sword's edge. He had slain not only his natural enemies as any man must, but had ordered his father strangled and had himself been foremost with his own lance in the slaughter of all his uncles as well as his twelve elder brothers – and some younger too – all to gain the Emerald Throne. Though he had scoffed when the people muttered of dynastic murder and had won them to him with grand largesse and great spectacles and broad conquests, the Great King was, in his old age, as much troubled for the peace of his own soul as for the peace of Kamardol. The crafty monk, at once obsequious and imperious as an itinerant merchant playing upon a great lady's jealous greed for rare jewels, offered the King surcease for both his fears.

Sins done in ignorance, the monk explained, could condemn even a king to rebirth in the vile form of a serpent or a scorpion as surely as crimes done in full knowledge. But all hope was not closed to a king who had sinned unwittingly, as it was to one who had sinned willfully. He must open his heart to the first glimmerings of enlightenment. He must undo those crimes he could. He must, above all, broadcast the Buddhist truth, the Dharma, and the realm must be ruled in accordance with the Dharma. Since he could not undo the murders he had done nor restore the blood he had let flow, the Great King's future lot could not be perfect. Still he could be reborn to an equal state, and he could move closer to Nirvana, which is the Buddhists' great consummation of blending with Eternity. The Great King had rejected that last promise for a time, swearing mightily that his own goal was not extinction, however peaceful. At last, he had appeared to accede.

The Old Queen, however, whispered to Tamar that it was not wholly concern for his soul's fate that led the Great King to his compact with the Chief Monk. He only half heard the monk's warnings, she said, and dismissed the promises because he knew absolutely that *his* soul would endure forever, separate and proud, unmixed with the rude stuff of common Eternity. But, she added, the Great King's desires for his earthly realm of Kamardol ran well with the Chief Monk's proposals, which so muddled the matter of this world and the other worlds – as the Buddhists do – that no man could distinguish his present reality and their future reality.

Let the Great King, the Chief Monk said, revert to the ancient practice of the realm by retiring from the Throne after appointing his successor. Only by such a deed could he ensure that power would pass without strife. Thereafter his living presence, though withdrawn, would deter his sons from overthrowing his chosen heir. Only the Monastery of Ghokrao, the Chief Monk added, could provide refuge for the Great King, a refuge that was in part within this world and in part without it. Let that successor, he suggested, be Chandra, the only one among the Royal Princes to be known to all Kamardol as a man of peace. Chandra was, of course, the Chief Monk acknowledged candidly, a friend – though by no means a convert – of the Buddhists. He added gently that he ventured to suggest Chandra as the choice most politic, though the Great King's wisdom might well set upon a successor more fitting. Promising orderly rule, Chandra would be supported by the bureaucracy, by the merchants, and by the Buddhist Sangha. Against that array the adventurous, wild elements – Gupta and the unruly princes, the Army and the nobles – would be almost powerless, particularly if Gupta's wild energy was absorbed by the onerous ceremonials of the Vice-royalty. The Great King at length agreed. No one could read the secret pages of his mind. But despite his certainty of his soul's security, he seemed not averse to buttressing that security while simultaneously contriving the security of his earthly realm.

'After all,' Tamar smiled, 'he is an old man, and not even the Great King knows what lies beyond. He has, therefore, gone a long way down the Buddhist road. He has actually sponsored some of the reforms the Chief Monk asked. The Pariahs are now called human beings, and it is ordered that they may drink from public wells and walk the roads without crying out warnings lest their shadows pollute the twice-born Brahmans, who have come to their sacred state by progression up the ladder of human lives – and then have been sanctified by the Rites of Rebirth. But, of course, they do not. And the Great King's grace is not without end. He turned his face when the Chief Monk ventured that he enlist Pariahs in the Palace Guard.'

She shuddered delicately, too nice to talk overmuch of such perversity, and leaned the shining curtain of her pale-brown hair over me. Her quick tongue searched my secret parts. At that moment Harrap's voice sounded below. His rumbling tones blurred his words, but my mother's clear reply floated up to us, 'He is above, lying with the Lady Tamar, Highness.'

'Come up to us, Harrap,' I called, 'but give us first a few minutes.'

'Later, my love,' I whispered, kissing Tamar. She said nothing, only smiled as she wound her skirt around her hips.

Harrap overfilled the small chamber with his commanding vigor, though he wore neither sword nor mail, but a simple short-sleeved tunic. His arms, I saw, were blotched with a chain of small purple bites, like those that would soon blossom on my own. He smiled, lifted Tamar from her deep obeisance, and asked courteously, 'Good sport, my children?'

The priest came panting slowly up the narrow, winding staircase in Harrap's shadow. When Tamar murmured farewell, it was he who said abruptly, 'No, do not go! Stay with us, Lady Tamar, if it pleases you. We have no secrets.'

'Do us the honor, Tamar,' Harrap added hastily.

Reverting without thought to the ceremony of the Court, we stood attentive till Harrap sank down on the cushions and motioned us to join him. I poured white wine from a curved silver flagon that came dripping from the sunken pool of cold water in the corner. The priest waved the wine aside, asking for plain water. He took a sweetmeat wrapped in a palm leaf and silver foil from the wallet that hung at the cord girdling his yellow robes. The acrid odor betrayed the stuff of his dainty, which was largely bhang. Some courtiers prefer hemp to wine, though I have always found the confusion it breeds extreme. The priest, who would neither eat meat nor sip wine, rolled the cud of bhang between his yellow teeth.

We chatted for five minutes like casual acquaintances who had come together out of social need or mutual boredom. I inquired anxiously if the wine pleased, and Tamar chattered about the latest scandal of the Great Palace. Two ladies-in-waiting, glowing with too much wine, she smiled, had sought to seduce a pair of sentries on the wall, though they were but common fellows of the mountains. Failing to overcome the guardsmen's caution, the ladies had lain together in a sentry box, where they were surprised by the duty captain. We laughed, and I was proud of the ease with which Tamar played the grand hostess.

When I grew impatient, I took the privilege of being both host and junior to observe, 'We have contrived the opposite of all we sought. Chandra is to be Great King and Gupta Viceroy. Neither will welcome disruption. If there is to be no Seeking, what of us? What can we make of the years that lie before us?'

'I do not know,' answered Harrap dully. 'But I . . .'

'You are too quick in your surrender to despair, my young Yakir,' the priest interrupted. 'It is by no means certain that

Chandra will be Great King and Gupta Viceroy – nor that the Seeking will not flame across the world. There are many . . .'

'What is this new nonsense?' Harrap interrupted.

'Just this, but no nonsense,' the priest snapped. 'Neither Chandra nor the so-called Chief Monk of the heretics has seen the reports of the Scavengers of Knowledge. Indeed, they could not, because that channel is still truly secret and still in the hands of true believers. The itinerant priests, the sly peddlers, the prostitutes, the barbers, and the servants who go everywhere and hear everything – all have garnered one conclusion: except for the Pariahs, who do not matter, the common people are aghast at the prospect of rule by the heretics. They fear an era when no man can pursue his natural pleasures and every man is bound by a host of odious rules. No more Bacchanalias, no more sacrifices, no more spectacles. The village elders see their authority threatened by the bureaucracy, and, of course, the true priesthood is enraged.'

'What meaning has this gossip of the mob for us?'

'Simply this,' the priest laughed, though his hands were clasped before his face in the attitude of prayer. 'Chandra cannot rule a discontented mass unless he breaks with the Buddhists and their ways. But he cannot break with the Buddhists, who are his chief support. Only if the Army stands firm behind him can he force his will on the people.'

'And the Army . . .' I began eagerly.

'The Army,' the priest continued, 'is in no mood to shed the blood of citizens so that a monk upon the Emerald Throne can lay a pall of gray upon Kamardol and call it peace and order. The Army will follow only the man who sits here with us.'

'Go on!' Harrap ordered.

'To me, Highness,' said the priest with exaggerated respect, 'this muddle suggests one great possibility. If Chandra is wise, he would rather have half a throne than no throne. Let him exalt Gupta as Co-King, let him abate the infamies of the heretics, and . . .'

'. . . let him proclaim the Seeking,' I finished eagerly.

'It is not impossible,' Harrap mused. 'But there are too many details. We would have to talk with Gupta . . . and eventually with Chandra.'

'Let us begin, Harrap, let us begin,' I begged.

'What of my father's wishes?'

'He that was Great King is in retirement from this world. He will not return to chastise his sons if they reach a new agreement that gives peace to the City.'

'But he charged me to follow his will.'

'Highness,' said the priest, extending his bony hands, palm up, 'I tell you, as a priest, that it were no sin but a duty to alter your father's wishes – if you, so doing, advance their purpose and maintain the true religion. He has been seduced in his old age by the heretics. His purpose is clear, but his means are awry.'

'Perhaps,' Harrap said slowly, 'perhaps that is true. Still, I would not . . . And why should Chandra – or even Gupta – order the Seeking once they sat side by side on the Emerald Throne?'

'Because the Seeking is the price of the Army's support – as it was when we played upon Gupta's single-hearted greed for the Throne to gain his backing for the Quest. Though the Great King has made this decision in error, neither Gupta himself nor the lay of forces has altered truly since your princely brother agreed to back us if we would back his thrust for power.'

'But what,' I asked, 'if the Army should remain constant, hailing the King only when he was crowned?'

'The forces arrayed against Chandra are restless,' the priest answered. 'The Army *must* move – if only to prevent disorder. And by moving, the Army must choose. Besides, still another prince might move. He who holds the Army this day holds the succession. He who would sit on the Emerald Throne should have sat with equal ease and relish beside far campfires. He should have fashioned hedges of spears – since he must walk through avenues of spears to the Throne.'

Harrap set his goblet down. It rang on the floorstones, and I feared for an instant that it would shatter.

'Look you, Brahman,' he swore. 'I do not want the Throne against my father's command. I do not seek the Throne – certainly not now, if ever . . .'

'Prince Harrap!' the priest sought to placate him. 'I was not suggesting . . .'

'. . . I desire only the Seeking.' Harrap ignored the priest. 'And I do not see why my brothers should give me that joy once they possessed the Throne.'

'Gupta,' smiled the priest, 'agreed to our Quest because he wanted the Throne. In the confusion that followed the Great King's death – had the Great King died – Gupta would have offered the people the Seeking . . . and taken their support.'

'But,' I interjected, 'he would not wish the Seeking if he sat as Co-King with Chandra, no matter how he had won the prize. The risk is too great. It was worthwhile when it was his only road to the Throne. He would not risk all if he had already come to the Throne by another road.'

'Yakir, there is no other road for Gupta, nor even for Chandra,' the priest answered. 'If they denied the Seeking, another prince might still come to the Throne by offering the Seeking – particularly if the Army lay sheathed in the scabbard of that prince.'

'I have told you, Brahman, that I do not seek the Throne,' Harrap rumbled.

'I have not suggested that you do, Prince Harrap. But your brothers – expectant or enthroned – could never be easy, though you told them truly twenty times a day what lies in your heart.'

'You are indeed devious, Brahman,' said Harrap. 'Your plots are so subtle they pass beyond disloyalty into new worlds of deceit.'

'Thank you, Highness,' the priest smiled.

'But disloyalty remains to me disloyalty. It is not my way. My father has spoken . . . and I will not disobey his command. Besides, your plot is too complex . . . too subtle to succeed. Even should I follow your tortuous road, it would not benefit us. The Co-Kings would move their hands – and we should all vanish. Why should they order the Seeking, when a stiletto could find a path through my ribs?'

'Because, Highness, the promise must be given to the people before their joint Enthronement . . . because the Army's good will toward them must endure if they are to rule. Despite the great risk of the Seeking, both Chandra and Gupta would welcome it. How else can they command the Army's good will? How else can they dispatch Prince Harrap and the unruly flower of the Army beyond the borders of the realm for an entire year with some luck – or forever with great luck?'

'You are plausible, Brahman,' Harrap mused. 'But it is still not my way. I would not gain my desire by trampling on my father's last command. And the Seeking, so gained, would invite not the Gods' favor, but Their retribution.'

'Leave it to me to read Their will, Prince Harrap. That is my vocation. I promise you, the Seeking, however attained, will gain immortal favor and will dissolve all disobedience.'

Tamar rose. Pulling the free end of her pink garment over her head, she said, 'If I may, Highness, I must wait upon the Queen.'

Harrap stared abstracted at her as if he had forgotten her presence, before he nodded his dismissal. We sat silent while her skirt rustled down the narrow staircase, and the door closed on her soft farewell to my mother.

'No, Brahman, it is too complex for me,' Harrap finally said. 'Your ways are not mine. Even if I wished to follow your road, we would need to talk with Gupta. And Chandra would need to learn our thoughts, though we could not tell him. Put this fantasy away. Perhaps later the Gods will give us the Seeking.'

'What better way for the Princes to learn than through the women?' the priest cajoled as if he had found agreement, rather than rejection.

'She will not speak,' I said hotly. 'Tamar will not betray us.'

'Who spoke of betrayal?' the priest asked. 'But if necessary, the Princes will, nonetheless, learn through the women.'

Six

The Rites of Disenthronement were over, and the City emptied with the great gout that relieves a reservoir engorged with the angry waters of a month of storms. When the sluice gate was opened, the peasants and their families flowed into the countryside to take up their accustomed lives on the earth. Freed of their multitude of cousins from the land, the townspeople shook off their exhaustion and returned to their trading, their squabbling, and their chasing after pleasure.

Within the City, but above it, the Great Palace was dark and still. Only the cooks, the lackeys, and the men-at-arms went briskly about their tasks, feeding the Court, keeping it clothed, and guarding it from perils that might arise without. The courtiers themselves shambled through the canyoned courtyards and the constricting maze of passageways, pent in the unmoving mill of the Court that had once ground out all power and all delights. Eyes dull with self-concern, they performed their duties by rote until they realized that they did not know what their duties were and simply stopped. The feeble, dying company was served by lively varlets, who each day grew more pert and more thieving. The women of the Great King locked themselves away, and I saw Tamar only for intervals so brief they leached all the savor from our lovemaking. The patterns of life were wrenched awry, that progression of days and those duties of the Court so hallowed by time that they had themselves become sacred ritual.

The torpor that lay over the Great Palace was more profound and more enduring than the solemnity men would have assumed had the Great King died like his predecessors and been mourned by the hallowed rites. The traditional rites would have comforted by their familiar demands; the savage, self-abasing sorrow attendant upon the mass interment of the King, the Queens, and their servants; the spate of sacrifices till the earth surrounding the hundred and eight altars was sodden as a dyer's crimson sponge; the bloodletting enlivened by gifts to the common people and by gorgeous entertainments recounting the birth and the life of the Gods; and, at the end, the cycle of games, bullfights, gladiatorial contests, and the great lotteries that would enrich families for generations. All these were meant to betoken the beginning of the rebirth that later would culminate in the joyful Enthronement of the new King. The great Brahmans of antiquity had prescribed the ritual, each elaboration heavy with meaning, so that neither nobility nor commonalty might stray from its set duties, so that neither grief nor lack of occupation might render men too weak to endure the dismal spectacle of the great caravan of days that must pass after the old lord vanished while the new sun still lay below the curve of the earth.

By going freely from the Throne, the Great King had thought to secure an ordered transition to a new era of peace that would fix his own fame. He had in double measure opposed his will to the Gods'. He had defied Them by invoking his own dynastic death before his proper time and, again, by seeking to fix upon his successors – and upon the Gods – a new order contrary to all that had gone before. Still, we heard that the Great King was content in the Monastery of Ghokrao, cosseted by false reports from smiling monks while Kamardol atoned his vanity. But the Court and the people groped through the fog of insecurity that should have been dissipated by cycles of ceremony.

No catastrophe, however vast, could have kept the priests from their sacred books and their sacrificial altars. But so many centuries had passed since the last abdication that the priests could not agree upon the proper forms of rites. The more they searched the old texts and the more they read the omens, the louder swelled their contention. Calling itself the 'conservors of tradition,' one group asserted that the full ritual must be celebrated as if for the Great King's death. Another school, self-appointed 'the true orthodox,' argued that the transition 'from life to life, without death intervening' could not be marked by the sacrifices prescribed for the death of kings. Casting their own interpretations of the Vedas and certain obscure Brahmayanas, they warned that calamities would fall upon Kamardol if any ritual but their own were celebrated. Other schools offered their own truths that combined the rites of death and birth. Few men understood, as my father remarked, that it was in truth not important *what* ritual was performed – as long as *some* ritual was performed.

But Chandra lay back on his pallet, piously sipping cold apricot cider and waiting for the power that was his by right to pass by right alone into his hands. Either his natural lassitude or the counsel of his new advisors kept him from grasping the authority ordained for him. He did not deign to intervene in the dispute among the priests, though the deepening bitterness troubled the faith of the townsfolk and even the peasants. Perhaps Chandra did not realize that he must himself decree the correct rites if he would rule. Perhaps his Buddhist henchmen advised him to hold his hand until the controversies had scattered the priesthood of the Old Religion, rather than take a premature decision that would certainly raise against him all groups except the one he favored.

Nonetheless, the torpor that lay upon Kamardol, a black cloud split from time to time by the fretful lightning of the priests' polemics, would at length have lifted had it not been for the Buddhists. They entered the controversy over the rites as if they had not, two centuries earlier, denounced the Old Religion and the realm that was its form on earth. They exacerbated the controversy by proposing a milk-and-honey form of the rites whose potency flows from blood and wine. If their purpose was indeed to hasten the disintegration of the ancient priesthood, they miscalculated. Other forces sprang up, as abhorrent to the Buddhists as to the Old Religion.

The priest of our Quest was allied with the 'conservors of tradition' in demanding the celebration of the full ritual prescribed for the death of a king. But he appeared to desire no quick resolution of the controversy when I met him hurrying through the corridors of the Great Palace. We spoke briefly several times, though Harrap refused to see him and even forbade me to do so.

'It is cracking!' the priest said on one occasion, grinding his sharp knuckles into his cupped palm. 'It is cracking! It will not be long to wait now. The Great King is dead, and the new King is not yet born. The keystone is gone and the mortar is rotting. It must soon collapse.'

I asked his meaning, though I expected no clear reply.

'In the countryside the peasants are returning to the cult of the Mother Goddess. I have heard of youths and virgins sacrificed to Her. That is an enormous and a terrible sign.' His words were grave. But his lugubrious features and melancholy eyes glowed with delight. He would say no more.

Harrap ignored the portents of catastrophe. Bound by his oath to his father, he would not meddle in great affairs. Instead he sought escape in vicious pleasure.

I remember particularly one morning when we had been abroad in the City for three days and three nights. We had slept in whatever corner of pot shed, hall, or crib exhaustion finally struck us down. In cramped shanties on slimy back alleys, sitting among Pariahs, mutilated beggars, and hereditary thieves, we had drunk raw spirits of millet and new wine of the grape that stank of half-cured skins. We had taken bloated, unkempt women on heaps of coarse sacking and greasy cotton coverlets. Some were girls of the shops, avid in their own drunkenness for the honor of lying with noblemen. Others were the sweepings of the City's whores, women who coupled in deep doorways or under storage sheds because they lacked either protectors or beds. Even those were still glutted and sore after their great trade with the influx of countrymen. The more loathsome the women, the more Harrap desired them. Once, it was only by some force and much cajoling that I kept him from the withered arms of a leper crone.

Even Harrap's bull-like tenacity began to decline after three days, and I stumbled through a mist of exhaustion. After lying half the night, inhaling the fumes of that distillate of the poppy the people call the 'great smoke,' Harrap arose in disgust.

'Let us get a little fresh air into our lungs, Yakir,' he bellowed, overturning two stools laden with drugs, almost splintering the door, and knocking over the frail proprietor with a flung purse. Out of the wreckage a tall, lean cutpurse came at him with naked dagger. Harrap did not break his stride or draw his own dagger. He negligently reached out a hand and brushed the assassin aside. I heard bone crack as the man fell. Later, when I spoke of the assault, Harrap looked at me unremembering.

Perhaps it never happened. My own memory of that time is still an erratic alternation of light and darkness, the sun suddenly appearing through drifting clouds and as suddenly covered over again. I do not know how we came there, perhaps in a peasant's bullock-cart, though I remember clearly our loud descent on a cavalry station near the walls. First delighted by Harrap's coming, then affrighted by his manner, the sentry ran to wake his captain, who was properly abed at two hours past the crest of night.

The captain knew Harrap and blanched at his demands. It was he who would be impaled if the prince smashed his skull on a drunken nighttime ride. But Harrap had his will, playing the captain with alternate threats and appeals to the soldiers' camaraderie. Five minutes later I was hurtling through the sleeping streets toward the Old City on a rough-haired, half-broken charger. Harrap bestrode a rawboned devil.

'The wilder they are, the better,' he had sworn. 'I must ride the filth out of my blood.'

Three cavalrymen spurred desperately to keep us in sight. Harrap rose in his stirrups at the full gallop and shouted, 'Ho, brothers! See if you can ride with me!'

He pulled his horse off the high street and threaded a maze of alleys, culs-de-sac, and courtyards he knew from the mad nights we had spent in the Old Quarter. We jumped fences, splintering their tops, and knocked tiles off the roofs of sheds as we flew over them. The cavalrymen gave up the chase, but we startled several patrols of the City Guard. Hearing us clatter through a field of earthenware pots, one patrol lowered a fence of pikes across the alley. But the sergeant grinned and struck up the pikes when he saw Harrap's wild face in the torchlight. 'Good riding, Highness!' he called after us as we skidded around the corner.

The mad race might have ended only when the horses toppled had I not, feeling myself swaying in the saddle, called out, 'Hold, Harrap!'

He pulled up hard, the charger sliding and almost falling to the cobblestones. He turned a calm face to me and said, 'That is a little better. What is it, Yakir?'

'Where are we going?' I gasped.

'A moment and we'll be there,' he answered, slapping his horse's hairy flank.

We clattered off the cobbles into the sucking mud of a lane that twisted between stone walls broken by massive wooden gates. Harrap pounded his dagger's hilt against a gate studded with silver nailheads.

'Open!' he bawled. 'Open! We are in need of refreshment.'

When he had pounded and bawled full five minutes, the postern opened a crack. A gray-bearded old soldier bearing a lantern in one hand and a spear in the other blinked sleep from his eyes.

'Tell the maids to wake your mistress,' Harrap commanded. 'I have need of her conversation.'

The veteran leered sleepily, and I heard the bolts clang open. The gate swung open, and the watchman saluted. 'Hail, Highness. The lady has gone to her bed, but I need not ask if she will receive you.'

'Good, Corporal, good!' Harrap cried, flicking a silver coin into the air. 'Drink my health and I'll drink yours.'

A fountain in the center of the courtyard alternately sank to a riverlet and soared to a vertical jet, filling ten silver streams that spilled through serpentine channels toward the walls. Amid the orange hibiscus and purple bougainvillea, stone dancers and goddesses were one moment concealed and the next revealed by the shifting shadows of the limpid moonlight. Jasmine chaplets twined their dark heads, and full-blown roses lay behind their ears. Despite the multitude of blossoms, the scents were elusive, drawing men on subtly rather than enmeshing their senses. The enclosure appeared to extend endlessly outward, so cunningly was the shrubbery placed to yield only glimpses of the pale pink walls beyond. Two symmetrical streaked marble stairways, curving almost imperceptibly, embraced a small white door above our heads, but the mansion's bulk was hidden by foliage.

I sat upon the bench beside the fountain, lightheaded with the utter clarity that follows total exhaustion. Each odor, sight, and sound slid across my senses distinctly, but somewhat distantly, as the barber's knife slips to slit your cheek before you feel it move. Behind me Harrap plunged his head into the fountain, splashing like an elephant calf sporting in a river. Somehow, his snorting was not gross, but a gay peal of springtime that transformed the cultivated beauty into a grove tended only by nature's erratic grace.

The white door opened above us, and a maidservant came timorously onto the landing where the stairways met. Her blue saree was awkwardly wound, and she blinked in the feeble yellow light of her lantern.

'My mistress bids you enter,' she quavered, turning her eyes from our torn and filthy garments.

We followed her through halls paved with black and white marble squares. Miniature fountains played sibilantly. The walls were hung with big-figured carpets that framed niches where statuary groups stirred in the restless light of butter lamps wrought in gold. Those lamps stood on silver stands, and the bloom-filled vases on onyx tables were carved gold set with sapphires. The house outshone in its intensity the indiscriminate wealth of the Great Palace itself. Court wits said the Great King received his tithe of the spoils of conquest only after Ambiala had chosen her share. The maid tapped on a white door screened by blue silken hangings on golden filigree.

Ambiala stood in the center of the great bedchamber, her crow-black hair caught loosely into a single heavy tress that flowed over her right shoulder and down her hips. Her infinitely pleated robe hung around her ankles. It seemed at first cut of some dense white cloth, but the fine silk was transparent when the pleats opened with her movements. She wore no other garment, aside from a girdle of red silk ribbons caught low on her hips and knotted at the juncture of her thighs before falling in a short fringe. Although the young courtiers, self-conscious devotees of the new fashion of slenderness, sneered that Ambiala's lushness evoked the ancient Mother Goddess of the Earth, she was a fleshly recreation of the bountiful hetaerae who lived in bas reliefs preserved from the time of the Great Conqueror.

I stood entranced, but Ambiala's mood was not complaisant.

Her black eyes snapped against the unexpected whiteness of her skin, and her heavy lips were drawn taut. Even the gentle curve of her nose was, this once, forbidding.

'You are welcome to my house!' She spoke the ancient formula, adding with her famous candor, 'But I tell you, Harrap, if it were not for the love I bear Yakir, as well as yourself, you would not have been admitted at this hour. What need do you have of me? Are you hurt?'

'We are chiefly in need of rest, Ambiala,' I interrupted. 'But first, perhaps, a few words with you.'

'That is all you will find here tonight,' she said severely. 'My sisters sleep, and I will not wake them – even for you.'

It was, as ever, strange to hear her speak of her sisters, this waif cast out of the desert of the north, bought by a brothel-keeper of Taxila like a trussed duck, and trained like a performing bear until an admirer bought her freedom. She followed the new custom of the courtesans, living together with a pair of women, almost as accomplished as herself in the arts of love and discussion. These she called her sisters.

'But you are here now,' she added, casting off formality like a cloak, 'and I am too much awake to sleep again without a goblet of wine.'

While we lowered ourselves painfully to the floor cushions, she laughed, 'A goblet of light wine – very light wine – for you two, I think.'

She clapped her hands, and the maidservant appeared. While the servant brought wine and grapes and cold chicken, Ambiala chatted lightly, telling grotesque tales of the confusion brought upon the City by the horde of bumpkins. When the maidservant withdrew, she said, half mocking and half grave, 'I am delighted that you two travelers have at last come to call. It has been long since your return. How, Harrap, goes the training of your new racehorse?'

Harrap chose not to catch the note of malice in her question.

'The Colt,' he answered, 'waits in my stables, growing fat and lazy.'

'But that,' Ambiala persisted, 'is no proper training for the racecourse, is it?'

'The Colt is not for the course.' Harrap's brusque reply startled me.

He was, in truth, saying what everyone knew, but it was the first time since he had rejected the priest's proposals that he had spoken of the Seeking.

'I am deeply grieved, Prince,' Ambiala said with true gravity, 'that the dice have not fallen for you. But, if I may?'

She paused until Harrap's slow nod granted permission to continue.

'I am puzzled by your passion for another longer and even more wildly uncomfortable ride across the frozen mountains into the gritty deserts. All my guests who know of such things tell me that your chances of return stand as one to ten chances of death or capture – and your chances of success as one to a hundred chances of disgrace. Whence stems this passion of yours?'

Obvious as it should have been, blatantly obvious as it now appears, Ambiala's flat question startled me much more than Harrap's permitting her to speak of the Seeking. Some matters are so much part of us that we do not dare even to think of thinking about them.

It came to me first that I thirsted for the Quest because it was Harrap's obsession. But I heard a sly whisper that I myself was never wholly at ease in Kamardol and therefore longed to ride among the strange civilizations beyond. In every way the normal course of my life was so narrowly prescribed that I could see my end clear before my beginning was fully shaped. But why, I wondered still, was Harrap so obsessed? He was a great prince of a great realm, honored and pampered; his interest in other lands stopped at their infantry and cavalry drill that he might plan how to defeat them. It came to me, further, that the Seeking promised no great conquests, heavy with treasure and glory, but only a bitter, devious Quest commanded by capricious fate while dishonor stalked every mountain pass and every crossing of trails.

'I would not rot here,' Harrap answered, his thick voice cutting through my reverie.

'Would you be King?' Ambiala spurned the taboo.

'No,' he said curtly, a glint of amusement at her presumption breaking the glaze wine and drugs had laid over his eyes.

'But the Quest . . .' Even her daring would not name the Seeking. 'The Quest cannot make you more royal than you are.'

'That is true,' answered Harrap, enjoying the litany.

'Then why not take the command of the Armies, if you desire either glory and fame or spoils and power. Surely, it would be better to take the command and wait until you can make a reason to use the weapon. Surely you could find a reason.'

'I could find a reason,' agreed Harrap.

'Then why not take the command?'

'Probably I will – in my own time.' He laughed abruptly. 'But Yakir wants to travel . . . and I cannot bind him to my service unless I too travel.'

Ambiala ignored his evasion, which I realized was not wholly evasion. She waited silent till he burst forth, half in anger.

'Look you, Ambiala, I do not seek power and spoils – or glory and fame. They are too easy.'

'Too easy, Harrap?' I prompted.

'Too easy, Yakir,' he laughed, good-humored again. 'Together we could conquer where we would – till the world rang with our names and we wallowed in the booty of a hundred empires. That we could do merely by my taking the command and forcing a reason. I could not hold my father's charge to keep Kamardol safe without campaigning far from our borders. But glory, fame, and loot – they are not my purpose.'

'Would you, then, obedient, make your brother great and be yourself greater in his light?' Ambiala pursued him.

'That one is as far from greatness as a mole's burrow from the eagle's crag. Sooner will a yellow hen sprout peacock's plumage than he even learn to recognize greatness.'

'What do you desire?' Ambiala persisted, still skirting the taboo she had laid upon herself.

'Something that is not easy – a Quest to try our hearts and sinews – the Seeking.'

Stretched upon the cushions, his eyes closed, Harrap completed his answer. His voice was so muffled even I could not tell whether he spoke in earnest or in jest.

'Besides, the Gods have willed it!'

Seven

We rode wearily back to the Great Palace through the silence that lay upon the City the next afternoon, when all solid burghers and their servants napped behind bolted shutters and even the beggars, swathed to their heads in rags, slept in the shelter of walls and bridges. Storming down the valley out of the heart of the continent, the wind scourged the red-stone buildings with a lash of fine brown sand and buffeted our aching bodies. We sat heavy in our saddles, our cloaks pulled across our faces to keep the driven sand from clogging our eyes and nostrils. Even the horses, who had not joined our carousing till its end, plodded wearily up the broad glacis that guarded the Palace. Harrap was beyond speech, but the madness had gone from him and the somber cast had left his features. The black waters of exhaustion had filled us completely, submerging all feeling and all thought. He curled his left leg around the pommel to ease himself and rode sideways like a woman on a pillion.

'It's like a horse,' he complained. 'Exercise is good, but too much play leaves it tender and shriveled and useless.'

Within the courtyard he slid from his saddle like an old man and gestured stiffly to an attendant to take the horses. Still he laughed with an echo of his normal gusto when two cavalrymen, tired and fearful, loped out of a doorway to claim the chargers.

'Discipline, Yakir, discipline – and a fine regard for the quartermaster's ire,' he said. 'It has been good sport, but I think I shall rest now. Farewell for the moment.'

Ranbir later told me that instead of resting, Harrap made for the stables and, for two hours, curry-combed the Horse and whispered to Him. I was halfway across the courtyard when he hailed me.

'Yakir, I think I'll tour the camps for a few days. Look for me when I return.'

Surprised and a little hurt that he did not want me to accompany him, I was nonetheless glad of the respite. I could gladly forgo the hard riding between camps, the hard bread, the sour wine, and the sour soldiers' jokes. By some miracle of his own being, Harrap would return refreshed from a journey that would have undone me completely. Besides, I wanted to wander alone through the crannies of the Great Palace, searching for the future. The profound lassitude that lay upon the Court could not, by its very nature, long endure. It must either break of itself or be broken from without.

The five days of Harrap's absence were, at the beginning, blessedly empty. I was alone, for my parents had returned to their villa on the hillside. They were loudly thankful to be gone from the slow-festering intrigue of the Palace. I lay long on my cushions that first morning while my mind darted aimlessly about, furtive as a gray mouse searching for crumbs in an unused larder. I pulled my errant thoughts back firmly each time, as if I held them on a lead, but they scurried away again the next moment. At length I resorted to the 'mind-emptying postures' the priest had taught me on the trek. I had conscientiously made myself into a cobra, a plough, and a scorpion when a maidservant entered with a flagon of wine.

Whatever she may have been seeking when she failed to knock, it was not a naked fakir tottering on his head. She placed the flagon on the floor and skittered from the room, undoubtedly rehearsing her astonishing tale of my posturing like a professional holy man begging for coppers at a fair. Dissolved by laughter, I thumped onto the cushions, all hope of attaining detachment flown.

Drops of snow still clung to the flagon's silver sides. I poured myself a goblet of wine before lying back under the net of sunlight, resigned to following my thoughts wherever they tended.

The Harrap who had revealed himself to Ambiala was utterly strange to me, perhaps because I had never wished to know him. There was, it came to me, a strain of condescension in my love for Harrap, as there was in his for me. When we began to run together fifteen years earlier, easy contempt had bound us, as well as familiar devotion. Harrap, youngest of the Royal Princes, could not hope to excel his brothers in weaponry and the chase. Just two years younger, I was a butt made to take the flashing arrows of his superiority. Still I was no dullard in the management of weapons, but a worthy competitor – if always his marked inferior. Besides, my skill with song and the lute did not encroach upon him. Beneath my own admiration lay the smug conviction that this flashing creature was dependent upon my counsel. I loved the young prince as one loves a dauntless staghound, which never pauses between perception and action. But I knew it was harder to play the true man, who reflects before he acts. Since my mind ever interposed itself, I was slower to move, but more certain. Harrap was a prince, but after all a Kshatriya, no more than a hereditary man-at-arms, while we were Brahmans, men of letters, though by choice not practicing priests.

My restless thoughts still strove to pierce the enigma of the man I believed I knew best of all men. I had thought that Harrap simply yearned for the glory – the renown and the adulation – a triumphant Seeking would bring him. It had seemed self-evident that neither his brain nor his soul made a deliberate choice, no more than a dog ponders before he abandons one bone for a larger. Yet it should have been self-evident, as he told Ambiala, that fame and poets' praise and riches must surely come to him if as Generalissimo of the Armies he conquered in the name of defense.

Alexander the Macedonian had wept that there were no more worlds for him to conquer. But we lay amid states whose habitual hostility would give Harrap pretexts for attack, while their different weaknesses, skillfully utilized, would make conquest certain. We had between us become expert in opening wider the faults in our neighbors' political and military fabrics – and in turning their customs and their ways of thought so that they destroyed themselves. Yet Harrap's presumption was greater than the young Alexander's. He spurned the worlds that lay open to conquest. His pride bade him hazard name and life within the constricting laws of the Seeking that made him at once vulnerable and a mark for all to shoot at. He would offer himself, naked but for his own sword and a few companions, as a plaything to the Fates.

But, I wondered, was it in truth pride that goaded him to unreason? 'Besides, the Gods will it,' he had said to Ambiala. Were those words the superstitious soldier's bow to the powers he acknowledges without truly feeling their force within himself? Did his assertion carry no more feeling than a punctilious salute to a superior officer? Was it, perhaps, the pretext he was unknowingly shaping for disobedience to his father's final command? To believe the reverse was hard for me. I could not quite conceive that Harrap had been visited by divine inspiration denied to me. But my skepticism was sustained neither by logic nor by fact. The words he had mumbled as he entered the little death of sleep were robed with a portion of the sanctity of the words men speak just before entering the great death itself. Few men lie to their pallbearers.

I could not crack the kernel of the puzzle. Harrap had always taken the quickest road to his desire. Why should he now reject the easy way that was the certain way and choose instead an infinitely circuitous way whose likely end was disaster? Why – unless he believed himself inspired?

We had never been religious, Harrap and I, never known the wild ecstasy and the pain of possession by the Gods that came upon some youths. We had, of course, always believed, I more than he because it was my birthright and because I knew more of the sacred books than he. But we had always found ways to bend the strict will of the Gods to our own needs, rather than permitting Them to shape our lives through Their appointed heralds, the priesthood. Our belief was a formal convenience, not possession that compelled us.

My thoughts were long that bright winter morning. They meandered like a dog that rolls in the sunlight, then races off to chase fragments of colored paper across the wind, but always returns to the same dark burrow where a rat has gone to earth – though he cannot get his prey between his teeth for all his scratching, his whining, and his paroxysms of threats. I could not begin to crack the riddle then, and I have not, even to this day, ever fully understood what forces compelled Harrap.

I soon came to that contemplation of myself that was, in those days, never far from my awareness. Ambiala had awakened doubts I did not know slumbered within me. Until she spoke, I had believed I longed for the Seeking because Harrap wished it – and we had always done as Harrap wished. But that morning I pondered what truly moved me. Was it merely habit, my will moving with Harrap's as the chorus follows every gesture of the chief dancer? Was it merely a greedy curiosity regarding the lives of men far different from us – a debased form of my father's profound scholarship, which he felt I could not share? Or was it simply that I felt myself circumscribed by the life of Kamardol, at once too rigid and too familiar? I knew too well that no divine fire had transmuted the crude ore of my soul into the pure gold of dedication.

I believed, of course, in the divinity of the Seeking, but I saw that Quest as merely the prelude to the contest between the Gods and men that would be played on the broad chessboard of Central Asia. Each would seek his own purposes, ours known to us and perhaps to the human antagonists we would meet, the Gods' known only to Themselves. The Horse and the soldiery were splendid chesspieces, which would move by the rules we and, presumably, the Gods Themselves accepted. The spiritual crux of the Seeking was to me the search for understanding the manner in which Gods control the lives of men – and the means by which men may control their own lives and the Gods'. Mine was vile curiosity, like the prurience of yokels who give their coppers to see monkeys or dogs couple with women at fairs. It was not religious, not even sacrilegious, but in essence a denial of the supreme power of the Gods.

My pledge to Harrap was by no means explicit. Nor could honor compel me to the Seeking. Indeed, my own honor and my own duty impelled me to remain. In the way of the Kshatriya, Harrap had already taken two wives, daughters of neighboring kings. He gave them little attention, but enough to get upon them four sons. My parents were aghast that I, still unmarried at twenty-three, had given them no grandchildren. We Brahmans, of course, marry only once. Could I undertake the Seeking still unwed and childless, though I might vanish from their eyes forever, a stone dropped into a ravine?

I was all but resigned to what my father would call my duty. I would no longer struggle against the coils of precedent, compromise, and timorousness that had crushed his vitality. I too would pay in subservience for petty advancement. I would tender my services to Chandra, sure of his pleasure at my desertion of Harrap. To please my parents and honor them, I would take a wife, the good Brahman girl my mother unceasingly urged upon me. She would, at least, be of my own choosing, though heavy with the solid Brahmanical virtues. She would be no creature of flashing delight like Tamar. Our children would bear traditional names and would be reared in the strictest orthodoxy. Their minds would be tormented by neither the curiosity nor the confusion my father's laxness had bred in me.

I was wondering if I might grow a beard in the old fashion so that I might measure my years by its slow blanching, when Tamar came into the tower room trailing the sunlight on her skirts. Through the rest of that day I found in my delight that my beard was not yet white nor my spirit in chains.

Eight

When we lay, drained for the moment, beneath the silken coverlet, her head on the thick of my arm, Tamar said lightly, as if she were resuming a conversation interrupted a minute earlier, 'Only one thing is decided. The old Queen will retire to a villa outside the walls, where she will live simply, withdrawn but honored.'

'Not to a nunnery?' I asked idly.

'No,' Tamar answered greatly in earnest, 'she has absolutely refused to enter a nunnery. She hates the Buddhists for taking the Great King from her, and she is spitting angry because she will not ever be permitted to suttee.'

'Why not?'

'The Buddhists say the Great King is already as one dead to her, but the old priesthood all agree that she cannot suttee while he still lives. And if the Buddhists have their way, she will never know when he dies. They believe that suttee is evil, rather than the crown of a woman's life. Now she wails that her soul will never be reunited with the Great King's.'

'I do not understand why.'

'Because she will not have been a faithful wife, though it is not her fault,' Tamar answered, still utterly serious. 'Besides, the Great King will go to a Buddhist Heaven. He has been promised. But the poor Queen will be driven down to one of the deepest Hells of the Old Religion – and perhaps be reborn as a lizard or a beetle. She sits crying all day, her hair hanging uncombed over her swollen eyes.'

Amusement must have tinged my voice when I asked, 'How can there be two different sets of Heavens and Hells, one Buddhist and one of the Old Religion? Men do not make new Heavens and Hells when they change the form of their prayers.

The Gods do not come in infinite sets like sarees you can put on and off. The priests and the monks do not make Gods, but only try to read Their nature and Their will. Sometimes they are right, and sometimes they are wrong.'

Tamar propped herself on an elbow and gazed down at me in horror. She lay back slowly, squirming until her head fitted comfortably into my arm again. Only then did she smile, though reproach colored her rejoinder, 'Yarie, for a moment I did not know you were joking. You should not mock me so. Of course a new religion must have its own Heavens and its own Hells.'

I could say no more without entering theological dispute, and I had learned that it was maddening to match logic against her female simplicity and her unthinking piety. I envisioned all the space above the disc of earth crowded like a summer bazaar with the thousands of Heavens created by all the varied religions of the world and the space below the disc as tightly packed with Hells.

I waited silently for her to go on, for she was telling me more than she knew. She alone had certainly not achieved that enchantingly simple reconciliation of the conflicting claims of the two religions. Some more subtle mind had contrived the rationalization. The courtiers, as ever supple as serpents, were apparently remaking their consciences against the day when two suns would shine in a single sky. Chandra's Buddhist supporters, it seemed, were preparing their road to power. I would not ask, but I hoped she would tell me of her own how far beyond the women's quarters the easy new belief had made its way.

I was disappointed. Twining a golden-brown lock of her hair around my ear, she spoke with the artful ingenuousness of a small girl wondering aloud whether her father had happened to pass a toy stall on his way home. 'But didn't you know of the Queen's decision? Where have you been?'

'In the Old City with Harrap for a few days,' I replied, equally ingenuous.

'And what did you there, Yarie?' she asked.

'What do we always do in the City? A little drinking, a little play, a few fights . . . that was all.'

'Oh! I thought you seemed a bit tired.'

76

I flushed at the rebuke, though she was justified, better justified than she imagined. I could not remember each woman with whom I had lain, but I wondered then how many had carried in their filth the sickness that makes a man's private parts drip like a cracked flagon and rots a woman within. The priest had told me that a man, lying with a woman so diseased, could pass the evil to the next woman he lay with. I prayed that if I had lain with such a woman, she was not the last, and that the sickness had already passed to another slut.

I feared that Tamar would divine my fears, as she had in the past. But she was heedless, apparently intent on some purpose of her own. 'Then you do not know, either, that the old Queen takes only ten or fifteen of her ladies with her? The rest are to be freed of service, I among them.'

'That must be a relief to you. There has been too much gloom around the Queen these past days, too much wailing.'

My reply was apparently not the one expected of me, for she remained silent. Apprehension suddenly struck me, and I forgot that we were playing a game whose rules only she knew.

'That doesn't mean you'll be leaving the Court, does it?'

'No, there's no question of that now, though . . .' Her voice trailed off, and her eyes fixed on the knot she was tying in her tress that encircled my ear.

'Though . . . what?'

'Though . . .' The word escaped segment by segment, through pursed lips. Her fingernails stabbed my earlobe, but I barely noticed the pain.

'Well . . . it's really nothing, but my father is beginning to give me that isn't-it-about-time-you-were-married look. He's beginning to talk in that we-must-really-do-something-about-it tone. It was the same with my elder sister before she was finally betrothed. Oh, it's nothing, but . . .'

It was nothing, she said, but she was already seventeen and overripe for marriage. Should her father insist – as he had every reason for doing and every right to do – she could not long resist. I looked upon our liaison as it must appear to her, and I was not reassured. A golden springtime of freedom was yet granted to the noblewomen of Kamardol, though not to them of Hindustan.

Yet she could not waste her life unwed and childless until the barren husk was consumed by the crematory flames. And she must marry within the next year, or she would, in all likelihood, never marry.

Tamar waited. I could not see her purpose clear, but I was growing wary at the way she tended.

'And what have you said?' I asked.

'Nothing yet, because he hasn't really begun to press. Mother's a darling, you know. She says, "Leave the girl alone. There's plenty of time for her to marry and breed. Let her enjoy herself now." That keeps my father still for a while.'

'Well, that's fine,' I said heartily.

'Yes,' she smiled, dismissing the matter. 'There's nothing for us to worry about now. I only told you about it because you asked.'

'That's fine,' I repeated. 'Let's have another goblet of wine.'

But I could not dismiss my concern as lightly as she had her own. I was at once sheepish for suspecting her of guile, and fearful for the first time of the future. My thoughts dwelt on that new puzzle, though we lay content in the sunlight, sipping the flinty wine and tasting the joys of our first unhurried hours together since my return.

Tamar had other reasons to be thinking of marriage beside her father's haste. She had already undergone two abortions at the sanctified hands of the Queen's physician, as was only proper for an unmarried girl. They had been of little interest to me at the time, since there was no strong reason to believe that either child was mine rather than another's. But the priest had told me during our long talks on the trail that more than two abortions would almost assuredly prevent a woman's bearing healthy children.

I placed greater trust in him than in any other physician, though he had not won wide reputation because he chose not to amass riches by curing noblewomen of imaginary ailments – and flattering their husbands. Tamar must know of the danger from the women's own secret wisdom, but I resolved to remind her later. I would not, though, tarnish the luster of that radiant afternoon.

Even that resolution I abandoned when it was but half formed. She could only reply, 'What shall I do? Shall I marry?' And how could *I* answer that question?

Her own perversity must make her dilemma more painful. She had told me on my return, laughing in self-disparagement, that she felt no desire to lie with other men. Though she knew I would be glad to hear that her inclination had altered, she had not since then spoken of any change. I knew that she could not long conceal our unnatural liaison, though she might dissemble for a time. But rumor, with the force of truth behind it, must soon echo through the maze of empty minds and avid ears that was the true structure of the Great Palace, more enduring than the stone and the mortar, the jewels and the statuary. Branded by her abnormal attachment to one man, she would, despite her father's wealth, find no one willing to take her to wife.

If she had not unwittingly shown me that she entertained no hidden purpose, I might have wondered. Could she be dreaming of marriage to me, a prospect so wholly impossible that we had never discussed it? Regret clutched me by the throat, and I knew that I would sacrifice all else to be with Tamar all the days of my life rather than the brief hours we pretended were so utterly delicious because they were but passing.

Since I *was* thinking about it, the prospect of our marriage was quite evidently *not* unthinkable. It was nonetheless impossible. Despite our lack of wealth, her father might yield, for the Kshatriya hold it an honor to marry their women to Brahmans. But I could not imagine approaching my own father. His pride was not only in our pure Brahman line, but in our Aryan blood, untainted by Dravidian or Central Asian strains for a thousand years. Knowing that he looked down on Harrap for his mother's blood, though it was the blood of the royalty of the high mountains, how could I propose a woman who displayed an unmistakable strain of the Greek? The children of his firstborn, his first grandsons in the direct line, to be borne by a half-caste? I would sooner ask him to commit my mother to a nunnery or even to burn his library, rather than beg him to welcome Tamar to our altars.

The range of thought, so cumbersome to relate, passed in an

instant. But I must have betrayed my preoccupation, for she asked quietly, 'What are you thinking about, Yarie?'

I smiled, feeling the set muscles of my face move again, and replied, 'Of you and me.' It was, after all, no more than the truth.

'Pleasant thoughts?' she asked idly, tracing a pattern on my chest with her fingertips.

'How could they be anything else?' I dissembled.

'I'm so pleased, Yarie,' she smiled, and we lay silent for long, silken minutes. 'There *is* something else,' she said very low. 'I did not tell you earlier because you were so beastly, rushing off to the old City with Harrap when I wanted you.'

A rush of rage hammered within my temples at her petulant assumption that I must be in constant attendance upon her needs. Was I a page to sit at the feet of his mistress when she gossips with her friends and hover attentive to her commands when her maidservants are bathing her? Rage passed as swiftly as it had come, and sudden alarm raised the hairs on my neck. Had her first reassurances been given only to prepare me for another threat? 'What is it?' I asked briskly.

'Now, don't be angry,' she coaxed. 'It's really nothing . . .'

'Nothing again?' The harshness in my own voice startled me.

Tamar's luminous gray eyes half closed in anger, but her voice was light.

'It was nothing to do with you and me, Yarie. It's just some more gossip.'

'Oh,' I answered, through an outrush of breath. 'Please tell me.'

'My father said the Old Queen had Chandra in a net, when I told him. You know, the people demand the rites for the Great King before Chandra is enthroned. Still Chandra cannot make up his mind. His advisors fault every form of ritual as soon as it is suggested. Some forms, they say, would undermine his own prestige. Other forms, they insist, are too perfunctory to celebrate the transition of supreme power.'

'What of the Old Queen?'

'I'm coming to that. Chandra wished to proclaim that the rites would be celebrated according to the Buddhist forms alone. It was mainly a gesture to win the Pariahs, who, it seems, are more numerous than I ever thought. Chandra thinks he can build his power on them. But he didn't think he would have to go through with it. He was sure the Brotherhood of the Priesthood would compromise with the Buddhists, agreeing to mixed rites, rather than let the Buddhists become the chief religion by enthroning the new King alone. Then, the polemics would be finished and Chandra enthroned with general support.'

'But the Old Queen?'

'It's really funny,' she giggled. 'All the big men in their colored robes helpless before one small old woman.'

'Yes?' I prodded patiently.

'The Queen hates the Buddhists.' Tamar's voice was suddenly brisk. 'She has obeyed the Great King. She has not protested his retirement. She has not tried to suttee. Now, if Chandra declares he'll be enthroned by Buddhist rites, she swears she will suttee. She will suttee not only because her husband is dead to her, but because her son has trampled upon the True Religion. She will suttee for the death of the Dynasty – the death of Kamardol.'

'It is interesting, very interesting, even frightening,' I said severely. 'But hardly comic, as you seem to find it.'

'I'm sorry,' she giggled. 'But every day all the old men come to call upon her – and even Chandra himself. She stops weeping for a few minutes, just long enough to send them away baffled. I think she's secretly enjoying it. She really wants to suttee, so they know she's not just threatening. But, above her own soul, she is determined to preserve the True Religion from Chandra.'

I shuddered at the chaos that would engulf the City if the Old Queen carried out her threat. It would be not mere folly, but self-destructive madness to allow her to suttee in expiation for the death of the Dynasty. Chandra could never permit her to suttee. Would he yet begin his reign with matricide?

'I hope she is well guarded,' I said.

'Yes,' answered Tamar, grave for the moment, 'her food is tasted, and old Ranbir has posted a double guard. Someone warned him that he was intruding himself into internal affairs, setting at naught the very reason for recruiting mountaineers for the Royal Guard. He shrugged and answered, "By no means. It is my duty to guard the Royal Family. Besides, she has always been good to me, and I am, after all, an old man." '

'That was all he said? Nothing about Harrap?'

'That was all. Why Harrap? Oh, I think . . . yes, I see why you asked. This skein is becoming almost too tangled to unravel, isn't it?'

She let the coverlet fall from her breasts and twined herself around me, her arm lying across my chest, and her face in the hollow of my shoulder. Her lips brushed my skin, and her voice was muffled when she asked, 'Oh Yarie. Must you . . . must you go with him if he does go?'

'I do not really know, Tamar,' I answered slowly, stroking her hair.

My thoughts were still enmeshed with the chaos the Old Queen could invoke by immolating herself in protest. Even if the cult of the Mother Goddess did not still run strong beneath the sophisticated beliefs we called the Old Religion, the mob would have been in the streets. The enraged peasants, converging on the City with their crude weapons to defend the orthodoxy, would be joined not only by gangs of thieves, wastrels, panders, and barbers, but by the mass of solid citizens. The Queen's defiance could destroy Chandra and cast the realm into anarchy – until a strong prince imposed order again.

I wondered, half resentful, if the Queen's concern was truly for the Royal Family and the Old Religion. Harrap had long since claimed her heart with the charm that seemed to bend all women to him. When his own mother died in his infancy, he had become the child of the Queen's old age. Was the life of Kamardol now imperiled for the memory of his dark baby-locks?

I was about to ask Tamar if the Old Queen ever spoke of Harrap, but she brushed my earlobe with her lips. When we lay back, exhausted and drenched, a half hour later, the thread had drifted from the surface of my mind.

Nine

The five days I passed while Harrap toured the camps still glow in my memory like gems – not cold like gems, but forever warmed by the pure joy caught in their depths. Even today I take them out and fondle them whenever depression besets me.

I realized on the first day of my freedom that I had not ceased from constant striving since we rode out to seek the Horse. The unending tension had set my spirit and my body against each other. In the presence of Harrap's obsessed dedication, I could not question his purpose nor even see that his passion was in any way extraordinary. I had lived so long on the heights, I did not know until I descended to the lowlands again that the harsh and sterile upper air starved my spirit even as it goaded me to efforts ever more violent.

With Harrap's going I came down into the valleys, and my commonplace spirit was at ease. For almost a week I drank their abundant warm air. Because my course was not mine to choose, I was free even of the petty irritations that haunt our busy days when we believe ourselves in command of our ends. I but awaited instructions, indifferent whether they came from the Gods or from men. I could do nothing for Harrap but wait, since I knew neither what he did nor what he desired. Savoring my own perfect inaction, I saw – but did not feel – the rising dismay of the Court.

My euphoria was, somehow, untouched by my knowledge that our miniature world of favor and comfort, our complex Court of lust and greed and grace, was breaking up. The hum of talk and the scuffle of feet through the corridors was as charged with anger and despair as the frantic rasping that blights the summer afternoon when men gathering honey thrust their torches into the hollow trees where the wild bees have built their cities. Great officials and pert pages, cocky subalterns and untried concubines – all knew that the common people of the City and the countryside were sullen to the edge of revolt. Yet Chandra still held his hand.

Only once during those days did I perceive a feeling that did not touch upon Tamar, but was nonetheless stronger than the passing irritation of a spectator at a play badly performed. When I came to his villa on the third afternoon of Harrap's absence, my father pulled distractedly at his beard while denouncing my cheerful listlessness. Amid Kamardol's anguish, he said, I was as cold and unfeeling as a visitor from China, which was to him always the most remote and most contemptible of nations. I was briefly ashamed that I did not care. Only a few minutes later, however, I strolled gaily out the gate, bidding my usual adieux to the twisted pines that framed the path. Perhaps the message of the Gods was that there would be no message.

Tamar came to me often during that demi-week, and, I suppose, the particular flavor of our slow days and nights together dominated all my senses. I can today recall little of our passages. The matter of our talk and the nuances of our lovemaking are no longer distinct in my mind. But, sometimes, standing in the sunshine on the bluff above the crimson City or watching the trout leaping among the blue rocks of a mountain stream, I feel the distinctive texture of those five days against my fingertips – and a tide of joy rises within me.

I have never discussed those moments with any man. I do not know which revelation I would find more distasteful – discovering that everyone knows such moments or discovering that no one else does.

As I try to re-create those days in words, one specific moment does come back to me in full. I remember now, I believe, because I was so astonished at my realization of the true emotion at the time – before I pushed the revelation from me. After the first morning Tamar did not speak again of her own future. When, foolhardy in my anxiety, I begged her for a word, she only smiled and said, 'Yarie, I promise I will stay with you as long as you need me – or as long as I can.'

It came to me then that I had been foolish in my facile assumption that the perfection of emotion lay in its isolation, the perfection of a single pearl on black silk. If there is no future, I became aware, neither joy nor grief can come to full flower in the present. The present, winnowed of the seeds of the future, is itself barren. Yet there was no future for Tamar and myself; we could neither spin hopes together nor together plan to defy perils. Since our love – I finally used the word, though only to myself – could not seek to perfect itself, it was blighted before it was ripe. But as I have already said, I thrust the revelation from me, since I was gluttonous for the lesser pleasures of the moment.

Yet I was not cast down by my isolation from all the fears and all the hopes of the future that shape the present. My perfect euphoria was not unlike the state the Buddhists call Enlightenment, the total suspension of desire the individual must experience before he can attain that unity with the universe they call Nirvana. My own inadvertent way was to satisfy all the demands of the flesh, rather than to deny them as the Buddhists preach. I later learned with no great surprise that at least one school of Buddhism seeks to extirpate desire by glutting the senses. I have, however, met no acolyte who succeeded by that technique before he was sixty – though many persevere. Besides, perfect Enlightenment still seems to me a sterile purpose, supremely selfish in its apparent self-denial. If a man denies this world utterly, the next world will deny him.

My own Nirvana was not spiritual, but temporal, and its end was soon upon me. Six days after Harrap's departure, the maidservant brought us our breakfast of golden melon, wheaten cakes, and mild beer. She said breathlessly, 'The Prince Harrap returned between the crest of night and the oncoming of the day. He now lies abed.'

My grunted response must have offended her, since she too was obviously rapt by the spell Harrap casts on all females. She glared at me reproachfully before clattering down the stairs, her tray swinging by her side.

My stomach tightened convulsively, and all my insides shrank, leaving a beslimed, cold cavity within me. It would be hours before Harrap summoned me, perhaps another day if he were still in the peculiar temper that had sent him forth alone. But the days of my joy were done. Though I had had no sign, divine or human, the decision would soon be forced upon me. I could no longer suspend my choice. I must either make formal submission to Chandra or follow Harrap wherever he went.

I turned fiercely toward Tamar where she lay, showing only her eyes and her forehead spangled with shining hair above the pale-green coverlet. Half awake amid the warm exhalations of perfume and sleep, she slipped her hands around my back.

'Do you go with him, Yarie?' she whispered.

'I do not know . . . I do not know if he goes!'

Intent and blind, I laid my lips between her breasts to stupefy myself with her musk-and-flower scent. When I rose to thrust myself urgently between her thighs, she looked at me sadly, as if in farewell. I may have imagined that look, for she clasped me to herself with both her arms and her legs. She cried shrill and loud in release, her nails raked my back.

Disentangled, we lay silent in awe, so silent I thought I heard a distant roaring in my ears. Dismissing the fancy, I looked down upon her face, which was wholly open to me though her lids were drawn over her eyes.

'Yarie, do you hear something?' she asked, sitting up.

'Only great joy slowly receding. It is that we both hear.'

'No, there is something outside. Please look.'

Grumbling at her fancies, I slid from the warm bedclothes and climbed shivering onto a stool beneath the high grilled port. The flaming sun of the morning overpowered my eyes, and at first I could make out only the hazy towers of the City glazed with gold. Soon, however, amid the glare I saw a black throng heaving at the foot of the glacis, and I knew that it was their shouting we heard. As my eyes cleared I made out a file of troops strung across the glacis, halfway between its foot and the gates of the Great Palace. Their round helmets and their stature marked them as regular infantry of the Palace Guard, rather than the squat mountaineers of the Royal Guard.

'What is it?' Tamar asked.

'I'm not sure. Come and see.'

We pressed together on the stool, the coverlet draped around our naked shoulders, my hand clasping the warm curve of her hip.

The mob was flowing slowly up the smooth, steep surface of the glacis, its progress as implacable as a phalanx of soldier ants. The ragged fringe at the front opened and closed with a life of its own as individuals slipped and fell. But the great wave itself moved upward unbroken.

The roaring became more distinct as it became louder. Straining, I could hear the words: 'Give us . . . orphans . . . our King! Give us . . . our . . . King!'

Individuals stood out in my sight as the throng drew closer. The yellow robes of lower priests shone in the somber mass like pale raisins in a curry. The dark richness of matrons' sarees and the pastels of unmarried women flecked the predominant dun and brown of the men's cloaks like pungent spices.

'Give . . . us . . . our King! Give us . . . orphans . . . our King!'

Chanting, the wave rolled upon the file of soldiers. I did not hear the command, but I saw the infantrymen's pikes drop in a single movement like a drawbridge swinging open to form the bristling 'steel hedge of Kamardol' upon which a hundred mailed charges had broken and dissolved. Beside me, Tamar gasped.

The mob came on still unwavering, the chant swelling: 'Give us . . . orphans . . . our King!'

The citizens of Kamardol advanced implacably upon the terrible hedge of pikes. A bar of light no broader than a man's finger separated the darkness of the throng from the glinting silver line of spearheads. Tamar's nails pressed into my hand. The bar of light vanished, the spearheads were lapped by the forefront of the mob, and her nails drove deep into my flesh.

No screams of anguish rose to our ears, nor did the throng reel back broken. The soldiers . . . it was impossible, I thought, but the soldiers were slowly falling back. The infantry was falling back, the infantry of Kamardol that had for centuries maintained its stark motto: *Here we stand, Here we die!* The infantry was falling back, the infantry that had died in full companies, each man in his alloted place, rather than retreat before the onslaught of Alexander, the infantry that had perished rather than break the hedge of steel.

'Give us . . . our . . . King!'

All single sounds were swallowed by the distance and the mad chant. Half deaf, as in a nightmare, I imagined I could hear the despairing commands shrieked by junior officers in their shame. I would not have stood closer to that cauldron of disgrace for the sway over all Asia – not for all the knowledge of the entire world. Minute flashes of silver rose and fell at widely separate intervals, and I knew that the officers were using the flat of their swords. The officers were beating their men, the free troops of Kamardol. They had not used the flat for more than two centuries, not since we stood before Alexander himself at the Ford, and afterward more than a hundred officers had died, some slain by their own men, others strangled by order of the Great King. It is still said that in their shame they went gladly to the relief of death.

The drama was still to be played out by the lunatic puppets so far below us, both groups maddened by anger, remorse, and fear. The bar of light opened again between the helmets and the dark throng. The infantry, their great pikes shouldered, trotted toward the gates of the Great Palace. Only the half-dozen swords of the officers still flashed amid the throng. One by one, these darting points of light vanished as the officers were pulled down. Still at the same slow, unrelenting pace, the dark throng rolled toward the gates of the Great Palace. It seemed a small eon, but I knew that no more than ten minutes had passed since I had first heard the distant roar.

The infantrymen were straggling through the gates – into their own hell of savage recrimination and vicious punishment that they had created by their refusal to kill their fellow citizens. Through their broken ranks bobbed the square blue helmets of the Royal Guard. My grief turned to terror for Kamardol, and my heartbeats rasped in my throat. Still, the mountaineers had left their pikes behind and their swords in their sheaths. Their closed square swept into the throng, their crests set to swaying jauntily by their bowlegged half-trot. The guards were using their round shields with the pointed bosses, pushing against the unarmed citizens.

'Give . . . us . . . orphans . . . our . . . King!'

The chant swelled higher. The dark mob flecked with pale dots did not break, but rolled around the square drawn by the blue helmets. The blue lines wavered, and the short swords of the

Royal Guard glittered clear of their scabbards. The bars of light rose and fell time after time with the slow rhythm of farmers threshing wheat. It was full five minutes before the chant died, and the mob began streaming down the glacis in separate dark rivulets. The mountaineers halted, and I saw that their blue square was fringed with the sombrely clad bodies of citizens, the yellow of the priests, and even a few pastel and wine sarees.

Tamar's nails had gouged four red pools in the back of my hand. I drew my hand away from the white welts my grip had left on the tender skin of her hip. She leaned her head against my throat and drew the tight bands of her arms around my chest.

The common people gave many contemptuous names to the Royal Guard, calling them foreign barbarians, the King's tame monkeys, mountain lice, and mocking the tribesmen's awkward gait and lisping speech. For the first time the King's monkeys, duty perhaps sweetened by revenge, had slain men and women of Kamardol. It did not matter who had given the order. No matter who had commanded the confrontation, the Court, the Army, the King-designate himself were all set against the citizens. The Royal Guard had but one function, to keep the King safe from his own Court, from the nobles, and the Army. Guardsmen might, therefore, not settle in Kamardol when their service was done, lest they form a new community given to intrigue. They were an extension of the King's own hand, and the King had turned his hand against his own people.

It would have been better to suffer the throng's entreaties rather than march the regular infantry out to oppose them – and far, far better to have permitted the citizens to hammer on the gates and storm into the outer courtyards rather than fling the Royal Guard into their midst with bloodied swords. Someone, blind with panic or distended with malice, had given the order, and all the pride and order of our world had fallen away. The structure of Kamardol was disintegrating as the baked-mud walls of a Pariah village vanish when the spring floods sweep upon them.

Tamar and I stood clasped together and trembling. We were witless as children who stir an ancient crocodile from sleep amid his own stench of decay and escape by an instant his red-eyed rage behind a wall. I felt her tears wet on my shoulder, though she did not pull away to wipe them from her cheeks. I remembered then that her father was Colonel-in-Chief of the Palace Guard.

Ten

The summons came within the half hour. From that time onward the momentum of action forced its decisions on me, nor could I consider my own dilemma between Tamar and the Seeking. The summons was borne by Harrap's favorite page, a stocky boy whose round head was capped by a pelt of thick hair the tender orange of ripening mandarins.

Tamar and I pulled apart from our despairing embrace when we heard the soft rush of his slippers up the stone stairway. His haste carried him through the door in the same instant we heard his knock. Seeing us lying together, half covered, he wheeled about to stare up at the barred port. Red and white blotches mottled his cheeks, and his hands shook, imparting their trembling to the slender sword he clutched by its scabbard of gold embroidery, the jeweled hilt tight against his chest.

'Yes, Orberk! What word do you bear?' I asked as gently as I could in my surprise.

'Master Yakir,' stammered the boy, his eyes searching the cracks between the floorstones, 'His Highness charges you to meet him at the south postern with all haste. Put on your richest garments, he commands, but neither arms nor armor – only this sword of ceremony, which he presents to you.'

Thrusting the sword at me, the boy rushed down the staircase even faster than he had come. With half an eye I saw Tamar smile at his confusion, female perversity overcoming her tears. But I could not give her another glance. Leafing through the folded garments in my low chest, I was only half aware that her deft hands were directing them into my own. Only when I was fully dressed and she slipped the sword through the links on my belt, only when she rose, all naked, on her toes to kiss my lips, was I again awake to her presence. Halfway through the door, I turned to clasp her, and she twined herself around me despairingly. As I ran through the dim corridors, my eyes saw not the familiar red-stone blocks, but Tamar, her cheeks tearstained, her body half drooping before the tangled bedclothes where we had lain together a few minutes earlier.

When I came into the sunlight of the courtyard, my peacock-blue cloak streamed out behind me in the wind. The red-gold frogs, set with chip emeralds, flashed like the iridescent feathers of a crow's wings as he dives at the morsel in a man's hand. But that glitter, spied at my eye's rim, was paltry when I glanced down at the flaming splendor of the diamonds and rubies in my sword hilt.

Tense beside a pair of chargers at the postern, Harrap wore an identical sword. I saw with a start of pleasure what should have been obvious the instant Orberk came into my chamber. Harrap had presented me with one of the twin swords of ceremony bestowed upon him by his father after his victory over the Jats at the pass. Immensely valuable, as much for the cunning workmanship as for the gems, they were useless as weapons. They were, however, essential to a gentleman's formal dress – if the gentleman happened to be wealthy beyond imagining or a prince of the blood.

He mounted when he saw me. He did not speak until we were hurtling down the glacis at a pounding gallop. His personal banner flared from its golden staff in the hands of Orberk, who perched desperately atop a gray charger.

'Delighted . . . see . . . you . . . Yarie,' Harrap shouted over the pounding of the hooves, the wind snatching the words from his lips. Grinning with the delight of action, his eyes slitted into invisibility, he reined his horse. His words were more distinct in the relative quiet.

'No time to talk now, but later. We ride into the City. I have taken the appointment . . . Generalissimo. You are my personal adjutant . . . Good day, Colonel.'

'Good day, General,' I parroted, and we kicked our horses into the gallop again.

Even had I been able to make myself heard, I would not have echoed Harrap's joy in my new title. I thought of my father's disgust at my taking military rank, the twofold disgust of a scholar and a Brahman. Not even the plea of the realm's great peril would make it acceptable to him. At that moment I knew I could not, but I resolved that I would later tell Harrap he must take back the rank.

When we came to the first narrow street beyond the meadows girding the glacis, Harrap reined in hard beneath the fretted wooden balconies that leaned wearily toward each other and cast the cobblestones into perpetual dusk. Above the horses' panting, he said, 'Yakir . . . you'll not mind, this once? Orberk, give the colonel my standard. You will wait my return here!'

I took the banner from the boy's limp hand. His face was mottled white and red, and tears stood in his eyes. His mouth worked as if to protest, but Harrap was already away at the gallop.

My first – and last – mission as a Colonel of Horse was curious indeed, I mused as we clattered over the cobbles between the shuttered houses. We were attired in fragile silks like fops making for a grand dinner, and we were unarmed except for the whip-thin swords of ceremony at our belts. We rode into a City that should have throbbed with life in the autumnal forenoon, but was as silent as a summer afternoon when all its citizens are besieged by the heat within their barricaded houses. Yet we rode into jeopardy, for the City was arage with sullen resentment that waited but the spark of a single word to flame into violent revenge. Had I not seen the massacre myself, I should have known our peril from the hard gaiety in Harrap's every gesture, the antic joy he brought to battle.

We galloped through the deserted streets, unhindered as if we chased along a country lane, and came upon the Central Bazaar twenty minutes after the postern had closed behind us. A swarthy priest in mustard robes that were bleached almost white gesticulated from the roof of a vegetable stall. His forced pulpit twang resounded across the multitude of upturned faces and rang back in the pent silence from the ancient red-stone buildings that hemmed them. We reined in beside an oxcart to hear his catalog of wrongs.

'. . . desecrated the True Religion in numerous, odious ways.

And the Old Queen weeps all the day and through the night. They have turned the King's monkeys against us. They have slain innocent citizens of Kamardol. Free men have fallen beneath the sword. They have spirited away our true King against his will. Why else do they refuse to crown their new King, except that they fear the wrath of the Gods for their deceit. They must give us orphans back our true King!'

He paused. The palpable silence lying over the unbreathing throng held the citizens in a vast net. I felt my pulse throb in the stillness and began counting without deliberate thought: forty . . . fifty beats . . . sixty . . . seventy . . . eighty beats. The priest, no artless orator, must have been counting his own pulse. On the instant, shrill as a bird's shriek, his voice raked across the throng again.

'We must march . . . on to the Great Palace again! We must demand our King, we free men of Kamardol! And . . . this time . . . we shall not . . . we shall not . . . be turned back!'

'To the Palace! Give us our true King!'

Voices scattered at great distances among the crowd took up the cry. The chant rose, slowly at first, then spreading from the claque and swelling into the full-voiced cry of a mob in rage. Harrap glanced at me, and wordless we mounted the oxcart. Standing erect, I gave the banner to the wind.

'Fellow citizens!' Harrap's hoarse cry would have arrested a squadron of cavalry at the charge. 'Free men of Kamardol! I would speak.'

The throng responded with the sloth of a feeding elephant disturbed by a jackal's distant cry. Heads near us turned, and the wave eddied slowly toward the distant fringes. The green-and-gold banner cascading in the wind compelled attraction, marking the point from which his cry came.

'Fellow countrymen – and countrywomen – I would speak to you!'

The mob was turning toward us, the brooding silence that followed the chanting pinked by an occasional cry of recognition. A pale youth no more than fifteen feet from us stooped to the cobbles. His face contorted, he came erect in a single flowing motion, hefting a cobblestone. When his arm reached the top of its swing, a stout middle-aged man knocked it down. I shuddered. We would have been torn apart if the stone had struck Harrap and released the rage of the mob.

'Silence for the Prince Harrap!' the stout man cried. 'Prince Harrap, silence!'

'Free men and women of Kamardol, I bring you your King!' Grasping the instant, Harrap spoke. 'I, Harrap, promise you your King. Go in peace to your homes. You shall have your King. He shall be crowned by all the old rites, the proper rites.'

'Hail Harrap! Hail Harrap!' Again the scattered voices cried out, and I saw with amazement that the youth who had hefted the cobblestone was shouting with the rest. Within seconds the entire vast assemblage, as capricious as sudden summer rain, was chanting, 'Hail, Harrap! Hail, King Harrap!'

My prince raised his arms. The tight silver sleeves of his tunic framed his dark face, and his scarlet cloak wind-flared into an undulating rosette.

'Hear me, free men of Kamardol!' he bellowed. 'I would take this honor from your hands and wear it like a crown beyond all other crowns in value – if I but could. But it is not my fate to be . . .'

'Hail Harrap! Hail King Harrap! Harrap, the Great King!' The torrent of chanting submerged his solitary voice.

I spoke into his ear. Again Harrap raised his arms for silence, and I made the green-and-gold banner dance upon the air.

'Free men and women of Kamardol, did you truly love the Great King, my father?'

'Truly!' The single word beat upon us like a cloudburst.

'Then hear me, my countrymen! The Great King has laid his command upon us all. You, even as I, must show obedience to . . .'

'Hail, King Harrap!' Again the chant. 'Harrap, the Great King!' But this time, a little less forceful, subsiding more readily at Harrap's gesture.

'My fellow free men and free women of Kamardol, I cannot be your King. Another task is laid upon me by the Gods. It is a great task that shall honor us all – a task I cannot yet reveal to you because the Gods do not yet permit. But this I promise you, by my sword, I promise: the guilty will be punished. You shall have your true King.'

The Gods still reigned among the common people. The exhortation to loyalty had but half won the throng, yet the appeal to faith won them wholly. We still had to turn aside a few shouted questions, but the mob was already dispersing.

Some two hours after we first rode out, we turned our horses' heads away from the quiet Bazaar. Harrap smiled and waved, but his hectic delight in peril had faded. He did not speak to me until we were almost clear of the narrow streets that ran with the quicksilver of cheering crowds. Just before we came upon the page, Orberk, waiting by the meadow's edge, he asked, his voice despairing, 'Well, Yakir? Our dream of the Seeking, you can see, is finished forever now. But what else could I do?'

I handed Orberk the banner, and the listless monotone droned on: 'I was still asleep. I did not see the incident. Chandra himself came running to wake me. He was gibbering with fear. He sobbed that I must take the command our father had ordered. He begged me calm the people.

'What else could I do? We have taken up the burden my father decreed. We shall never ride through the center of the world behind the Horse.'

I found in myself no great sorrow at abandoning the Seeking. Still, the disappointment raging in Harrap found an echo within me. I answered, 'Perhaps we shall still find a way.'

'No, Yakir. It is finished! I am grateful for your riding with me. I know you hate it, but you had to be a colonel – and it will be essential for some time to come. We must still winnow out the crop my brother has reaped – and the winnowing will be slow. By Vishnu, they made a frightful mess in just a few days.'

Startled that he should have divined my repugnance for the title, I swore to myself to play truly the role of adjutant and counselor I had begun with my whispered advice in the Bazaar.

'It would not, perhaps, have come to this, Harrap,' I said, 'if you had stayed and supported Chandra, as the Great King charged you. It would never have gone so far. There would have been no killing.'

'I am flattered by your confidence, Yakir,' he answered, the initial surprise in his voice giving way to amusement. 'But my father did not appoint me nursemaid to my fat brother. He charged me only to obey Chandra. That I have done.'

The postern gate was guarded by four pikemen of the Royal Guard. Their flat faces were closed against the world, and their salute was ponderously formal. Behind them, Ranbir waited.

'Hail, Highness!' he intoned.

'Hail, Captain Ranbir Bahadur!' Harrap replied with equal gravity.

'The High Prince Chandra bids me say that he is overjoyed at your safe return.'

'My humble gratitude to the High Prince Chandra. When may I wait upon him?'

'He charged me to express his sorrow that he cannot receive Your Highness immediately. He has retired to prayer, but he will summon you as soon as he can. He would, however, have word of your mission.'

'Tell the High Prince that all is quiet – for the moment.'

'Yes, Highness,' Ranbir said. His sword flicked to the salute, and he turned away. But in the moment of his turning I saw that his face suddenly aged beyond belief, it was crumpled and seemed like an apple left overlong in the bin.

'Why didn't you let me take a couple of my men with you?' he cried facing us again. 'Or even me alone?'

'And have us all brained with pavingstones, Ranbir?'

'I swear to you, Harrap,' Ranbir persisted, 'my men would have been overwhelmed out there on the glacis. They would have been pressed down by numbers and trampled. I had to use the blade.'

Harrap did not answer. The old mountaineer, usually so short-spoken, assailed the stern silence with a charge of words.

'The Colonel-in-Chief told Chandra not to use troops. I heard him myself. He pleaded with Chandra. He begged Chandra to let the people come to the gates and then speak to them himself. But Chandra was mad with fear, and he would not listen. Then came our turn. I begged him to let us stand to the gates. I told him it was not our proper task to go among the people with arms. But he commanded me. And then what could I do?'

Harrap's face was sallow with anger, but his voice was gentle. 'Father Ranbir, I promise you that you will not suffer – nor your men – if it is as you say. Remain here. I go to Chandra now myself.'

He strode down the corridor and into the courtyard, his soft-leather boots sighing on the stones. I followed because I did not know what else to do.

Before we came to the private apartments Chandra still tenanted, the King's quarters remaining vacant, our way was blocked by the priest of our Quest. His red robes were of heavy silk and his girdle was of gold rope. He moved like a sleek old bull, his features were slick with self-satisfaction, and his demeanor exuded the consciousness of power.

'Hail, Highness! Hail, Colonel!' He mocked me with the title. 'May an old companion of the trails have a few words with you?'

'Hail, Brahman!' answered Harrap. 'Later. I go now to Chandra.'

'Let him wait,' counseled the priest. 'My words are more important. The moment of triumph is the moment to pursue.'

'You know what occurred in the Bazaar?' I asked.

'Of course I do, but he,' gesturing toward Chandra's door, 'does not. Let him wait and wonder.'

Harrap raised his hand to wave the priest aside, but I interjected, 'Harrap, let us hear him out. Let Chandra rot in his own stinking fears for a time. Five minutes' delay will not slake your anger.'

'If you wish, Yakir,' Harrap conceded coldly.

Even before we were seated in his own apartments, Harrap asked, 'Well, Brahman, what is it that could not wait until I had spoken to my brother who is to be King? Do you bring me word from your spies that will help me pacify the people? Since you know all, you know that only this morning I agreed to undertake that task of pacification, forsaking all others.'

'I would not, O Prince, worry overmuch about the people,' the priest replied. 'The people will be still when they have their King. I have come in all haste to urge you to assure the Seeking, now that all auguries are near perfection.'

'Do not mock me, Brahman!' Harrap's words were sharp, but

his manner displaying no more than the passing irritation of a man who will no longer discuss a child's fantasy. 'I forbid you to speak of the Seeking. Even if honor did not forbid, it is not politic. The command I have taken I must discharge. I have given away all my advantages.'

'How do you say all the auguries are near perfection?' I asked, fearful of the priest's shrewdness. 'The auguries of earth here in Kamardol or the auguries of the Heavens?'

'Both, O Colonel, both. I have read the stars again – most carefully, as I am bound to do. Not in eight hundred and twenty-two years have the planets stood so favorable to the Seeking. It is ordained that the Quest will bring us not merely deathless fame, but . . . it is almost sacrilegious to say the words, though it is written in the stars . . . we shall sit, now and hereafter, almost beside the Gods – and far above men.'

I waited in vain for Harrap to speak. Finally, I put the question I had expected him to ask.

'And the auguries of earth? The Prince Harrap has said that all hope is passed. He has laid down the weapons that might have won his will. He has assumed a new task. We are now powerless to compel the King-to-be to the expense and peril of the Seeking.'

'On the contrary, O most valiant Colonel.' The priest was in high good humor and supremely certain of his arguments, or he would not have permitted himself to be quite so patently offensive. 'The tasks are one, and the means are one. Only the Seeking can bring tranquillity to Kamardol.'

'How so, Brahman?' growled Harrap, annoyed at the priest's levity, though lured by his promises.

'Look you, Prince Harrap! The High Prince Chandra sent you to face down the danger he had created. Did he expect you to be slain or did he expect you to prevail? For which end did he hope? I do not know.'

The priest paused like a conjurer about to transform a sow into a golden statue.

'But it has come to this. You are alive, and the people are quiet for the moment. But they are quiet only because of your promises: that they should be avenged and that you would undertake a great task on the Gods' command. Chandra must proclaim the Seeking – or you must be King in his stead.'

'Nonsense!' Harrap tore the word from his throat. 'I promised the people their rightful King. He is Chandra, the Gods help us. I said nothing of the Seeking. And they accepted Chandra from my hands.'

'Accepted him only because you declared for a greater task.'

'I said "a great task" was laid upon me, not a greater task.'

'A task that prohibits your taking the Crown from the people's hands must be a task greater than the Kingship. How else? Is it not so, Master Yakir?'

'He does not speak without meaning, Harrap.'

'Go on, then,' Harrap commanded. 'How is it that only the Seeking can bring tranquillity?'

'Let me go at my own pace, O Prince. It is slow and perhaps circuitous, but it makes the path easier.'

'Then go at your own pace, but do not halt on the road.'

'Thank you, Highness,' the priest purred. 'In his concern for the people, the Great King, your father, forgot the people. My men in the throng cried, "Hail, King Harrap!" They set off the acclaim. But they would have awakened no response if the desire had not stirred in the people's hearts. We can only move the mob a mite faster. We cannot force it to go where it does not wish to go.'

'Your men?' Harrap asked.

'Just helping, O Prince, just helping. Now, I say to you that you must be King yourself or undertake the Seeking if Chandra is to be allowed to rule. The people will accept no less.'

'But my honor stands. I promised my father that I would support Chandra. And I all but promised him I'd let the Seeking pass.'

'Honor!' the priest expelled the word from his lips as if it were a pellet of rat dung in his rice. 'Honor! There has been too much talk of honor here in Kamardol in these past days – and too little true concern for honor. You promised to see Chandra safe on the throne and the realm at peace. Would you now follow your honor to the destruction of Kamardol? And the Old Queen, will she for her own honor destroy the City and the true religion that

100

she would cherish? If she suttees as she has threatened, she will destroy Kamardol. Yet you both would act according to honor!' The slack contours of the priest's face drew tight in disgust as if he still tasted the rat dung.

'What proposal would you put?' I asked.

'A sensible question at last,' the priest smiled. 'We Brahmans understand the true nature of honor, do we not, Master Yakir?'

'Get on with it, man.' Harrap's patience was dissolving in his perplexity.

'First, the Great King did not forbid the Seeking, did he?'

'That is perhaps strictly true,' Harrap conceded. 'But he did not wish it.'

'It would not, then, be explicit disobedience to undertake the Seeking?'

Harrap nodded reluctantly.

'For the rest, the Rites of Enthronement are already fixed. I have fought it through the Brotherhood. We will even permit the Buddhist heretics a small part to keep their credit with the Pariahs – and to keep the Pariahs quiet.'

'The old Priesthood will compromise with the Buddhists?' I asked.

'I hate it,' the priest answered, 'but we must. Gautama himself ignored the Gods, but his followers create new multitudes of Gods. The Buddhists began by proclaiming they would make Heaven and earth better for all men. Now they intrigue for power more skillfully than ever we did – and with even fewer scruples.'

'If possible,' Harrap observed. 'But get back to your plan.'

'The ritual is fixed, though Chandra has not been told. It requires, however, two Co-Kings to replace in force the Great King who is not dead, Chandra *and* Gupta in other words.'

'You seek to force my hand, Brahman,' Harrap warned.

'No, merely to save the realm and the Dynasty, Highness. I leave it to you to calm the Queen and bring the Army to heel. We of the Brotherhood shall assist in pacifying the people, the mission you swore to the Great King and have just promised Chandra.'

The Priest let his words fall into the wall of our silence.

'But the Seeking is the capstone. Without the Seeking the structure falls. Chandra and Gupta must buy the Throne with treasure and peril. The treasure, of course, will be not theirs, but the people's. The peril will be not theirs, but yours and mine. But consider only this: Would they sit easy on the Throne if you remained in Kamardol?'

'It almost seems fated, Harrap,' I agreed reluctantly.

'I have never yet bowed to fate,' he answered. 'I shall not begin now!'

'Though it is your own desire, O Prince, and the only salvation of Kamardol?' the priest asked low-voiced.

He rose, and backed toward the door, bowing deep. His hand on the door thong, he said, 'And, Prince Harrap, one more thing. Your brother, the Prince Gupta, bade me say to you that he awaits you this evening at the house of the courtesan Ambiala.'

When the door closed, Harrap asked in perplexity, 'What do you think, Yakir?'

'What is your wish, Harrap?'

'Truly the Seeking! Forever and always – the Seeking!'

'Then,' I answered, playing fate's laughing fool and my own blind judge, 'the priest is right!'

Eleven

I met Tamar by chance that evening as I hastened to my appointed meeting with Harrap through dim corridors lit at intervals by oil-soaked torches smoking in their iron brackets on the red-stone walls.

Her face was shadowed from below by the butter lamp she dangled on a silver chain to lighten the gloom. She drew a face of mock disgust, and the black shadows of her raised cheekbones filled her eyesockets. She was, for an instant, a lovely ancient statue grotesquely weathered into vacant blindness. The illusion shattered when she sniffed the scented oil I had lavished upon myself to play the part of a young rake seeking his pleasure in the Old City.

'Pfew!' she laughed. 'A fat ram anointed for the sacrifice.'

'I thought you'd like it,' I laughed back.

'But you have not anointed yourself for me, have you, Yakir?' she asked, her lips drawn into a prim bar across her face. 'Harrap seeks his pleasure. And you are off to Ambiala's with him, forsaking me, are you not?'

'It is not that,' I explained, sheepish in my finery. 'It's not pleasure. We go into the Old City on other . . .'

'I know, Yarie, my darling, I know,' she interrupted, the pendulum shadows of her lamp swaying across the gentle curves of her cheeks. 'I know why you go. I should not mock you.'

She rose on her toes. Her lips brushed the angle of my jawbone, lighting softly on my lips.

'My darling,' she whispered, 'I pray for the good fortune you deserve. May the Gods bring you whatever you truly wish.'

'If we must go, it will still be six months till high spring!' I answered. 'And your father? What word of his punishment?'

'Only silence from on high.' The bitter lines around her full

103

mouth were, this time, no playful pretense. 'But, Yarie, darling, perhaps you . . .'

'I hope so. We deal for empires tonight, but perhaps . . .'

I held her for an instant before opening my hands as one gives wing to a captive thrush. Forgetful of the waiting Harrap, I watched her slender back diminishing down the long corridor. Her shimmering blue skirts, swaying with the movement of her hips, were a column of alternating brilliance and darkness till she turned the corner.

Litters and torchbearers waited in the courtyard. We must leave our horses behind as would young gallants visiting Ambiala for pleasure. But Harrap was late.

I found him in his stables, gazing rapt at the Colt in the guttering light of his torch. Silent in the darkness, I watched his hand trace the shining arch of the neck and his fingers tangle gently in the white mane. The Colt nickered softly, and the domed eyes looked up questioningly. They were dark, almost black, in the gloom with sparks of reflected fire flickering in their depths, though they could be slate gray in the snows. He stirred under Harrap's hand, the neck muscles bunching and flattening as the broad head swayed restlessly.

'Soon, Little Brother, soon it shall be!' Harrap whispered.

At that moment, I accepted wholly what I had already perceived in part. Harrap had decided. He would make the Seeking. I knew too, startled at my pleasure, that I would follow him.

'Harrap!' I said softly. 'Harrap! Shall we go and make our arrangements, then?'

He grinned, unperturbed by my incursion, and he answered, 'By all means, Yakir, let us make our travel arrangements.'

Linking his arm in mine, he led me back to the courtyard and threw his torch to a footman. Before he let the heavy curtains of his litter fall around him, I spoke briefly of Tamar's father.

Alone in the darkness of the litter during our slow progress into the Old City I should, I suppose, have been beset by regrets and misgivings. But I felt only vast relief that the decision was taken. In my eagerness I regretted only that it would be full six months before we set out.

Ambiala herself waited before the double stairway when the bearers set our litters down and drew back their curtains to let in her perfumed garden. Her eyes were dark with kohl, and her black hair was caught up in intricate knots from which pendant pearls swayed above the round, many-folded collar of her slender crimson robe.

'Welcome to my house, young gallants,' she intoned the formula. 'Someone awaits you within – awaits quite impatiently.'

She led us through the corridor past the half-lit statues to the antechamber of the bath, where slave maidens helped us disrobe. They were half-budded virgins taken from the mountain tribes or the Dravidian folk of the south. Ambiala's slaves of the bath, she swore, knew nothing of our tongue beyond the few words necessary to her guests' desires.

Gupta lay alone in the bath chamber, baking in the steam rising from the hot streams that cascaded down black marble walls and between black marble benches. He was at once chiding two dark slave maidens and idly stroking their naked thighs with his long, boneless hands as they squatted to rub him with fragrant oil. His small face, bisected by a curved, slender nose, reared snakelike through the mist above his lean, dark body. The hair of his head was sleek with moisture, and the flattened curls on his limbs and body shimmered like gray scales.

He waved the slaves from the room and said reprovingly as the heavy door closed behind them, 'I have been waiting, my brother. What kept you?'

'Sorry, Gupta, I had something to attend to.' Harrap dismissed the reproach. 'I was consulting the auguries.'

'I had not thought to come so soon to the matter,' Gupta smiled guardedly, 'particularly since you have been at pains to avoid me since our father's withdrawal. But you yourself have spoken of the auguries . . . I'll ask then, "What do they portend?"'

'Should we come so soon to the end of our conversation, Highness?' I interjected. 'Even before we have agreed upon the road?'

Gupta lazily turned his head, swaying gracefully and indolently on his long neck. He stared without recognition from his small,

105

filmed eyes. 'Ah, Master Yakir!' he said at length. 'Good evening to you. How goes all among the scrolls and the lutestrings? And your father, the scribe, he is well I trust?'

Before I could contrive a courtesy as formal and as barbed as his own, he turned to Harrap and asked, 'I thought we would speak alone, my brother?'

'Yakir rides with me,' answered Harrap shortly. 'He goes where I go – if he wishes.'

Though I knew he needed me, I was grateful to Harrap for his intercession – and twice grateful that he refrained from citing the detested military rank to assert my new status.

Gupta, his apology at once negligent and unctuous, gave me the title. 'Stay then, Colonel,' he said. 'I was startled at your appearance, though I should, of course, have expected you.'

'I am here, Prince Gupta, only to be of service to Prince Harrap and yourself,' I replied, stressing the stilted, mock-humble formula. 'I shall remain only as long as I can render service.'

'And we'll need him too, my brother,' rumbled Harrap.

'I'm sure of that, my brother,' Gupta answered, his smile negligent.

Although I had inadvertently been forced forward, I waited for Harrap to begin as we had agreed. When he spoke, I was reminded of the old tale, told half in laughter and half in admiration. Harrap's mother's family, they said, had won by conquest an area no larger than a manor and had then, by trading and by marriage, made it the greatest kingdom of the high mountains. They had fought only when they must, but then they had fought well.

'I am sorry, my brother,' Harrap said, 'if I seemed to be neglecting you, but my heart was full. What can I do now to make amends?'

Gupta flowed into erectness, the great hamadryad rising alert. His hands rested palm up between his thighs, and his long, oiled body swayed in a gentle circle so that he had us both in his vision constantly.

'I thought,' he began, 'that we could talk better here than in the Palace. Should the meeting become known, the content will, at least, remain our own. I have, of course, already gone over much of the ground with your emissary, your chaplain . . .'

'The priest is neither my chaplain nor my emissary.'

'Can I at least assume that he has communicated certain proposals to you?'

'We have,' I answered with caution, 'heard a number of thoughts notable largely for their antic air. As for specific plans or proposals – we have heard none!'

Gupta's tongue darted between his thin lips. Smiling without mirth, he essayed, 'Can I assume that you are familiar with the general course of events since your return from the Quest?'

'Of course, you can assume that, brother,' Harrap laughed, 'And we are grateful for your support in our quest for the Horse. But, naturally, all that is finished now.'

'Finished? I thought it had just begun anew!' Gupta's constant undulation was momentarily halted by his perturbation.

'Of course it is finished,' Harrap replied, his normal deep rumble rising in surprise. 'As you know, I have accepted the command – and there is much to be done.'

He knuckled the sweat from his eyes. Half vanishing in the steam, he pulled the heavy door ajar and shouted for cold wine.

'Yakir,' he asked, 'would you too like a massage?'

'Keep those girls out!' Gupta snapped.

'Surely, if you wish,' Harrap answered, holding the door open for a slave maiden who bore a silver flagon and silver goblets. 'But why?'

'Ambiala can be trusted. But these others, no. They are bound, in time, to learn more of our tongue than they admit.'

'As you wish, brother,' Harrap answered carelessly. He sighed with regret as he watched the firm brown buttocks sway to the door. 'Though it would appear that there is little to talk about.'

Gupta's body continued its restless movement, his sleek head swaying amid the rising steam. The long muscles on his gray arms were hard with tension.

'Harrap,' he asked harshly, 'would *you* be King?'

'The suggestion has been made. But no, not particularly. Why?'

'Because – I would have you know – you cannot. If you took

the Throne, the nobles and the Pariahs would rise against you, odd coupling though it be.'

'I imagine, Prince Gupta,' I interjected, 'that the Army and the people, who offered Prince Harrap the Throne only this morning, might play a role.'

'And tear the realm apart with civil war?' Gupta smiled. 'Do you wish that fate for Kamardol, my brother? Shall the leopard and the elephant destroy each other while the ring of jackals gathers outside?'

Harrap and I were silent.

'Of course you would not,' Gupta went on. 'You are too honorable. But you know that Chandra and I would not hesitate to arm the nobles and the Pariahs, rather than let you take the Throne.'

'The Army holds the High Prince Chandra,' I observed mildly. 'They are his guards.'

'That *was* true. But Chandra rests tonight at his castle outside the walls, guarded by his household troops.'

'Why, O Prince, do you say always "Chandra and I"? Why should the High Prince Chandra prefer you to Harrap as an ally?'

'Because he fears Harrap more . . . because Harrap is superficially more powerful . . . because it appears to him that Harrap could be King alone, as I could not . . . because he cannot understand Harrap, while my greed is like his own and, therefore, wholly intelligible to him . . . and, finally, because he needs me.'

'How precisely does he need you, O Prince?' I pressed.

'The priesthood, the Brotherhood, has finally agreed upon the ritual to mark the passing of power. They have found that two men must be Co-Kings, the elder as well as the younger brother, the elder to be spirit-in-flesh of the Great King, who is dead but not dead. I don't follow the rigmarole, but it works out well for me, you'll agree.'

'That rigmarole,' I raged impolitic, 'is clear and true – and beautiful beyond your understanding. That rigmarole has kept your dynasty on the Throne for centuries though you sneer at it and desecrate it.'

'Yakir!' Harrap's voice cracked in the red darkness that had come down around me.

'Sorry,' I murmured. The reckless anger still rang in my ears, though my voice was cool again. 'Then, Prince Gupta, only your pride and your lack of scruples stand in my prince's way. If we strangled you here, Prince Chandra alone would never dare raise the nobles and the Pariahs.'

The small, sleek head drew back as if to strike, but Gupta laughed, 'My honorable brother Harrap would never . . . Besides, I have fifty men in the lanes outside. Their orders are to kill anyone – maid, courtesan, Brahman, or prince – who leaves the courtyard before I do.'

'Enough!' Harrap's command cut across our anger. 'I have said that I will not be King. My father forbade it. And I do *not* wish to be King. Be at peace, my brother Gupta!'

'What *do* you wish, then?' Gupta asked softly.

'Our father's wish – peace for Kamardol – and glory too.'

'One word mocks the other, but no matter,' Gupta laughed. 'Yet for yourself, what do you wish?'

'What do you offer?' I put in.

'The Seeking!' Gupta answered. 'The Seeking for you, but not only for you. It is now the only way to peace for Kamardol – and perhaps to glory as well.'

'I have heard this plaint before, my brother. Show me, then, that it is true – and you may be Co-King yet. But it must be well proved.'

The sudden flare of my anger had cleared the air as does a brief summer storm; even the steam-wreathed room seemed no longer so oppressive. Having traversed of his own will the pass to which we had driven him without his knowledge, Gupta was all grace and limpid sincerity. We tried him further with mock resistance. He put all the priest's arguments with eager clarity and slowly persuaded Harrap to the course Harrap had already chosen when the encounter began.

'Your argument has weight – as far as it goes,' Harrap finally said. 'But what of Chandra? Only he can make it real.'

'Chandra awaits us at his castle. We can ride at the crest of night.'

'And place ourselves in your power?' I objected.

'One thing is clear, Colonel,' Gupta laughed. 'Harrap must

talk to the people again – or there will be no realm of Kamardol to apportion. And he must lead the Seeking. Seek no false dangers, Colonel. We have enough that are real to occupy us.'

The slave maidens massaged us, and afterward we sported with them in the cold pool like country urchins. We came tingling into the chamber where Ambiala waited. In my impatience I little marked what we ate and drank, and I was almost deaf to the skillful banter that passed between Ambiala and Gupta while Harrap offered an occasional lazy word.

I do remember, though, Ambiala's asking, 'Have you, then, agreed, gentlemen? May I send out a few flagons and some roasted meats to your men, Prince Chandra? And to yours, Colonel Yarie?'

Gravely, I gave permission to feed the bodyguard she had called up with words alone. Yet the two princes believed in its existence. Gupta looked long at me, between speculation and respect. Harrap glared his annoyance.

Before our departure Ambiala asked, as she had a week earlier, 'Harrap, can you tell me in honesty why you wish the Seeking? We have all here in Kamardol that any man could desire, and you have more than any other man in Kamardol.'

'Yes, Harrap, tell us,' Gupta added. 'I too have wondered.'

'Ambiala,' Harrap answered slowly, half smiling, 'ask my brother Gupta why he would be King. As Viceroy he could have the best of Kamardol – all glory, all power, and all pomp without responsibility. He loves responsibility even less than he does power, but he now pursues both.'

Gupta shrugged sinuously, replying, 'My brother is right, Ambiala. I would not rule. I would rather talk and drink and invent new ecstasies. But we must live in this world, not in the Heavens. In this world a man – or a woman, I imagine – must do certain deeds he little desires to do or lose the power to enjoy that which he does desire. I act as my ancestors ordained. But Harrap's way I still do not understand.'

Harrap ignored the challenge. He was silent through the long, cold ride that took us beyond the walls to the hill where Chandra's castle frowned in the moonlight.

Gupta had been alternately elliptical and mock-candid,

threatening one moment and cajoling the next, as ever an excellent negotiator. While we waited in the anteroom to Chandra's bedchamber I wondered about that prince, whom I hardly knew. Harrap had never been much with him. He was forty-eight, but the twenty-three years that lay between them were a greater barrier than the twenty-five that separated Harrap from Gupta, with whom he shared a certain recklessness. Chandra was unlike either, and no man knew him well. Men laughed at his enthusiasms, his devotion to the Buddhists and his desire to remake a world most found quite satisfactory. But no man knew his thoughts – or the springs of those thoughts. He neither gave his confidence nor revealed himself inadvertently. Yet it was Chandra who held the reins of fate in his plump hands. Gupta might propose, but only Chandra's word could confirm, since he still held whatever formal power endured in Kamardol.

He came heavily into the antechamber, pulling a white robe around his bulk, his white feet flabby in soft leather sandals. Even Gupta and Harrap rose, standing until Chandra had subsided into a mound of cushions. His light-brown eyes staring protuberant from his pallid cheeks, the Sub-King took our salutations with a heavy nod. When he finally spoke, I was startled that he allowed himself a waspish petulance that should be displayed only by him who exercises certain and absolute power.

'Who is this?' he asked querulously, singling me out with a pale, flexible forefinger like a blind grub.

'Colonel Yakir, my personal adjutant, Chandra,' Harrap answered easily.

'Why did you bring him? This was to be a private talk – a family talk about family matters. Is that not what you wanted?'

'I requested no talk, private or public,' Harrap said lightly. 'You asked me to come to you. Nevertheless, Colonel Yakir is here because we will need some record and because he is the only man I trust utterly.'

'I don't like it,' Chandra persisted.

'Why not, then, send for your own aides as well. Between you – you and my brother Gupta – there must be one man you trust.'

'All right, let him stay,' Chandra conceded. 'There are more

111

important things to discuss. You know, my brother Harrap, you have not behaved well toward me. I waited for hours this day for word of your mission. It was finally brought to me by a gossiping page, though I had ordered the Captain of the Royal Guard to report to me. You countermanded that order. I have, of course, ordered Ranbir strangled this dawn, but, still, it was a long and wearisome wait.'

The rush of blood stained Harrap's thick neck, and his eyes slitted. 'It was by my order that Ranbir waited. I will not have him executed – if I am indeed Generalissimo of the Armies.'

'All right, Harrap, if you insist,' Chandra replied, waving his plump hand negligently. 'But, still, you should have come to me. In any event, the Colonel-in-Chief of the Palace Guard must be strangled for discipline's sake. I'm sure you'll agree. That debacle was, after all, his fault.'

I glanced imploringly at Harrap, hoping this once to see his pent anger burst.

'I will not have it, O Prince!' he swore. 'If the Army is not mine to command and discipline, you can disentangle your own raveled skein. Come, Yakir!'

'Sit down, Harrap, sit down!' Chandra commanded. 'Let us talk about this.'

'There is nothing to talk about,' Harrap replied. 'Either I command or I do not.'

'If you had been here to command when you were needed,' Chandra said bitterly, 'there would be no mess.'

'You, my brother, gave the orders that set my soldiers against our people. You are breaking my Army. My men are sacrificed to your fears.'

'Be that as it may . . .' the Sub-King began, and I saw Harrap's hands clench in renewed anger.

'Brothers,' Gupta interrupted, 'perhaps this problem is, after all, the best place to begin. Assuming agreement here tonight, Harrap, what's to be done with the Palace Guard?'

'I'll take them with me – the Palace infantry, the Royal Guard, and their Colonel-in-Chief as well. If you punish them harshly, you break the Army's will. If they remain, the people will riot again and again.'

'That is reasonable, is it not, Chandra? Anyway, we'll be happier with our own household troops for a while.'

'Agreed,' said Chandra. 'Will you sit down, Harrap?'

Harrap lowered himself to his cushion, and I sat behind him.

'You have, I take it, agreed to the Seeking?' Chandra asked.

'Gupta has convinced me that I can thus best fulfill our father's will, maintaining you on the Throne and bringing peace to Kamardol. But if you do not wish it . . .'

'It will be very expensive,' Chandra complained. 'The gifts to the priests alone, and the games and gifts for the people . . .'

'I'm afraid you'll just have to pay,' Harrap answered.

'And the danger you bring upon the City?' Chandra mused. 'Are we strong enough to challenge the world? Do we not court disasters greater than those we may avert tonight? Why, Harrap, are you not content to stay beside us and help us build the new Kamardol?'

'Gupta contends that the Seeking is now the only way to make Kamardol secure,' Harrap answered uneasily.

'And so it is, my brothers,' Gupta interjected.

'But perhaps we could find another way,' Chandra continued, ignoring the scowl that crept over Gupta's dark forehead. 'Do you not see, Harrap my brother, that the challenge here in Kamardol is greater than any you may find on your road? We have always ruled by arms and by custom. But our father has seen a vision – and I have glimpsed a fragment of his vision.'

'What vision is that, Chandra?' Harrap asked gently.

'A vision of a realm at peace with its neighbors and at peace with itself . . . a vision of a realm that brings to all men an equal share of the good things the Gods have given men upon this earth. Thereafter the vision is less clear to me. But I see a realm where all men are at one with another and none is set above another except by need agreed upon, but not by custom or by force. All men strive to know the will of the Gods and their own natures, to praise the Gods in statuary and song . . .'

'But, Highness,' I interrupted, shocked, 'it is ordained by the Gods that men shall live in their proper places, serving and being served. Even the Pariahs, who are not quite men, have their place, the True Religion teaches. There is beauty in this appointed order.'

'*Have* the Gods so ordained, young man?' asked Chandra. 'I am not so sure.'

'I cannot see your vision, my brother,' said Harrap, soft-voiced as if he too were moved as well as bewildered by Chandra's words.

'No, I suppose not,' the Sub-King sighed. 'Perhaps, someday, you will . . .'

'Shall we return to our problems of this day?' Gupta asked briskly.

'A moment, my brother, a moment!' Chandra waved him to silence. 'Or, rather, yes. I spoke of the challenge you would give the world. As you know, the Brahmayanas are explicit. Only he who is in truth all-powerful may claim the title of World Monarch by proclaiming the Seeking. If he is less than all-powerful, it were but a foolish gesture that will bring his enemies ravening down upon his weakness.'

'I know that, Chandra,' Harrap replied. 'But all the signs of Heaven and earth command that we proclaim the Seeking. Who knows his power that has not tested it?'

'And Harrap is no fool to stray too far from home,' Gupta assured him. 'You would not, would you, brother?'

Harrap did not reply.

'I do not understand why it is so difficult,' Chandra's plaint continued. 'All I want is good for my people. But it has become so complicated. You, Harrap, your desire . . . my mother's mad anger merely because I speak with the good Buddhists . . .'

He sighed deeply, scratching the flaccid, dull-white surface of his inner thigh, which was exposed by the open skirts of his robe. Strangely, I began to fear him for the first time.

'Life is complex, my brother,' said Gupta. 'But we will manage. Harrap, I know, can guarantee the Army, and he will also speak with our mother – the priesthood, the Brotherhood, will support him. But why she won't listen to us, her own eldest sons . . .'

'As you say, my brother, life is complex,' Chandra avowed. 'And the people, what of them?'

'We thought Harrap might, within a day, assure them that the succession was fixed,' Gupta answered. 'He could promise them the Rites of Passing, the Enthronement – and, finally, the Seeking. We thought they would then be quiet.'

'It will all cost a terrible lot, but I suppose we must,' Chandra agreed.

When we came to details, each point required an eternity of talk. It was full dawn when we two rode down the stony path from Chandra's castle.

'Well, Yakir,' said Harrap dully, 'we seem to have stitched together a new kingdom. My brothers will both be kings. And you'll be taking that long ride you so much desire.'

After the tumultuous night, I felt weariness for the first time. And, for the first time, it came to me that we were fully committed, I to Harrap as firmly as he to his brothers.

'And out of all this haggling and corruption, perhaps . . .' I answered.

Harrap turned in his saddle, looking at me in surprise. 'Corruption?' he said. 'I smelled no corruption.'

Twelve

When the fate of peoples lay heavy upon us, it was perhaps petty to fret over the military rank Harrap had forced on me. Although it rubbed upon my conscience, I could not make the occasion to remonstrate that I would serve him just as well if men did not call me Colonel. When the occasion finally rose of itself, I already knew that the rank was no empty formality, but was essential to executing the duties he heaped upon me.

During the nineteen months that passed between our compact with the two princes and the climax of the Seeking, I earned my rank with strenuous labors. It was not by display of valor that I reconciled myself. Who could compare with Harrap in valor? Instead, I won my sash of rank by taking on myself all the essential details of organization and by offering counsel he would take from no other. Toward the end of our Quest I heard the despised title with a certain complacency and, sometimes, pride.

Since he was bound to the City by his promise to calm the people, Harrap sent me out the evening after our meeting in Chandra's castle. Ranbir and his three hundred men rode with me, as did the two hundred infantrymen who had broken before the mob. There was no rancor between the two groups. They obviously felt themselves the victims of a common tragedy, despite the antagonistic roles they had played. Under Ranbir's firm hand the Royal Guard displayed neither self-justification nor remorse. The infantrymen were listless under their burden of shame for the deaths of their officers, whom they had abandoned. Even the Colt trotted docile by my side amid the strange soldiers. He was yet not anointed, but He was chosen, and I would not use the leading rein as long as He returned to my familiar voice and odor.

Since my ill-matched charges presented none of the problems

I had feared, I thought much of Tamar during the march. Our abrupt departure prevented my seeing her. Instead, I had sent a short note in simple language I knew she could read. It told her little beyond my going and her father's reprieve. Perhaps, I thought, I should have said more.

We made for the southeast, where the realm stretched first into plains and then knit together into long valleys between spurs of hills. It was six days' march before we found the valley we sought, far from the City. It was guarded by rocky cliffs, and the neighboring valleys were planted, though thinly, with farms that would feed us. Well protected and well watered, the isolated valley gave ready access to both plains and mountains, as Harrap had directed. We built a shed for the Colt, open on one side so that He could wander as He wished, and a priest of Ranbir's race consecrated it with wine and the blood of a black cock. Afterward, we laid out our own camp, so that when Harrap came to us ten days later, all was well begun.

The people, he told me in some bitterness, had received the proclamation of the joint succession with joy. They were avid for the spectacles and the gifts that accompanied the Rites of the Passing of Power. They had, he said, quite forgotten their demand that he be King in their avidity for the more splendid games and richer gifts that would attend the Enthronement and the consecration of the Horse to the Seeking. The priest, who visited us from time to time in our exile, assured Harrap that he still held the people's affection above all his brothers. But I wondered if the priest's spies might not be ensuring their own rewards by telling him that which would please him most. Nonetheless, the Seeking was assured because the Co-Kings could not withdraw from their promises without enraging the people. For the rest, Harrap and I had no interest in their maneuvers as long as they did not imperil Kamardol.

We were far from the City, and the City was far from our thoughts. The labyrinthine intrigue that had given us the Seeking had never been revealed to us in the full intricacy of every convoluted turning and every remote chamber. In our narrow valley between the mountains and the plain, memory lost its edge, and our recollections were soon as hazed with forgetfulness and contradictions as the tales of other men's adventures heard but once around the campfire. Besides, Harrap's intensity drove us to exhaustion in our own small realm on the edge of the inhabited world.

Harrap had brought with him a hundred sons of nobles, all of whom claimed princely rank. Most of the threads of descent were so long and so tangled with unproved couplings and loudly sworn illegitimacies that we came to call them the Presumptuous Bastards. Princes they must be to partake of the Seeking, and princes they would be if they foreswore the honor of every female ancestor for the past five hundred years. Happy to have his choice from the thousand or more clamoring candidates for the troop of princes, Harrap had not examined their bloodlines with care. He was content that the men he chose could somehow be shown to conform to the prescription of the Brahmayanas. But when we were alone, he took to calling me 'Prince Yakir.' Himself he called the 'Fallen Brahman.'

'Surely, Prince,' he remarked, 'since it is clear that every female of every ancient family of Kamardol has been wanton in adventurous and fruitful adultery for the past ten centuries, it is hardly likely that we have escaped the cross-breeding.'

'With certainty, learned Brahman,' I answered. 'But before you interpret me a disputed verse of holiness, answer me a question. What use do you plan for our valorous Bastards? Shall we send them forth before us to charm the rooks from the passes, to shift the glaciers from the courses, and to call up springs in the deserts by their shameless eloquence?'

'No, that is your function,' Harrap laughed.

'Then perhaps they could be our vanguard. They, who lie so well, could lie terror into the heart of even the Great Emperor of China, so that he would disarm his men and present us with his treasury.'

'It may come to that later. But now I have another use for these Bastards. They shall be the point of our spear. It would be wasteful to seek to discipline them, though not wholly impossible. Instead they will ride before us, reporting what lies ahead, but not enduring in battle because that is not their virtue. Some of them shall always be with the Perfect Stallion, His sworn guardians.'

Since coming from the City, Harrap no longer referred, half contemptuously, to the Godlet. Instead, he spoke always of the Stallion. But in my thoughts He always remained the Colt, though sometimes, on my tongue, the Horse.

So we disposed of our troop of princes. Harrap himself taught them the elusive tactics he had proved with the regular light cavalry. He also taught them to descend out of the night that lay on the hills in one sharp charge and then, dispersing into twos and threes, to disappear among the ravines, the water courses, and the sand dunes. He armed the Bastards lightly, taught them to live on mutton jerky and dried beans, and led them on rides that tried even their superlative mounts.

Since such tactics depended on speed and endurance, our agents ransacked Kamardol and the adjoining kingdoms, going in the guise of itinerant horsemongers. Harrap paid from his own purse for the cross-breeds between the war chargers of the plains and the shaggy ponies of the mountains. They were ungainly to the eye. Broad withers capping shortened legs and heavy, unshorn coats gave them the square, half-formed look of the toy horses the peasant carves from a fallen bough for his infant son. But the club-headed beasts could almost match a racehorse over short distances. And they endured. By the Gods, how they endured, spinning off seventy to eighty miles a day over rocky passes, through sucking mud, or across the hot sands, where a war charger might collapse after no more than forty.

'You will ride four times as far as the rest of us,' Harrap told the princes, 'seeing all, remembering all, doing fearful slaughter when attacking, but never standing to defense and never remaining engaged for more than five minutes except by my own specific order.'

Ten of the Bastards kept watch on the Horse. We placed no let upon His ranging, and He would often lead them a week's ride through the hills He loved. Knowing that the Bastards would keep Him in sight or die, although He could outrun all their horses and outlast most, we did not worry that He would escape us. Besides, He knew the encampment waited with fodder and the accustomed scent of men and their horses. I did not fear His fleeing us. But I ever knew a moment of glory when the white God appeared in the cleft above our camp, the sun tangled in His mane; and I knew great thankfulness when, neck arched, He picked His haughty way down the stony path to His temple. All the while, He grew toward the Perfect Stallion Harrap already saw. He would be almost two years old, coming into His early prime, when the Seeking was consecrated.

From time to time Harrap would displace one of the Bastards, himself riding the trails the Horse found. From time to time I took the same ride, leaving Harrap to govern the camp. A few times we rode all together out of the hills, seeking to turn Him and marking how He wheeled and flowed away like a driven smoke.

'It is fine preparation,' Harrap explained. 'I must know His every move and how He behaves on different ground and in evil weather. I am forbidden to train Him, but I can certainly test Him.'

The glory of the Horse and those long chases through the hills just below the clouds could not divert me from the management of the camp, which daily grew in magnitude and complexity. There came to us during the first weeks a hundred knights, a troop of a hundred archers who were the sons of archers, and another troop of a hundred yeomen who were the sons of yeomen. Such, with the prince, was the array prescribed by the Brahmayanas. Joined to Ranbir's three hundred guardsmen and the two hundred infantrymen, those groups should have raised our strength to just over nine hundred. But, somehow, newcomers ever appeared of themselves, and the central group, what Harrap called the 'main shaft,' was never less than ten hundreds, and sometimes it rose to eleven hundreds. Besides, certain regular units were ordered to join us – always the most unruly. By the end of the third month, when our strength was complete, we mustered almost twenty-five hundreds of prime fighting men.

It was by then winter, the blue-cold and powder-dry winter of the hills. Our warriors were denied the winter's respite, during which they had expected to divert themselves with their own women – or with the camp-followers who had come to us despite

Harrap's orders and had made in the next valley a disorderly encampment almost as large as our own. Instead, the troops worked harder than they had in the autumn, as each unit was trained to its assigned place and duties. All learned to manage the three hundred camels and five hundred yaks Harrap had brought from his mother's country. Ranbir's mountaineers were still struggling to sit their horses, their short legs and long bodies ludicrous in the saddle. Harrap insisted that they learn to ride as well as the men of the plains, though the Royal Guard and the regular infantry would not fight in the saddle. The Bastards alone excepted, the entire force made arduous practice of infantry tactics. Tamar's father shook his heavy head in distress and prophesied disaster if the swift cavalry of Kamardol were used as footmen. Harrap twitted the old border-raider – reminding him how they both had fought afoot when their mounts were killed – until the handsome head, with its mane of white hair, rolled in laughter.

'Why, Mirab,' Harrap added, 'next you'll be telling me the mountaineers will never fight on foot again because I've taught them to ride and thus opened the road to flight.'

To my surprise, we heard no complaints at the new tactics from the young cavalry officers, those scented gallants who never hid their certainty that the subaltern of the cavalry of Kamardol was the crown of humanity. Foremost among them in ardor was Anand, the sub-lieutenant who had greeted us so sourly at the Towers on our return from the first Quest. Despite my misgivings when he came to us with his unit, Harrap had allowed him to remain.

'No harm having a few Buddhists with us,' he said, 'though I'll wager this one's a cavalryman first, then a soldier, and only last a Buddhist.'

When it finally came, the cavalry's protest was not of the rigors and the monotony of the constant exercises. But they sulked after Harrap ordered them to destroy the snug huts we had thrown up of stone, sand, and thatch. Fumbling, they made out that they could not master the setting up of the yurts we had seen north of the mountains. Those structures were, in truth, simple enough – notched withes that were bound together to make a hemispherical framework over which triangular pieces of heavy felt overlapped, and perhaps a woven reed outer wall to keep the wind from the felt. The riders of the steppes kept one yurt for a family of five or six, each member carrying a few parts behind his saddle. But Harrap ordered that twelve men share a yurt for lightness and for warmth. Nonetheless, two troops of light cavalry preferred, they said, to sleep in the snow.

We held our peace for a week, the malingerers growing the more stubborn the more their comrades mocked their love of discomfort and the more they suffered with fluxes and fevers. On the eighth day Harrap scanned the sky at dusk and ordered the two troops – two hundred men including the sick – on a forced ride of a hundred miles in two days. When they failed to return after four, we two followed their trail with ten of Ranbir's men. Rolling with our camels' splay-footed gait, we found them in the pass where the snowstorm had overtaken them twenty miles from camp. The horses had mired in the soft snow, and the cavalrymen, who had disdained to carry the yurts, huddled among blankets and cloaks in holes scooped from the snow. The crippled troops came home slowly along the trail packed by the camels' broad feet.

We lost twenty-seven men and more than fifty mounts, their legs broken or their nostrils stopped with ice, but Harrap never regretted the loss enough to talk of it. Even before permitting the cavalrymen to dismount, he assembled the entire force and told them, 'The mountains and the steppes make their own demands, different from the plains. In a year's time you will remember this winter and your fancied suffering as the silken and scented luxury of the Heavens themselves.'

From time to time, we sent units out with instructions no more specific than: 'Find something that will surprise us.' Sometimes a second unit trailed and ambushed the first. Harrap bore down my objections, insisting that the constant alertness the men learned was cheaply bought by the few deaths they inflicted before they realized whom they were fighting.

My favorite among the trophies those hunts produced was a veined block of many-colored stone the weight of twenty men which Anand's cavalrymen brought back on a reed sledge dragged behind four horses. The sub-lieutenant explained quietly, 'It's a chip from Shiva's footstool.' He would say no more.

The most striking, though, was the catch made by the mountaineers, a strange shaggy creature that seemed half bear and half monkey. Larger than the largest man, it was covered with coarse reddish hair, not fur. Even after lying three days bound across a horse's back, it made gestures that seemed to have meaning. When the creature died the next day, Ranbir laughed with glee. Three of his men had died of the wounds it inflicted before it was bound.

A few days after the bear-monkey's death Harrap called all our officers together. We met in the single building Harrap had left standing, a hall built of stone and wood. Ordinarily, we two used it as a central office. The craftsmen Harrap had assembled also worked in the hall – farriers, blacksmiths, tailors, carpenters, armorers, and the like. Coarse jute bags of grain, polished horse furniture, and square heaps of clothing were piled along the walls, and the burnished heads of pikes and arrows threw back the yellow rays of torches. Standing behind Harrap in the half-darkness, I saw the image of the diversity we had brought together for the Seeking. Cloaks of matted sheepskin parted over the carved breastplates of cavalry officers, and jeweled sword hilts lay against rough breeches of dun felt. Beneath their square blue helmets, the slanted eyes of Ranbir's lieutenants watched unmoving. The wide-set blue and gray eyes of tribesmen from the northwest roamed restless over the assemblage. Lean hawk noses in sharply honed faces pointed inquisitively at the flat features of hillmen from the east, and the range of complexions from wheat-gold to teak-brown revealed the dozen races of Kamardol.

'Gentlemen!' Harrap's rumble sawed through the chatter. 'Gentlemen! And I include princes, Brahmans, even cavalrymen . . . Gentlemen, we all know our purpose, insofar as we may know our purpose. Not even I, nor Colonels Mirab and Yakir, not even, I dare say, the priests themselves know our whole purpose. But what we do know has brought us here.'

The laughter awakened by his sally against the cavalrymen fell when he spoke of our unknown purpose and rose again when he mocked the priests.

'Gentlemen, I cannot tell you what I do not know. I cannot tell you our whole purpose. But I can tell you how we will seek it. Perhaps you will then be more tolerant of the mad maneuvers you have endured at my command these past few months. I know some of you believe that it was not in the maneuvers but in myself that the madness lay.'

Shamed relief tinged the renewed laughter, and several cavalrymen gazed intently at the chased helmets in their hands.

'There has never been a venture like this of ours. There have been conquests, and there have been Seekings, some wholly spurious, some deliberately directed away from danger. We do not march to conquer, but neither will we turn aside from the trail of the Stallion. We are puppets of the Gods. This, I believe, you knew, knowing me.'

His voice sank lower, compelling strained attention.

'But I believe the Gods would have us seek by all the means given to men to preserve ourselves – and to serve Them better. Since we go into the unknown, we must know ourselves – our strengths and our weaknesses – as perfectly as we can. That is true of each unit, each officer, each sergeant, and each soldier. I shall speak to the soldiers later.

'Picture a broad spear shaft with a diamond-sharp head that strikes as heavily as a boulder hurled from a precipice. Perfectly balanced, despite its weight, it is responsive to the slightest movement of the man who wields it. That man is myself.

'Then picture not a single, solid shaft, but a shaft made of a multitude of arrows. Each arrow is perfectly obedient to the will of its master – yourselves, gentlemen. We are a single shaft, but we are also a host of swift arrows, each directed by its own intelligence when there is need to attack individually – or to flee.'

We had shaped that speech with much care, Harrap and I. We sought to convey in the simplest words our concept of a force so swift that it struck the enemy before he knew of its existence, so constant in movement that the enemy could no more bear it down by mass attack than he could find a skein of smoke. The assemblage gasped when Harrap told them we would, on occasion, flee, and I knew that he would need to explain to them again and again.

Nonetheless, we both left the encampment the next day, I to the City and Harrap to tour the camps of the standing army. Mirab remained to command, though he was admonished to act only to avert catastrophe.

'Let them make their own mistakes for a time,' Harrap told Mirab when his feet were in the stirrups. 'They have been subjected to mine too long.'

The comforts of Kamardol were full welcome – as was the excitement only a great city generates. Still, my mind dwelt much on our rude camp, which was more real to me than the stone buildings and the effervescent life of the City. I was caught up in bargaining for our needs and in consulting with the priests on the coming consecration of the Horse. Tamar I saw for but a few hours. It was her time of the moon, and we could not lie together, but neither did she reproach me further for my loyalty to Harrap and my commitment to the Seeking. Instead, she gave me thanks for her father's life and, since we could not speak of our own future which could not be, she gossiped of the Court. Chandra and Gupta, even before their Enthronement, were of wholly different minds on many matters, but the people seemed content. It was a singularly empty visit for me, and I was pleased to ride back to the camp.

Harrap had returned a day earlier, but he stayed only a few days – just long enough to ride out once with the troops – before himself journeying to Kamardol. One of us must stay with the force, and his presence was commanded at the Enthronement. I was myself quite content to remain in camp.

Harrap reappeared after twenty days. The priest of our Quest rode beside him, still as awkward and strained in the saddle as he had ever been. It was apparent that they had come to a new understanding, and they spoke of the Enthronement in alternating sentences, equally relishing their ribaldry. Listening to their account, I was suddenly aware that Harrap and I had also struck a new balance. Since I had assumed duties which were of right Harrap's, we were no longer two enclasped parts making a single whole in thought and action. I had become more than the 'unswerving shadow and wiser echo' he once called me.

The Enthronement, they told me, had surpassed all previous spectacles in the volume of blood and gold that flowed, for even miserly Chandra would spend to bind the people to the Throne. He had taken as his personal sign the Bull Elephant, and Gupta the Hamadryad, each renowned for wisdom as well as strength.

'But some call them the sow and the viper, deeming those animals more fitting to their separate natures,' Harrap said. 'Now have I done all I could do to honor my father's command.'

The priest spoke chiefly of the form and the sacrifices. Speaking to me as another Brahman, he explained in professional detail the shaping of the ritual to enthrone Co-Kings. I was, however, more concerned with the temper of the City, which he passed over. Still, I was amused at the minute pleasure he took in describing the mock sacrifice of a Pariah to the Mother Goddess, the ancient earth deity he had earlier feared.

'They whirled the fellow around in a cleft bough,' he recalled, 'stopping well short of death. Only a few ribs cracked where the cleft held him fast. It was, in a way, a pity to revert to the ancient rites, though it would have been interesting to see it carried through. Still, it was necessary. She is, after all, the Goddess of Destruction and of Birth, the Fountain of Multiplicity. How else could we have appointed two Kings at once?'

'And our own affair?' I finally interrupted. 'The Seeking, how stand the signs?'

'Oh, the Seeking,' the priest's complacence was startled by my question. 'All goes magnificently. How else could it go?'

'Chandra did not seem enthusiastic to me,' I observed sourly.

'Nor is he,' Harrap answered. 'But what choice does he have?'

'He *must* allow us to march forth,' added the priest. 'He has promised. If he did not, Gupta would force him. They have ensnared themselves. Besides, both desire Harrap's absence above his counsel or direct support.'

'Both, of course, will contrive as many obstacles as they can,' Harrap said casually.

'Obstacles?' I echoed.

'Of course,' said the priest, 'that is expected. They will try to

126

keep us on strings – even as children are given sharp-edged toys to buy their silence, but must be kept from injuring themselves with those toys.'

'Even now,' added Harrap, 'they are assembling a herd of one hundred ancient nags. Chandra will insist that they accompany us, since it is so written in the Brahmayanas. Yet we could not move more than a few hundred miles in their company.'

'What can we do?' I asked, stricken. 'We cannot refuse the nags since they are prescribed. Perhaps the people can be roused to press for our freedom.'

The afterthought pleased me. I was, I felt, becoming as adept as the priest in intrigue. But he smiled in pity.

'The people, Yakir, want only the forms and the gifts and the blood sport of the Seeking. They care even less for the reality than do Chandra and Gupta, who win glory if It succeeds and are freed of Harrap if It fails.'

'Then what?' I persisted, feeling myself a novice again. 'Are we, in truth, entrapped?'

'There are,' answered the priest, 'other texts and other interpretations.'

'And,' Harrap laughed, 'only the Gods command us when we are gone out of Kamardol.'

Thirteen

Spring came creeping over our hills, taking us with tactics half learned, stores half amassed, and weapons half shaped. Or so it seemed to me, so closely was I pitched to the daily rhythms of the camp. But Harrap laughed at my quick dismay when the deep snow melted and men and beasts crashed through the brittle crust to flounder helpless in sucking slush with the half-frozen water choking their nostrils.

'Yakir,' he said, 'you are too true to your new role. No force has ever been fully prepared for action since warfare began among men, and no adjutant has ever felt his force more than half prepared. Go into the hills for a while with the Stallion and the Bastards, forsaking all our petty turmoil here. Take your lute and charm the spring flowers from beneath the snow. I yearn to see them.'

I gladly left the encampment where I awoke to each day fretting over missing harnesses and spears or weighing new remedies for colicky ponies and lamed camels. In the warm, moist air of the spring hills, I forgot the quarrels among men of different regions and the intrigues of their priests. And I began to make a great 'Song of the Seeking.'

Only two days were given to me to follow the Colt through the awakening hills. He was listless and timorous, afraid to trust Himself to slopes that changed their shape under the weight of His hooves. The Bastards were bored. Only repeated commands and constant vigilance kept them from chivvying the Colt toward our own valley. But on the second day He turned His head toward the valley, and we followed Him. I was reconciled to taking up my tasks again, and the Bastards longed for the pleasures of the encampment – wine-quaffing matches, tossing sticks for gold, and fighting over the women in the next valley.

The encampment had vanished, utterly swept away. The Council Hall and the Horse's temple floated awry like foundered boats in the lake of black mud that lapped the edges of slopes frosted with purple freesias. The fetid yurts toward which the Bastards yearned had disappeared – together with the pennants, the weapons, and the stores – into pack saddles and baggage carts.

The entire force was strung out along the ribs of rock that caged our valley. The soldiers lay half naked in the sun, their clothing and weapons spread around them to dry. Most were using the respite to pick the lice from the seams of their garments, and a few hacked at each other's long hair and tangled beards with daggers. I heard the women wailing in the next valley, bemoaning Harrap's command that they could not follow us to the City.

'Ho, Yakir!' Harrap hailed me. 'I have done your job for you. Now, come and do mine for me. Get these fat, lazy fellows moving!'

I unloosed the lute from my saddle, and, after testing the strings, struck into 'The Warriors' Return':

> We have drawn a curtain of fears
> Between this bright City and the foes of the King.
> We have borne the magic power of his ring
> To the skybound cave, where the years
> Lie sleeping till the earth, their dam,
> Wakes each – to rule and to die.

When I sang the opening lines, silence crept over the clatter of the force. Harrap first and then others joined in the chorus:

> Oh, you maidens of Kamardol,
> The warriors return from the kill!
> Hear, you slow townsmen's wives,
> The warriors return from the kill!
> Bearing, empouched, ten thousand foemen's lives
> To lay between your soft thighs,
> And breed up more warriors still!
> The warriors return from the kill!

On the first chorus, the soldiers began to grin and stir. On the last, hoarse chorus, the harsh echoes from the hills, already softened by the sponge of moisture that overspread all, were lost amid the jangling of harnesses, the regular clash of scabbards against armor, and the mewling of the newborn foals. We were, at last, on the march over the earth that still labored with the spring.

We moved at first with the slothful undulations of a serpent that crawls, half blind after his winter's sleep, out of the thawing swamp. Though the consecration still waited, the Seeking was at its true beginning, but even my first sally from the darkened City with the stricken core of our force had been more vigorous. The joints of men and beasts were stiffened by their reluctance to depart from the valley that the habit of six months, if not inclination, had made their home. Nor could we cut ourselves free of the long train of camp-followers – the wives, harlots, children, peddlers, soothsayers, acrobats, dancers, and players who had passed the winter in the next valley. Their presence half seen, but never unheard, dragged at the soldiers' will as if their wrists were bound. The horsemen held their reins slack, and their mounts were sluggish.

Yet Harrap's fierce good humor was so free of all the world outside his own purpose that he neither displayed impatience nor goaded the soldiers to haste. I knew from his demeanor that it was not yet time to try the effect of my new 'Song of the Seeking.' Besides, the song was not yet made complete. Only the priest, bloated and pale after the long winter, muttered his fears of coming to the arena after the appointed hour of the appointed day. He consoled his impatience by praying us toward our fixed destiny, commanding his Gods to hasten the column despite its general's carelessness.

So we came slowly over the burgeoning hills toward Kamardol. After five days, when Harrap detached the units to be conse-crated, the rest, who had originally been so slow to move, shouted their protests at once more enduring the boredom of an encampment. Relenting his stern prohibition against the ines-capable, Harrap advised them to enjoy the services of the camp followers for the last time. While Mirab stayed to oversee the main body, we three – Harrap, the priest, and I – rode toward the Towers of Kamardol with the chosen four hundred bellowing their exuberance behind us – the princes, the knights, the archers, and the yeomen. In the City, which was gaudy with lights and banners and pungent with swollen bullockskins that dripped wine at every corner, the four hundred halted in the Grand Bazaar for orders.

'You'll disperse now,' Harrap bawled. 'Make the best of this night and the next. One day past tomorrow, just after the noon rest, we meet, bleary-eyed and heavy of head, at the edge of the glacis.'

The priest had vanished as was his practice, and we two rode toward the Great Palace, the Colt between us. He was even more shy of the turmoil of the City than He had been on that night almost eight months earlier when He first came to test His fate. The people lined the noon-bright streets to cheer our dwarf procession. Like the Horse, I felt that the wilderness, though it were seeded with enemies, was less frightening than this, my own City.

Our brief homecoming denied itself in its first moments. I cannot remember the time when I did not know the Great Palace. The dank corridors and butterfly clouds of courtiers, the subterranean kitchen and the scullions' greasy faces bronzed by the soaring fires – these were the substance of my early years. Their unchanging pattern was so fixed so deep in my being that I could neither identify nor believe the uneasiness I felt when we came to the South Gate.

His body rigid with distaste, Harrap jerked his chin toward the sentries and said, 'It's an odd sight, eh?'

I had passed through that gate thousands of times, and each of those times I had been admitted by Ranbir's stocky mountaineers in their square blue helmets. But that day the men of Chandra's personal guard, soft-bodied and hard-faced, stood in their places. They punctiliously tendered the ceremonial salutes due us and as punctiliously summoned their officer to pass us in. He was a short captain with incongruously heavy shoulders and a great paunch, more like a strangler than a guardsman. While the mock captain concluded his deliberate examination and gave us his salute, a tide of regret submerged me. I yearned for the days of the Great King and for the certain order we had known before his retirement and the Seeking altered the world. I felt older than my own father and utterly defeated.

When we came out the long passageway into the courtyard, Harrap lifted his hand in casual farewell. I said nothing, but ignored the dismissal. Together we showed the Horse to His stall, lingering to watch the grooms fill His bin and His trough before rubbing His flanks and combing the filth from His mane.

'Ever the adjutant, eh Yakir?' Harrap grinned at me as we parted in the doorway.

'No, it is not that,' I said, turning his jest. 'But He is a good horse.'

'Yes, He is, isn't He?' Harrap answered softly.

We parted then, and I went directly to the baths. The attendants – neither as young, nor as beautiful, nor as naked as Ambiala's – giggled and mocked me as a greasy, sun-bleached barbarian while they combed my matted hair and shaved my beard. They scrubbed and rinsed me twice before they would let me enter the scented pool of hot water, but the water slowly turned gray as the filth worked out of my pores. Though the bathmaid strove with brush and stone when she trimmed my nails, grime still engraved my knuckles and the callouses on my palms.

A page brought me a kilt and a plain tunic, both of white cotton, for I was weary of coarse garments and loath to risk my silks in the fevered City. I left the Palace through the North Gate and turned toward my father's villa. My old tunic was tight across the chest and shoulders, and the earth rocked gently beneath my feet. I had not gone more than a few paces on foot for months, and this was no day to try my cramped muscles in the tumultuous streets of Kamardol. I had seen the Holi many times before that day, but never before that day had I seen the Holi with eyes that had in the endless hills lost the measure of the confining buildings.

Before I had gone a hundred paces, my clothes were stained purple and green and red by the dyed water, the sacred urine, and the cow's blood the revelers squirted from the bladders of pigs and sheep. Beside the great wineskins, where all might drink, stood small altars – and upon the altars the images of the

Gods and Goddesses shaped in clay. Whether elephant-headed, pig-snouted, many-armed, or hung with breasts like a pine-cone, each dripped crimson with the blood of the sacrifices that twitched on the altars – white kids and dappled calves, brown pigs and black dogs. Greater in number than they had been at any other Holi, more profuse than the images of all the other Gods, were the images of Black Khali, the Slayer and the Creatress, whom the common people confuse with the ancient Mother Goddess. All the Gods received the same total tribute, and swarms of flies encrusted them all, droning somber black and iridescent green on their pilgrimages.

Priests, carrying sharp knives as if they were scepters, walked majestically through the streets, their sodden robes splashing blood onto the cobbles. At every corner a priest stopped to take a silver coin, the blood money of the Gods, and to slit the throat of a sacrificial animal held in a noose. Eyes rolling in anguish at the stench of blood and the cloying incense that displaced the spring air, the animals raised a fearful chorus. The bleating, the lowing, the squealing, the barking, and the insane cackling rose over the gay shouts of the revelers and the hoarse quarrels of those already drunk.

On smaller altars, set in the roadway itself, only piglets and rabbits died. The power of fertility, so strong in their blood, anointed enormous phalluses, a full yard high and five hands' breadths around, or vulvas shaped to receive them. Some were of the ancient mode, simple shafts or hollow ovals of stone worn smooth by the devotion of generations. Others were painstakingly carved of wood and painted in the boldest lines. Every detail was perfectly reproduced as in life, though so manyfold larger – the swelling heads and pendant globes of the phalluses, the convoluted lips of the vulvas. Those latter were fringed with the coarse hair of bulls and cows. By evening all would be the same, half dripping and half clotted with the red and brown of blood, as would the smaller phalluses and vulvas the dancers in the streets had strapped over their brief garments. All images are sacred at Holi, and all deeds are sacred.

Some celebrants had already passed into ecstasy. They capered naked in the sunlight. The sex organs of the men were stained purple and their backs were painted with scenes from the copulations of the Gods. The thighs, buttocks, and breasts of the women glistened with a scarlet dye. From time to time a couple would break off the dance and lie together in the street, striving to emulate the infinite intricacies of posture practiced by the Gods. Their fellows danced around them in a tight ring, shouting ancient chants to encourage their invention.

Many women – and some men – walked aloof among the frenzy of the throngs. They were muffled in many-colored robes that hung to the ground from pointed fools' caps, and they wore masks that hid their features. Those were – or pretended to be – Brahmans or Kshatriyas, whose pride of caste kept them from the open revels of the simple folk. From time to time a woman so muffled would crook her elbows to part her robes and reveal that beneath them she was naked and painted like the commonality. Only the masks were fixed.

As I pushed through the throngs as laboriously as a traveler plodding through the loose sands of the desert, masked women whirled before me to display flanks and breasts glistening with sweat and desire. I felt the tightening of my loins and the swelling and heat in my private parts that even the matronly bath attendants had awakened after my long abstinence. Why I did not pause I cannot tell. But each time, I saw with relief, the woman found a partner within seconds.

One masked woman lay on a heap of grain sacks in the roadway, her golden-brown knees drawn up and apart while at least ten men waited to enter her. Carters, porters, merchants, servants, and such common folk, they cried loudly, urging the man at the head of the line to greater dispatch. There was something, not precisely identifiable but nonetheless familiar, about the woman's slight, dripping form and quivering thighs. I wondered for a moment, with bitter distaste, whether she might be Tamar. But I mastered myself and walked on, marveling only at my own concern, for all deeds are sacred at Holi.

On our low hill the tumult subsided, and I came in peace to the row of gnarled pines before my father's house. Behind shuttered ports my father sat at his books. I endured my mother's overwhelming solicitude until she withdrew to find what food the

134

servants had prepared before going off to their revels. After her effusiveness it was a relief to submit to my father's astringent questioning. He did not ask after my welfare, but how we had trained and organized our force. I answered in minute detail, for I knew that he, as Court Chronicler, would record the Seeking for the *Royal History of Kamardol*.

At length, he laid his pen aside and kneaded his cramped fingers. 'I see,' he said, his mild eyes fixed on me, 'you have let your hair grow like a Kshatriya. And I hear you are called Colonel.'

My mother came into the room on the tail of his sentence. She bore the inevitable black earthenware bowl of mutton broth on a polished wooden tray, and she was effusively silent.

'I must be called Colonel,' I answered, keeping my voice level, 'if I am to command troops. The long hair is merely convenient. It masks my difference from other officers – and requires less care. I have not thought much about it, but I will have it cut properly if it will please you.'

'That's a good boy, Yarie,' my mother gushed. 'Your father and I will . . .'

'No, Aminsa,' my father interrupted. 'He must do as he thinks best. He has taken the task upon himself, and he must discharge it as best he can. Later, when he returns, of course . . .'

'As you say, my dear,' said my mother, unusually submissive. 'Still, it's a terrible shame that he couldn't have married before he left. So many fine Brahman girls would just love . . .'

My father's white eyebrows rose, portending a thorned reply, but I broke in to ask what treat waited in the kitchen. My mother's eager answer turned their imminent quarrel. My father's disapproval of my actions had been so mildly expressed it could be taken as faint approval of my purposes – if not my means. I could not bear that they should smother my relief with one of their interminable, self-absorbed quarrels. Yet I, who should have been the pampered guest, was forced to exert all my tact to prevent their despoiling their own grace.

The afternoon passed pleasantly despite the latent strain. When the shadows deepened without, I evaded my mother's insistence that I spend the night at home and gratefully accepted my father's offer of his litter to bear me back to the Great Palace. I did not wish to walk again through streets that would be seething toward the climactic abandon of the Holi. My father took from me a fresh promise to keep full notes for his records, and I was finally done with my mother's tearful farewells.

My own Seeking truly began when I passed out of the avenue of pines before my father's house, though Tamar came to me in the apartments at the Palace that evening. I greeted her with an air of light surprise, for I was determined to ride out no more storms of feminine emotion.

'What is this?' I mocked. 'Not out enjoying Holi?'

'Somehow, I didn't want . . .' she began to answer as lightly.

We embraced, and all our artifice was shattered. Our love-making that night was almost savage. The long separation just passed and the longer separation that lay before us inflamed our bodies so that, beyond our own will, they clung and pressed together as if to join themselves forever.

We did not wake to the first sun of the morning, for we had not slept in the night. I returned to the full light of day to behold Tamar gazing down at me. She appeared at once ravaged and radiant. Violet petals of exhaustion lay beneath her eyes, but their gray luminescence was at once soft and arid. A hot wind rising within me swept away both discretion and propriety.

'I am going because I must,' I said, my words stumbling beneath their weight of total sincerity. 'Believe me, Tamar, my love, I would – ever so much – rather stay with you.'

'But will you return?'

'The Gods willing, I shall return and . . .' I paused abashed.

'And then?'

'And then . . . if you wish it, we shall find a way.'

'Shall I . . . wait . . . then?'

'If you wish it . . . wait,' I answered, drawing assurance from the certainty in my own voice.

'Oh, Yarie my darling . . . if I can . . .' she sighed, her lips against the hollow of my throat.

We made love again, long and luxuriously, and afterward I told her again what I sought on the long road. She did not speak of our own future again, and I was grateful that she did not soil

136

the moment with uncertainty. Only after she had gone, smiling through the tear courses on her cheeks, did I wonder what I had promised.

I could hardly call Tamar back to ask her. Besides, I had actually promised nothing. The promise, as she might interpret it, would keep her content in my absence. But the passage of a single year, even a year of miracles, could not make the impossible possible. It could certainly not make the impossible likely.

As I put on my coarse campaign clothes, I forgot those vexations. I forgot Tamar herself when I rode down the glacis to the field where the sacred four hundred were assembled – the hundred princes, our Presumptuous Bastards, in burnished breastplates; the hundred knights, somber in black armor; the hundred archers, their arrowheads polished to mirror brightness; and the hundred yeomen twirling their steel-headed staves. I knew from the gray semicircles under their eyes, from their drooping heads, and from their sodden silence that they had partaken of all the pleasures Kamardol offered.

We rode through streets that still bubbled with revelry, though the people were tiring on this third day. The throngs parted to let us pass, and only from time to time did the spearmen who rode ahead lean over to prick an entwined couple from our way. Harrap and I rode behind the spearmen, the Horse between us bound to our saddles by leather traces. A black scarf covered His eyes, but He tossed His head and reared at the stench of blood. When we came to the arena midway between the City and the Towers, His hooves dripped red.

We staked out our horses and made our camp on the broad meadows north of the arena, which was silent after the bull-baiting and the gladiatorial contests. We had come to the austere purity of the Consecration after the orgies of self-gratification and blood-letting the City and the arena had encompassed during the week past. After the anguish of death and the fever of copulation, it was fitting that the ritual rebirth should be of limpid simplicity. The meaning was not in the splendor of the trappings, nor in the heat of our actions. All meaning was in the essence of the deed, which would bind men and Gods each to the will of the other so that each would be one with the other and together they would be one with the universe.

I was given much time for such reflection, since I remained with the Horse and the four hundred while Harrap and the priest went into the arena. The preparatory rites, which had been in progress for a week, were to culminate that night.

All was made ready. The priests, four hundred in number, had prepared the sacred grains and the great cauldrons of soma, the drink that carries men beyond intoxication, and beyond narcosis, to the exhalted contemplation of crystalline visions of the world – as it was, as it is in reality, and as it shall be – all glowing within an aura of perfect rainbow hues. The priests had braided the rope that would lead the Horse, and they had greased it with refined butter, the fiery spirit that is sacred to Pragpati, the premier God of the Rite. They had chanted the soma hymns and the hymns of adoration to Khali, the Destroyer and the Creatress, and they had presented the Co-Kings with golden dishes of rice and pounded wheat, which is the seed of the world and the seed of the Horse. The Kings, had in their turn, bestowed upon the priests four hundred grains of gold, which is the seed of the universe. That much gold would buy four thousand cows, but they had granted the priests four thousand cows as well.

I pondered the profound miracle of the expression of creation in earthly forms, but a chance thought made me laugh aloud. Chandra was now paying as he had known he must pay when he complained that the Seeking would be horribly expensive as well as horrifyingly perilous.

I lay outside the great currents that night. Within the arena the priests were divided into the Invokers in mustard-colored robes, the Sacrificers in yellow robes, the Chanters in saffron, and the officiating High Brahmans in orange – each hundred priests representing one of the four points of the world. They were divided into four groups, and four groups would attend the Horse, because four times four is sixteen, the sacred number of the parts of Pragpati and the parts of the world. To each of the priests three servings of rice were offered – 'four bowlfuls, four handfuls, four double handfuls, being, in all, twelvefold,' as the Brahmayana declares. Twelvefold is the year in its months, and twelvefold is the rope that leads the Horse, twelve units in length. The rope contains the entire year of the Horse, the Seeking that encompasses all, since the Horse is all – the creator and the created, the Gods and man, the earth and the Heavens, the priests and the nobles, men and beasts. Out of the coming together of the sixteenfold, the twelvefold, and the fourfold arises the one that is the perfect unity, which is the universe and the Gods and man.

When the priests had eaten of the sacred rice and drunk of the soma, the Co-Kings again gave them gold, each King bestowing upon each of the four Chief Priests of the Invokers, the Chanters, the Sacrificers, and the officiating High Brahmans a gold disc of one hundred grains in weight. Thereupon, the first priest of the Sacrificers declaimed, 'Fire thou art, O Kings, light and immortality!'

Since gold is fire, light, and immortality, the first priest thus repaid the Kings' gift by commanding the Gods, 'Bestow life and transcendent strength upon these Kings and their consorts.' The Queens were hung with gold, which is seed; they were again in fours, four Queens to each Co-King.

When the evening rites were done, the Kings retired, each to his private place behind the Great Altar with his four wives. They put off their rich garments, and they stripped themselves of their jewels and lay down naked to rest together. Each of the Kings was commanded to lie with erect member between the thighs of his favorite wife, but neither to enter her nor to spill his seed. Should he spill his seed by either intent or failure of self-control he would spill the seed of the world, which is the Horse. The good fortune and supreme power that the Seeking brings to him – to the King, above all others – would be turned into misfortune, and the power of the realm would rot.

Whether the Kings were true to the command or not, I do not know. Nor do I know whether, during the year of the Seeking, they were true to the command to abstain from all sexual congress, just as the Stallion must not know the mare. As I followed the rites thus far in my mind, another chance thought whispered that Gupta looked with no great joy upon the Seeking because of the injunction to abstinence, just as Chandra was stricken by the outflow of gold it demanded. Each was true to his own love.

Were this account a guide for young Brahmans who will never themselves see the Consecration to the Seeking, I should recount every moment of the morning rites. Were this account not the tale of our Quest, I should tell of the further gifts of the Kings and the libations of soma, wine, milk, and ghee poured out while four hundred priests chanted a ring of hymns propitiating the Deities of the four corners of the earth and particularly Varuna, who is the spring and the Seeking, and Pushan, who is the lord of all roads and is the earth itself. I shall not, since that lore is stored in a hundred books. Besides, my tale is drawn not for priests, but for men who are charged to rule other men, even, perhaps, those who are not of our race or religion. I shall therefore record only that which I myself saw when, at the head of the four hundred, I came into the great horseshoe of the arena through its open northern end.

I led the Horse myself, since I was again for that moment a Brahman, as well as a warrior.

The tiers on either side were fields of many colors shimmering in the morning sun. The people, in their proudest garments, had filled the seats during the night, speculating with heavy jests on the ordeal of the Kings within their tents behind the Great Altar. When my four hundred halted at the four points of the world and I rode forth with the Horse, the tens of thousands in those tiers gasped all at once. Harrap and the priest of the Quest rode to me.

I heard the Chief Priest of the Invokers chanting: 'The Horse is marked with all colors. He is perfect in speed. He is of the value of a thousand cows, nay, tenfold a thousand cows. And the Horse is without match under the yoke.'

We rode toward the shallow pool scooped out before the towering mass of the Great Altar, where stood a figure in the dun shirt of a Pariah, holding a dog under one arm and dangling a club under the other.

'He is marked with all the colors, being white,' the hundred Invokers chanted. 'And he is marked with all the colors so that the Sacrificer Kings may obtain all, for color, being that which is seen, is all – and the Seeking is all. He is perfect in speed, for speed is vigor, and He shall give His vigor to the Kings. And He is worth a thousand cows tenfold, for the thousand encompasses all that exists, and the Kings shall obtain and rule over all that exists. Above all, He is without match, so that the Kings shall, in Him, obtain all, even the sun, which is without match. There is no one to rival the Horse, and no one will rival the Kings.'

I shuddered at the blasphemy that arrogated matchlessness to *two* Kings, a reality that cannot be either in logic or in inspiration. But the rent in the seamless fabric of the rites seemed invisible to the others.

The Pariah, squinting crosseyed as he knelt in the pool with the dog under his arm, was a rough fellow whom I knew. Son of one of the whores of the Grand Bazaar, he was a thief, a hired bully, and, some said, a murderer for pay. I led the Horse into the pool and left him standing free before the Pariah, who dropped the dog into the water. The dog swam yawping for the edge, its head bobbing so that the black patches above its eyes winked as if it had four eyes.

The son-of-the-whore raised his club and smote the dog on the skull. I heard the bone crack, and blood eddied in pink ribbons through the shallow water as the dog died.

The Horse had been standing quite unmoving, calmed by the Spirit. But the stench of blood stung His nostrils. He tossed His head and flung out His hind legs. One hoof struck the Pariah on the temple, and he crumpled into the pool. When the priests came to bind the sacred rope around the Horse's shoulders, the priest of the Quest stepped into the water and turned the Pariah over. He released his hold, and the Pariah rolled back on his face.

'It is good,' the priest whispered to me. 'The whore's son is dead. We are blessed by the twofold blood offering, and all evil is driven out.'

The priests led the Horse to the foot of the Great Altar, while we waited beside the pool where the two carcasses floated. The ceremony was long, the anointing, the chanting, the bestowing of new gifts on the priests, and the renewal of commands to the Gods to serve the Co-Kings in all things. When the last echo of the last invocation had died, the priest of the Quest and I came forward again. I whispered into the right ear of the Horse, while he whispered into the left.

'Abundant is Thy mother and full of strength Thy father, for Thy mother is the earth and Thy father the sky. A Horse Thou art, a Charger Thou art, a Steed Thou art.'

The eye, gray that morning, rolled back to look at me, and the strong neck trembled.

'Child Thou art called,' we whispered, 'and speediest of all. Thyself, the best of all horses and the compass of all men. And in Thy shape, the shape of the earth itself.'

Priests roped the hundred and eight sacrificial beasts to their stakes for the slaughter. Harrap and I bowed to the Co-Kings and their wives and then led the Horse to the center of the arena. The priest of the Quest, mounted and garbed for the journey, bestowed upon us the golden threads of dedication, enjoining us in secret words to be true to the Seeking even as he fixed the threads on our foreheads. His voice rose to penetrate every corner of the arena, and he declaimed:

'O Ye Gods, guardians of the four regions, guard Ye this Horse, consecrated to the Gods. O ye men who ride with the Horse, the Gods of the four regions look upon you. Guard Him well and let Him run ever forward for a year. Were he to turn back, all would go backward to ruin here in Kamardol.'

The awful words reverberated in the stillness.

'Those who go to the end with Him will become sharers of the power of Kamardol. The Sacrificer Kings will become the greatest Kings Kamardol or the world has known. Those who do not go to the end will become peasants and Pariahs. And should you meet a Brahman on the road, ask him, "O Brahman, what is the Seeking?" And if he cannot answer, you must despoil him and slay him, for he is no true Brahman that does not know the Seeking, which is all.

'This is the meaning of the Seeking. You shall go forth, following where the Horse goes and never turning aside from the path He chooses, nor choosing for Him the path. For His will is the Gods' will, and you shall follow Them in Him. And the Gods will guide Him back to return to this same Great Altar when the appointed year is past.

'Wherever He goes, you must go. In foreign lands, those princes who know the will of the Gods will not seek to hinder the Horse on His road. Instead, they will worship Him and smooth His road, and they will offer tribute to the Kings of Kamardol, who are their true lords. Princes and Kings who do not know the will of the Gods, or spurn Their will, may seek to keep the Horse from passing or to capture Him. Then must you fight them for the Horse's passage, so that He goes unhindered. And when He goes free over their lands, even impious princes will be subject to the mighty King of Kamardol. That is your task before the Gods. Go now!'

Released from the rope, the Horse bounded through the open end of the arena and toward the north. He fled the arena, where He had been made God, He fled toward the broad fields of the north impelled by His other nature, still equine.

He had chosen, and we would go northward. Squadron after squadron, the four hundred formed up and galloped after Him, all thundering toward Alexander's Road and the high mountains.

Book Two

Book Two

Fourteen

The torrent of pink rock that was Alexander's Road flowed through a valley gilded by the morning sun. The villages and fields of our youth fell away from the pounding of our horses' hooves. Spattered with many-colored bunting and the white cloaks of gaping countryfolk, the home valley shone like a burnished copper cauldron in the fierce rays. The shimmering intensity of light melted the shapes of houses and trees into lovely grotesqueries and, like shining copper, gave us back disjointed, wavering images of ourselves. The fires of the morning hid men and beasts, almost consuming them behind curtains of flame, but we heard the nervous throbbing of drums, the thin squeal of pipes, and the braying of the village dogs hailing the passing of our cavalcade.

As the intervals between villages stretched longer, Orberk, Harrap's bright-haired page, watched his master's hand. When that hand dropped, he dipped the gold-and-green banner thrice. The four hundred checked their pace, and ten horsemen broke from our ranks to gallop after the Horse, still fleeing wild-eyed from the terrors of the arena. Just before they were lost to sight, ten more horsemen hurtled after them. Another ten would follow them and still another ten – if the Horse did not grow weary – until the hundred Bastards, riding one by one if necessary, formed a living chain between ourselves and the Horse. We had drilled them until they moved as swiftly and unthinkingly as a child snatches his hand back from a hot stove. The princes loved the task, which let them ride free – before all the rest and in the place of greatest danger. The knights, too, had been schooled in the maneuver, though we preferred to keep them beside us rather than see our most aggressive fighting men extended over fifty miles of mountains and valleys, weak and vulnerable links in the living chain. But we could not, above all else, lose the Horse.

Harrap's tawny skin was flushed with a crimson underglaze, and his heavy, oblique eyelids were drawn wide. By his fresh stare of wonder and the sweeping grandeur of his gestures, I knew that the ritual soma was filling his vision so that it soared far beyond the bowl of our mountains. Even the three cups I had taken were working within me, suffusing the familiar rocks and huts with the inexpressible glory I have ever sought around the next turning – and have so rarely found there.

Still Harrap spoke in his accustomed rumble. 'Well, Yakir, we have begun – and we have already done all we can. The courier rides to alert the main body. From this moment we are but thistles in the wind of the Gods.'

'I would rather be an arrow.'

'Certainly, that too, my fierce priestling. Though by the time this year has passed, you'll be hating swords and arrows.'

'Thistles in the winds?' I persisted. 'Is that all we have become with all our labors, our sacrifices, and our intrigues?'

'Do not, pray, mock me with your Brahmanical sophistries. I am content to be a thistle.' Harrap half smiled. But the smile broadened into a grin. 'Of course, a fine, fat thistle – an enormous, heavy thistle that sinks its barbs deep in the flesh of whoever would stay its course through the free air.'

'But always to go where the Horse's will takes us?'

'Of course. The Gods' will through the Horse's will. That is our fate – the fate to which we are consecrated.'

'Might we not lay a rein across the Horse's neck from time to time?' I taunted him. 'Or turn Him in other ways, so that we ride toward our own purposes?'

The imprint of mirth was on Harrap's tawny face, the green eyes slitted by the high arches of his heavy cheekbones. Beneath his ravaged nose, scarred white and purple and scarlet like a broken butterfly, the fleshy crimson curtains of his lips were drawn apart from canines crooked and lupine. I saw again how simply planed, almost primeval was his broad face, so straightforward and so fixed upon its own desires. His face altered as I watched. The stamp of joy remained, but the clarity and power his fierce will imposed faded as if a sponge had been drawn across his features, minutely reshaping the contours, almost imperceptibly blurring the hard outlines.

'Do not mock me so this day,' he answered, his voice weak and troubled. 'I was wrong. It was never permitted to us to bind Him. Now, of course, less than ever.'

He twisted in his saddle, craning back to survey the armored squadrons that moved to his command. Perceiving his thought complete, I thrust another question into the sun-swollen air between us, 'Harrap, our purpose, what then . . .'

He faced me again, his eyes wide and his lips relaxed and grave. When he spoke again, his voice was stronger, but still troubled. 'Purpose? You talk of our purpose? I do not know our purpose as we *will* it, except, perhaps, that it be to have no purpose. If I knew where this year would lead and how it would end . . . if I sought goals I knew . . . I should not be riding beside you.'

He fell silent, perhaps carrying on in his own mind the argument he had from the beginning addressed not to me, but to himself. After a time he spoke again to me, and his tone was that of a patient teacher who strives toward knowledge hand in hand with his pupil.

'I know already, Yakir, that I can command men, that I can manipulate events. The glory – the adventure, if you will – in this, our Seeking, is that we seek no known goal, either by command or by manipulation. Even more, the glory is to be free of all desire to control our course. I command these men, but I have surrendered my own will to other commands.'

Feeling again the chafing awe of that morning in Ambiala's bedchamber when the unknown Harrap first spoke in my old playmate's voice, I railed, 'Harrap, my prince, Harrap, my brother, this is sophistry indeed. It is Brahmanical beyond the Brahmans and mystical beyond the soothsayers, who speak always of some reality. Worse, it is heretical.'

'How so, Yakir, my conscience?'

'Do not the Buddhists seek blessedness by surrendering all will and all desire, by purging themselves of such dross of humanity?'

'I do not know their doctrines,' he replied, moved neither to anger nor to laughter by my goadings. 'But I believe that the Buddhists' purpose is always the self. They desire to know no desire in order to attain blessedness for the self. Is that not true?'

'As I understand them, that is broadly so,' I replied, startled that our accustomed roles were reversed, he leading me onward with artful questions.

'Then the divergence is enormous between their heresy and my own true belief. My purpose is not my *self*. I seek neither future blessedness for my soul nor the rewards men give to other men whom they call great. The first I could attain far better in a monastery, the second more surely at the head of an army of conquest.'

'What, then, do you seek?'

'I have told you, Yakir, I seek nothing,' he answered, irritation at my persistence putting a jagged edge on his words. 'I have given myself to the will of the Gods, grateful that it is embodied – made palpable and manifest to my poor perception – in the Perfect Stallion. As far as I can tell, I feel neither pride nor the satisfaction of sacrifice in that surrender. The *self* is not in this.'

'You desire nothing for yourself?'

'As far as I can tell, no. If you would speak of rewards, I suppose they are to know, and to try ourselves – against whatever we are willed to encounter. But I shall not grieve if there is nothing more given to us to know – or if we are to circle peacefully for a year, being granted neither obstacles nor enemies to try us.'

'But in our trials . . . if we meet trials?'

The splendor of laughter flashed across his face, so long set awry by the uneasy flow of words rising from those unknown springs within him. He had listened intently as he spoke, cocking his head as if to read his own heart from his own words. But he laughed in relief and answered, 'That is another matter, my friend. If trials are granted to us, I am sure the Gods will guide my hand. But I would be false to them if I failed to use all the strength, all the skill, all the guile, and all the weapons They have bestowed upon me.'

The priest rode abreast of us, but a little apart, having fallen so soon into his old practice. He pulled his piebald gelding closer, awkward even in that simple movement. 'There is a purpose, of course,' he said conversationally. 'But it is, perhaps, so plain that you have not seen it.'

We waited, but he fell back into silence broken only by the small grunts that escaped his lips when the gelding jogged him. When he began to draw away, still silent, I asked, 'What is this purpose that has escaped us?'

'Simply to restore the True Religion and the ancestral beliefs. We are charged to build up again the great altars of the true Gods and to erect Their thrones again in the hearts of the men of Kamardol. Then the Gods will know again Their ancient splendor and Their primeval power – and the men of Kamardol will again know Their favor as They bend Themselves willingly to our desires.'

'What has that to do with us when . . .' I began, but Harrap, taking up my words, finished the sentence as if we were again eager boys, both speaking at once, '. . . we are separated – wholly detached – from Kamardol this year?'

The priest sighed demonstratively. The air hissed between the violet folds of his broad, beautifully carved lips, so oddly set under the sickle of the jutting nose in his swarthy face. Holding the reins loosely, he crossed his long fingers on his pommel, and I marked again their unwholesome puffiness between the swollen knucklebones.

'It is,' he said with asperity, 'sometimes difficult for me to know whether I ride with warriors or with apprentice philosophers. I might better have remained behind in comfort, teaching youths who have yet to receive the red thread of manhood or debating with those who comprehend all knowledge because they have worn that thread for a month or two.'

'What does this plaint mean, O Brahman?' Harrap rumbled, his good humor once more in flower. 'We know that warriors find it hard to think beyond themselves. We also know that priests hate reason and abhor thought as a diversion of the Devils.'

'You have been sitting at Yakir's feet again, Harrap,' said the priest, his mouth twisted between a smile and a sneer. 'Who else

151

but our young paragon, half priest and half warrior, knows both worlds so well – and so contemptuously?'

'Be that as it may, my masters,' I broke in, obscurely troubled by the priest's continuing, careless use of Harrap's name without his title, 'please tell us, as shortly as you can, what lies behind your plaint – and what is this, our purpose, revealed only to you.'

'As for the first, my kinsman,' he laughed offensively, 'we are not now detached from Kamardol – and we will be no further from Kamardol in six months' time. Your adolescent philosophizing confuses deed and intent. Were we walking forth, the three of us, barefoot, with pilgrims' staffs and mendicants' bowls, determined to leave Kamardol forever behind us in our search for reality . . . were we thus, then we would be truly detached from Kamardol though we were still within the gates. But, given to the Seeking, which is Kamardol, we carry Kamardol with us. We are Kamardol wherever we move. We shall never be more than ten minutes' ride from the Great Palace, though we perish in the frozen steppes that lie beyond the Mountains of Heaven, the mountains we may reach after we cross the Desert of Desolation.'

'I do not fully understand you,' said Harrap.

'Perhaps, Harrap,' answered the priest gently, 'you read my words too subtly. My meaning is not complex. It is this: We are a living arm of Kamardol because our impetus is of Kamardol and our deeds will exalt Kamardol. Detachment is an illusion. And to speak again of our purpose, it is to rid Kamardol of the curse of the Buddhists who defile the True Religion and would alter the proper order among men the Gods have decreed.'

'The Buddhists?' I asked. 'What have we to do with the Buddhists?'

'Look you, Yakir,' the priest answered, all mockery leached from his voice. 'What occurred in Hindustan when the Emperor Ashoka submitted to the Buddhists? The imperial armies halted their southward progress, and the land, which was almost made whole in grandeur, remained divided. The Gods' purpose was thwarted.

'Ashoka spurned the Gods' commands to conquer and to rule as a Kshatriya should. He sent out missionaries, some of whom planted the pernicious life- and heaven-denying doctrines among us. So it came about that while the false religion soon began to die in Hindustan, it grew in Kamardol and in other realms on the borders of Hindustan.'

'We all know of Ashoka's faint-heartedness. We all know the Buddhist scourge in Kamardol within the past generation. But, I ask again, what have they to do with us?'

'If they triumph, the Buddhists will overturn the ordained order among men. They will make us a race of women. They deny that the Gods employ men for Their ends, and they deny that men can either themselves aspire to *their* own ends or command the Gods. Their end is dissolution.'

'Oh, Brahman!' Harrap's impatience broke through the harangue. 'What, as Yakir asks, is this telling us what we know well to do with the Seeking?'

'Simply this – and this brings us to our purpose. If Kamardol is to live, the True Religion must prevail over Buddhism. The True Religion must triumph completely, since truth cannot live divided,' the priest pressed on, his great voice sonorous. 'We are the sword of the True Religion. We are chosen to prove the truth again to men with our might. When we return in triumph, the Buddhists will perish under the avalanche of the people's joy.'

'That is *your* purpose,' Harrap mused. 'I am content to follow the Stallion.'

'That is enough for this time,' the priest answered. 'Our strength lies in this – that we have no fixed purpose beyond our grand purpose. By submission to Their will, we are purged of all weakness.'

I knew, of course, that the Gods were in the Horse. But I could not believe that the busy Gods swooped before His hooves, sweeping aside each stone that might lame Him. Nor could I believe that They constantly directed His inclination to that single one of all the trivial temptations to stray from His course which would answer the divine purpose. I did not know how fate would work upon us, but I knew the sacred year was not, as the priest implied, precisely fixed. Were all ordained to the last cast horseshoe nail, the Quest would be no Quest, but little more than a grindingly costly and hideously dangerous performance by a troupe of witless players who did not know their own lines. To abrogate chance by asserting that all was predestined was to make the Seeking no more than a meaningless exercise – even though the climax was not revealed to us till the end. Neither knowledge nor glory, neither exaltation nor grace could arise from such a campaign. If it were already ordained either that we were made infinitely strong to surmount all obstacles or, alternately, so flawed that we must fail, we were ourselves not more than particles of dried dung on the winds, and the Gods were fools to harry us so for Their petty pleasure.

The priest's vision was to me as erroneous as it was childish. But I, least of all, could cast up the true balance of forces. I could only wait, striving to discern their reality as it appeared. I was, if not content, reconciled to finding reality yard by yard as it unfolded beneath our horses' hooves.

I could not thrust the dagger of my skepticism into the full-blown bladder of Harrap's serenity, for I loved him still. Nor could I present a reasoned alternative to the priest's assertion of the grand design, though I was already weary of his flatulent foreseeing. His visions were at once as mundane as a peddler's haggling for half a copper and as wildly pretentious as a hemp-mad fakir's description of all the diverse Heavens, even to the patterns of the carpets and the shape of the lamps that light the thrones of the Gods.

We had almost come to the ford. The village called Alexander's Rest was already behind us on the plateau's rocky face. A little way before the road dropped to the river bank, a pair of herdsmen cantered out of a copse of thin-leaved poplars on our left hand. Their sheepskin tunics were free of their shoulders in the morning heat. Their lean torsos were burnt nearly black against the gray fleece.

'Highness,' the elder said, his impudent eyes light gray in the seamed leather of his face, 'we bring a hundred horses to you at the command of Chandra, the King. You may find them already a little tired.'

'Where are they?' Harrap asked.

'In the shade of the trees. Better out of the sun.'

'I take them from you. Your job is done. You may go.'

Staring at us with bold eyes, the herdsmen offered a casual salute, their palms pressed together for an instant. They turned their rough-haired horses toward the City. At Harrap's low command Orberk, the flag-bearer, swayed the standard from side to side to order a halt. Harrap, the priest, and I rode toward the poplars, Orberk behind us.

'Two herdsmen to drive a hundred head,' Harrap remarked as we entered the copse. 'They must be prime stock indeed.'

No more than ten or fifteen of the horses were standing, their flanks and withers blotched raw red with ulcers a hand's breadth across. The rest lay in emaciated exhaustion among the rocks between the trees and the cliff's edge. Their galled shoulders heaved, and their yellow eyeballs were rolled back in their granulated sockets.

'Khali's thighs!' Harrap swore. 'Did I say we'd go no more than a few hundred miles with my brother Chandra's nags? Only the greatest good fortune the world has ever known would carry us a hundred miles in all our year. The few strings of meat left on those chalky old bones . . . they're not worth the slaughtering.'

'He must have searched long to find these proud steeds,' I laughed. 'Such utter decay, yet still alive, must have cost Chandra much gold.'

'Surely not that, Yakir. Remember, this is Chandra's gift. I know my brother, and I know he spent no gold to contrive this trap for us.'

Harrap slid from his saddle and, strangely irresolute, prodded the nearest nag with his toe. Dirty gray in patches where the coat was rubbed, and moss green along the ripple of protruding ribs, the black mare barely stirred. Only an ear twitched to shake off a blue-green fly, and the jutting shoulder bones heaved as she settled her forelegs into the hollow between two boulders.

'I hadn't really thought of this,' Harrap mused, 'even though the slaughterers wait with the main body. I hadn't thought he'd really . . . Besides, they'd hardly stand the drive.'

'When need compels . . .' quoted the priest. 'But more, the hundred nags are a late addition to the rites, contrived by timorous kings to curb the spirit of the warriors and draw the risk from the quest. They are no part of the original conception.'

'So be it,' said Harrap slowly, '. . . if you are quite certain?'

He did not wait for the priest's nod to give his orders to his flag-bearer. Silent we watched Orberk ride through the screen of trees, and silent we waited until silence was routed by the scuffling of hoofs and the clatter of armor. The four hundred were coming to us.

Between the trees and the ancient nags the troops formed a line bowed like a sickle. When Harrap lifted his hand, a dozen archers raised their bows. The twang of the bowstrings resounding in my ears, I watched the arrows arch high to fall around the standing horses and prick their flanks. Panic arched the weary necks, and a red glaze diffused the yellow eyes. The herd moved with sick deliberation that plucked my nerves. Sinews and muscles answered the alarm with bone-cracking anguish. The feeble scrabbling of ancient hooves in the dust mocked the grace and strength that is in horses.

Harrap dropped his hand, and the sickle cantered forward. Spears were leveled at the shambling horses; the archers bayed the hunting call of the gray wolf that is their totem; and the yeomen pounded the stinging stave-points toward the cliff's edge. When the foremost nags came to the verge, the weight of their fellows behind them – and behind them, the weight of men on vigorous steeds – carried them over. One by one and then in clumps of three and four, the exhausted nags fell toward the boulders below, tumbling in slow, graceful spirals while their frantically windmilling hooves sought support in the yielding air. High-pitched vibrato neighing shrilled over the thud of hooves in the dust and the shouting of the soldiers. Silence swelled when the last nag had tumbled over the cliff's edge, but I still heard the cries of terror.

'A proper business this – for Pariahs!' I said, low-voiced, to Harrap.

'It had to be done,' he answered, 'did it not?'

Of their own will the four hundred turned toward the highroad. The stragglers who had ridden to the edge to peer down at the carnage returned faster than they had gone. Two minutes after the last shriek died, we were galloping down the highroad toward the ford. The horns sounded in the sun-spangled air, and I ran my hand over the strings of the lute at my saddle-bow. But no one spoke.

I knew as we splashed through the ford, which was chill with the spring thaw, that the last tie was cut, the last pretext shattered which might have kept us close to Kamardol. I plucked again at the lute, calling out a jangle of remote melodies. Then my hand conjured forth a pure, high strumming, and I saw beyond the green valley through the ice-heaped passes and across the blue glaciers to the golden deserts men said lay to the north and the east. The vision – if true vision it was – sprang from no roots in my own experience or in the experience of our race. We had gone north and west to find the Horse, but no man had ridden beyond the mountains and returned to Kamardol to tell what lay north of the ranks of purple peaks with the white snow on their heads and shoulders. I shivered in the hot sun, and my hand dropped from the strings.

One of the Bastards waited above the sloping bank, his crimson crest cocked arrogantly against the green hillside.

'Highness,' he shouted, above the splashing and the clatter. 'He has taken the right-hand way. He has left the highroad, spurning to return toward Ferghana whence He came with you.'

Rank by rank, the four hundred rose dripping from the white-flecked stream and turned their horses' heads toward the northeast. Beyond the gray ridges, patched with cold shadows as the sun fell away in the west, lay the lands of darkness, lands that even our legends knew not.

Fifteen

The Horse never stayed his pace, though the dreadful arena lay far behind Him, and I did not see Him for five days after the main body under Mirab joined us beyond the ford. But I knew His every moment from the Bastards' reports. He ranged free before us, often circling deep into the foothills to graze among the spring herbs that laid the hollows with lime-green carpets set with orange poppies. Yet the weight of the high mountains beyond ever forced Him back onto the narrow ledge along the river gorge that twined toward the northeast. He used His freedom with moderation, never seeking to elude the horsemen that followed Him, but halting often upon outcrops to look for the mailed figures in the distance and let them come up to Him.

The priest heard those same reports with satisfaction, a complacent smile swathing his pendulous cheeks and drooping on his violet lips. Harrap seemed to me troubled by the Horse's lack of spirit, though the others could read little from his occasional stifled grunt of disappointment. On the third night after our departure we squatted beside the fire where roasted the flesh of the big-horned mountain goats the archers had shot.

'Ho, priest, what of the Quest?' Harrap demanded, propping his long dagger against a rock, though it still impaled three chunks of crisp meat entwined with a string of the small wild onions of the mountains.

'The Quest?' replied the priest, spitting a sliver of gristle into the fire. 'The Quest? What of it?'

Although Harrap's meaning was plain to me, who had been watching his irritation swell, I kept my silence whole. The confrontation delighted me. For the first time in the year I had known him the priest was caught in a web of bewilderment, neither a grave aphorism nor a light sneer ready to his lips. I gulped a mouthful of koumiss, the sour fermented mare's milk hardly stronger than wine, and leaned back to listen.

'Yes, the Quest – what of it?' Harrap insisted, scrubbing the grease from his lips with the edge of his cloak.

'I do not wholly take your meaning, Prince,' said the priest.

Harrap snatched up his dagger and bit off a chunk of meat. Grinding the fibers between his teeth, he spat out the words.

'Is this a stallion we are following or a gelding? He goes like a mare in foal, heavy of foot and fearful of losing the escort. Where is the fiery inspiration, the imperious will of the Gods? We chose Him as you said we must, and you promised . . . this?'

'Be of good patience, Harrap,' counseled the priest. 'We are hardly begun. The will of the Gods will manifest itself when it is meet. Have you ever seen a horse run without a cause? They are lazy beasts!'

'But this is no horse. The command of the Gods is embodied in the shape of a horse.'

'Did you not say as we rode out from Kamardol that you would be content even if we met no trials?'

'Yes . . . if it were the divine will. But no will at all works in that lazy beast.'

'He is the consecrated Vehicle,' the priest answered in his most portentous tone. 'I swear to you, the will and the spirit will flame forth when the appointed time comes. Have I, till now, led you astray?'

'No,' Harrap said shortly, apparently content once more.

I marveled at the alternation of childlike pique, more in the manner of my old Harrap, with the serene insight he had shown us directly after the Consecration. It was a most curious creature my old playmate was becoming, mercurial and inexplicable. But I had little chance to watch him close, for we had already fallen into the order of march we would maintain to the end.

Harrap rode with the four hundred in the vanguard, leaving the main body to Colonel Mirab and Captain Ranbir, those old companions-in-arms. I ranged between the two groups to keep a picture of the whole force in my mind and to decide questions either too trivial or too immediate to refer to Harrap. I found to my surprise that I enjoyed the tension, as well as the power of decision. My task would later prove physically punishing. I had to press my mount to the utmost toward the vanguard, though I could rest while I waited for the main body to come up to me. In those early days the constant needs of the two thousand men of the main body compelled me to ride with them much of the time. The four hundred of the vanguard had already become a balanced spear in Harrap's hand. Gradually, however, the main body was to become as supple and responsive as we could hope, hampered as they were by the baggage-carts and the pack animals. Always behind them straggled the camp-followers, their numbers dwindling through accidents and illness, but never less than a few hundred.

The Horse, as I have said, was not once in my sight during those first full days when the troops were fitting themselves to the trail. I was too busy to ride ahead to seek a glimpse of Him. I pronounced upon disputes over forage ground, distributed rations, assigned craftsmen to repair shattered wheels or broken girths, and kept the soldiers' petty quarrels from bloodshed. I set my mind several times to completing my 'Song of the Seeking,' but I was always summoned by the pressing needs of men and beasts that must be fed and gear that must be made whole. I felt myself the chatelaine of an enormous, peripatetic household rather than the gallant officer or the lyric singer, and I knew the sharpest sympathy with the great ladies who somehow contrive to subdue the sea of details around them without sinking beneath the waves.

Yet the constant petty assault upon my detachment carried its own peculiar reward. Since I could not give myself to making my song, my brief intervals of freedom were quite empty. I rode in a daze of peace along the narrow valley of the ice-crowned river we called the Khunyar, which means the Unknown, through the ever rising mountains no man of our race had seen before us. The sweet tang of the spring flowers and the faint bitterness of the wild garlic on the warm breezes softened the chill impact of the blue massif that towered before us. In the afternoon's clarity the stark slopes seemed so close that one could lean forward in his saddle and push the crag-spired barrier aside. In the morning's mist the blue-gray cliffs receded, and we knew not how many days' ride would bring us to the first slope.

Always in some remote cave of my mind I felt the presence of the Horse. I had last seen His silver form top a rise on Alexander's Road and glance back with tail and mane streaming in the wind. He had then sunk into a hollow, His train of princes floating behind Him. Yet I knew far better than the bare words of the princes' reports that He moved steadily ahead of us, drawing our small array ever onward, for I could feel the beat of His questing hooves in the throbbing of my own pulses. I did not believe with Harrap that He led us to a bright inevitable destiny, Himself knowing the will of the Immortals and helping to shape Their will. But an undefined conviction of purpose rose from my constant inner vision of the Horse moving before us into the wilderness. That conviction gave form – indescribable, though palpable and coherent – to our journey.

Both ended just after the crest of the fifth day – the quarrels among the soldiers and my own exaltation in the unreal peace of the deep gorge that stretched forever into an unknown world without bounds. I was weary of the constant petty problems that Mirab, with contemptuous good humor, invariably referred to me because he, the born warrior, disdained them. Lifting my horse into a gallop with knees and spurs, I came sooner than I had expected upon the four hundred who had dismounted to squat among the strewn boulders. Threading my way among them, I found Harrap sitting on his horse a few yards in advance of the column.

'Ho, Yakir, well come!' he hailed me. 'We have been waiting two hours for the Stallion to choose His course, though one trail seems from here no more than a crease. But there He stands.'

I looked upward, and my breath stopped. Upon the hillside before me He shone, a living statue of veined milk-marble. His escort waited in a broad crescent a hundred yards lower on the slope. This was an Avatar to follow to the lip of the Heavens – if He would but move.

'Two hours,' repeated Harrap, 'and the priest has retired to seek guidance. I don't want to force His choice, but, by Pragpati, we'll mount and ride if He does not stir in the next minutes. I would not waste this good going.'

I saw then that we were in reality almost upon the great blue massif that had beckoned us for days. Its crown was veiled by clouds, but the tangle of stunted pines on the sheer slopes had become single trees to the eye.

'We must get as far as we can before nightfall,' Harrap fretted. 'It will still be His choice. We'll just hasten the choice a bit.'

He spoke to the page, and his banner bobbed up and down in the signal to mount. The horns chortled their shrill, macabre mirth, and the four hundred trotted forward toward the unmoving Horse. I gasped, and my throat ached as we drew closer. The Colt's sides were streaked with blood that had at a distance made me see a statue of veined milk-marble.

'He bleeds,' I cried, anguish cracking my voice.

Harrap's answer dismayed me as much the Horse's grievous wounds. 'Of course,' he said casually, 'He bleeds.'

'Did He fall? Has an avalanche caught Him? Are there hostile archers in the hills?' I asked, scorning to mask my horror with the light tone Harrap had chosen. That He still stood, though His wounds were so grave, proved that I saw a dire miracle.

'Of course He bleeds,' Harrap repeated, laughing aloud.

'What has happened, Harrap?' I demanded. 'How can you laugh?'

'I'm sorry, Yakir, truly I am,' he snorted, twisting in laughter. 'But you look like a tormented ghost. Have you so soon forgotten whence He comes?'

'No,' I answered, still truculent, though I felt memory, insistent though insubstantial, seeking release within me.

'The blood-sweating horses of Ferghana, Yakir!' Harrap said less raucously, though bright laughter gilded his words. 'The thousand-league horses of Ferghana!'

'Perhaps, now, I do remember,' I answered, feeling foolish, though my awe of the miracle lingered. I did remember; indeed I could hear the oily voice of the Uighur horse dealer cautioning us, 'Gentlemen, after exertion in their own high altitudes, my horses bleed in streams. No one knows why. It seems to relieve the pressure they build up by their feats of speed and endurance.

The bleeding is their strength, not their weakness.' I laughed in relief, but added stubbornly, 'Still, it seems a miracle.'

'Perhaps, Yakir, perhaps it is.'

We had, all the while, been drawing closer to the unmoving figure. We were upon His escort of ten princes when the Horse tossed His mane and skittered down the hillside to the ledge beside the gorge. Spurning a narrow ravine that led almost due west, He galloped northeast toward the blue massif. The four hundred surged behind Him, the clatter of their hooves resounding from the depths of the gorge, where gray boulders and patches of yellow soil gave refuge to a few clinging shrubs spiked with dark-green leaves.

The slopes on either side trailed their cloaks of snow ever lower, the air grew chill, and the way was steep and narrow. I was glad to ride with the vanguard, rather than the two thousand. I wondered if I should turn back to see how Mirab and Ranbir fared, but laughed at myself for an officious fool. If the old campaigner and the captain of the mountaineers could not make their own way through these fledgling mountains, our journey would never be done. Besides, Ranbir and his men had almost come up to us during the halt.

My hand was on my lute when the way opened into a flat, ice-rimed hollow hedged by sheer walls of rock. I felt I could again make my song to the Horse, where He trotted no more than a hundred yards ahead toward the shadowed cleft in the rock where the way narrowed again. But my hand lay unsinewed upon the strings. A boulder fell from an overhanging crag to splinter a few yards in front of the Horse's hooves, and He halted. Another boulder fell even closer, and a flight of arrows hissed through the cold air, studding the ground around Him.

'Up shields!' Harrap shouted. 'Princes, forward and cover!'

The hundred Bastards hurtled forward to make a wall around the Horse, those nearest Him joining their broad shields into a roof over His body. They swept the Horse toward the far cleft, which would give them shelter.

The archers shot at the palisades of rock that surrounded us to give the Bastards what aid they could. But the cliffs rose so steeply that we could see no more than the tip of a spear or the quiver of a bow's head. Hemmed by our raised shields and feeling the arrows clatter on them, I feared that the mountains themselves, enraged by our temerity, had thrown a host of Devils against us. The human enemy was as invisible as he was unknown and unexpected.

The Bastards recoiled from the cleft, and were galloping toward us, the Horse in their midst.

'Barricaded, by Vishnu!' Harrap swore. 'Pass them through!'

Loosing arrows and even more futile spears at our unseen tormentors, we eddied slowly backward. Five times horses screamed and fell. Three archers did not spring free, but lay still, one clutching the arrow between his ribs. When the overhanging cliffs gave us the slight shelter the open expanse had denied, Harrap halted us.

'The fools,' he laughed, 'they should have closed both ends of the purse. Yakir, get me Ranbir. Hurry!'

Somehow I did not crush a dozen men against the cliffs as I spurred through the narrow passage. I came through, only glancing at the Horse where He stood, flanks heaving and bright with blood, among His princes. Just beyond, Ranbir waited, delight beaming from the intricate seams of his face and his three hundred drawn up, ordered and fresh as on parade.

'Hail, Yakir, my son!' Ranbir entoned. 'Can I, perhaps, be of assistance to the young gentlemen?'

My excitement checked, I grinned at his recalling the mock formality of address he had used when Harrap and I were small boys. I answered in the same tenor, 'Hail, Father Ranbir! We have met a slight difficulty. Prince Harrap would be glad of your counsel.'

'A moment,' Ranbir answered. 'Ambush, is it?' I nodded, and he asked, 'How lies the land ahead?'

With a pointed twig on a patch of soft ground I sketched the dwarf valley, feeling as if I were again a small boy venturing for the first time into the mountains with Ranbir as teacher and guide.

'You're sure,' he asked, 'quite sure there's no way up or down once within the cliffs that hedge the vale?'

I nodded again, and the old mountaineer spoke in the lisped

gutturals of his own tongue to two lieutenants. As he and I turned our horses' heads into the choked passage, the guardsmen slid from their saddles, cast off their ornate blue helmets, and swarmed up the precipitous slopes on either side of the trail.

When we came up to him, Harrap said gravely, 'Ranbir, I should have come to you. Are your men climbing?' Taking Ranbir's nod, Harrap added, 'Let us ride to them, then. You'll take the left body. I'll take the right. Let us move now. I don't fancy the climb if your hill monkeys get too far ahead.'

Ranbir and I checked our horses, and I moistened my lips to argue that I should take the right flank while the general remained with the troops. But Ranbir spoke first, drawling his words lazily, 'I had thought, Harrap, my prince, that you might keep with the troops in the defile. Indeed, I am growing old, and I had also thought that perhaps Yakir and I could loll below, letting my young men deal with this difficulty.'

Harrap's face darkened, and the black peak of hair on his forehead drew down toward his eyebrows. But his anger dissipated before it was fully formed. 'You're right, of course,' he said lightly. 'But I'll be happier if you give up your ease. You on the left and Yakir on the right.'

'I was afraid of that,' Ranbir grumbled as we rode back. 'A nasty climb, instead of a rest.'

But he was off his horse and climbing the hillside faster than his young spearmen. He turned and halloed at me, 'Remember, slowly when you come to the ridge.'

I waved in acknowledgment, so soon too winded to reply, though a young mountaineer climbed on either side to help me. The guardsmen ahead were climbing cautiously, their gray-brown cloaks blending with the rocks, and we came up to them after half an hour. Still it was an arduous ascent. Whenever we came to a patch sheltered by the intervening crags from even the keenest eyes among our ambushers, the guardsmen stood erect. But they could see nothing, and they resumed the climb, clutching their short horn bows and holding their swords lest they rattle. Thrusting their heels into the ground, they went up the slope as if it were a staircase, and I was glad of the supporting hands of my two young escorts.

Crouched just beneath the ridgeline, I saw all the forces displayed beneath me like children's wooden soldiers. Across the defile Ranbir and his men were a reflection of my own unit, like us clutching the ground for concealment. Behind us on the trail, the main force under Mirab was still coming up. Before us Harrap, the Horse, and the four hundred sheltered in the mouth of the defile. The dwarf valley before them was empty except for five fallen horses and three archers, one impaled by a long arrow shaft. At the far end a heap of boulders blocked the cleft. The archers in the defile blindly flung their arrows at the cliffs where our ambushers lay.

Some two hundred men were concealed in pockets of rock atop the cliff walk. When they rose to loose their arrows or pry a boulder loose, I saw that they wore bearskin cloaks and beaten-iron helmets from which sprouted the horns of the mountain goat. It was fighting garb of the warriors of the Little Kamar, Co-King Gupta's chosen tribe, who normally kept their flocks far from the City. In a ravine that pierced the cliffs to the east, its mouth screened from men on the flat by an outcrop, I saw several hundred riderless horses and mounted tribesmen to the number of at least a hundred. All the Little Kamars were so intent upon the troops in the defile that they glanced neither upward nor behind them to mark our progress across the rocks.

We moved slowly, keeping always behind the ridges, until a great circle had brought us directly behind the ambushers. The light began to blur as the sun dropped behind the western mountains, and our breath hovered before our mouths in dense cloudlets when we came into position.

A gray-bearded warrior rose out of a hollow at my feet, the horizontal rays of the sun impaled upon the horns of his helmet. His mouth was a huge straining circle, and I could see deep into the red cavern of his throat as I snatched at my dagger. Before he could shout, a guardsman sprang from behind me, his half-moon knife flashing, the circle of his bare brown arm crushing the warrior's throat. The knife point slid into the sentinel's belly, and the broad blade glided inward and upward, emerging with a quick jerk to the left. It was the stroke for disembowelling the wild boar.

The strained mouth flapped closed, and the astonished face, a foot from my own, turned gray. The guardsman, a youth of no more than sixteen, lowered the flaccid body to the rocks and plunged the half-moon blade twice into the ground to wipe it of blood. He smiled shyly at me.

I saw Ranbir rise for an instant above the opposite ridge. On the signal, we loosed our swarms of short arrows, and the keening war cry of the mountaineers sounded from the ridges. Above the warriors we shot our bolts at short range, and they could hardly twist in their cramped holes to meet our impact. When they rose to shoot at us, the archers below whooped their joy at finally seeing the invisible enemy who had been tormenting them. We were, on each side, a hundred and fifty to their hundred.

It was quick work when we hurtled down upon them, and the half-moon knives flashed in the retreating sunlight. I called out to my men to spare the chieftains. But my cry was too late.

Pushing aside a warrior from whose throat the bright blood still spurted, I leaned over and hallooed to Harrap below. Awaiting his answer, I saw that the warrior's right hand bore the blue-serpent tattoo of the Little Kamar.

'Horsemen, a hundred,' I shouted, pointing toward the hidden ravine. The knights galloped out of the defile, and I followed my guardsmen in their race along the ridge to the heights overlooking the enemy cavalry.

We came up too late to loose more than a single flight of bolts before Harrap and his horsemen closed. The skirmish boiled at our feet in the strange clarity of light that precedes dusk in the mountains. Horses whinnied in blood anguish, and men fell from their saddles into the snow as we slid down the slope to join our knights at the kill. We came too late, though our descent took no more than five minutes.

His scar livid purple against his golden skin, the flat of his short-hafted axe encrusted red-mottled gray with brains, Harrap confronted a warrior of the Little Kamar, a chieftain from the double horns on his helmet. The man's right hand was half severed at the wrist, and a cavalryman supported him, fist jammed into his armpit.

'. . . stationed six units . . . one at every pass,' he was gasping, his old-fashioned country accent oddly comic. 'Gupta's orders . . . seize Horse to keep him enclosed . . . or kill Harrap. Better both. . .'

'Gupta's orders?' snapped Harrap.

'Gupta's orders,' sighed the chieftain. 'For Khali's sake, and the wine we drank by the Indus, bind up my arm.'

Harrap shook his head, and the cavalryman stepped back, withdrawing his fist. The chieftain sank to the ground, bright blood spurted in regular gouts from his wrist onto the stained snow. His soft-leather boots scrabbled in the wet for a minute, and he died.

'The Gods,' Harrap said, exultation in his voice, 'send us trials – assisted by my royal brothers. Will Gupta believe we vanished upward into the Heavens when no kinsman of his returns from this ambush?' His tone became bitter. 'Parsimony and policy! Chandra sent us the ancient nags to keep us safe. Gupta sent us his kinsmen in ambush, thinking it better that we never returned. Both true to their natures – and both, as ever, ineffective. The Gods send us more enemies like my brothers.'

We made our cramped camp in the dwarf valley after stripping the corpses and staking out the horses, which were restive amid the blood scent. When we had lit our fires and cooked our meat, Harrap spoke again: 'On the whole, I prefer Gupta's way. At least, he sent us *fresh* horse-beef.'

Sixteen

The Horse fled in the night. His unshod hooves thudding dully through the half-light of the moon and the low-hanging stars, he fled the sweet stench of torn flesh He abhorred.

The sleep-thick swearing of tired men and the jangle of harnesses half awakened me. The tumult rose from the far end of the dwarf valley, where the Bastards slept beside their horses. When the first decade had followed the Horse, shouting insults at each other and rattling their swords in spite, I squirmed luxuriously within my sheepskin cloak. Twisting my hip away from the sharp-edged stone that had, as ever, lodged beneath me, I fell back into sleep.

A delegation of princes waited upon me before the night had quite passed. The flat disc of the moon was dissolving from shining silver to misty white, and the stars were wisps of gray fleece stuck to the vault of the skies. The sentinels of the heavens were changing at the dawn, and the orange rim of the sun was appearing through the jagged eastern peaks. Three princes came to me. Their breastplates shone dully, and their eyes were red-rimmed with foul temper and lack of sleep.

No more than half the hundred Bastards remained, the rest having followed the Horse through the darkness. I was about to congratulate them on the discipline that had dispatched successive decades from the encampment as they were needed to keep the Horse in view. But the foremost spoke before I could proffer my compliments. Their spokesman was a shallow, lanky fellow with a straggling cheek beard, pretentiously named Gorbabordol by a father who ruled a mouse-sized manor in the arid southwest. Although his claim was no more tenuous than half the princes', Gorbabordol asserted his rank with contentious hauteur. His normal temper was so inflamed that Harrap would have rejected him but for his gift of bitter humor that emboldened his fellows with laughter when the battle was most perilous. There was, however, little humor in the princeling Gorbabordol that half-dawn.

'Master Yakir!' he cried shrilly to fix my attention. I started at the Brahmanic form of address and almost called him to order. Still I chose to wait, largely because I remembered how reluctantly I had taken military rank.

'Master Yakir!' he repeated. 'We would not harass the General – yet. But I am bidden to say that we princes are dissatisfied.'

'How so?' I asked coolly.

'We are assigned duties better fitted for grooms.' His voice rose and fell in the regular rhythm of one who has memorized the words he speaks. 'We cannot sleep after battle for chasing after the Horse. Worse, when battle comes, we are excluded, for we must guard the Horse. Ours is not a fitting task for princes such as we are.'

'I am glad you came to me, gentlemen, rather than to the General, who might not welcome your words. But I am more patient, being neither of his blood nor his choler.'

'Therefore we came to you, Master Yakir, knowing that you would advise us. We are . . .'

I interrupted, ignoring the implication that I might advise, but not command: 'Let me ask this of you. Is the task easy?'

'No, by Vishnu,' Gorbabordol replied, 'it is not. That is what I have told you. It is grinding and unfitting for . . .'

'Could grooms truly perform this task, then?'

'I suppose not,' he conceded. 'But still . . .'

'But still . . . you will have fighting aplenty in the future. Only the archers and the mountaineers used their weapons honestly yesterday. For the knights it was a slaughter, not a battle.'

'I suppose that is true, but we would have liked . . .'

'Gentlemen, I promise you many battles and much blood once we are again on the flat, where you excel. Till then, yours is the most arduous, the most demanding, and the most important duty. To keep the Avatar safe – is that not a task for princes?'

'If you put it that way,' he granted me. 'But it's still hard – and undignified. Next we'll be collecting His manure for little gardens.'

His followers chortled at the thought of their noble hands soiled by manure, hands that were fit only for blood. I made a promise to myself, but smiled my gentlest and answered, 'Not that, I assure you.'

'All right then, Master Yakir . . .'

'Colonel Yakir,' I snapped. 'You will call me Colonel as long as you are under this command.'

'Surely, Colonel,' he answered, his long mouth curved down in mock surprise. 'But you *will* remember when we come to the plains . . .'

'I promise you many deaths.'

Their stiff-legged strut demonstrated that they were but half placated. I tilted the skin of koumiss to my mouth and chewed a stick of horse-jerky to change the taste of my awakening. But the beginning set the tone of the dreary day that followed.

We buried our four dead and dressed the wounds of thirty more. I left those tasks to the priests, merely noting the numbers and thanking the Gods that by turning surprise against the ambushers we had carried the battle at so little cost to ourselves.

The corpses of the Little Kamars, three hundred twenty-two in all, we threw into the ravine, and upon them heaped snow and rocks. Their weapons, their armor, and their bearskin cloaks we divided among our men. The horned helmets we set on the rocks of the gorge as an offering to the Gods and a warning to men.

I liked least the slaughter of the horses. The injured horses we could of course but kill, and we picked out fifty of the best to replace our own losses and to add to our reserve. But we butchered the remainder, nearly two hundred head. Our troops gorged on roasted horse-beef at noon, their boots and sleeves caked with dried black blood. Each soldier reserved a sodden packet to hang from his pommel. The horse's heads, with their staring eyes, and the bones, with their glistening, transparent carapaces, we left on the rocks for the birds to strip.

Two more archers died of their wounds that noon, and the priest warned that another three would die if they were not granted a day of ease. The princes were not alone dispirited, for

171

all the four hundred and even the cavalry and the mounted infantry of the main body were weary beyond any reason after their brief penetration of the edges of the high mountains and their first glancing battle. Glutted with meat, they lay listless in the sun, their eyes half closed in gray pouches. Only Ranbir's guardsmen were untarnished by the malaise of the spirit. They were men of the eastern mountains, barbarian mercenaries hired to guard the Royal Family from the nobles. Only the guardsmen could stomach the dull numbness that sickened all others, though no man spoke of it. There was nothing more to say after saying that the tribe of the Little Kamar, who are called the royal kinsmen, had attacked us at the command of Gupta, the Co-King.

As a Brahman, I was free of the fine-spun web of loyalties that bound the warrior caste. Still, I felt their shock myself, and I knew that the most phlegmatic men-at-arms were rent by rage and bewilderment. Our fathers and their fathers before them had built a City and, beyond the City, a realm bound by submission to common Gods. They had become a people, and all men of Kamardol had felt the life of one as the lives of all. Gupta had broken the sacred compact that had created Kamardol. We had been hurled backward to the age of contending tribes, before Kamardol existed, when each man's life was his own to guard as best he could and all other men's lives, families, and goods were his to take if he could.

Harrap alone seemed untouched. He waited no more than half an hour after the last horse was slaughtered to pass the order to mount. 'Enough of this idling,' he called to me cheerfully. 'The Seeking is but begun. Should we lie about stroking our wounds mournfully after every skirmish, we will never come to its end.'

I urged that we not ride onward till the morning, that we reserve the rump of the day for rest. Perhaps, I added, the three sorely wounded archers might live if we gave their bodies but an afternoon's grace.

Anger seamed Harrap's forehead, and he raised his clenched fist. For a full minute we stood silent, glaring at each other. I had never given way before his rages, and I could not give way without destroying all that lay between us. In the end he dropped his hand, flexing his whitened fingers with deliberate restraint.

'Yakir!' His voice trembled in fury. 'If the Gods demand the three archers, They shall have them. Our task is only to go forward, following the Stallion as He goes, halting only when He halts. Order the men to mount.'

I was astonished, not by the quick anger I knew so well, but because Harrap raged, who alone among us had been unmoved by the fratricidal attack of the Little Kamar.

'Harrap,' I answered, holding my voice level, 'is it certain that the sacrifice is demanded? These men are consecrated to the service of the Horse. Should we, to gain ten miles, extinguish three lives that may yet preserve Him?'

His face softened, and I hoped that his love for the common soldiers would move him to rescind his command. But he repeated stubbornly, 'Order the men to mount. Or must I?'

Resigned, I turned to give the order to Orberk, the flag-bearer, who would pass it to the trumpets. But Mirab, who had come up with Ranbir to watch the spoils divided, spoke in the chill silence. 'Highness!' His voice was hoarse, no more than half his normal bellow. 'Highness, I would suggest . . . my men are weary. Their sickness is of the soul. Give them this day of ease and let the priests cleanse them of fratricide. They fear, even now, that our Quest is damned.'

'Prince Harrap, think on the Colonels' words,' Ranbir offered his own counsel. 'My monkeys can, of course, go on. But it is not good even for them to feel that the others are at war with themselves.'

I saw my opportunity in Harrap's clenched lips, though they were drawn not by indecision but by the realization – which was ever irksome to him – that other men were weak.

'Harrap,' I said, 'can we not let the men rest and order the priests to sacrifice wheat and milk to cleanse them? Can we not pause to pray that the Seeking will exalt the City, rather than divide it.'

We should, I think, have pleaded in vain had not a courier of the princes cantered into the camp. Assuaged by the report that the Horse grazed quietly fifteen miles away, Harrap gave the day to the soldiers to rest and to the priests to pray.

I lay down to sleep away the feast, while Mirab and Ranbir returned to their command. Harrap plodded a little way up the slope, where he sat silent, turning a doubled-horned chieftain's helmet between his palms. The beaten iron was split by an axe blow.

In the late evening, when the fires had dwindled to a glow of embers, and the clouds driven by the north wind had drawn a curtain between the earth and the bright heavens, Harrap came back to my side.

I saw where he stood because the blackness was barely darker against the embers' glow. His voice whispered out of the blackness as it had when we were boys punished for crimes that transgressed the indulgence granted our mischievousness. So had he spoken when we were beaten with saddle girths for spearing the sacred carp in the pool of Shiva or for taunting the sacred bull of Krishna.

'Yakir, I am sorry we argued – and I regret even more that we did not go on today. Can you not understand that we are sworn to go on – until all of us fall, if that be the Gods' will?'

I did not answer, and the anguished whisper resumed: 'Yakir, I would have given that chieftain of the Little Kamar his life. I had but to nod instead of shaking my head . . . He rode with me against the Jats, and we looted their palaces together. But I could not, for he had cursed himself and all his people by striking at the Stallion. He died to keep our Quest pure. It was not my gesture, but the will of the Gods that condemned him.'

'I take your meaning, Harrap,' I answered. 'Did I not honor your purpose, I would not ride beside you. But all men are not as you. Other men must rest and pray.'

'No!' The sore pride of the Royal Kamars flared in the hoarse whisper through the darkness. 'No, I suppose they are not. Of course they are not, and well it is for them that they are not.'

'Good night, Harrap.'

'Good night, Yakir,' he answered with sudden tenderness. 'The Gods keep your sleep.'

Our morning came early, though the light did not attend it.

The black-streaked clouds still hung low, shaming the sun and pressing the heavy winds upon the cold earth. My commanders and my craftsmen came to me before I had gulped a mouthful of koumiss. The pause had broken the rhythm of the march, and I was beset with new details. Where to stow the arms of the Little Kamar? Could we not delay again because four bull camels had savaged each other during the night? Must we abandon two carts with broken wheels? The drift of petty problems rose almost as high as it had when we broke our winter encampment.

The priest came to me last. The three wounded archers, he said, might live even if we rode. I was thanking him for that single good word when Gorbabordol burst from the far defile, scattering men and horses. His pony was caked with dried sweat, and his own sallow face, red eyes glaring, was a long skull purged of all laughter.

'Colonel,' he shouted from his saddle, 'the Horse is away! He fled in the dusk as if all the Devils drove Him. He is at least fifty miles away and still going. By Pragpati, His father, it seems He'll never stop.'

He wheeled, shouting at the remaining decade of the Bastards to follow him, and was gone. Half amused at his haste, I walked toward Harrap, who was examining the feet of his rough-haired dun.

'We should be ready to ride in half an hour,' I said. 'And the Bastards report the Horse is away, fifty miles away, and still running.'

Harrap dropped the hoof as if it had been transformed into a viper. He hurled himself into his saddle, shouting, 'Mount and ride! Mount . . . and . . . ride!' He glared down at me, and his voice was low and venomous. 'Damn you, Yakir, damn you! What if we lose Him? I told you we must not pause. You bring up the main body.'

'But He is still in sight,' I reminded Harrap. 'The drill is working perfectly. We will not lose Him.'

He ignored me and rode out, bellowing again, 'Mount . . . and . . . ride!'

The last princes swept into the defile while it still echoed Harrap's hoofbeats. The knights, the archers, and the yeomen followed them within ten minutes, while I waited for the main body. All that day I knew that Harrap still raged ahead of us, pursuing the Horse. The pace was so fierce that Mirab, at my suggestion, sent half a squadron of cavalry forward to keep the vanguard in sight.

Harrap's passion bore us untrammeled over the blue massif that had for a week towered in majestic impassability before us. We climbed ever higher and away from the river in the track of the Horse, but the ascent was slow and the way broad. When it briefly appeared that there was no passage through the broad battlement of cliffs, the cavalrymen in the lead showed us the way the Horse had found. We slipped around the gnarled façade as smoothly as the tiger glides between the gray flanks of the elephants when the master of the mahouts has failed to close the interval. The massif seemed no more substantial than the mirages of the hot sands that promise either shaded ease or fierce hostility and disappear when the traveler rides headlong at them, charged either with credulous hope or desperate courage. Even the balky camels climbed the gentle slopes without groaning, and the carts rolled as if they were on the highroad.

We came around the flank of the massif at noon on the second day after Harrap's raging flight from the dwarf valley. The river again appeared on our right, shining like a twisted flaw deep in the green jade of the pine-encrusted gorges. Below us, though full fifteen miles ahead, the four hundred spiraled down to the river through the crystalline light. I thought I saw Harrap, the priest, and the banner a few paces in advance. I even thought I saw the white flash of Harrap's teeth as he smiled. I knew he was content again for I saw too the chain of princes in yellow cloaks spilling down the slope. Pendent from the last golden link was the translucence of the perfect pearl that was the Horse.

Beyond the gorge white battlements of mountain ranges stretched away to the far horizon all around, purple-tinged and splotched with wild green and red gashes. Beyond the first row of peaks, another rose higher, and then a third, and still another, summoning my eye to the frontier of infinity. Putting away that fancy, I surveyed the prospect with the eye of an adjutant. For each descent that lay before us we would encounter a sharper ascent, each stage leading us ever higher until we crossed the last and highest range – if, in truth, the mountains ever ended. Unless the ice-enfolded ranges mounted to the top of the world, we should find the golden cities of men beyond them.

I did not rejoin the vanguard until the following day. I wished to allow time to turn Harrap's rage to remorse that festered within him. Only then, I knew, would he offer a generous apology.

As I had expected, Harrap welcomed me with a half smile. 'A fine land, eh Yakir?' he said. 'Though better suited to birds than men. The Gods themselves must have cast up these breastworks of rock in Their battles.'

'A fine land, Harrap,' I agreed and waited.

'How goes the main body? All well?'

'All is well,' I answered and waited again.

His face darkened for an instant like a forest when a cloudlet scuds across the sun.

'It has not ended in disaster this time, Yakir. It was my fault more than yours that we halted. We go forward now, never pausing but to strike down the enemies of the Stallion who defy the Gods.'

I forced down my outrage and bridled my voice. 'If you ride too close, you'll force the omens, I'm afraid.' Disdaining that his persistent rancor should divide us further, I added cheerfully, 'But, of course, you command.'

'That is true,' he said brusquely. 'But, come, tell me how it goes with the main body. I have neglected it too long.'

I made my formal report, not dwelling overlong on the minutiae and concluding, 'They are ready to fight whenever they are needed. The cavalry, I fear, are growing restive for lack of action.'

'They'll all have their action – soon enough and blood enough for all. The Gods will see to it – if we are but obedient and follow Their Perfect Stallion without tarrying. It is well, though, that it was the guardsmen who fought on the hill and not troops of Kamardol.'

'That is clear,' I answered, feeling for the firm ground of understanding on which we had always stood.

177

'If it had been a unit of Kamardol,' he mused through my interjection, 'the others' jealousy would have been fierce. But Ranbir's men never crow. To them battle is a welcome diversion. But it is only part of their work, like standing guard or mounting parade. They go into combat like a merchant going to the market – and count their profits or losses with less wailing.'

'But, next time, we should give our own people the lead,' I reiterated. 'And now, Harrap, if you are done with me, I shall ride back.'

'I am done with you, Yakir,' he answered, a half-smile on his fleshy lips. 'For the moment, that is. But stay another moment . . . What of this nonsense about fratricide? Do the men still grumble and fear?'

'There have, of course, been the sacrifices . . .'

'That I know, Yakir. But what do the men think?'

'I do not know, Harrap. They do not tell me their thoughts. I am set apart from them by my birth. And you have set me above them by rank.'

'I must know their thoughts. Then I can make them see that the Gods lead men to glory by twisted paths. Then I can show them the higher purpose that sets all normal laws at naught.'

'I shall do the best I can,' I answered, giving him a half-salute, such as any colonel-adjutant might make to any general commanding.

He was startled by my formality, though his hands rose, palms together of their own will as I turned out of the line of march.

I sat my horse beside the trail through the peaks and waited for the four hundred to pass. The princes rode with arrogant ease, their helmets and breastplates varied and fanciful, their voluminous yellow cloaks streaming over their horses' hindquarters. Behind them came the knights in their shorter scarlet cloaks, their blue-gray chain mail more menacing for its lack of ornamentation. The ranks of knights were irregular and wavering, but still ordered ranks, rather than the melee of the princes' progress. The archers and then the yeomen rode last, both groups in green cloaks and both keeping a tolerably regular order of march. Their half-helms hung at their pommels; their slung bows and steel-tipped staves made twisted peaks under the cloaks.

Here a fur cap with turned-up earpieces broke the rough uniformity, there a white scarf flaunted or a tigerskin saddle cloth.

Watching the regular cavalry of Kamardol trot up the pass ten minutes later, I saw again why Harrap had divided the force into two separate bodies. Helmets and breastplates polished so highly that the sun cast its reflection from exactly the same point on each, their green-and-scarlet cloaks draped at precisely the same angle, the cavalrymen could have halted on the instant for a royal inspection of their spear-straight lines. Though the mounted regular infantry and the Palace Guard lacked the cavalry's insolent grace, each man's garments and weapons were identical with his neighbor's, and the ranks were cleanly aligned.

For fifteen minutes or so I had both halves of our array in view from my slight eminence beside the trail. The way of the Horse miraculously led forever onward through the jagged upheaval of mountains, through the splendor of colors, amid the sudden bursts of red and green and purple and even orange and pink, though the cold whites and blues lay over all. The enormous vista at once drew the soldiers onward through illimitable space and enclosed them within impenetrable walls. Our moving columns were at once infinitely small and lost against the gargantuan backdrop and infinitely large and powerful. They grew great as the arena by the courage that had brought them into its unknowable perils.

During those protracted minutes, I could almost partake of Harrap's exaltation. New as at the birth of time, the great amphitheater was unblemished by the works of man. Had I made those ranges, I would choose them as the arena in which to work my miracles.

I pondered again the sources of Harrap's rising passion. Did the implacable splendor of the land confirm his conviction of holy mission and alter his innermost nature? Did direct inspiration fix his single purpose so that he saw only that purpose, as a hurtling eagle sees only his chosen prey? Did he speak with the priest during the long stages, feeding his own fires with the priest's prophetic frenzy?

I did not know. But a curious revelation of the nature of the

Quest came to me while I waited beside the trail. I felt that the Horse was but a horse despite His divine consecration. Though He was touched by the Gods, He was impelled more by Harrap's will than by Their will. The true greatness of Harrap's purpose was, it came to me, that he himself had all unknowing created his own purpose. Knowing the Colt mortal and, beyond human mortality, deaf to his own nature, I loved Him consumingly for the weakness that made His strength. We were the pawns of the will that worked through Harrap, and the Horse was the pawn of pawns, infinitely to be cherished.

I shivered in the sunlight and pulled my cloak about my shoulders. Composing my face into a smile of casual greeting, I pulled into step beside Mirab. Set off by his white hair and white mustaches, his blunt features glowed with untroubled good will.

Seventeen

After piercing the massif, the Horse led us down into the gorge and across a ford into a broad valley that each morning overflowed with the sun's golden hoard. Everywhere around us the mountains challenged the sky, but we had come into a secret realm of ease. The clouds were high and scant, the air was limpid and cool, and the Horse trotted eastward as on a highroad. The overwhelming soft spell of the green land among the peaks remained constant even when the broad river that ran between its wide cupped palms veered to the north.

Ring-necked pheasants rose from the brush at our horses' feet, so curious and unafraid that I thrice saw men reach out and catch them with bare hands. Rabbits, wild chickens, and hedgehogs swarmed in unending abundance and, like the yaks, the long-haired cattle, and the small, brown deer, they did not flee our arrows. Seeing the beasts dazzled by the green splendor of spring, our hunters disdained to chase the agile mountain goats, and the dried horse-beef hardened in our saddlebags. Cascades of berry bushes rolled down the hillsides among plantations of twisted trees. The elongated, smooth-skinned fruit of those stunted trees glowed yellow-green within foliage so darkly green it shone silver. The streams sparkled cold with the torrent's speed. Plump with the tender spring grasses, our mares gave us more sweet milk than we could drink or ferment.

Five times during those entranced days we saw the smoke of distant fires or glimpsed round hovels cobbled with pelts. The nomads of the mountains were near. Our joy was a little diminished by the knowledge that not we but the nomads of the hills were the first men to enter the valley. Harrap forbade the cavalry to ride after them. They were not true men, he said, but no more than animals, Devil worshippers who possessed neither

Gods nor lands of their own. Since the nomads did not seek to bar our way, we would not molest them. He commanded our priests to mark each confluence of streams, the joints of the living land, with ritual sacrifices and commanded my craftsmen to carve upon flat rocks beside the streams a record of our progress. Beneath those texts he incised a replica of his own seal, which read: *Harrap, Prince of Kamardol, Regent and General for Chandra-Gupta, Kings of Kamardol and Sovereign Lords of All Lands Where His Hoofprints Fall.* Chandra's elephant symbol and Gupta's cobra he omitted because, he said, they would require too much time for the carving.

Twice during those days wild herds of shaggy ponies rolled across our horizon. On the first encounter the Horse was so far ahead that He did not mark their presence. On the second He galloped close, circling the herd that would have been His cousins had He been wholly mortal horse. It was the season of bearing, not the season of begetting, and He did not pursue the startled herd, but kept docilely to the straight road of the valleys as if driven. I wondered fleetingly how we could keep Him from our own mares when their time came, but banished the doubt. It was of the same inferior metal as Harrap's earlier fears that the Colt's apparent need for the company of men had curbed His bold, free spirit. If the Gods so ordained, then that was Their purpose.

While crossing the massif, I had thought I was granted a revelation of the true nature of the Seeking. The spurious clarity of my vision of ourselves and the Horse alike compelled by Harrap's will faded during our journey through the valleys. Our very presence beyond the mountains that had always been the edge of our world was itself an irrefutable demonstration that the beliefs of our fathers were as firm as they had ever been. Unless the Gods drove us, why were we there?

I knew then that I had earlier been misled by the ageless Brahmanical compulsion to perfect men's imperfect communion with the Gods. Although I might ponder the intricacies of our conduct toward the Horse and the Gods' conduct toward us through Him, immutable reality was unaffected by my willful musings. The Gods' hands led Him forward, and it was our apotheosis to follow Him of our own will. The first choice to follow Him or not was perhaps each man's own choice, but it was a grave error to see in that minuscule exertion of human will the negation of the divine will. The great will lay upon us all the days of our Quest, closer to half-blind men because its vessel was in the shape of a beast. The Horse Himself felt Their purpose purely, since no impulses of the self-pride men call reason interposed themselves. If He was, as I had judged, placed beneath men by His lack of reason, the unhampered working of the divine will set Him, finally, far above men.

The golden certainty of the spellbound valley laid its balm even upon Harrap's sore passions. His incoherent rages had passed, assuaged almost as much by the miracle of the valleys as by the fratricidal clash with the Little Kamar which had so frightened the troops. The tribesmen's attack was in his mind the Gods' promise that we would be tried again and again until our bodies and our souls shrieked in an agony of striving. Suffused by that faith, he was content as long as the Horse led us onward. The anger and the scorn that had lain between us thawed in his new warmth, and we talked again as we had talked before the divine will sundered us.

The true glory so filled those days in the valleys that there remained no space for either fear or doubt. I myself was free of petty cares for the first time since I had led the dishonored Palace Guards and the blood-guilty Royal Guard out of the City by night. Neither Harrap nor the troops had particular need of me, for our column rolled forward as majestically as the broad Ganges. Little by little I cast off the character I had assumed, half warrior and half storekeeper. Little by little I became almost what I had been before the Seeking.

So a warrior feels when he puts off a full suit of armor piece by piece. After the first joy of release from the burden, the muscles of his arms and legs move clumsily, at once longing for the accustomed weight and hampered by its memory. There was hardly, of course, time enough to put off all the armor of my spirit, much less to teach myself to run and leap unencumbered. Nonetheless, I rode apart, and after the first day I unslung my lute. The words came hard, but still they came, and they grew into my 'Song of the Seeking.' It was a simple song to which men

might ride and, later, chant in the taverns or croon to their
grandsons:

> The Horse, He was born in the north,
> In the white land that lies above
> The last great curve of the sky.
> Where men of our blood go but to die
> Unless bound by the will of the Gods and Their love.
> The Horse, He came out of the north!
>
> The Horse, He was brought from the north,
> By Harrap, a prince of our line,
> And others who rode by his side;
> By men so proud beyond pride
> They took the Gods' goads as gentle kine.
> The Gods brought the Horse from the north!
>
> Our Kings' will became the Gods' will,
> That commanded us in Their name
> To follow Him and to kill
> Even the Brahman who knows not His fame.

I fashioned those lines, just fit to begin my song, after
discarding many false starts. Somehow, the words did not soar,
and my lute did not sing. My spirit yearned for a sign that the
Gods would lead us not only to great deeds, but to a triumphant
return. Other lines came to me, lines that should have awaited
the deeds that would give them life.

> All our days lead us to eternity
> Be the pace hard or be the pace slow.
> We seek but a token to show
> That the Quest is not vain,
> That we shall come back again
> From the crumbling edge of calamity.

I did not really hear those words until I had fitted the last line
into its place and repeated them all aloud. Though the verse
needed much smoothing, I was gratified by the twofold meaning
entwined in the last three lines. They subtly questioned both
man's passage through the visible world and our Seeking itself.
I sang the verses aloud again to feel their texture on my tongue
as a sculptor caresses a new statue with his eyes and his fingertips.

Was it, I wondered, just a device of prosody, this calling-up of doubts to scatter them in the end? Or was some doubt sealed in my heart thrusting itself into my Song?

I was troubled, and I knew I could make no more that day. When I heard the thudding of hooves behind me, I slung my lute and let my horse walk. It was a cavalryman, astride one of the great dapple-gray chargers I thought should have been left in the plains. I feared that the heavy beasts would slow our way through the mountains by their lack of agility and our progress across the deserts by their lack of hardihood. Harrap had preferred to keep them, because only the powerful grays could carry cavalrymen in full armor. He had preferred to hazard on the chargers' adaptability rather than upset the cavalry's discipline by remounting and re-equipping them.

The single rider wore his crested helmet square on his head, and his shield was precisely hung at his saddlebow as prescribed by regulations. His cloak was draped with millimetric accuracy, even at the gallop, and he wore the white scarf of a sub-lieutenant. I saw with pleasure that it was Anand, the lieutenant who had received us so churlishly when we brought the Horse to the City. Later in the encampment he had surprised us by his ardent support. He and I had talked together often during the last few days, at first because I sought to assess the temper of the troops as Harrap had commanded, but soon because I found pleasure in his conversation.

'Hola, Yakir!' he smiled, raising his hand in casual greeting.

'Hola, Anand!' I answered.

We had already cast off the burden of titles since we were so nearly of an age and our thoughts ran so eagerly together, though hardly in agreement. Originally of my own Brahman caste, Anand had become out-caste, first by accepting Buddhism and then by becoming an officer. Since my own caste was uncertain, I felt at one with Anand. I also admired his confidence in his own choices. We had, therefore, tended easily together, though the priest warned against him, muttering that he must be a spy for Chandra and the Buddhist monks.

'Hola, Anand,' I repeated, my spirit suddenly buoyant. 'What

185

new cares do you bring to heap upon my overburdened shoulders?'

'Not a straw, Yakir. Mirab grumbles to his captains and Ranbir mumbles to himself like his own grandmother beside her fire. All, therefore, goes well. I just thought I'd ride ahead.'

'You are welcome to ride by me,' I answered, and we trotted together in pleased silence for some time.

I marveled again at the decisiveness within this new companion of mine who appeared so commonplace. Despite his youth, his body was pudgy with the thickness of middle age. His thin lips were hardly darker than his sallow olive cheeks, and the bridge of his thin nose curved to a sweep of gristle that framed the shallow pits of his nostrils. Hair the hue of smudged sand grew thick over a fleshy forehead, robbing him of the distinction the broad swell of his temples might otherwise have conferred. A reddish wisp of beard covered a chin that, I suspected, receded sharply. Set deep under heavy brows, his eyes were normally an opaque black. But they glowed with the secret heat of flameless coals when his mind quickened and the vivid sentences spilled from his mouth.

'Well, Yakir,' he asked abruptly, 'how go your researches? What have you reported to the General of the state of our souls?'

'Nothing yet. But I'll have to say something soon.'

'And then?'

'As good as can be expected,' I laughed. 'I don't know what else I can say. Then, of course, he may hand the glove right back to me . . . Not that you've been much help.'

'Well, you know, we Buddhists don't credit the long bonds of caste stretching unbroken back to Khali's first spilled blood. For me, if I must kill, I'd just as soon kill Kamar – or Little Kamar – Kshatriyas as anyone else.'

'There speaks the true apostate,' I laughed again. 'Trust a fallen Brahman to delight in slaying Kshatriyas.'

'Or a falling Brahman,' he riposted.

'That's not true,' I answered seriously. 'There's more wit than truth in your words. I took no pleasure in our defeat of the Little Kamar.'

'How could you not? They sought our deaths.'

186

'They were,' I summoned my feelings deliberately, 'men of our own realm. We were bound to them by common purposes and by our long stand together against outsiders. For that reason – and that alone – I was appalled. I neither rejoiced because they were Kshatriyas, nor shrank from the deed because of their caste.'

'Now, that is truly another matter. I was half joking. As you know, we Buddhists believe that caste does not bind men together, but rather sunders the bonds men themselves have woven through the centuries. Not the Gods, but we ourselves have brought ourselves together by our own efforts. I believe we weaken our common purpose and our common humanity by preserving the distinctions priests pretend the Gods have put upon us.'

'Are all men the same, then – the dullard and the scholar, the merchant and the warrior, the peasant and the priest?'

'Of course not. Men could not live together without distinctions. Even among the beasts there are leaders and followers. Assuredly, men are not born alike. But we – I myself – do not believe that the Gods impose these distinctions by birth, so that one family must forever clean latrines and another forever interpret the divine will.'

'How else can we make those necessary distinctions? If we reject the distinctions that are ordained, we accept pure chance.'

'Each man must do what he can best do. I was born a priest, but I have become a soldier. That is what I do best. Of course, it was easy – too easy – to go downward. It should, however, be just as easy to move upward.'

'What would this random movement accomplish?'

'I must reply in parts. First, there is pure justice, fairness, if you prefer to call it so . . .'

'I do not understand,' I interrupted. 'Justice is what the Gods have ordained. It is just . . . It is just because it is so . . . that this one is a tanner of hides and I am a priest. It is just because it is ordained . . .'

'But you are not a priest! You are our colonel-adjutant.'

'No, I am not now priest or scholar,' I replied hesitantly. 'But that is only for the moment – and in obedience to a greater command of the same Gods. Later, I shall . . .'

'Perhaps you will . . .' he interrupted. 'We shall see. But let us pass by the question of justice for now.'

'If you will, though you reveal the weakness of your logic when you will not pursue it. Fine, then – I ask again: Where does it lead, all this random movement – warriors becoming scholars, scholars becoming peasants, even peasants becoming warriors, or Pariahs becoming priests, to be utterly absurd?'

'I agree, Yakir. It is hard to talk of justice. But you mistake my words. We Buddhists say that there should be – that there are in truth – no hereditary warriors, priests, peasants, or even Pariahs. The Brahmans have invented those distinctions. They are not imposed by the Gods. We say each man is born to do what he can best do, providing, of course, that his own energy or his father's wealth enables him to reach the goals toward which he yearns.'

'That is absurd, Anand. If all men were in constant motion, no man would know what he was or what he must do. No man would be secure, either in himself or toward others, and the realm itself would know no security at all.'

'The spirit within would guide each man more surely than do the laws of caste without. And the realm would be infinitely stronger – against enemies without and discontent within.'

'How?' I asked shortly, helping him tumble into the pit he had dug for himself – with my sly encouragement.

'Today, Yakir, men's spirits are bent by vast burdens of resentment, and their minds are bound by the ties of caste.'

'That is the proper order. Our security depends on restraints. Their minds must be bound.'

'It is false security, for it is division. Men strive for the good of their castes, not for the good of the realm. The realm is weak because it is riven. Men cannot use their full powers for their own good or for the good of the realm. They are fettered by priestmade distinctions. We are many who should be one! Being separate, we are weak!'

'I cannot,' I objected, 'imagine any other way. Men cannot live together unless their functions and their places are ordained.'

'You cannot because you have never seen it, not because it is unimaginable. In the ancient days, we were not so divided.'

'And it was progress, movement toward civilization, when men recognized and accepted the divine distinctions in their prayers – and in their lives. Beasts are alike, not men.'

'I think not, Yakir. And I warn you that we are weak. Kamardol is perilously weak. Someday we will be destroyed by a people that is strong because it is not divided by caste.'

'Your case is weak if you must resort to prophesy – and without the Brahmayanas to guide you,' I deliberately diverted the stream of our argument. 'But let us return to the present. What of your own cavalrymen and the others? Do they still fear that our cause is cursed because we slew the Little Kamar?'

'In this green land,' he evaded me, 'who could see anything but blessings?'

'I do not understand you,' I persisted. 'Can you not tell whether there is still fear in their hearts?'

'I meant this – we ride through a land that the Gods have blessed. No man in our force but thinks that the blessing falls also on our Quest and on himself. Later, when we are imperiled, then the doubts and fears will rise again – if not the curse of fratricide, then other curses, for each man carries his own special fears in his heart as each seed carries its own particular flower.'

'Then I can tell Harrap that all is well?'

'Assuredly, for this moment. But when the time of peril is upon us, it will depend on why each man rides.'

'Why each man rides?' I echoed. 'Assuredly, we all ride because it is ordained that we ride and there is honor and glory in our sacrifice?'

'Do you really believe that?'

'Of course not,' I laughed. 'Except, generally, that we all ride in a common purpose. Each man, of course, rides for his own reasons as well. Some to escape their wives, others in search of loot so that they may acquire wives. Just so Harrap was unmoved by the slaughter of the Little Kamar because he *knows* that he was but the arm of the Gods. He *knows* he was commanded to slaughter them because they would have barred the way of the Horse.'

'And the Bastards, as you call them?'

'Patently, they ride for the lust of the trail and the fight – and, of course, in hope of loot. For that matter, the Royal Guards and the Palace Guards ride because it were death – or at least disgrace – to remain.'

'And why do you ride?'

'I am not certain, yet,' I evaded him in turn. 'But I shall try to tell you when I know.'

'That will be good,' he answered gravely.

'And Harrap?' I persisted. 'Why, think you, does Harrap ride so wholly obsessed?'

Anand did not reply for the time it took us to go perhaps a hundred yards. The land was still green and fecund. But, it seemed to me, the evergreens were set a little further apart and the brush was somewhat sparser, somewhat less resilient beneath the horses' hooves. A bank of clouds blocked the broad mouth of the valley, and we were climbing a slight rise that reached into those clouds.

'It seems colder,' Anand finally said, 'and I thought I saw a mountain peak thrust above the clouds that lie before us.'

I looked long, but saw nothing except the swirling gray mass, a curtain before the sunlight.

'Harrap . . . Harrap, I think,' Anand resumed as if I had just put the question, 'rides for the same reason I do.'

'How so?' I asked, a little affronted by the comparison.

'Because each of us seeks – each in his own way – to do deeds that are beyond himself . . . beyond the experience of men and the commands of the Gods as we know them.'

'I do not wholly understand you,' I said, this time truly puzzled.

'Look you, Yakir!' Anand replied with crisp decision. 'What I have said is this: Man – each man – is what he is, regardless of the will of the Gods. Once They have shaped a man, he will act in accordance with his true nature. Even the Gods can but seek to guide him. Therefore I said caste was nonsense, since it is nonsense that every son in each family will be the same, much less every man – and woman – in each caste and subcaste.'

'I do not agree, as you know, about caste. It is a distinction above each man's individual nature – and some, like the Pariahs, are not men, having no individual spirit. But assuredly I will grant you that for us Brahmans and the Kshatriyas at least, your words are true. Each man is quite different.'

'Let it be so, then. I will not dispute with you regarding caste again today.'

'And Harrap?'

'Yes, Harrap. How shall I say it? Look you, Yakir, Harrap could have been King, but he did not want it. Is that not correct?'

'Yes,' I conceded. 'It is perhaps not strictly true, but true enough.'

'He refused to be King because he wants more than to be King. Like me, Harrap seeks a purpose that will make him greater. But not necessarily greater in the common forms.'

'And the Seeking?'

'In the Seeking he has found his purpose, just as I have found it in Buddhism. The Seeking is its own purpose, though Harrap will, I fear, come either to a great triumph or to utter defeat.'

'That may be,' I answered. 'I think you were right about the mountains. Look ahead.'

The curtain of clouds had parted. Before us we saw a barrier many times more forbidding than any we had stormed. The mountains soared forever upward so that we could see neither their peaks nor any light between them and the dark skies.

Eighteen

I slept fitfully that night. Harassed by the phantoms of doubt Anand had called up, I was harried back and forth between sleep and awareness by the night sounds of the encampment – the nickering of the horses and the coughing of the camels, the jangling of harnesses and the sighs of sleepers who shifted each time the sentinels called the hour.

Although the night was black, without moon or stars, and my fleece cloak a warm cave against the chill winds, I came wholly awake two hours past the crest of the night. The soldiers were straggling back from their revels among the few hundred camp followers who still clung to us as obstinately as a tick to a dog's rump. Cavalrymen shouted threats at infantrymen, swearing they had been cheated in the tossing of the sticks. Others sang, the chants of the march and the ballads of love blurred alike by tongues swollen with wine. Some boasted of their feats in the flower tents, their own endurance as prodigious as the beauty and art of their harlots. I was annoyed, but I laughed at the fantastic descriptions and the constant soughing obbligato as each man counseled his friends in a booming whisper, 'Be careful . . . Not so much noise . . . Don't want to wake everybody up.'

Abandoning sleep and the sleeping Mirab, whose silver mustaches bristled alert under his blunt nose, I rolled up my gear and led my horse out of the circle of light inscribed by the smoldering fires. The dawn still slept in the east, but the snow on the slope caught some distant light. Through the night of the fifteenth day after the ambush in the defile, I rode toward the vanguard. I hoped to come up with them before they began to move. My report to Harrap on the morale of the main body had been long delayed, but, beyond duty, I longed to ride again with the four hundred and capture the Horse in my own sight.

The dawn was a faint rent in the black cloak of night. But I found the way where hooves had packed the sod. The trail was again rising sharply, and we were drawing out of the enchanted valley. When the sullen gray dawn split the night, I saw the four hundred camped on a rock-rimmed plateau a half mile or so to the north and a few hundred yards above me. The dull dawn filmed the bright banners of the vanguard, and their morning fires were pallid-yellow patches beneath pillars of spiraling soot. Beyond the plateau lay a savage and desolate universe of ice and snow and rock. Had I still believed – as even scholars did a century ago and women still believe today – that the earth was a flat disc floating in dark oceans of air, I should have shaken with unnameable fear. The mountains, rising even higher to imprison the northward-seeking eye and palisading the east and west, might have been the last barrier set to rim the edge of the world. Though I knew the earth was shaped like a vast egg from which few men fell, my heart still started – half in awe and half in terror of the magnificent citadel we challenged.

A host of massifs mustered their jagged cliffs to the east. Even at the great distance the cliff faces were gnarled and jagged, the black and gray surfaces lightened by neither vegetation nor snow. All the enormous range seemed the refuse of an immense quarry enlarged a thousandfold and tenthousandfold again. Far in the west a complementary range marched to the cloud-smudged horizon. Its contours were obscured by a heavy veil of snow, though patches of sheer cliff glowered through that veil. Black rock gave roothold to drifts of green – whether shrubs, stunted evergreens, or only hardy spring grasses I could not tell.

Seven separate mountain ranges were enclosed by the titanic amphitheater. Uncountable individual peaks rose precipitately from the scarred floor of the amphitheater to form those ranges. Aside from ridges and depressions carved upon them by wind and hail, each peak was a perfect cone, while each range was parade-ground straight. The children of the Gods – or the young Gods themselves – had heaped up an immense encampment of peaked tents in their play. A broad trail ran across the gargantuan panorama, winding through the snow-streaked sides of the mountains.

The wind trumpeted through the gorge, driving the hard snow against my eyelashes and assailing my nostrils with the mixed scents of heather and smoke. I drew my cloak across my face and mourned the green valleys behind me. But I praised the Gods for the path They had laid before us.

The clouds lifted from the gray ridges to the east, and a hundred shafts of morning sunlight streamed down in benediction. The entire amphitheater ran with molten light, and the thousand mountains glowed. All the hard, bright colors of all the world woke in that celestial dawn – greens and whites, reds and ebonys, purples and blues – and all tumbled in the waves of light like an endless torrent of gems.

I gave thanks again – for the transcendent glory of the morning and for the way through that glory. The lines came unbidden to my lips, 'Oh, Varuna, who made the sun and is the sun; Varuna, whose bright Child we follow . . .' But my wandering eye quenched the song with fresh discovery. The broad track among the mountains gleamed cold blue and infinitely deep where the sunlight smote it, and I saw that it was no road for us, but a terrible twisted barrier of ice. I saw in my despair no way through the barrier, and I was convinced that we must turn back or wander forever through the wilderness. The Gods had spoken directly to us, showing us that we must not attempt to go forward.

The clouds lifted higher, and the unwavering light froze the mountains in their multitudinous brilliance. I saw the Horse poised on a crag a little distance from the camp, an ivory image washed with gleaming platinum that left its radiance upon each taut muscle. Ten princes sat their barbarous ponies around Him, and their yellow cloaks were the golden tribute pilgrims bear on their backs to the Gods. The Horse was quite still, as if Himself awed by the forbidden splendor He had revealed to us. Beyond Him and beyond the seven ranges, new peaks, till then unseen, shone forever white and forever sharp until my eye gave up its power and I could see no further into the cold north.

The vision endured but a few seconds. Then the Horse vanished as the clouds fell again, and fog enveloped me, filling the amphitheater and englooming the encampment. I rode toward the sound of voices and the scent of smoke, where lazy figures loaded deformed beasts among undulating ribbons of mist. I found Harrap where the bustle was loudest.

'Hola, Yakir!' he grinned, his incisors gleaming through the dullness like the great dog teeth of an old wolf hunting by moonlight. 'You are come just in time. We ride on the instant.'

He thrust his left foot into the stirrup and lifted himself into his saddle as straight-backed as if he danced on the marble floor of the Great Palace. The jewels on his scabbard and hilt gleamed through the mist, and I was suddenly aware that I wore the twin of his sword of ceremony, each fragile and priceless. Harrap clung to his axe for battle, but I preferred to keep a short infantryman's sword under my stirrup leather.

'I am glad you are come up to us,' he greeted me. 'Here, gnaw on this if you've not breakfasted. Then we can talk.'

I took the delicate haunch of mouse deer, savoring the juice that still ran sweet though the meat was cold. This attention was obviously intended to show that the anger that had lain between us was past. It was Harrap's pleasure to forgive my transgressions – as long as I did not further oppose his will. We picked our way through the mist, the priest and Harrap and I riding abreast, and the flag-bearer just out of earshot. I cracked the venison bone and sucked out the dark marrow before tossing it away. When I had tucked my leather flask into my saddlebag, Harrap spoke again. 'Now, Yakir, how does it go with the regulars?'

'Well enough,' I answered carelessly. 'But how they'll come through this Devil's soup in this Hell's cauldron, I do not know. Or how we will, for that matter.'

'Do not waste yourself on idle fears. It was worse than this when we came up yesterday.'

'And the Horse, can He find His way . . . our way? Does He go without fear though He is blinded? He was close to the encampment this dawn, as if reluctant to go forward.'

They answered me at once from either side.

'The Child of the Gods is never blinded,' the priest swore in his high-prophet voice. 'He moves in a pool of constant light, though we should clamor in unbroken night.'

'He will go!' said Harrap. 'He will go! There is need neither to urge Him onward nor to hold Him back against mishap. It is *promised* that He will find *my* way.'

The Seeking had come down so soon to the divine pair – Harrap and the Horse. Amused though not surprised, I said nothing, finding nothing to say, until Harrap asked impatiently, 'Well, Yakir, what of the main body? No misfortunes, I'm sure – or I should have heard. But what of their spirits? Do they still sweat in foolish fear over what they call fratricide?'

'You would indeed have heard,' I replied. 'No, there has been no misfortune. And the spirit seems strong, the fear flown.'

'Good! Tell me more.'

'There is no more to tell, Harrap. The men are in good spirits. What fears hide beneath their everyday faces I cannot tell. But I have not seen the downcast eyes or the mumbling lips of fear. Nor have their own officers. But ride with them for a day and see for yourself.'

'It would, of course, be useful, but I cannot,' he answered portentously. 'It is ordained that I must ride always in the vanguard upon the heels of the Stallion.'

'By whom ordained?' I asked without pause. 'I remember no such command in the Brahmayanas.'

'It is ordained,' he answered stubbornly. 'I know it. So, Yakir, you must be my eyes – as you have been these many years.'

'As you say, Harrap, it is ordained,' the priest responded to his interrogative glance.

'So be it,' I replied. 'Can I tell you more? It may be that the fear sleeps because of the ease of our passage through the fruitful land that lies behind. But I feel it is not dead. It could awaken, hungry and furious, in the mountains that lie before us.'

'What you say must be true,' Harrap mused. 'It is the way of soldiers – the braver in battle, the more timorous before the perils they imagine.'

'But we must . . . there must be some way to raise the spirits to the deeds they must do,' put in the priest. His broad, beaked nose, his tremulous jowls, and his lips pursed in concern put me in mind of an uneasy matron wondering how she might keep her servants' thefts within reasonable limits.

196

'There should be a way, indeed,' said Harrap. 'Your words, Yakir, are consoling, but how can we inspire these soldiers as we ourselves are inspired?'

'Inspire ... soldiers?' I asked scornfully, distaste for their purposeless chatter riding over my amusement at Harrap's nice distinctions. When he spoke of the divine favor, it was always *I* and *my* and *mine*, but when it came to difficulties, it was *we* and *our* and *ours*.

'Yes, inspire soldiers ... common soldiers,' he flared. His conviction of divine mission had not conferred serenity upon him, but had kindled a smoldering rage that was ever on the point of flame. 'Yakir, give off this damned Brahmanical hauteur. Common soldiers are men, as you and I are men. Their spirits, too, can soar to the divine purpose.'

'As you say, Harrap,' I said, uncertain whether the reply would soothe him or goad his rage.

But he had already passed out through the further gates of anger, for he continued softly, 'Perhaps, if I spoke to them ...'

'Perhaps later,' wheezed the priest, twisting uncomfortably in his saddle and easing the skirts of his rough red robe between his legs. 'At the moment, our strength is that we move without fixed purpose – or set fears. Let it be so for a time longer.'

'How so, priest?' I asked.

'Aside from our general purpose – in obedience to the Gods – we are bound by no fixed policy.'

'And that is strength?' I persisted. 'I see purposelessness as strength no more today than when you first discovered the notion.'

'Yes, Yakir, that is strength. Our strength is that we do not seek to impose our own desires on the future.'

'I can see,' I said, waving my hand at the fog that hid all of the world four horses' lengths beyond us, 'that at this moment our only purpose is to survive ... to go forward ... if we can, since we must. But I cannot agree that this aimlessness makes us strong.'

'Look you, Yakir, it is so,' the priest insisted. 'Once bound by fixed means, once directed to a certain goal, we lose half our power. Some purpose, of course, leads men onward through life.

But they ride between cliffs that rise ever higher along a path that grows ever narrower.

'So it is with almost all men. They are bound by their own wills, fettered unknowing by the free choices they believe they have taken. But we have escaped the manacles of that delusive free choice by giving our purpose wholly into His . . . into Their hands. By submitting to the greater bonds, we have broken the lesser bonds.

'Still . . . even now . . . even as we are . . . the first deliberate steps we take by choice will determine all our steps that follow – until we have attained the purpose we believe we chose . . . or fail of it and are again released from the bonds we have, unknowing, laid upon ourselves.'

'With most men that first step is birth,' I added, drawn unwilling by the thread of his thought, 'and the release comes only with death.'

'That is so. Most men think they choose. But most men cannot rise even to the limited choice we have gained by our departure from the life of Kamardol, by our breaking from the roles of conquering general, scholar, and domestic priest. But, of course, every step we take on this, our Quest, is also foreordained.'

'Then,' I asked, my talk with Anand echoing in the chambers of my mind, 'is it pointless either to seek to avoid commitment or – on the other hand – to choose a commitment? All is foreordained in either event.'

'Strictly, yes,' the priest answered. 'Strictly, you are quite correct, Yakir. It is an illusion to believe that we can choose even the first step that binds us. Whether it be the will of the Gods working within us or the will of the Gods working upon us, it is fixed. He directs . . . They direct even the first step, which determines the road we must, thereafter, follow to the end.'

'Then why do you seek aimlessness – this being empty of purpose, which you say is our strength at this moment? Our course is, in any event, traced upon some great map as far as we shall ever go.'

'Simply this – our course is marked broadly in space and in deed, but not precisely in time. By preserving our purposeless-ness, as you call it, or, better, by failing to commit ourselves – we gain time. And we avoid the anguish men suffer when the Gods force them to retrace their false steps.'

'I am not sure that I understand you wholly,' I said, nor was I.

Harrap, who had been attending to some inner voice rather than our tortuous dialogue, said with decision, 'So be it, then. I shall speak to the troops when we have come through this trial of the mountains. There will be need then.'

The priest and I picked at the bones of that conversation during the terrible three weeks of our ordeal in the mountains. Like gluttonous jackals, we ever came back to rip another scrap from the stripped carcass. Unyielding in his assertion of certainty, the priest was mild in disputation. I believe he knew that I walked the verge of an abyss, incapable of surmounting the barrier that divided me from Harrap and finding no firm footing in the Seeking itself. Nonetheless, I drew little consolation – and no certainty – from the priest's adamantine conviction. There was more sustenance even in Anand's persistent and, to me, inexplicable faith in men.

Harrap took no part in my talks with the priest, though he listened tolerantly when he was near us. His mien – at once attentive and withdrawn – was that of an aged philosopher who permits his green pupils foolish speculation. *I* know, his smile said, but you must find out for yourselves.

Those talks were but a small part of my days. I went constantly back and forth between the vanguard and the main body. I was driven back to the regulars by duty and by weariness with Harrap's self-locked smugness. I was as often drawn forward to the vanguard, not so much by my duties as by my need to look upon the Horse – and, paradoxically, to draw strength from Harrap's leadership. His demeanor toward me did not alter, being compounded as ever of rough cordiality and unthinking harshness. Constraint remained between us, but he carried me forward by the vigor of his will, as he did all the company.

It was the time of the trials Harrap had invoked. Not men nor the high Gods, but the earth itself contested the way with us. Spring was just penetrating the high mountains, whose granite battlements had held winter captive while the plains were already in flower. Spring was the most capricious, the most treacherous of times in the mountains, for all the world was in flux. For an hour or two the clouds would lift and the fog would disperse to reveal the full terror of the Devil's realm through which the Horse led us, somehow always finding a way through a gully or along a spur of solid rock among the streams of ice, the sliding snows, and the heaped barricades of boulders larger than elephants. Then the fog and clouds returned, hurling their arrows of sleet at our aching bodies. Yet darkness was a merciful relief, hiding the bottomless crevasses, the sword-edged cliffs, and the deceptively solid spires of snow that could crush us all if alertness faltered for ten or twenty heart strokes.

The soldiers grumbled endlessly. At first they only muttered, but after a time they cried out their fears without shame. They knew that I but pretended not to hear their constant complaint: 'Fratricide! We are being punished for fratricide! We shall all perish. The Horse is not led by the Gods, but ridden by a thousand Devils!'

I could neither despise them for cowardice nor exhort them onward, knowing the same terrors myself. Each day two or three riders would feel their mounts lurch beneath them, and men and beasts would vanish screaming beneath the cold pall of gray mist. It was far worse when the watery sunlight let us see the ledge crumble beneath imprudent hooves – and watch horse and rider fall gyrating through the cruel light until both were consumed by the depths.

Only Ranbir's men were unawed. Perhaps they felt themselves secure in the great mountains where their Gods lived. Perhaps their stern discipline prevented their displaying fear. Perhaps they were so stolid, truly 'half men, like beasts without pounding hearts,' as the regulars swore, that they felt no fear. Yet the Royal Guards, who had learned to sit their horses only a few months earlier, suffered but a tithe of the regulars' casualties, losing no more than five of their number. The cavalry, in particular, refused to lead their horses across bad patches as did the Guards. They would die in the saddle if they must die, they swore, but they would not dismount. I think in truth it was not pride that made them so stubborn, but that they were afraid to trust their own feet.

The Bastards were initially too proud to speak of their fear, even to each other. But I could see from their sideward glances into the abyss that the ravens plucked at their hearts too. On the sixth day Gorbabordol came to me. He was their spokesman, since they acknowledged no leader.

'Colonel Yakir,' he said, 'two of us rode forward today. The Horse was lost in the mist ahead, and they were the first link in the chain. As I watched, the solid rock vanished beneath their feet. We shall never see them again.'

'I am sorry,' I said, 'but what can I do? We all bear the same perils.'

'Can you not speak to the General?' he pleaded. 'Could we not wait until the fury of spring has abated? Or, better, could we not turn back? To what goal, after all, do we journey in such haste? Why must we press forward so fast? Better let the priests prove the will of the Gods in their solid temples than perish chasing an illusion.'

'Turn back?' I asked without pausing to reflect, for I had pondered the matter myself. 'The perils that lie ahead cannot be worse than those we have already passed. Or pause? To await death here? No man knows the way of these mountains, and their fury may last forever – or become worse. Is it better to go forward. At least the Horse guides us.'

'The Horse!' he spat. 'If I live, I shall never sit in the saddle again after we return. I'll walk or be carried in a litter like an old lady. But gladly and willingly will I sacrifice horses to the Gods – tens of horses, hundreds of horses.'

I gave the same answer to each of the captains who privately brought me his fears during the next two weeks. The others lacked Gorbabordol's self-mocking laughter, but all had to take the answer – whether with grace or without grace. None, I knew, was content with my answer, but all recognized its truth. And all in some measure, directly or deviously as they were made, echoed Gorbabordol's complaint that the Seeking was the folly of men, rather than the quest of the Gods. No officer grumbled to Harrap himself, even when the second week ended and the mountains seemed just beginning. I heard one captain mutter that he preferred the faint chance of life by obeying to the solid certainty of death by rousing Harrap's wrath.

But my answer convinced myself. As each succeeding day conjured new terrors from beneath its gray cloak I became inured to the constant peril and, finally, exalted by it. If the Horse were not led by the Gods, how could we have come so far through unremitting hazards? Was it not the Gods' blessing that the danger was veiled, since looking upon its naked face might have frozen our resolution? Only a power infinitely greater than His own dumb will could drive the Horse onward through crags the mountain goats shunned. Hardship convinced me, as ease had failed to convince me.

Even Anand's skepticism could not depress me when we talked, gnawing our dried meat and filling our mouths with snow against thirst. We could not hunt, and the mares had gone dry. He argued cheerfully but stubbornly against my renewed faith. The Horse did not turn back, he said, because the troops blocked the way. He went forward because the Bastards were forever at His heels, pricking His timidity into motion. I laughed and asked Anand if he had ever seen a horse choose – actually choose – to gambol through a landscape of death. The Horse, I reminded him, was free, quite free to go as He willed.

Twice Harrap was forced to give the order to halt. Once, we huddled beneath an overhanging cliff for three nights and two days while the wind swept torrents of snow past us. The second blizzard, four days later, drove us to shelter in a defile for only a day and a night, but it was even fiercer. The mountains themselves split, and we heard the Devil's roar of snow peaks falling above the anguished screaming of the wind. The hurtling icicles were as long as our pikes and sharper than our swords' edges.

The storm died three hours past the crest of night, and the dawn was brilliant. I saw in the fresh clarity that we had come as far as we could. Ten miles ahead a sheer white wall loomed so high that I could not see the tips of other peaks behind it. The flattened summit supported the gray sky, and the mass was balanced so precariously I marveled that it did not crash down upon us. The base of the mountain was so high that the flowing skirts of snow and ice that draped its massive flanks were unrent by the thaws of spring.

Harrap could still surprise me. Any other general would have permitted his men to rest after the terrible night, but he laughed and ordered the trumpets to sound the advance. Dazed by the wild night and by his audacity, first the four hundred and then the main body mounted and followed him.

The Horse was in clear view, for He too had retreated into the defile with us. He went forward almost as if reluctant, the Bastards only a few lengths behind Him. I would have cried out to Harrap, warning him that he forced the divine will and imperiled the Seeking by driving the Horse, when He began to trot along an almost imperceptible crease toward the face of the mountain. So He drew us on to the impasse. I knew that we would go a wearisome way back before resuming our Quest, since even Harrap must learn within the few hours that this road led but to destruction. Seemingly unaware, he approached the confrontation that could break the soldiers' slender faith and shatter even his power to carry them onward.

'We move again, Yakir,' he shouted above the shrill wailing of the winds that keened for the dead storm. 'The Gods are generous. Bring me up Ranbir and his men. I may have need of them. I ride with the Bastards today, a pace behind the Perfect Stallion.'

I returned three hours later with the mountaineers. The four hundred were already trailed across the glistening white skirts of the monstrous peak, a ribbon segmented green and scarlet and gold. The Horse, with Harrap and perhaps a third of the Bastards, had vanished. As I watched, the ribbon was drawn slowly upward, and another inch disappeared behind a broad fold of ice-spangled rock.

'Father Ranbir,' said Harrap when he came up to him behind the concealing rock, 'hold your men near me. Your snow monkeys may have to show us how clever they are.'

'It will not be an outing for young girls, Harrap. But I believe we can manage,' answered Ranbir, squinting along the draw that zigzagged up to a natural glacis, half ice and half snow. Beyond the glacis opened a cleft in the wall of rock.

I marveled that Harrap's luck still soared triumphant to find a way through the impenetrable.

'No, Ranbir,' he said, 'I was not concerned about your men. But it may be that you can help the others. Yakir and you must decide, for I ride ahead.'

After four interminable hours of exhausting toil we came to the edge of the glacis. The mountaineers almost carried us all. Staking out their horses at the foot of the draw, they climbed on foot, soaring upward as lightly as eagles. Having found a way, they returned as easily and helped the Bastards pull their horses upward. Harrap climbed with the Stallion, sometimes leaning over to whisper into an ear and run his hand along the quivering neck. So the Horse went first, neither impelled by force nor wholly deterred by fear, but cajoled up the precipitous slope.

The semi-glacier, which seemed a glacis, was still to cross before we came to the saddle, which must, I prayed, give us a way through. The mountaineers stretched a rope across the glacier, tying it to javelins hammered deep into crevices in the rock and ice. When Harrap and the Horse had crossed to the saddle, the first twenty Bastards followed, five men clinging to the rope and pulling each horse. I went up also, with my trumpeter, to speak with Harrap. Since he would follow the Horse whatever came, the task of moving the remainder of the force was mine alone.

His arm encircling the Horse's neck, Harrap stood at the bottom of a cleft hardly wider than a man's shoulders. 'Come a little higher, Yakir!' he shouted into the wind. 'Come a little higher and behold a new world.'

The Horse between us, we climbed till we could just see through the cleft. Before us lay a frozen ocean of white peaks, jagged, rough-cast and precipitous. But all the way led down, and all the peaks were lower than the pinnacle on which we stood. Far beyond the mountains, yet appearing almost beneath our feet in the unearthly clarity that surrounded our heights, glowed a strip of brown earth. It was barred with bright green.

'See the others across,' Harrap shouted as casually as if he were sending me off to drill a platoon of recruits. Then he clambered through the cleft, the Horse following him. He found shelter from the wind in a coign of bare rock and waited for the Bastards to come over to him.

I stood beside the split rock for nearly an hour while the yellow cloaks of the princes and the hindquarters of their weary horses flickered through the cleft, one at a time till forty had crossed over. The Horse led them onward, slowly at first, then rejoicing, His hooves dancing over the easy downward slope. Above Him masses of snow were piled higher than the great Towers of Kamardol.

I was turning wearily back to the task of bringing the others across, when white movement flashed in the corner of my eye. Wheeling back, I saw that one of the great snow towers was cracking at its base. Sides casting off a feathery white spray, it leaned toward the slope where the Horse capered with Harrap behind him. I opened my mouth to shout, but the keening of the wind would have overwhelmed even the shouted rage of the Gods.

'Sound the alarm!' I cried to the trumpeter.

Once, twice, thrice, the shrill call screeched out of the brazen mouth, the trumpeting of an enraged bull elephant, the screeching of the peacock when hawks circle overhead.

Harrap looked back at me, then up where I pointed. Hurtling forward with drawn sword, he laid the edge across the Horse's loins. The pair stormed across the slope as the tower of snow broke and fell.

I waited for minutes, staring anguished into the white cauldron, before the torrents of snow subsided and I could see again. On the far side of the avalanche I saw Harrap and the Horse with eight of the princes. On my own side of the avalanche, I counted an additional eighteen yellow cloaks. Fourteen princes had been swept away.

Praying that the Gods of the mountains and the spring had taken Their last sacrifice, I went back to shepherding the force across the summit. Though the guardsmen worked as if fatigue and discouragement alike were words they had never learned, it was two full days before the last of the main body had passed through the cleft. All that time Anand was at my side, sustaining my will and taking all but the chief decisions on himself. The pack animals were unloaded and their burdens carried across on men's backs, while the light carts came through the cleft's slit in pieces. The heavy carts I abandoned, though Harrap's anger was certain since he had reserved them to carry loot. In the dying hours of the second day, I invited his anger again by bringing across the two hundred or so who still remained of the original six hundred camp-followers.

All that time Harrap, our commander-in-chief, rode gaily onward behind the Horse. I finally came to him, myself wholly exhausted, a week after we had first spied the climactic mountain. He waited in a rock-strewn valley, tinged with the green spring grasses, which lay just one ridge above the broad plain we had seen from the pinnacle. He accepted my report lightly, saying only, 'I knew you'd manage, Yakir. But it is a pity about the heavy carts.'

Disheartened, I turned my horse, intending to return to my post with the main body without speaking again. But he checked me, saying, 'Perhaps it would be well if I addressed the troops now.'

'As you wish,' I answered.

Mirab and I drew up the force. Standing on a boulder overlooking the valley, Harrap began to speak: 'Princes, knights, archers, yeomen, mountaineers, and my own dear troops! Warriors! We have come through the cauldron of the Devils by the grace of the Gods.'

He flung back his massive head, and the shining black hair cascaded across his shoulders. His voice grew heavy: 'Some of you swear at our losses. Some of you weep – as I have wept. We have taken grievous losses. Eighty-three men and beasts are dead. More than twice that number are injured by the malevolent mountains and the cold blasts of Hell.'

His voice crashed proudly against the overhanging crags. 'But I tell you . . . I tell you that we are shielded by the grace of the Gods . . . Otherwise, ten times that number would have perished. Never have men come through such perils so nearly unscathed. Never, in truth, have living men come through perils such as you and I have overcome – by the God's grace and the spirit of the Perfect Stallion!

'Warriors, we will, it may be, take greater losses still. But after this ordeal, nothing more on earth – or in the Heavens – can frighten us while we bow to the Gods' will and partake of Their grace.

'Warriors, we will win great renown and take many fair captives and trickle the wealth of empires through our fingers.

'Warriors, our triumph is certain!'

The troops were silent for a full minute while the echoes of Harrap's words rolled across the valley, and I feared that they would raise their weapons against him in their anger. But they cheered, tossing their spears in jubilation. They actually cheered, as if Harrap had led them to a victory, rather than forcing them to the edge of disaster.

Nineteen

A vision of warmth and ease swelled in our eyes, growing sharper and more vivid with each ridge we topped in the Gods' great staircase that fell away before us. I did not feel myself free of the icy grasp of the mountains until we stood on the last slope with all the Devils' wilderness at our backs. Then finally we saw before us only the brown earth and the green plants, their glowing life unmarred by the black rock and white snow that had imprisoned us for almost a month.

Still, it was a harsh land, this fringe between the mountains and the sand to which we had come on the track of the Horse. Even where the narrow rivers ran it was hot and dry by day – yet so cold by night that the animals' breath froze on their muzzles. The plants were sparse and shallow-rooted.

In all our wandering we were never to discover the Perfect Kingdom at the heart of the continent, the realm, the fables tell, where a hundred kinds of vines and trees hang heavy with the sweet fruit of everlasting summer, and broad, cool rivers are engorged with gold. It must lie elsewhere, that Perfect Kingdom, where all men live free of pain and disease, dying only with the centuries, so secure in perpetual peace under wise and learned kings that they maintain neither armies nor city guards. That realm we all yearned to despoil, but never found.

Yet we knew so much joy in those first few days after our release from the mountains that we might indeed have come upon the Perfect Kingdom. Even Ranbir's Guards, who had passed through the ordeal as if on parade, rejoiced, lending their strength and their skill to the rest. Even they laughed and shouted like boys on their first hunt and hewed at each other with their lances in pure exuberance. For the rest of us it was total delight to ease our aching muscles by walking on the plain, unafraid that the firm ground might collapse beneath our feet or peaks of falling snow bury us.

We had five soft days in the sun to rest and let our wounds and our broken bones heal. Gaunt after their trials, the animals grazed and slept. Small hunting parties flushed deer and small beasts unknown to us, providing fresh meat and a little left over to dry. When the mares' milk began flowing again, we could make koumiss. Anand and I marveled together at the fickle temper of the troops and wondered how long their new confidence would endure the next trial. But we too exulted that the ordeal was done, and that the soldiers, buoyant again, muttered no more of being cursed by their fratricide.

'The General is right,' they told each other. 'We move in the light of the Gods!'

The Horse gave us the respite, not Harrap, who might have conceded us a single day of rest – though no more – after we came out of the mountains. But the Horse was reluctant to leave the foothills for the narrow bars of living green that lay across the dead sands of the desert. Each morning, the Bastards reported, He would trot away from the encampment, and only a few miles distant graze and roll in the small, secret meadows cupped by the low hills from which streams inched into the sands. Each evening He would return to the encampment as if He had been trained all His life to the routine of a farmer's ox. The fire of inspiration that had brought us safely through the mountains seemed to have died in Him. Unlike the lesser beasts, He had grown stronger through our ordeal. His skin was soft and shining, His energy ever flowing when we came out of the mountains. But after a few days of rest, the taut contours of His muscles blurred, and His jaunty paces dragged. It was as if He had aged greatly in those days. The questing spirit, which wavered in the Horse, was constant in Harrap, and after three days in the encampment he grumbled to me, 'Nearly two months have gone by – one day in every six allotted to us. And still we have done no great deeds.'

'Not quite two months,' I said lightly, too sunk in ease to feel alarm – or give him close attention.

'Two months near enough, Yakir. I have almost decided to move the Stallion along a little.'

'And force the omen?' I asked, alarmed. 'Shatter the shape of Their will?'

'It would not be that, Yakir . . . Just a little gentle prodding to set Him on the proper road again,' Harrap replied confidently enough, though I knew I had stirred his ever present fear of spoiling the Seeking.

The priest, coming up behind us, spared my urging that men and beasts needed still more rest. Wearied by the constant task of restraining Harrap imposed upon me by the Gods, I had no heart for a new argument.

'I cannot, on my part, agree even to the gentlest prodding,' the priest said sternly. 'How can you doubt that it is the will of the Gods that we pause here for a time? You have seen the true miracle. The Avatar led us – wholly miraculously – through the mountains, never pausing in His eager progress though we were blind. Now He pauses – and we must abide.'

'Just a little gentle prodding to remind Him of His mission, O Brahman?' wheedled Harrap with the sly glance of a child pleading for a toy.

'You command, O Prince,' the priest replied. 'But the auguries tell me that it would be disastrous, marring our perfect Seeking beyond restoration by all my skill.'

Harrap's flush of anger deteriorated into the pout of a child denied. But the black fear of failure that was the other face of his mindless dedication kept him from acting or even retorting.

On the morning of the sixth day, the Horse turned of His own will at the river's edge and trotted eastward. Later, when I was beyond surprise, I learned that the priest had contrived the respite, because he judged that the men and beasts would founder if they did not rest. Swearing Gorbabordol and two other princes to keep the secret from Harrap, he had revealed to them that the Gods commanded a pause. Exactly how he convinced them that they must gently restrain the Horse I do not know, but they could have been no great challenge to his sophistry, those arrogant, unlettered nobles. Each of the five mornings they had galloped their own horses straight to the patches of lucerne that lay in the meadows, and the Horse, drawn by curiosity, had remained to graze like an eager colt.

When I charged him with his deceit months later, the priest explained, 'It was necessary to hold the force back from action, both to rest and to avoid commitment too soon. But I did not interfere. No one touched the Horse. If the Gods had wished Him to go on, it would have been impossible to stay Him.'

I did not pursue the question. When he finally so confided, I was all but convinced that the priest either believed in nothing or kept his true beliefs apart from us all. That realization came to me long after our descent to the desert, and perhaps I should have reserved it for the proper point in this narrative. At the time he worked his deceit I was simply grateful for the respite, and it did not occur to me that the Horse had been manipulated. Perhaps He would have stayed to rest in any event.

We parted from the foothills on the morning of the sixth day. We were refreshed and gay, and our spirits danced when we left behind the mountains that had tormented us. During those days on the plains the men were shielded by their gaiety from the daily plunging and soaring of the temperature, from the monotony of the shifting sands on either side of us, and even from the portents of approaching hunger as birds and animals became ever scarcer. Few, I believe, wondered – as Anand and I did – how we should come back again. Their renewed faith in the Horse, stronger because they had doubted Him, filled them utterly and crushed their fears before their minds could shape them into words.

It would be both wearing and pointless to recount each moment of the long, empty stages we rode behind the Horse during the months that followed. It is better to keep to events that were themselves significant to our purposes, or that, at the least, cast oblique light on our ends. It should, therefore, be enough to note that the desert was monotonous and that our petty cares soon become wearing. Squeezing the truth of those days from my memory, I must remind myself that protracted vacant periods intervened between our perilous encounters and our high trials. I would not have it appear that the empty desert swarmed with warriors or was alive with cities. In reality, men and their works were no more frequent and no more imposing than the tracks of worms upon the broad pastures of the Great King.

For the first twelve days we crept across the desert, ourselves as blind as worms, coming upon few animals and no men. Vegetation grew sparser with each passing hour, and the pale amber sand on either side squeezed the strip of green along the creek's banks ever narrower. But we had fodder and water enough as long as we stayed beside the channel. Only the heavy cavalry chargers suffered sorely, not having recovered from their ordeal in the mountains. They found the heat exhausting and the dry plants little nourishing. Their coats grew dry and coarse, their breaths stank, their gaits limped, and on the tenth day they began to die, swollen with noxious gases. The mountain ponies and the crossbreeds, which looked so clumsy and so stunted beside the cavalry mounts, thrived on the coarse feed that rotted in the chargers' tender stomachs. More beautiful than the chargers, swifter and more enduring than the ponies, the Horse floated joyously ahead, often showing Himself over great distances as a vision in the sky. The priest, Harrap, Anand, and I knew these appearances for tricks of light above the level sands. But the white Image against the blue heavens gave the soldiers further proof of the Divinity they followed. Even Harrap said, only half smiling, 'Yesterday, I saw two of the Bastards riding behind the Perfect Stallion through the sky. Only the greatest miracle could elevate those fellows.'

'That's true enough, Harrap,' I laughed, happy to meet him this once on the sunny plains of agreement. 'But no miracle can keep them long from falling to their natural level.'

'It is reasonable, though you jest,' the priest interposed. 'It does not seem a miracle to me, but I cannot prove that it is not. If the soldiers want a miracle, they may have it.'

'I suppose it helps,' Harrap mused, 'but it's hardly necessary. We know!'

Finding him so amiable, I yielded to my adjutant's instinct and put to him the matter of the cavalry horses.

'There is nothing much we can do, Yakir,' he answered, as equably as if he had not contrived the problem by refusing to remount the cavalry. 'Do whatever you can, of course. But if they must die, they must.'

'I'm remounting them from the reserve, but there won't be enough by . . .' I began, when a yellow-cloaked courier drew rein before us.

'A party of nomads, General,' he announced. 'No more than fifty men they appear, with women and children.'

'The Horse is guarded?' Harrap asked. 'Then I'll ride forward and talk with them.'

Uninvited, I rode beside Harrap, and we trailed the hundred knights behind us. When we came upon them an hour later, the nomads cowered in fear quite different from their normal fierce defiance. But they were otherwise as we expected. Filthy with soot and grime, their gaunt bodies were wrapped in uncured hides. They carried on the ends of long poles the skulls of the bears that were their totem.

We sought with much effort to find common words with the nomads from among the barbaric languages of the center of the continent, while our noses, hardly delicate after so long on the trail, still wrinkled in disgust at their stench. After striving for nearly an hour, we thought we understood the bearded chieftain's meaning: 'Hannya . . . the scourge . . . three days' ride behind . . . Killing all before them . . . Perhaps . . . two times ten tens.'

'Let them pass,' Harrap ordered, and the knights opened their ranks for the fleeing nomads.

'Hannya?' he asked. 'What does that mean, Yakir?'

I could only shake my head in bewilderment, not knowing whether the Hannya were men or beasts. Three times in the next day we came upon similar groups of nomads, one numbering more than two hundred men of fighting age, with their women and children. All were fleeing in the same direction. They told the same tale, but from the second group we thought we learned that Hannya were 'Men . . . terrible warriors . . . Sparing nothing, but for gold . . . Never turning back . . . men like beasts.'

Harrap shrugged, deprecating his own caution, but ordered, 'Take the knights, the archers, and three hundred cavalry, Yakir. Put a screen before us. Put scouts before you and couriers behind. Above all, keep me informed and keep the Stallion from harm.'

They came out of the sun on the second morning, those Hannya, disdaining artifice, nor even putting out scouts. They rode, heads low behind their ponies' necks, with the massed power of a pack of wolves running down a gazelle. They were relentless as a column of red ants that surges forward in unbounded dumb confidence that it will overwhelm any being in its way. They came up so fast at their deadly, tireless trot, the sun behind them gilding their conical helmets and casting their figures into blackness, that they were not half an hour behind my scouts' warning. I had no more than dispatched a messenger to Harrap and drawn up my forces before I met the first impact.

A hundred yards from my formation the Hannya slowed momentarily as a tiger gathers himself to spring. A canopy of yellow dust rolled above them, concealing their number and sweeping up in a golden cock's tail behind. In the instant before the implacable column began moving at the full loping trot again, my line broke. I had given no order, but forty yellow cloaks and shining helmets, all the princes who had joined my force, hurtled forward with lances leveled.

They will die well, I thought, noting that my disciplined cavalrymen were shifting to close the hole. The two forces collided within seconds. The Hannya, who wielded only swords and axes, were checked for an instant by the thrust of the lances. In the next moment their ranks swallowed up the forty, and I could see only a fierce undulation in their midst to show that the princes still fought. They could not live long.

I nodded at the trumpeter and Anand beside me. The archers' bows twanged behind us, swelling into a single chord, and their rain of arrows began to fall on the Hannya. The knights in the center and the cavalrymen on the wings hurled their javelins, then lowered their lances to take the shock of the coming charge.

Shaking themselves free like dogs doused by a swift stream of water, the Hannya came on again. In the single pulsebeat before they were on our lance heads, I saw they did not appear quite human – those round, ochre faces with their slit eyes and flat noses, the screaming mouths and long, thin mustaches between the conical helmets and the small round shields. Then they were upon us. Some were impaled on our lances by the shock of their own charge and the pressure of their fellows behind them. Others slid between the lances or thrust them aside and came at us with their longswords and axes.

We opened the flat wall of our long shields so that we could use our swords. Our line held, falling back slightly as I had ordered. For two or three minutes I could see nothing but the shifting bodies and darting swords in the arc of sight immediately before me, and my weapon was no longer the entire force, but only my own short sword. The pressure lessened abruptly and the Hannya began falling back still shouting their guttural war cry. As rapidly as they had come, they withdrew.

I knew that the rain of arrows, falling upon their rear, had broken the charge, and I exulted. We had held the warriors who never retreat. It was as unexpected, as nearly impossible, as hurling back a horde of warrior ants. But like such ants, they would return to the attack again and again until they overwhelmed us or they were themselves all slain. We had won not a victory but a respite, and they were at least three times our number.

The Hannya drew up just out of range of our arrows. I could make out a small knot of men, chiefs by their look, talking in the center of the line while the rest unslung short saddle-bows. Our ranks opened on my order. Our archers dismounted to give play to their longbows and loosed coveys of arrows, not in rising arcs, but fast and low. The bright morning stank of dust and sweat and blood.

The new flights of arrows, when they had thought themselves out of range, goaded the Hannya. Spreading wide, they charged down upon us again. Most of the short bolts they loosed without halting rattled harmlessly upon our shields. But a knight screamed and fell beside me, and his horse twisted in panic, breaking our line. Before they were wholly upon us, I put aside the temptation to stand and fight. At my order, our ranks spread wider. We trotted a hundred yards to the rear before turning to face them again, still moving slowly backward to draw the impact from their charge.

Again the Hannya broke through our hedge of lances, taking fearful losses, and again they themselves broke under the rain of arrows. But their front rank remained closed with us until every man was cut down, and the rear rank raised their targets over their heads against the arrows. Though their shields were too small to protect them wholly, I saw that we could not hold them again.

Anand confirmed my feeling, saying in a light voice, 'We have lost too many. If we remain massed to protect our archers, they'll roll us up on either side. If we spread out, they'll break through and ride our archers down.'

I saw with surprise that he was binding up my forearm where the blood gushed from a ragged axe cut. A mist of blood fell into his thick eyebrows from a shallow gash on his forehead. He dashed the blood away in a fine spray, and I suddenly felt dizzy. For the first time since the Hannya had appeared in the dawn, I felt the sun warming my night-chilled face. The rays parched the sands around us. Only for the slight breeze rustling the long grass, all nature was silent. But men swore amid their groans, and dying horses screamed.

'Help me . . . ohh . . . Indra!' The shrill, inhuman shriek rang from the sand hillock where the Hannya huddled irresolute. At least one of the reckless princes had lived to be tortured.

The desperate cry lanced my dizziness, making me cold again. 'Spread out as far as we can,' I ordered. 'We'll fight and pull back slowly till Harrap comes up.'

For almost an hour, we stood and retreated alternately. The ferocity of the attacks did not lessen, though the Hannya losses were great and they charged over their own wounded, who did not cry out. Our flights of arrows were thinner to conserve our dwindling stocks, and we fought with little hope. In my exhaustion, I wondered why the Hannya did not break off. We were too weak to pursue them, though we broke their attacks and savaged them sorely. Though they could simply have disengaged and sought easier prey, they hurled themselves at us as a mauled dog will fling himself at a bear. We were, I reflected with cool detachment that surprised me, met in the ancient battle between

216

civilization and barbarism, our discipline and tactics against their dumb tenacity and frontal assaults.

At that moment I heard Harrap's war cry and saw our heavy cavalry chargers pounding down on the Hannya flanks. In a single pulsebeat shut out of the combat, I slumped over my saddle-bow. I was too exhausted even to watch. After a minute, I said to Anand, 'I suppose we should go in and help finish the slaughter?'

He gestured silently at one of Ranbir's young officers waiting patiently before us.

'Hail, Colonel!' The guard's sword came to the salute with parade-ground punctiliousness. 'The General bids you wait with us in reserve till he has need of your force.'

We fought no more that day, nor did the mountaineers. There was no need of us. The Hannya resisted with the viciousness of trapped wolves, but with little of the wolves' cunning. Repeated charges from either side battered them, but they did not turn and flee to the open rear. They flung themselves first to the north where the infantry stood with pikes leveled, then at the hedge of pikes to the south. Hurled back time after time, they huddled under the rain of arrows, which lifted only to allow our cavalry to charge.

Weary of the slaughter and sick at our own losses, I turned my head aside. In that moment, I almost hated the white glory of the Horse, quietly grazing within a ring of princes. When I turned back, Harrap sat beside me, wiping his brow with a blood-drenched cloth.

'It will be finished in another half hour,' he grinned, the flat white scar of his nose pulsing with his heavy breathing. 'You did beautifully, Yakir. Held and drew them in upon us beautifully.'

At his praise the rancor that had been between us fell away. I took pleasure from his praise – and greater pleasure from the knowledge that we had contrived the victory between us, just the two of us, as it had always been in the past.

'Hail, General!' I laughed. 'Behold the warriors who never retreat! Behold the scourge of the continent!'

'They won't retreat,' he answered gravely. 'And they won't

ask for quarter. They must, of course, die. But I hate to lose my soldiers in the executioner's work.'

'Then let the bowmen finish the job,' I suggested.

He spoke briefly to Orberk, his flag-bearer. The tawny-haired youth made the green-and-gold banner dance, and the trumpets sounded the recall. When Harrap had given his orders, the cavalry withdrew, but the infantry closed the hedge of pikes around the few hundred Hannya remaining. Behind them, the bowmen methodically fitted arrows to their strings and let fly.

It was nearly an hour before the slaughter was done and we rode among the dead and dying. Their cloaks of many pelts crumpled around them and their short felt-wrapped legs twisted in the red dust, the Hannya were smaller but more terrible in death. Broad hands still clutched ponderous longswords with the lean deer figures arching their golden backs upon the hilts. Not one round face I saw looked surprised at death or even fearful, but all were set in the same dumb determination I had marked at their first attack.

A Hannya rose to his knees almost beneath our horses' hooves. I saw in the instant that he flung his axe that his cloak was clasped with a double gold chain and his conical helmet was barred with gold. Harrap and I swerved aside, but Orberk was slow to move. The axe cleaved his forehead as Harrap spitted the Hannya with a javelin flung as casually as he would stick a yearling boar.

The warrior slumped forward, but he spoke in a strange shrill language, emitting deep gutturals like growls. As the last Hannya toppled forward into the red slime, his body held half erect by the javelin that transfixed his chest, I heard a voice speak behind me in the liquid Sanskrit of East Hindustan. 'We have not retreated,' it said. 'We have died! This is not our land yet. But it will be our land. All lands shall be ours. Then we shall be avenged. Mark you well: We are the Huns!'

I wheeled with my sword raised, but checked the downward stroke. The warrior who tottered before me wore the cloak and helmet of the marauders, but his hands were empty and his skin was dark.

'Quarter!' he gasped. 'I am no Hun to die rather than ask

quarter. My name is Barniar, and I am a man of Hindustan. Give me my life, brother.'

I sheathed my sword as he fell among the corpses. At my command, two infantrymen lifted the strange figure and carried him away.

'See that he lives, if he can be saved,' I shouted after them.

'I would not countermand your order,' Harrap said in my ear. 'Though he should have died. He stood against the Stallion! But the revenge has been so swift we can spare one life as a token.'

'Perhaps we may learn something of these Hannya from him,' I said.

'Perhaps,' Harrap agreed, and we turned from the slaughter, leaving it to Mirab to see to our own wounded and to strip the enemy.

It would be three full days before we were ready to move on again, and Harrap, exulting in our swift victory, made no objection. The princes, the forty-six who remained, rode tirelessly behind the Horse as He fled the place of slaughter. The knights were also assigned to His escort.

When Mirab finished his count, I recorded two hundred and sixteen men of Kamardol killed, in addition to the forty princes who had flung their lives away. Of seriously wounded we had fifty and of other wounded nearly three hundreds. The Huns, to call them by their true name, had numbered almost sixteen hundreds, and every man had died fighting. We took their sturdy ponies, those that were not maimed, to remount the cavalry. We laid the cavalry's heavier armor on the remaining baggage carts and slaughtered the proud cavalry horses. The Huns had carried a great quantity of gold and jewels, each man keeping his own share in his saddlebags. This treasure we distributed.

After two days Barniar, the man of Hindustan who had ridden with the Huns, threw off the coils of fever for a brief time. Garbed as one of us, his thin, arched nose and his dark-wheaten skin marked him clearly as no barbarian, but a man born south of the mountains.

'I am,' he told me haltingly, 'a Brahman of East Hindustan and a physician. I was taken with six companions when we ventured into the mountains, seeking herbs and secret medicines made of the parts of the white rhinoceros. The mountain men took us, but later ranging north for pillage themselves, they were attacked by the Huns. The Huns spared only me. They slew all the rest, but spared me to serve them as interpreter and physician. For six years I have ridden with the Huns. I have seen their tents spread across the empty steppes of the north from horizon to horizon. They are as many as the fish of the Ganges and as deadly as cobras. They are so many that they will not miss this raiding party you have slaughtered until their spring convocation of all the tribes almost a year hence.'

'Where do they lie?' I interrupted, seeing that he was weakening.

'Fifty days' march to the north their pastures begin, but they are always moving. Do not ride north. They would crack you as easily as I crack a louse between my fingers . . . Give me my life, brother, that I may serve you and someday return to Hindustan. Let me follow the sacred Horse with you.'

'And their Gods?'

'They have no Gods, yet all things are their Gods – rivers and rocks, birds and beasts, even lances and spears and fires.'

The priest waved me away, placing his finger upon his lips to signal that the man must talk no more if he were to live.

When I repeated Barniar's words to Harrap, he rejoiced. 'A Brahman who would follow the Horse? Then he must live. The Gods speak through him, granting us another miracle by his appearance to us.'

We laid Barniar in the finest litter reserved for our own wounded officers. It was many days before he could talk at length, but then and thereafter he told me many strange tales of the Huns and the other curious peoples he had known.

Before we rode forth again, hastening to come up with the Horse, Barniar told me briefly whence his party of Huns had come. 'We had taken tribute of a city that lies perhaps two weeks' ride away. The people preferred to pay us, though they are many. They call themselves Hellenes and they call their city . . . It is hard to say . . . They call their city Cosmopolis.'

Twenty

Full fifteen days we followed the green-girt stream across the shifting sands toward Cosmopolis. Even before we saw the city we knew the people must stem from the armies of the great Alexander. They too had called themselves Hellenes, though we call them Greeks. I wondered how such men could have offered tribute to the Hunnish raiders, rather than crushing them. Still, I thought, we would see the splendid capital of a great empire, a city that might make Kamardol itself seem small and cramped. I knew from the little my people still remembered of the language of the Greeks that Cosmopolis meant 'the city – the capital – of the world.' I learned later that the Hellenes took it to mean 'the city where all the world meets.' Thus they reconciled the proud claim of their city's name with their own degenerate weakness, since they could in truth assert that in Cosmopolis the peoples of the world met each other in peace.

The Horse was wholly free to go as He wished. So soon after the Gods' help in the slaughter of the Huns, not even the priest would tamper with His will. 'Now it is wholly in the hands of the Gods,' he said to me cryptically after the encounter with the Huns.

But the Horse, being wholly free, seemed to have surrendered His will to the will of the land itself. Day after day He trotted steadily to the northeast along the green strip the narrow watercourse had conjured out of the desert. Though we thrice crossed other streams that led due north and even westward, He ignored those routes. Our progress was easy after we had become accustomed to the constant silent menace of the dead sands. But for the groans of the wounded in their litters, the stench of their wounds, and our daily halts to bury our dead, we might have been a peaceful caravan of traders seeking only better markets, rather than warriors consecrated to the divine Quest.

After five days Harrap saw that the Horse would not alter His course. Mindful of Barniar's warning that we would be upon Cosmopolis within ten days, but doubtful of the Hindustani's assurance that the Greeks would not fight, he sent Mirab with three hundred light cavalry to ride before us. The old colonel was charged to keep a moving wall of armor before the Horse, as well as to stretch the range of our eyes. By his constant grumbling he won the assignment, which I had coveted.

'You finally let me raise my sword against the Huns, but then what?' he complained. 'A picker-over of the dead, a damned undertaker, that's what I became!'

Annoyed by the unending repetition of that formula, Harrap was glad to send Mirab out of earshot. But he was back on the dawn of the twelfth day, followed by his personal guard of forty lancers.

'Strange fellows I met,' he blustered after making his formal salutes. 'Thought I better come back and talk to you myself. Damned strange fellows.'

'And the Stallion?' Harrap asked, his cheeks dark-flushed and his fingers plucking at his jeweled sword hilt.

'Oh, the Horse,' Mirab replied. 'He's fine. No need to worry about the Horse. I left most of my people to look after Him to make sure. But there's no need to worry. Now, let me tell you about these odd fellows.'

Grimacing in hopeless resignation, Harrap dropped onto his saddle beside the morning fire. He gestured to Mirab, the priest, and myself to find seats on the gear that lay scattered about.

'Have you eaten, Mirab?' he asked with strained courtesy.

'By Vishnu, now that you mention it, I wouldn't mind something, wouldn't mind it at all.'

'Bring the Colonel hot milk and dried rabbit,' Harrap instructed his new flag-bearer. 'And now, Mirab, if you are comfortable, perhaps you'll begin.'

'Decent of you, General, very decent indeed. Now, let me see. Oh, yes. Well, we caught up with the Horse and His princes – no trouble at all, an easy ride – in a day. Good riders, my boys, and those Hun horses, they go beautifully. Not weight carriers, though, more's the pity.'

'The strange fellows!' I interjected. 'O Mirab, my senior in years and in rank, what of the strange fellows you were going to tell us of?'

'Don't rush me, my boy. Do you think after all these years I don't know the proper form, don't know how to make a report?'

'It would be good to know, O esteemed counselor and mighty warrior,' Harrap murmured.

'I'm coming to that, General. Just a minute now.' Mirab was unperturbed by Harrap's elaborate courtesy. 'Well, as I was saying, we overtook the Horse with no trouble at all, easiest ride I've had in years . . .'

Resigned to allowing the old man to proceed at his own pace, Harrap lifted his leather flask of koumiss to his lips.

'Then we rode for a couple of days with no incident to report,' Mirab continued after blowing the milk foam from his mustache. 'Nothing remarkable happened at all. But in the next couple of days we saw three bands of nomads coming toward us. Three or was it four times? I can't remember exactly, but it doesn't matter, does it?'

'As you say, Colonel,' the priest agreed before Harrap could speak.

'Of course not. It doesn't matter. Well, I sent a squad to ride them down, examine them. But my people couldn't catch them. Every time my people approached, they turned and rode as if all the Devils were chasing them. Odd, wasn't it? Never seen anybody ride so fast. I simply don't understand.'

'The strange fellows, Colonel – and the Stallion?' Harrap spluttered.

'Oh yes, that comes next, doesn't it? Thanks for reminding me, General. Well, a couple of days later, off in the dusk we saw a bigger party. Couldn't tell at the distance what they were, but they didn't turn and run. Scouts came back and reported they weren't nomads, but called themselves Hellenes and seemed peaceable enough. Only wearing swords of ceremony, no real armor and all that, you know.

'Well, there they were, all drawn up like fellows receiving a royal embassy, long robes, heralds, fellows bearing gifts . . . I've got some things for you, General. Silks, some pretty little trinkets, gold and jewels, you know. I can send for them in a minute, if you'd like to look at them now.'

Mirab picked the last shreds of meat from the delicate rabbit bones and flicked them into the fire. He drained the black-leather cup of milk, his head tossed back and his Adam's apple bobbing slowly up and down within his corded throat. He picked his back teeth with his dagger's point, waiting for Harrap's reply. His blunt nose and chin shone with self-satisfaction in the firelight, and his innocent eyes were wide with pride.

'Get on with it, man,' Harrap snapped. 'What did they say?'

'Say? Oh yes, what they said. Well, General, they had a fellow who thought he spoke some Sanskrit . . . devilish barbaric, it was, too. Lucky for me I remember a lot of the Greek I used to speak with my grandmother. That's what they were speaking . . . Greek, you know. They're very proud because, they say, theirs is the blood of Alexander's generals . . . Well, between us, we sorted it out. Lucky about that Greek, though, or I'd be there yet, trying to understand that fellow's jabbering.'

He paused again, waiting for us to swell the tide of his self-praise. But under our combined glare, he hurriedly went on.

'Let me see, now. Seems they think we must be good friends . . . or should be. They'd heard from the nomads what we'd done to the Huns. One fellow, prince of some sort, said, "The enemy of my enemy is my friend." Makes sense, doesn't it . . . devilish clever to put it that way.'

'It is not precisely a new idea, O Colonel, though undoubtedly well expressed,' the priest answered, even his habitual detachment shattered. 'But pray continue!'

'Well, there's not much more to tell. They said if we came in peace, they would meet us in peace, receiving us as honored guests, maybe adding more gold to show their solidarity – and for what we did to the Huns. In short, gentlemen, they seem to want to take us on as allies. From what I saw, it's a big city . . . pretty powerful . . . and we're still a little worn. I'd recommend taking up their offer.'

'We cannot, Mirab!' Harrap's voice cracked with exasperation.

'Don't you understand that I cannot command as I might wish, but only as I am commanded? And what have you done with the Stallion?'

'The Stallion? Oh, of course . . . the Horse. Well, first, as I told you, He's perfectly safe. My people watch as He grazes in the circle of green fields around the city. They've got wells and plenty of water, you know.'

'And His reception?' I asked.

'Well, one of my young fellows thought we ought to talk about the Horse. So I asked them straight out, could He go where he wished and graze as He pleased? And they answered, "Why not?" So my young fellow . . . a little careful, you know, because we were only a few hundred . . . the young fellow told them He wasn't just a horse, but a God and they'd be making submission to the God if they let Him graze and wander as He pleased. And again, they said, "Why not?" So I reckon everything's all right and . . .'

Harrap and I turned our backs to the flood of Mirab's words. I wished to meet the Hellenes in peace, and I feared Harrap would try the favor of the Gods by challenging them. But we both waited for the priest's judgment. His lips glistening wetly in the firelight, he spoke briskly and negligently. 'Gentlemen, the augury seems clear – as far as we can understand it. If these Hellenes wish peace and give the Avatar free passage, thus making submission, we cannot attack them. To attack would be as flagrant a transgression as retreating from a challenge.'

'But it is not wholly clear yet, is it, O priest?'

'No, Harrap, it is not wholly clear. But until we learn otherwise, it appears that the omen is for peace.'

'We will ride forward warily,' Harrap decided abruptly. 'We will ride in peace, but ready for battle if the Gods command. Thank you Mirab, you have done well. Will you return to the main body now?'

I had thought Mirab's self-approbation so great that no one else could either enlarge or diminish it, but his heavy torso swelled with pride and his silver mustaches bristled even more complacently as he and his forty lancers rode in stately procession toward the rear.

I was still troubled by the behavior of the Hellenes. It seemed they treasured – above all material treasures – their descent from the Macedonian's invincible soldiers. Yet they had paid tribute to the Huns, and they would apparently receive us interlopers with courtesies nicely balanced between those ceremonies accorded allies and those submissions tendered conquerors. Assuming that Mirab's report was correct, they were an unaccountable paradox. I let our forces flow past me, the men chattering of carousing in Cosmopolis, until the litters of the wounded swayed by between their patient mules.

Barniar, the man of East Hindustan, lay propped on his elbow. The curtains of his litter were opened to the sun and the breeze. When I approached, he waved cheerfully and greeted me with stilted courtesies. But I coughed uncontrollably when the first wave of stench rolled over me. I could see by the stains on the thick bandages around his right leg that the pus still flowed from the jagged tunnel the lance had bored through his thigh muscles.

'Hail, Barniar,' I said. 'The priest tells me that your chances are excellent – as long as the wound remains open and the pus flows. The wound must not heal over till it has cleansed itself. Then the pus must stop.'

'Assuredly, Colonel,' he grimaced. 'I am still ahope. I am sure that the wound will heal and the pus will stop in its own time. But as a physician myself, I fear my weakening body will not remain alive long enough to give the wound the time it needs.'

I smiled uneasily. What can one say to a man who lies in Khali's palm, except to assure him that his physician is unsurpassed? I told him so before I began searching with light questions for answers that might lighten my bewilderment at the Hellenes of Cosmopolis.

I said we still did not know whether we would ply the sword or the banquet cup. The smile did not fade from his bloodshot eyes, nor did his brown lips close over his teeth, which were as close-set, as square, and seemingly as massive as the row of stones that cap a parapet. But his face turned as yellow as the bile retched up by victims of the vomiting disease.

'Why should you fight?' he asked, his tone incredulous. 'I ask not only because it will mean death for me – in this crippled state

– if it comes to battle. I ask because I cannot understand why you should think of fighting.'

'Barniar, you are, you say, a Brahman of Hindustan. You must know the meaning of this Quest, the Seeking, upon which we are met.' My words were, perhaps, sharper than they should have been to a man of my own caste who had endured so long in barbarian captivity and now lay waiting for the Black Goddess to reveal her pleasure of him. I truly liked this Barniar the Survivor, but his obtuseness – so soon after Mirab's complacent irrelevancies – made me feel as if I were drowning in a vat of refined butter.

'I know the meaning of the Seeking, Colonel, though only from the old books,' he answered, his flat tones hovering between obsequiousness and indignation, but avoiding neither. 'I know that your deeds hang upon the Gods' will.'

'Then, by Vishnu, how can you ask why we should fight? The decision is not our own. We await Their command.'

'By Khali, Who holds me in Her grasp, the Gods' command is clear.' The fretful anger of the sick man matched my own. 'It is clear in what the Greeks have said – and what they will say.'

'What they have said, perhaps. But neither we nor you know what they will say.'

'On the contrary, Colonel,' he replied more calmly, 'their words are written in their nature. For more than a century Cosmopolis has survived by looking always to the power behind the single spearhead. The city paid tribute to my Huns' raiding party because it knew the might of the hordes that stood behind those few marauders. Cosmopolis knew the terrors that defiance would invoke out of the steppes that lie beyond the Mountains of Heaven.'

'And what is that nature of these Greeks that you speak of?'

'Their nature is to temporize. These Greeks have survived – and even prospered – by making themselves useful to all traders, by paying discreet tribute to all raiders, and, above all, by penning their pride, as one pens a fractious watchdog. They are violent only within their own compounds – and only to each other. Thus they at once make themselves smaller and keep themselves alive. Yet they are powerful enough so that most

227

prefer to deal with them rather than destroy them for the sake of their few fertile acres. And they are protected by the wastes that lie around their city.'

'But,' I persisted, truly puzzled, 'how can you be so sure that they will temporize before the might of Kamardol? They do not know us as they do the Huns.'

'Precisely because they do not know you – and would rather not. They will greet you fair – as they have done. They will make submission to the Horse and to your forces, in whatever form you wish – as long as they feel that their submission does not fray the strings of policy, and that small dignity on which their pride hangs.'

'But how can we be sure that their submission is true submission? Will it not be mere dissembling?'

'Tell me, Colonel, what is true submission and what dissembling? If their submission satisfies the Gods, how can you question its honesty? Would you open their hearts to read their sincerity there as priests read the entrails of a sacrifice?'

I took Barniar's words back to Harrap, who snorted at the Hindustani's sophistry. We rode ready for battle, but we left our swords in their sheaths when we met the Hellenes' embassy a day's ride from Cosmopolis. They spoke as Barniar had said they would. They offered us friendship and the ease of the city, and their words were reinforced by rich gifts.

Their friendship was proffered in good Sanskrit, though Mirab had led us to expect otherwise. Among the embassy were three old men in straight white robes who leaned upon smooth heralds' staffs painted with serpent's scales. Upon their breasts they wore plaques displaying a mouth and an ear embroidered in red, and among them, they said, they knew all the languages of all the peoples who came to Cosmopolis.

The priest, speaking for Harrap, who was mute as our customs dictated, thanked them for their welcome and put the ritual questions regarding the Horse. The Herald of Tongues did not trouble himself to repeat those questions to his masters.

'In Cosmopolis, O princes and O priests,' he answered straightaway, 'all Gods are welcome and all Gods are honored.'

'Our God in the Stallion is predominant – and must be

worshipped as such,' the priest insisted. 'Just so are our Kings above all other kings.'

'We understand and submit,' the Herald entoned. 'The God that is present is always predominant. Just so are the kings that are far away.'

I was not wholly pleased with that reply, and Harrap's hand plucked at the thong of his axe. But the priest, smiling, declared, 'We accept your submission.'

Before I discussed our reception with the Magistrates of Cosmopolis, Harrap cautioned me, 'We will keep the main body and, of course, the Stallion, outside the walls, Yakir. We do not know . . . Mirab will command the main body, coming within the walls only when you or I relieve him. Varuna grant us that the old man does not use his leisure to cast more lengthy reports.'

Warmed by Harrap's maliciousness, I rode with Anand to consult with the Magistrates. I was much pleased that this time we need not fight, and I yearned for the comforts of the city after our passage through the wilderness. I felt absolved for my lack of ardor, since the Gods had declared peace. Harrap hid from himself his anger that his sword must remain sheathed. The Gods had, this once, given him not more enemies to destroy, but only this eager submission.

'This is a gift, indeed,' laughed Anand as we came up to the Magistrates. 'I could almost believe that the Buddha too has blessed our enterprise. A city, peace, warmth, and no common brawling. Yet, like Harrap, I fear treachery.'

The Herald of Tongues attended us until it became clear that we had no need of his assistance. The little Greek Anand and I knew, together with the rough Turkyi tongue that all men commanded in the center of the continent and the small Sanskrit of the Magistrates, made a sturdy bridge between us. The structure was firm enough, though its lines were not graceful and occasionally we stumbled over a loose plank. But we came to understanding faster and more easily than we might have had we been compelled to traverse the titles, the formal courtesies, the subtle hypotheses, and the covert competition for place through which a common tongue compels men.

Only on one matter did the practical Magistrates seem less

than wholly rational. Before we came to the matter of our talk, they told us firmly that we must call them neither Greeks nor Hellenes, but Cosmopolítēs. They were not, they said, transplanted Greeks, but men at home to the entire world, like their ancestors who had marched with Alexander. Somehow I felt that only by insisting on calling themselves Cosmopolítēs could they justify their subservience to all who came in arms upon them. Besides, it was clear from their features that they were hardly more Greek than I, Cosmopolis being a curry kettle of peoples to which all the races of the continent had contributed ingredients. But I did not condemn them, knowing that, almost as much as their Gods, a people's name is that people.

Otherwise, the Cosmopolítēs were so accommodating and so practiced in receiving strangers that they took our work out of our hands. Their brisk and comprehensive concern for everything from fodder and wine through physicians and harlots to saddlery and food showed that they had accommodated many armies. Barely an hour passed before we had checked off the last items on our lists, and the consultation was done.

The main body, as Harrap had directed, would remain outside the city walls, where it would be provisioned by trains of carts. Harrap and his entourage, escorted by the hundred knights as honor demanded, would be accommodated in what the Cosmopolítēs called the Major Palace within the walls. Of the main body, no more than three hundred men would come within the walls at once for no more than twenty-four hours at a time, being then succeeded by their eager fellows. For all their professed friendship and their special gratitude for our destruction of the Huns, the Cosmopolítēs obviously feared our bringing in force enough to seize the city from within. No more did we wish to place our main body within the city and thus within their power.

Our God, they said, meaning the Horse, could remain without or come within as He pleased. They were surprised when I did not demand that He be worshiped in the great empty hall they called the Pantheon of Cosmopolis.

I do not remember the faces of the Magistrates with whom I talked in that gentle dusk, for I did not see them again. During our stay I left to Anand the lesser issues and to Harrap and the priest the greater issues.

I was weary when we finally came into Cosmopolis, not only from the long ride and the discussion of irksome trivia, but also from the anticipation of rest, which relaxed my muscles and myself till I was almost powerless. Swaying with weariness in my saddle, I saw little by the guttering flare of the torches in the hands of the guard. I noted only that Cosmopolis was a city smaller than Kamardol, a city that sought whiteness by artifices of chalkwash and shaved-marble façades, but was predominantly the red-brown of baked brick.

We came, after no more than twenty minutes, to the colonnaded building they called the Major Palace. Rejecting both the hot baths and the cold meats our hosts offered, I dragged the coverlet from the couch in my chamber and lay down on the stone floor. I twisted and turned because the stones seemed soft and yielding, and the enclosed air smelt dead. On my first night in months under a roof, sleep came slowly to me.

Twenty-one

We did not stay in Cosmopolis so long that my breath learned to come freely behind thick walls that spoiled the sunlight and blunted the wind's edge. My body soon learned again that it was no hardship to sleep beneath a roof, and, in the beginning, all my senses responded to the small luxuries of the town. After the first week, however, I abhorred even the air of that pompous market town that called itself 'the city of all the world.' I longed to ride again under the harsh and simple laws of the Seeking, which so precisely fixed both our own conduct and our attitude toward the outsiders we encountered. In Cosmopolis there was no certainty, not even in the smallest things, for all things were in flux – manners, customs, and laws. This outward flux awoke in me a flux of the spirit that was as debilitating and as painful as a flux of the bowels.

Even before I knew the citizens' utter baseness, I was glutted with the pretentious meanness of that 'city of all the world.' Behind the mansions' silver-thin marble façades lay cramped reception rooms set around meager courtyards and, behind those courtyards, the families' airless sleeping quarters. The shambling display diminished finally to mud kennels, where the slaves cooked meanly and cleansed perfunctorily, sleeping and fornicating amid their own filth.

The temples of Cosmopolis, too, were mean, unlike the spacious halls where the massively hewn and brilliantly adorned Gods of Kamardol receive our homage. Nor did they display the precision of outline and proportion that shape the perfect abodes of the Gods in Greece itself. There were, of course, images in those temples under the meager peaked roofs hedged by rows of round columns with cracked marble veneers. But they were pallid and prosaic, those statues of men and women who might have been thickening athletes past their prime and weary actresses from country troupes. Like the temples themselves, the images were filmed with grime.

No more than their squat buildings or the stunted dunes beyond their flat oasis did the imaginations of the Cosmopolítēs soar. They were a squalidly and nervously commercial race, affirming their reverence for all Gods and holding none in true reverence. Nor did they truly respect any man, since they held all freemen equal not only in their birth and in their private pursuits, but in the management of their city's affairs. So might a cook assert that all his confections were of equal savor because all came from the same pots – the infant's milky gruel and the rare dwarf pheasants basted with wild honey, larded with strips of yearling-boar hams, and artfully seasoned with delicate southern spices. So ridiculous was the belief of Cosmopolis, and the rest followed. Since there was no distinction among men, there could be no honor among men. In only two pursuits did the mongrel race display either vigor or ingenuity: their treasuries were heaped with the golden gains of a century of pusillanimity, and they pandered to the base pleasures of the flesh as if this world were not only real, but the *only* real world.

Suppressing my bilious distates for Cosmopolis, I had braced myself to withstand Harrap's impatience because the force required rest. I had expected him to demand that we move on well before men and beasts were recovered from their ordeal by battle and the mountains. But in the end Harrap's own sloth kept us full twenty days. Sensing my own eagerness to be gone, he answered, 'Look you, Yakir, the Stallion does not run. He moves as if held by an invisible hobble within this ring of green fields. Until the Gods bid Him depart, I shall enjoy the pleasures They have put in my way.'

I myself found even the pleasures tawdry, for my senses were set awry by the squalor of the city with the grandiose name. I resorted more and more frequently to our encampment outside the walls, allowing Mirab to enjoy the baths and brothels within the walls. Still preening himself on his brilliant negotiations, which he swore had procured our peace with the Cosmopolítēs, whom he called his kinsmen, Mirab wallowed in long, pointless, and half-comprehensible discourses with their elders. The soldiers took their pleasures more directly. The wine shops, the harlots, the gamesters, and the conjurers of Cosmopolis reclaimed much of the treasure we had taken from the Huns, as well as the city's own tribute to us. Harrap had ordered all distributed, except for the royal share.

Even the Horse was enticed by the tumult of Cosmopolis. Three times He entered the gates and wandered through the streets with the Bastards clattering behind Him. He pushed His curious nose into street stalls, temples, private courtyards, and even the women's quarters as if the Gods in His body were still curious regarding the city to which They had brought us. The Cosmopolítēs showed Him honor by hastening out of His path and by offering Him small sacrifices in their practiced way. Some I saw snigger into cupped hands at men who appeared to their simple understanding to worship a horse. Sooner would an elephant recite the Vedas than that debased race comprehend the intricate interplay of the mighty forces that made Him at once the Vehicle of the Gods and Himself divine, at once infinitely more than man and less than a stud stallion, but always our divine guide – at once our master and our child. I raged when I saw the street urchins make Him mock obeisances while miming His twitching ears with filthy hands half-cupped beside their heads.

My rage sprouted the fear that the degenerate Cosmopolítēs would corrupt not only our troops but our purpose itself, since we left unpunished their half-open mockery of the Gods in the Horse.

I could not consult the priest, for he was engrossed by the diviners and the oracles of the town. He was seeking to penetrate to the core of the strange cults the Cosmopolítēs called 'the mysteries.' Those cults promised total enlightenment in the here-and-now of this earth, an enticement wholly different from the Buddhists' so-called Enlightenment. Devotees who submitted to their secret disciplines were, they said, transported to the realm of the spirits – to return, unscathed in body and rich in knowledge and power, from that world beyond death to this world of life. How deeply the priest entered into their secret disciplines, which were forbidden to Brahmans, I do not know. He was, in any event, joyful because he had renewed his private stock of euphorics. The Cosmopolítēs make a potion more powerful than bhang from the thick, shiny leaves of a prickly plant that grows in the shelter of the dunes. Their 'mysteries' owe much of their hectic colors and inflamed visions to that potion.

Anand made small of my distress. He reiterated his conviction that only the form was important to the Seeking. We could, he asserted, hardly hope to alter the set of men's hearts with our swords and lances, which had only the power to still the heart's strokes forever. Nonetheless, he came with me to the bath at the Major Palace, where Harrap lay sipping wine and half asleep under the hands of the bathmaids.

In his lethargy Harrap did not comment on Anand's presence. When I began to speak of my fears, he stared at me unblinking, like a tiger basking upon a rock after gorging himself on an antelope.

'Harrap,' I warned, 'we are temporizing with these Cosmopolítēs. We are imperiling our Quest!'

'How so, Yakir?' he asked. He appeared no more disturbed, perhaps less, in truth, than he would have been by a report that a score of camels had gone lame.

'How so, you ask. I am convinced that these people have made no true submission, either to the Horse or to our Kings. We but deceive ourselves, who cannot deceive the Gods, when we pretend that this mock submission of Cosmopolis is the utter submission prescribed by the Brahmayanas.'

'Truly, Yakir, this is a matter for concern,' Harrap answered, though he spoke as if in sleep and grimaced in delight when the bathmaids pummeled his back. 'But as the priest has said and you have affirmed, we cannot deceive the Gods. If They are content, would it not be presumptuous – indeed impious – for us to assail Their certainty with our miserable doubts, knowing little of Their will as we do?'

He motioned the attendant to rub his neck harder, taking her hand lingeringly in his own to show her the spot before continuing, 'No, Yakir, you fret without cause. This is a true submission. It is pleasing to the Gods.'

'You are quite certain?'

'Quite. If the Gods were displeased, would they not loose powerful omens? Would the Perfect Stallion not race away or savage the people – instead of strolling majestically through the city which is His?'

'It is *our* task to read the God's meaning,' I objected. 'They do not force it upon us as a nursemaid admonishes a child to beware the adder or to drink his hot milk for sleep's sake. That were too much favor!'

'I cannot agree, Yakir. The Seeking is itself a mark of favor. It would be impious to seek to read Their secret meanings. We must wait humbly for Them to unveil Their meaning to us. What say you, Lieutenant?'

'I cannot say forthwith, O Prince,' Anand replied, his fleshy forehead contracting into wrinkles and his words coming slowly. 'I cannot read the will of the Gods, but I have thought . . .'

'Yes,' Harrap encouraged him. 'What have you thought?'

Knowing that Anand questioned the divinity of the Seeking, I waited in great anxiety for him to formulate his thoughts. Though Anand's skepticism proved my own faith, the new fanatical Harrap must not learn that such doubt afflicted one of his officers.

'I fear this, O Prince,' Anand finally said. 'I fear that the manner of the Cosmopolítes – their manner toward all things, not only the Stallion – I fear that it will infect our soldiers, weakening them as a hundre attles could not.'

'What do you mean?' Harrap asked, finally aroused. 'How can these city rats corrupt my soldiers?'

'Because, O Prince, they *are* city rats, as you have named them.' Anand's reply was quicker and more certain this time. I realized that he was speaking not for himself but for me, shaping my fears into hard, sharp words that would strike Harrap.

'The Cosmopolítes, as you know, give their obedience to neither kings nor priests – no more than rats know either the Gods or divinely anointed leaders.'

'That is true,' Harrap agreed. 'They live by an odd rule they call democracy.'

'Democracy means, in their language, rule by the people,'

Anand went on. 'It means, of course, that they are not ruled at all. They affirm not only that all men are the same, but that the Gods are no more than men – if, indeed, they acknowledge their own Gods beyond mock submission.'

'And,' I interrupted, 'it means further that man is their God, Harrap. They make statues of their so-called Gods in the shape of men, thus glorifying man rather than the Gods. They do not truly revere even those statues – as they should if they believed them truly Gods. Instead, they pay their homage to the outward beauty they see in the statuary – whether of men or Gods. Because their Gods are in the shape of men and women, they actually worship the human beauty of those statues – and the human creators of such beauty. They do not worship the divinity of their images, because there is no divinity in them.'

'And do we not also make images of our Gods?' Harrap asked.

'Of course, Harrap.' I replied. 'But we only rarely make them in human shapes – or animal shapes. Instead, we make them in a variety of shapes – often combining parts of men and animals. The vulgar believe that we worship those shapes, and the Buddhists call them grotesque. In reality, we give the different aspects of our Gods those shapes because we do not know their true shapes. And we worship the essence of divinity with which the Gods endow those images. We do not worship those images.'

'This is all fine, Yakir. What you call the new theogony I know. But how do the Cosmopolítēs differ from us, after all? Can they, too, not say that the divine essence is in their images?'

'By no means,' I replied hotly. 'The Cosmopolítēs worship the shape of human beauty in their images. Their legends speak not of true Gods. They tell of men and women who are more powerful than earthly men and women, but are subject to all the lusts and weaknesses of humans. They talk to their Gods as to men. And they themselves live only for the human pleasures. They find pleasure not only in the senses, as the Gods intended, but also in endless debates that seek by reason – by reason I assure you, though it is difficult to credit – to penetrate all the forbidden secrets.'

'This is, perhaps, true.' Harrap was weary of my discourse. 'But what does this have to do with us? How does it threaten us?'

'O Prince!' Anand took up the argument as if we had rehearsed our parts and suppressed his own heretical beliefs. 'They offend the Gods by their presumption. They, further, elect their leaders – that is, choose them by ballot from among all freemen. They mock the divine pattern of anointed rulers and preordained subjects. They have thrown away their courage, and they yield to any force that comes out of the desert, as long as it does not seek their destruction . . .'

'Enough of this moralizing,' Harrap interjected. 'I ask you simply: How . . . do . . . they . . . threaten . . . us – as you have said?'

'Harrap,' I interjected, 'imagine if our soldiers became exactly as are these Cosmopolítēs . . .'

'That is impossible!'

'Of course it is impossible that they should become exactly the same. But it is not impossible that they should, in many ways, become like the Cosmopolítēs. Not reverence and obedience, but license for all freemen . . . not submission to anointed rulers, but only contention with one's fellows . . . not dedication to hardship, but only to one's own desires . . .'

'That would be no army, but a sickly rabble,' Harrap agreed gravely. 'You are beginning to raise my fear that some danger may exist. What would you have us do?'

'Two things, Harrap,' I said quickly. 'Let us depart this bog of degeneracy as swiftly as we can. But first let us force the Cosmopolítēs to an act of true submission.'

'I must consider this,' he temporized softly. 'The danger may be almost as great as you fear.'

'As you say, Harrap,' I muttered, despair succeeding hope.

No words of men, it seemed, but only the anger of the Gods could strip away the green moss of sloth that had grown over him. He had truly surrendered both will and judgment to the Gods – as if They would command his every movement by clear portents. I too believed, but not that the Gods would lead us by the nose as the herdsman leads the bull. The priest, I was learning, would contrive his own omens, all the while avowing that he could read the hidden will of the Gods. And Anand – he believed at least in Kamardol, but hardly more. Our souls were ill met in the Seeking.

'As you say, Harrap,' I murmured again.

He must have read mockery in my low mutter, for he flung off the gentle hands of the bath attendants, and swinging himself upright on the smooth wooden bench, declared passionately, 'Yakir, I swear to you, if I but for a moment thought . . . if I knew that these people had not made a true submission . . . I would force them to such truth or destroy them.'

Hope quickened my blood. But his voice dropped, and he lay flat again as the passion flowed from him. 'Yet I cannot know, unless the Gods give us a sign. I shall think about your words. But I cannot act except by Their command. And the Stallion is content.'

I had cast and lost. I could do nothing more, but only wait for the Colt to weary of the green pastures of Cosmopolis. Perhaps my fears of corruption were, in truth, overblown, perhaps my eagerness to force a true submission upon the Cosmopolítēs actually sprang from nothing more than the overpowering distaste I felt for their profligate way of life and their vicious character.

The sign Harrap had demanded – the proof that the Cosmopolítēs' was but a mock submission – was given to us two nights before we departed. It was, of course, far too late. We had by that time taken much hospitality of the Cosmopolítēs and, worse, had bound ourselves to them as magnanimous overlords. To compel them then to a new act of submission would have mocked ourselves and belittled the Gods of Kamardol.

I did not know it was our final banquet in Cosmopolis for the Colt had not yet stirred when I went wearily to drink what they called 'double-burnt wine,' a raw spirit distilled from grape wine. The Cosmopolítēs had, throughout, thought to make us more amenable by making us drunk. They prided themselves on being great drinkers of their dark spirits.

I leaned across the low table where I sat opposite Harrap and the fat old man with pallid cheeks who was the Chief Magistrate of the year. I contrived almost to topple from my heap of cushions when I asked, 'Why, O Magistrate, did you accept us so easily as your overlords?'

'Why so easily?' he echoed, ruffling his white beard with the back of his hand. 'Indeed why not?'

'No, but truly, O Elder!' I insisted blearily. 'Why so easily?'

'It is a true submission,' he said anxiously. His faded blue eyes, the whites yellowed and bound with a net of fine broken veins, crinkled confidentially, and he added, 'Why should we not? We have accepted many overlords – the Chinese, the Huns, the Wusun, the Uighurs, and even the Khotanese. Why not you mighty warriors of Kamardol, in turn?'

Seeing Harrap frown, I pressed harder, 'But how can you pay true fealty to so many?'

'We give fealty to whoever comes upon us last – to him who can assert his claim,' laughed the Chief Magistrate. 'And it has not harmed us, but we have prospered. There are, after all, many overlords and many true Gods.'

Harrap scowled, and half drew his dagger from his belt. Having finally twitched truth from the web of deceit, I suddenly feared Harrap's anger. It was not the season for vengeance when our main force was beyond instant call.

Pulling a grave face and affecting the drinker's careful ponderousness, I warned, 'Elder Magistrate, we bear you nothing but good will. But look you well that someday the Gods do not take vengeance for your lightheartedness.'

'We shall guard ourselves, O Colonel!' he laughed as lightly as one laughs with a foolish woman. 'We shall guard ourselves, knowing that our overlords of Kamardol will protect us. Besides, we ourselves are not disposed to fight, but we *can* fight. I drink to your great Kings, who are now our Kings!'

So the issue was entangled in a web of ambiguities, while we were half stupefied by the double-burnt wine. It was, as I have said, too late to give back the oaths we had taken, or to take back the pledges we had given. The gray edge of futility crept over our quest, laying a film of slime upon our bright purpose. My unease was different from my earlier doubts and, unlike them, ineradicable. In the mountains I had doubted the divine authority of the Seeking. After Cosmopolis, though I *knew* that we were moved by the explicit will of the Gods, I doubted *Their* purposes.

But I sense that in my eagerness to come to the heart of the matter, I have outpaced my narrative. Before the revelations of that last banquet, our own behavior had entrapped us in a net of relations we could not lawfully break. Harrap drank with the men and lay with the women, ignoring my expostulations. For the first time since leaving Kamardol, he was no longer driven by the Gods. I found to my own perplexity that I rejoiced in his behavior. He was again the man I had known so long, the bold warrior and the gay carouser, unbowed by the burden of favor the Gods had laid upon him. Harrap and I drew closer, speaking idly of many things as we had in past years, not always and only of the Seeking as we had in the months just past.

I too lay with the women of Cosmopolis, finding them well made and fastidious in their persons and their speech. The great families sent their daughters to their overlords, deeming it both an honor and a duty that they should be with us. I found pleasure in the presence of those women and ease in their conversation, strained though it was through the coarse meshes of our lack of complete comprehension of each other's tongues. But there was no savor in the venery. To those women coupling had become much as the other natural functions, and it bestowed no more than the spasmodic relief which attends those functions. The light nature of the Cosmopolítes, at once cold and frantic, had corrupted even their women's bed manners.

I saw clearly the true nature of those self-claimed descendants of Alexander's warriors at the banquet. The Chief Magistrate, as I have said, revealed the base cowardice that determined their traditional policy of accommodation. They were debased beyond realizing that they were less than men in our eyes because they treasured neither their honor nor their Gods. They were blind beyond seeing that their traditional policy would maintain their ignoble freedom only until one of the great forces sweeping across the heart of the continent destroyed them.

When I had grasped the essence of the Cosmopolítes, I came to agree with Harrap and the priest that their submission must serve as it was. It would have been wasteful for us to force them to a profound submission, since their light nature was incapable of true reverence. Their wholehearted submission, could we obtain it, would be as meaningless as their persistent reservations. Either was without effect either in the real life of the Gods or in this illusory earth. The Cosmopolítēs were debarred by their own nature from deeds of significance as immutably as the mule is debarred by his nature from propagating his line.

While I still fretted over the empty submission and before the banquet, a party of three hundred officers, men-at-arms, and scholars had come out of the northeast. They called themselves Hans, after the dynasty that ruled them – not Huns, whom they called Hyoong-nyoo in their liquid cascading tongue. They were the men we call Chini – Chinese – after an earlier dynasty, and they were, they said, the outriders of a great army that marched from their Emperor's city of Loyang by a chill northern route to far Ferghana, where they had found the Horse. They claimed – and Barniar the Survivor confirmed that they spoke truth – that their forces more than twenty years earlier had turned back the Huns from their frontiers. They had set the fierce horde upon the great westward migration that swept the Uighurs, the Wusun, and other lesser peoples before them, as a tiger fleeing the hunters drives the lesser beasts before him.

These Chinese were as different from us as we were from the Cosmopolítēs. Our bodies were, of course, much the same, and we all spoke in words, each in his own way, as the beasts do not. Still, it was hard to accept that we Kamar, the Cosmopolítēs, and the Chinese were all – and equally – men. Perhaps different Gods with different purposes had called the three races into being.

It was apparent that the Cosmopolítēs held us Kamar for fanatics besotted by our Gods. They read as the madness of possession our decent submission, which was, of course, marred by occasional recalcitrance, but was dedicated to purposes beyond the brief unreality of this earth. The Cosmopolítēs themselves believed men to be as the Gods and the Gods as men, the Gods only possessing greater powers at the service of their essentially human passions. The Cosmopolítēs' own passage from this earthly realm would, they believed, carry them to another realm hardly different and hardly more significant. They argued that the exercise of what they call reason should properly be their chief pursuit in this world, as it would be in any other.

The Chinese were utterly different from both Kamar and Cosmopolítēs. While the Cosmopolítēs believe men to be as the Gods, the Chinese held men to be above the Gods, and they questioned the Gods' existence. I might have expected their conviction of nothingness to breed profound sickness of the spirit – in each man separately and in the realm entire – so that they knew neither laws nor purpose. Yet such was not the case. Convinced that man commanded the universe and that the Chinese were supreme above all other men in wisdom, virtue, and power, these Hans had, if reports were true, built an empire that was the most powerful in the world. We had heard many tales of the splendor of Han and, in truth, it appeared that their Emperor lived in grandeur unsurpassed since the unworthy heirs of the Great Ashoka tore apart their patrimony. Even Alexander, as even the Cosmopolítēs admit, was an itinerant adventurer beside the Emperor of Han.

The Cosmopolítēs could easily have annihilated the weak Han party, which rode with total confidence under the shadow of their great Emperor. But the Cosmopolítēs welcomed the Hans in accordance with their 'traditional policy of amity.' Since the Chinese did not claim suzerainty, but were content with a few gifts, we had no quarrel with them; the Horse had not led us to *their* lands. They were, for those reasons, offered revelry rather than battle.

We came at mid-afternoon to the great hall of the Citizens' Palace, one of the few buildings where the marble façade is repeated within, though baked bricks lie between the two shaved slabs. By our right as overlords we entered last – Harrap, the priest, Anand, myself, and twenty more princes and officers. We came upon the heels of the last Cosmopolítēs in their short, many-colored tunics who were strolling hand-in-hand toward their places, some even clasping each other's waists. I have perhaps omitted to record their belief that only between men can there be true and equal union. They keep their women for breeding and the arts of the courtesan. That sterile concept reflected the general sterility of their lives. They did not merely exalt such temporary unions as many Kshatriyas contract during campaigns, but they denied life by contending that only identical souls could mate.

With their closed features, their flat cheekbones and their veiled eyes, the Chinese penned all their thoughts behind their smooth maize-hued faces. But I saw contempt in the flick of a silken sleeve and in the brief comment from scarcely parted lips as they watched the lovers of Cosmopolis take their places at the low tables. Hardly another hint of their true reactions to either the Cosmopolítēs or ourselves did I perceive, though we sat together with the Chinese and his adjutant. It was, of course, true that we could communicate only through the aged Herald of Tongues who sat at the foot of the table. More than that barrier, the Han were so self-contained in their self-esteem that they had no need to show their true natures.

They punctiliously acknowledged our hospitality as overlords of Cosmopolis, and they inquired courteously with regard to our mission while the slaves poured the wine and offered grape leaves stuffed with meats and fruits. His proselytizing fervor aroused, the priest expounded on our Quest. The Chinese captain listened attentively to the Herald's rendering into his own language. Thin lips pursed, narrow hand stroking the black lapel of his blue silk robe, he asked, 'Will you sell your beautiful animal? I can pay well. He will do for the Emperor's stud.'

The priest's jowls shook, empurpled with indignation. His slack lips were drawn tight to suppress his anger, but he spoke courteously, ending, '. . . you see, he is not a horse, but an Avatar.'

I could not, of course, follow the Herald's trilling words to them, but the two Chinese seemed to understand the priest's explanation. The lean captain uttered just four seconds to his burly adjutant, and both rocked back in laughter.

'They say words I know, but I do not comprehend their meaning,' said the Herald uneasily. 'They say, "A white horse is not a horse!" '

I was asking the Herald to press for an explanation when the Chinese adjutant leaned over, still roaring with laughter that showed no more than a dozen yellow stumps in his mouth. 'You

244

are not merchants or you would sell,' he said. 'You are too small in number for conquest. So you must be pillagers. Why, then, gentlemen, do you not pillage?'

'Our Quest,' Harrap replied patiently, 'transcends such matters. We are in the service of the Gods, who know Their own purposes.'

'The Gods, too, I have heard, like a chunk of gold or a handful of gems – not to speak of perfumed flesh,' the adjutant persisted.

'Talk not business with thieves, nor theology with Pariahs,' I quoted the proverb to Harrap in a low voice and leaned over to reply to the Chinese adjutant myself. But the captain was already speaking: 'My lords, we honor your beliefs and your mission. Perhaps, some day, you may come to the court of our exalted Emperor and learn our ways.'

'What, then, are your beliefs?' the priest cut in.

'We know there are spirits,' the Captain answered, slicing the air with his hand to command his adjutant's silence, 'but they do not interfere in the affairs of men – except perhaps those of old women. Our belief speaks with the utmost clarity. We are fortunate in possessing the most profound insight. Our sages have divined the true purpose of mankind, and we live to fulfill that purpose.'

'And that purpose?' asked the priest.

'Man requires neither the favor nor the guidance of the Gods,' the captain answered. 'He need only order his affairs perfectly under the perfect laws our sages have revealed. With proper guidance from his superiors, he can win the approbation of his ancestors by behaving in the proper manner. Then, all in China being in proper form, all the world will be happy.'

'How does propriety in China make the world happy?' I asked.

'Because that is our mission, being at the center,' the captain replied simply. The adjutant had abandoned the conversation to give his full attention to the wine goblet.

'And how,' asked Harrap, as puzzled as myself, 'do you execute that mission?'

'We are at once blessed with wisdom and burdened by duties,' answered the captain, delicately raising the stuffed grape leaves in his lean fingers. 'We endeavor to make the world happy – to bring it to proper behavior – solely by example. Of course, when we meet disobedience or willful defiance, the great Emperor regretfully orders his armies to march.'

Although I was chilled by the Chinese captain's insouciant arrogance, I was in a fever of curiosity to learn more of his strange philosophy. But I was even more fearful that Harrap's temper might flare and consume us all in a sudden flashing of knives against the Chinese and the Cosmopolítēs. Regretfully, I put aside my curiosity and, feigning drunkenness, questioned the Chief Magistrate as I have already recounted.

Soon there was no need for anyone to feign drunkenness. The remaining hours of the banquet passed in a babble of half-understood chatter. The Herald became incapable of interpreting our words and passed the time crooning to himself in a broken medley of a half-dozen tongues. Only the priest, who drank no wine, and the Chinese captain, who drank little, were finally able to depart from the Hall of the Citizens without the slaves' assistance.

Twenty-two

I dared not open my eyes for fear that the act would dissipate the perfect pleasure I knew, a pleasure as intense as it was formless. Layer by creeping layer, the source of the sensation took shape in my mind. It resolved itself out of a floating globe of many colors until I saw it whole against my eyelids. A few moments from the welter of the banquet had, miraculously, been preserved entire in my memory.

I remembered chanting an endless ballad that seemed divinely beautiful, and I remembered the Chief Magistrate's leaning across the platters of picked-over food, the shattered goblets, and the puddled wine that strewed the low table like the debris of battle. Combing his white beard with oil-stained fingers, he essayed an avuncular twinkle that resolved into a filmy leer. Although his pale blue eyes mutinied against his will, his tongue formed the intended sentences – ponderously, but surely.

'Colonel Yakir, O astute scholar and mighty warrior, I have a secret to tell you. It will give you great pleasure. We Cosmopolítēs are famed for our gusto and our capa . . . cap . . . a . . . city – for how much we can drink.'

'And well deserved, O Magistrate,' I replied, raising my goblet to toast him.

'But we have a secret, Colonel. Our air is so dry and fresh that we never awake to the agony – the aching thirst, the granular eyeballs, the leaden head – that men call the Devils' carouse. You may drink deep without fear.'

I had drunk deep, slyly hugging the knowledge that I would be spared the torments of the next day.

Remembering the secret, I cheerfully flicked my eyes open to greet the bright sun. An instant later I lay back upon my pillows, a moan muffled in my larynx. Never had I drunk more or longer,

247

and never had the Devils caroused with such abandon within my shattered body. Bitter bile choked my throat, the sewers of Cosmopolis ran through my still-parched mouth, my arms and legs were beyond command of a brain sodden with sand and camel droppings. Only the headsman's axe could still the hammer stroke that burst asunder the bones of my skull.

Bitterly aware that the Cosmopolítēs were deceitful in all things – small as well as great – I forced my eyelids apart with my fingertips. The searing sunlight did not pierce my eyeballs as I had expected, for all was gray. I cupped my palms over my ears, and the hammer strokes no longer reverberated. They were actually repeated bolts of thunder. Dampness clogged the desert air that should have bubbled in my nostrils, and the sun was shrouded by dingy clouds. An enormous pressure lay upon me, so heavy that I could not have moved easily had I spent the previous evenings reciting the Vedas in abstemious solitude.

If the charm had failed me, it had also failed the Cosmopolítēs. Our attendant Herald of Tongues creaked miserably about the polished stone floors of the Major Palace, his hands trembling and his back bent, his yellow eyeballs hazed with blood and his tremulous croak a mockery of his normal sonority. He was an ancient whom the Gods had left decades overlong on earth.

'Not for twenty years,' he quavered, his normally polished accent abrasively incoherent. 'Not for twenty years have I seen such a day. The sun has deserted us. The well lines will collapse if it storms. Oh, Zeus, why is your anger?'

All the Cosmopolítēs tottered about the Major Palace in despair all that afternoon. To us, the thunder merely presaged a cloudburst, but to them it was an omen of disaster, a sign that their Gods, whom they held so low, had deserted them. For the first time I saw them pray in earnest. They prayed that the storm would pass them by. They prayed that – if it came – it would not wash away the intricate net of shallow ditches and deep wells that nourished their crops – and their lives.

The rain came with the night. Gusts of water alternated with spells of soft drizzle, and lightning cracked the black sky above the desert. When the jagged white bolts curved across the horizon to flare upon the tender earth, our attendant Herald and all the servants knelt again. Their prayers were fearful unto hysteria. They knew that their Gods were in a rage if They unloosed a thunderstorm, for Cosmopolis had known no more than a feathery drizzle in a decade. We men of Kamardol lay down early to sleep, enticed to memories of our own deep valleys by the bellowing thunder, the whiplash lightning, and the rush of water. The Major Palace lurched and cracked as rain seeped into the mud brick behind the marble, but we slept content.

An apparition woke me – the princeling Gorbabordol, his sparse beard drenched into scraggy tendrils that fringed his long, sallow face, which was blanched with the rain and fatigue. Malicious satisfaction glimmered in his small eyes like the decayed phosphorescence gleaming faintly in the depths of a well unused for years. He stood over me so that his sodden yellow cloak streamed onto my coverlet.

'Colonel,' he said mournfully, 'the Stallion is away, and lightning bolts crackle around our encampment.'

'The Horse away?' I repeated, still half asleep. 'And lightning striking around the camp?'

'As I said, Colonel!'

'How?' I asked, fully awake. 'And what have you done?'

'We followed till we were sure that He was not merely making a late excursion. Now, the princes ride behind Him, and Mirab is striking camp.'

'We must awaken Harrap and ride.'

'I would advise it. Else you may find yourself adjutant of a vanished army – and Harrap dedicated to a Quest no more divine than that compelled by the globes between his thighs.'

Harrap came awake as if he had been awaiting the summons. When we clattered through the streets no more than fifteen minutes later, the rain had stopped. Streams chuckled through the low places along the center of the road, but the high verges and the buildings were already drying in the sharp night air.

'I told you we would have a sign,' Harrap shouted with glee. 'And surely this is our sign. Did you command the Herald?'

'It is the sign,' I answered. 'The Herald will inform the Magistrates that they must await our orders.'

'They may wait a long while, but, then, they may not!'

The sand outside the walls crackled beneath our horses' hooves, for the thirsty earth swallowed the rain water as voraciously as a winning runner gulps down the ceremonial thimbleful of wine that is his reward. To the northeast, where our encampment lay, a roof of wispy white smoke hung over a pale band of orange that glowed just brighter than the oncoming sun. We spurred our horses into a gallop, though they snickered and would have turned aside from the stench of fire that filled their distended nostrils. We might have spared our fears, though the sparse desert growth was aflame around the encampment. The vanguard was already on the trail of the Horse, and Mirab, stolid as ever amid the smoke and the shouting, was methodically drawing up the main body for the march.

'Did I not tell you that the sign, when it came, would be unmistakable?' Harrap exulted. 'We are now commanded to move – as we were commanded to remain until now.'

The entire force was soon trotting northeast again, for the Horse once more loped in that direction as if He followed an invisible highroad. Men, horses, and camels groaned in protest at breaking their days of ease. Still, all were fat and rested, and the litters for the wounded were furled and laid across the pack animals' backs.

My own joy at leaving the sleazy corruption of Cosmopolis was high, and I rode in an aura of welling pleasure until Anand came up beside me. His pale face was severe, and he beckoned me out of the line of march. 'These Gods of yours seem to need human help,' he said, handing me a twist of cloth that was soaked with oil and charred at one end.

'Where did you find this?'

'I thought I'd have a look at the fire while my troop was saddling,' he replied. 'This rag was lying at the outer edge of the flames. It was quenched by a rivulet.'

'And you think the Cosmopolítēs . . .'

'Who else? They helped the omen along a bit. They were getting as tired of our presence and our demands as you were of them.' When I did not answer, he asked, 'What do you plan to do?'

'I don't know, yet. I'll have a word with the priest.'

250

But the resolution was half formed in my mind, and the priest agreed: 'If we show this squib to Harrap, he'll wheel back and attack Cosmopolis. Worse, it will shake his faith. Let's leave it.'

'That is what I would wish. But can we ignore this impiety?'

'Our task is to follow the Stallion. We are not charged to turn aside for revenge after the conquest. Your friend Anand may jest that the fire is no true sign, but manmade. But who can say with certainty that the Gods did not move the Cosmopolítes to arson to confirm the omen of the thunderstorm?'

Although I could not quite accept the priest's easy rationalization, I kept the knowledge of our new vassals' feeble treachery from Harrap. I had no heart to waste our strength in the sack of Cosmopolis. But I did not object to the purpose Harrap formed later that same morning when the Horse, having abruptly altered his course toward the northwest, led us back in a great circle through the fields where the green crops of Cosmopolis stood.

'Yakir!' Harrap hailed me. 'You were right – in part, of course – not wholly right. The submission was true. The Gods would not permit it to be otherwise. But you were right, the Cosmopolítes deceived themselves with the hollow reservations the Magistrate revealed to us.'

'I am glad you agree,' I answered eagerly, taking his words, only half grudging as they were, for a sign that the new closeness between us that had sprung up in Cosmopolis would grow until it was as vigorous as the understanding that had bound us before the Seeking began.

'I have this in mind, Yakir,' he continued. 'They must be punished for their doubts, but not too heavily. They have given us fealty, though it is not complete. What say you to filling the well lines as we pass?'

The well lines are the simple device by which the people of Cosmopolis, like most civilized dwellers in the deserts at the heart of the continent, distribute their sparse water so that they can grow food for themselves and their animals. The water is led underground from the springs of the central oasis, since it would evaporate on the surface. The builders mined the long underground tunnels by sinking well-like shafts every fifty feet and burrowing between them.

The tightly packed mouths of the shaft had half collapsed under the flailing of the storm, and it took no more than ten minutes at each to heave down enough soil to block the underground channel. Watching our work parties hack away gleefully among the tender growth of early summer, I was, for a moment, dismayed. When the young plants turned brown and withered for lack of water, the Cosmopolítēs would know famine. Since we had only blocked the northern tier of well lines, they would survive. But they would endure a winter of great toil and deprivation before the water flowed again. I felt no compassion for the treacherous Cosmopolítēs and hardly more compassion for their miserable, dispirited slaves who would, of course, suffer earliest and longest. Yet I wondered if we were justified in choking the fruits of the earth.

I did not show my disquietude to Harrap when he exulted, 'The Gods have commanded this punishment. Let all the impious take warning. We finish the retribution They began. And it will appear to the Cosmopolítēs that the Gods Themselves have done this deed solely by the sacred rains.'

The joy of injuring the city that had welcomed them suffused the troops for several days. But as the Horse cantered steadily toward the northwest where the mountains waited, the old fears rippled through our ranks. Each man, of course, carried his own amulets, secured by the prayers of his own priest and blessed by the particular Gods of his own village. Most amulets, I knew, included statuettes of the Mother Goddess of the Earth, though Her worship was officially proscribed. But the men worried that even the Mother Goddess might lose some of Her power so far from her own land. As we drew closer to the mountain walls and the air grew colder every day, the muttering began.

'The Horse leads us to a new ordeal,' the soldiers whispered. 'We shall not come safe through the great mountains again.'

'We have offended the Mother Goddess by destroying the earth's fertility,' others said. 'She is mightier than the Gods that guide the Horse.'

The men were still sleek with good living, and I little noted their muted complaints. After a week that was broken only by encounters with nomads, we found diversion in a small town, an offshoot of Cosmopolis, called Heliopolis. Although we stopped but a day to accept formal submission and tribute, the men were cheered by the easy loot and their grumbling stopped.

The Horse led us northwestward for another full week, until we came upon clusters of villages that skirted a great city. Since the villagers dared not oppose our progress, Harrap took their acquiescence for submission and swept onward toward the city. The mountains were very close, a constant presence of sheer blue and white beyond the level plain, and the buffeting of the trail had begun to wear the troops lean again. But they too exulted at the prospect of battle. Like Harrap, they had come to believe themselves invincible.

The baked-brick towers were thrusting their parapets above the horizon when the Horse abruptly swerved from the invisible highroad he had followed for two weeks. He chose to follow a stream so narrow that its banks were but a thread of bleached green against the sands. He pointed his head to the southeast as if that had been His purpose from the beginning. Like ducklings paddling obediently in the duck's wake, we followed Him. Harrap raged as the towers sank behind us, and the men swore. But none, I think, was so bereft by the denial of battle and spoils that he did not in secret rejoice at evading the terrible menace of the mountains.

The thread of green the Horse followed became a broad ribbon and then, for a time, a fertile valley, rich with the homes of men, their sleek animals, and their standing crops. As we swept southward into unknown lands, the chart the priest kept grew thick and dark with the names of rivers, wells, and towns. All but the most turbulent spirits among us forgot their regret of the great unknown city in their joy of the journey and the ease with which we rode down the occasional feeble opposition we met. Villages, towns, and small cities bowed before the passage of the Horse and paid tribute to the Great Kings of Kamardol.

Some few were still discontented, those who could not know themselves truly alive unless they were killing their enemies – and staking their own lives on the hazard of the enemies' swords.

Harrap himself grumbled to the priest and myself, for he distrusted the ease with which our sway expanded. 'How,' he asked, 'can we know ourselves if the Gods deny us trials? What virtue lies in this stately progress, as measured and as banal as parade-ground drill?'

The priest and I each gave his own answer. Their forms differed, but their purport was the same: 'This is the way the Horse has found. He has led us to these clean victories, blazoning the glory of our race across the heart of the continent. To complain of the largesse of the Gods is as futile – and as impious – as to curse Their malice when Their tasks appear beyond our strength.'

Harrap was not mollified, and he glowered in the midst of his triumphs. He longed for supreme trials, it seemed to me, not in humility – the conviction that he was unworthy of the Gods' easy favors – but in overleaping pride that challenged the Gods to contrive ordeals worthy of his immense powers. Fearing that only death – his own and ours – would content him, I still hoped that he might be soothed by a new voice. I persuaded him to talk with Barniar the Survivor, the Brahman from Hindustan, who knew the heart of the continent so much better than any of us, though the particular track we followed was new to him, too.

'O Great Prince, this humble worm is transfigured by your presence!' said Barniar, debasing himself with his own tongue in the manner of the men of Hindustan. 'O Royal and Supreme Highness, I have lived long among the barbarians. May I speak?'

'What have you to say to me?'

'But a little, Highness. It is the nature of these peoples, living exposed amid the deserts, to fight only when they believe they can prevail. The power shining from your array awes them into acquiescence. They dare not even think of resisting your Imperial splendor. To my imperfect eyes their submission appears proof of your supreme might, testimony far more magnificent than a thousand victorious battles.'

'I do not wholly understand,' said Harrap, and I heard longing for even more extravagant flattery in his feeble dissembling.

'Pardon, in your graciousness, my stumbling words, O Supreme Highness. I mean to say that only the strongest dare stand in your way. These others, who yield, are not worthy of your sword.'

Harrap accepted without demur that fantastic praise, such as

I could not give him and the priest would not. We all rode together southward and eastward behind the Horse. But Harrap rode alone in our midst, set off from us by conscious pride of majesty such as I had never marked upon the brow of the Great King who was his father.

Still, the measured triumphs of those days lent us all a small divinity. Men bowed to our will as if we were Gods as summer flared into brief, bursting ripeness among the wastes. Dates and melons swelled and dripped juice; the grain grew taller than our horses' heads within a week and hung heavy with life and fecundity; even the bees, fat and glossy, gyrated iridescent with demoniacal energy among the blossoms, which were spread red and orange and purple for their banquet on an emerald cloth. Never had we seen such intense abundance in our own land, where the earth comes to fruition gradually. We were granted a second spring, swelling in the instant into full summer, and our hearts were full as they had been in the first spring, which preceded our ordeal in the mountains.

The unending flood of petty problems that laps around an adjutant in peace or war, in triumph or defeat, in camp or on the march – all seemed to subside. The problems of ailing animals, quarreling soldiers, and broken equipment seemed to solve themselves or were resolved by junior officers who had learned to be confident of their own powers. Our train of followers had dwindled to no more than fifty or sixty hardy mountebanks and harlots, the rest having found themselves havens along the route.

Our relations with the tribute towns assumed a simple pattern. Their leaders saw that we were not marauders, who would sack their treasuries and slaughter their people, like locusts which know no compulsion but that to destruction. Their submission was orderly, and the token tribute we required was paid without demur. Anand came to oversee the details for me. Harrap, reverting to his obsession, could talk of nothing but the Seeking, while Anand and I had marked out the areas where we could not agree. I therefore found myself more and more often riding alone across the strips of ochre sand that separated the oases.

I forced my horse forward through the glowing days of summer, passing the foremost Bastards and coming up to the

Horse. I had become accustomed to the blood that streamed down His flanks when He ran, and I had become accustomed to the lonely bright courage – and more than courage – that shone from the Avatar we followed into the unknown. Still my breath caught and my heart faltered when I spied Him at a distance. All His perfection was so sharply sculpted that I could see each muscle and hair clear, though He was still a minute and distant figurine between the yellow sands fringed with living green and the burnished hollow of the sky, where hung the golden platter of the sun.

Sometimes He would pause to let me come up to Him – or even turn back, whinnying His greeting, to take the small brown cones of sugar I kept always ready for Him. Even when He frolicked foallike around me, demanding tidbits, His aura was pure majesty and more than majesty. I knew that He condescended when He gave me His love, condescension as natural as the Gods' own gift of favor. Each time I came up to Him the gray slime of doubt that had fouled our quest was sluiced away.

During those lonely and joyous rides beside the Divinity, I made my 'Song of the Seeking' whole. The old words I had made in the blessed valley of spring among the mountains would not quite serve. Starting from the old song, I made new verses I thought better to sing:

> Thus the white Stallion was given to bright Kamardol:
> The Stallion was foaled by the cold north wind
> In white lands that freeze forever beyond
> The mountains that guard the broad rim of the sky.
> His attendants, the dawn and the eagles that fly
> Without lighting, all gave to us men the command:
> Bring Him safe from the teeth of His mother, the wind.
>
> Thus the white Stallion was given to bright Kamardol:
> The Stallion was brought to the worlds that men know
> By Harrap, the boldest young prince of our race,
> With others, his servants, all sworn to the Quest:
> To ride without ceasing, to fight without rest –
> And storm, if the Gods will, the sun's molten face
> Across the bones of the pagans, through the blood of His
>   foes.

Thus the white Stallion was given to bright Kamardol:
We hung Him with garlands of roses and gold,
Anointed His mane with sweet oil and red gore.
We gave Him an escort of our bravest young sons,
All swearing to follow the Horse where He runs –
From white cloudbanks to chasms where Hell hides its door,
While the roses fall clotted with blood of His foes.

Thus the white Stallion was given to bright Kamardol:
The bravest are dying; the staunchest remain.
The Stallion leads onward to lands where our swords
Slaughter the barbarous and take tithes from the wise.
We could ride on forever, half divine in His guise,
Had we not sworn to our Gods in these words:
To close the year's circle, though only the strongest return.

There came between the verses the chorus, which I also shaped
to a harder, finer edge:

> Then the Gods' will is our Kings' will!
> And we ride out in Their name –
> To follow the Stallion and to kill
> Even the Brahman who knows not His fame.

The 'Song of the Seeking,' when I had made it whole, was
many tens of verses in length. Since it is sung today not only by
the Army, but in the schools and wineshops, by old peasants and
young rakes, there is no need to record all the verses again. But
there remained in my own mind – maddening as a recurrent itch
between the shoulder blades – a single additional verse that I
could neither forget nor fit into my ballad:

> All our days lead us to eternity,
> Be the pace hard or the pace slow.
> We seek but a token to show
> That the Quest is not vain,
> That we shall come back again,
> That our faith is more than perversity.

Today, of course, I know how foolish were my doubts. I have
had the best proof of all that our mission was divinely inspired
and we ourselves had been blessed manyfold by the Gods for our
constancy. But my vision was not wholly clear at those times

when the torment of the unending sands and the cruel white and black rocks of the mountains appeared more real than the will of the Gods manifest in our hearts. That single, errant verse remains the symbol of the agonies that rose, not from the malice of men or the elements but within ourselves. Since it demonstrates that doubts may afflict even the most favored, it may sustain those who know doubt even amid the abundant beneficence of the Gods we enjoy today. I should not, however, break my narrative for these reflections. I shall soon embody them in another work for the deserving people of Kamardol.

While I made my 'Song of the Seeking,' the plants were beginning to shrivel as if the earth had squandered all the water granted to her in the brief intensity of the avid land's ripening. The vegetation became sparse, and the days became so hot we broke our journey during the hours before and after the crest of the day.

The strips of sand between oases grew broader, and the cultivated fields shrank. We, who had been riding across a field of green plants barred with yellow sand, found suddenly that the field was yellow and the narrow bars lusterless green.

The cruel heat reached its greatest intensity as we approached the far edge of the sown land. Only three hours after dawn our men hid their faces in miniature tents they made of their cloaks. They preferred to swallow their own gritty sweat in the dark closeness rather than face the burning blasts of a wind that seared all moisture from the eyeballs so that they moved in their sockets like rasps drawn across splintered wood. Our noses streamed blood from time to time as if to relieve the aching drought from within, and we could touch our sword hilts only after wrapping our hands in rags.

The people of the last hamlets on the edge of the desert made their submission swiftly, tottering from hovels of baked mud roofed with brown reeds to gaze blinking at our array through the heat ghosts that spiraled upward like half-transparent serpents. Their heads were covered with filthy gray rags, and the tattered robes they wore against the unrelenting sun were encrusted with the fat and blood of animals so that they stank even in the arid heat. Seeing their poverty, Harrap excused them tribute, taking only their earnest submission to our might.

'Yakir,' he smiled, 'I think these will never be the wealthiest cities we are adding to my brothers' domains.'

The sun, I saw, had carved harsh furrows in the taut skin of his cheeks, which were baked the gritty gray-brown of old pots.

We had paused at a village called Kermat, where the dogs were too exhausted to snap at the green flies that ringed the hand's-breadth sores on their ribs. The old headman, when we demanded no more of him than fealty and water, kissed the sole of Harrap's boot and asked anxiously, 'My Lords, where does your road run from here?'

Full twenty minutes passed before we could make him understand that we knew not where we went. Barniar of Hindustan, of course, spoke best that mélange of Sanskrit, Turkyi, Greek, and a dozen more languages which the heart of the continent has used so long it has become a distinct tongue – even to its own syntax, so simple as to be cumbersome. The headman finally understood that we must 'follow our God,' as Barniar was forced to vulgarize our Quest.

The headman rolled his eyes in a show of terror, the dead, white opacity of the left gyrating with as much vigor as the red-rimmed, pus-dripping globe that was its neighbor. 'Do not go that way!' he screeched, pointing a twisted, black forefinger toward the southeast, where our journey tended. 'You will come upon nothing but sand, hotter each day till the world ends.'

'Where should we go, fellow?' asked Harrap.

'That way,' the headman said, pointing almost due west. 'We have heard that, many marches away, a great city lies. And there is water between.'

The priest opened his chart. After much twisting and turning and laying out of angles, he spoke a single word: 'Cosmopolis.'

'I would not, in any event, but we cannot go back – unless the Stallion wills,' said Harrap. 'It is in vain, but ask him the way thither.'

The ancient headman scratched his cheek with a puzzled forefinger, leaving a streak of grey across its black patina. Giving us no answer, he crept into his hovel to emerge bearing on his back a huddled shape. The eyes that could not see, the gullies and ravines that scarred the black filth of the face recorded an infinity of years, but his voice was astonishingly resonant.

'Perhaps my father can tell,' said the headman. 'He has heard much in his lifetime.'

'How old is he?' asked Barniar.

'We do not count well, but of immense age – at least sixty-five winters.'

Harrap strolled away, impatient with the protracted consultations and translations. But we finally learned that the two men of the desert believed that only four days' ride to the west began a series of oases leading down to the 'great city' the priest thought must be Cosmopolis.

'If we could but inspire Him, somehow, to the first oasis, the rest would follow,' I whispered. 'Is there not some way to . . .'

The priest motioned me to silence, jerking his chin at the approaching Harrap. Behind my teeth I almost cursed our thralldom to the Horse's will that led us toward death amid the sands. I could do no more than insure that all our waterskins were full and that we carried as much dried meat for the men and fodder for the animals as we could. That evening, of course, the Horse turned His head to the empty southeast. I knew before he moved that he would not lead us to the assured comfort – and promise of life – that was Cosmopolis.

We should have died in the desert but for Harrap's unbending will and the camels' stolid endurance. Though we marched by night and lay by day in the sparse shade the sand dunes offered, men, horses, and mules were tormented by cracked skins and thirst-swollen tongues that filled their mouths like the spiny leaves of the cactus, all dull with dust in the accursed seamless brilliance. Two, three, or four men died each day and, to save time, we carried the corpses through the night marches, burying them with brief services when we stopped to rest. The animals that faltered we butchered where they lay, the soldiers fighting to lap the thick, dark blood. As we had when we first entered the desert, we saw in the sky before us the white shape of the Horse, wading through an endless lake that shimmered just beyond our reach.

Only once, when we had been eight days in the Devil's kiln, did I urge Harrap to turn back before our supplies were exhausted.

'The Perfect Stallion,' he answered, seeking in vain to moisten cracked and blackened lips with his swollen tongue, 'does not turn back. We are pledged to follow Him, are we not, Yakir? Make good the boast of your song.'

I said nothing. Since no argument would turn his purpose, I disdained to point out that the making of songs and the survival of soldiers were not the same thing. Nor would it have served to remind him that the crux of our mission was to return at the year's end.

Uneasy in the silence, Harrap added more reasonably, 'Perhaps it will help to remember one thing, Yakir. He is horse as well as Avatar. He must be going forward toward water.'

We crawled six more days across the wastes like mites on an elephant's seamed flank before we saw more than single spikes of spiny desert plants. Twice cavalrymen thrust their lances through the riders in front of them. Each swore before he was beheaded that he had seen not a man but a fish. Each time I drew a cordon of Royal Guards around the headsman's block. I did not fear the men's grumbling at the executions, but their muttering that men's blood would quench thirst as well as beast's. The animals that died mysteriously without apparent illness or accident I thought it better to ignore. They were not too many, and their blood refreshed the men. The men knew that our supplies were so low we must all die if we turned back. They still hoped the Horse would lead them through the sands to his secret haven. My own hopes lay in the rough-haired camels that placidly nibbled the spiny sprigs and seemed, though leaner, to be fit to go on endlessly – as long as their loads were not too heavy.

The cruelest moment came toward morning of the eleventh day of our torment. Accustomed to the phantasms in the sky, we had learned to look through them, lest the vain promise of water destroy our senses. None of us did more than glance away, shaking our heads sadly, when we first saw another great lake perhaps five miles distant. Unlike the others, its blue expanse appeared to lie upon the sands, and I even imagined I saw a depression amid the umber wastes. As we drew closer, the lake remained fixed in place, instead of receding. The front ranks stumbled on, not daring to speak of the hope that throbbed in each man's temples. Still silent, we kicked our weary mounts into a rough lope. The beasts, thirstier even than the men on a cup of stinking, green-scummed water a day, still showed no eagerness.

No more than a half mile distant, all could see that it was indeed a lake – and no mirage. The blue waters, flecked with white, sparkled in the early sun. Marveling that we had lived so long with thirst that burnt our arms to withered sticks and our mouths to fire pits, we raced toward the shores of the blessed lake. Harrap – even the priest – forebore to remind us of the miraculous favor of the Gods that gave us water. Perhaps they knew that each man was renewing his faith and giving thanks in his own heart.

The lake was a broad salt marsh that had dried under the sun. Devoid of water as the Huns of mercy, the crystals sparkled in mock wavelets in the morning sun.

We cried our disappointment aloud, a great groan like the pleas of the dead before the doors of Hell rasping from two thousand throats as cracked and arid as the salt pan itself. Only one man in the host spoke intelligible words. His jowls hanging in a thousand loose corrugations and his eyes enormous where the skin had shrunk from them, the priest mused in a hoarse whisper, 'So it is true. The rivers shift, and the lakes disappear in this desert!'

I admired, though feebly, the priest's avidity for knowledge, but I no longer shared it. I was tormented by my efforts to keep the men moving. Twice I passed on Harrap's orders that the Royal Guards, the last buttress of our cracking authority, carry out mass executions. We beheaded five cavalrymen and fourteen infantrymen. They died for calling on their fellows to lie down and die beside them – and to struggle no more. We were seven and a half months out of Kamardol.

The Horse followed his ordained course, never deviating from the southeast. He nibbled the wrinkled leaves on the sparse desert shrubs, and he grew leaner each day. But he never slackened his pace. Each time I saw Him, He was more beautiful. The gross flesh was sloughing off with the water from His body, leaving only the imprint of the spirit like an ancient footmark upon granite.

On the morning of the fifteenth day, we came to an oasis called Gaustana-lezli. One instant we were trudging up the side of a dune as if we must go on into eternity. The next instant we came over the ridge, and green fields and cool watercourses lay beneath us.

Twenty-three

We had come upon Cosmopolis half unaware, our chance knowledge of its character largely dependent on Barniar's imperfect recollection of his brief sojourn with the Huns. In the far northwest we had seen no more than the high cupolas of the unknown city that lay in the shadow of the great mountains before the Horse drew us away from its conquest. I cannot even record its name, for we never learned how the people called themselves or their realm.

Neither distance nor the tangle of tongues obscured the fame of the great city of the southeast. We heard the name Gaustana from the men of the oasis almost as our beasts dipped their cracked muzzles into the shallow pond. Still dripping the water we sluiced over our dusty heads, our ears heard with joy a tongue much like our own Prakrit. It was somewhat like hearing whispering through cracks in a wall, for the accent was awry and the sense was adulterated by an admixture of words from the many tongues of the heart of the continent. The men of the oasis of Gaustana-lezli chattered as freely as they gave us of their scant stores, as much, I am sure, in pity for our misery as in fear of the weapons that trembled in our feeble hands. Never, they said, had so many men come out of the desert they called 'the endless dead waste,' but only two, three, or a dozen stumbling survivors of blasted caravans. Seeking to restore our moribund spirits, they told us then what lay before us: 'Gaustana, bejeweled Gaustana, the greatest city of the world.'

Fifteen days' ride to the southwest Gaustana lay, its splendor unveiled to the traveler with fitting deliberation as he traversed a great series of valleys, each subtly richer than its predecessor. At the end of the progressively opening horn of plenty lay Gaustana, where commoners lived like princes and princes like

Gods, where no man was oppressed by any other man and all men lived in harmony. In Gaustana the riches of the spirit were so much more abundant than the riches of the world that, by comparison, the people were impoverished materially, though even the wives of servants wore ladders of gold bracelets upon their soft arms on holy days and festivals. The men of the oasis told us many tales of Gaustana, but all their eager talk drew no more than a blurred picture in my mind. Perhaps the true glory was beyond the power of their words; perhaps they wished us to discover the perfection of the realm for ourselves.

We stayed for a week in that oasis, which the people called Gaustana-lezli, meaning 'the small star of Gaustana.' They were proud to claim kinship with the great city, though they worshipped other Gods and, in truth, knew little more of it than legend. The Horse, almost as worn as the lesser beasts, did not try the vigilance of His escort. He browsed and slept within the green triangle, no more than a half mile in extent, formed by two narrow watercourses extending from the central pond. It was four days before His awakening curiosity drew Him into the small fort the men of Gaustana-lezli had built for their security. Even Harrap was lethargic, content to let men and beasts rest after their passage through the fires of the sands.

I should, perhaps, not have been surprised at Harrap's acquiescence to the leisurely recuperation from our ordeal. But I was greatly surprised, for his obsession had come to dominate my own emotions, more real because more constant than the desert and the mountains or even Death, who had taken his assigned place in our formations. The Horse's quiescence renewed and refined the revelation that had come to me in the desert. The essence of our Quest – the true miracle of the Seeking – lay in Harrap's will. The divine will in the man drove the Horse onward, though he never touched Him nor chivvied Him with shouts or sudden charges or the brandishing of weapons. When Harrap's will was dormant, the Horse, obedient, halted. I recognized with reverence for Their subtle designs that it was Harrap, rather than the Horse, through whom the Gods worked. However, I did not speak of my new revelation. Anand, who no more than half believed in our Quest, would have scoffed at my conviction that divinity infused Harrap as well as the Horse. The priest, whose own beliefs I knew were more aberrant than they appeared, would have fobbed me off with resonant platitudes about the mysterious forces that inhabit all things. As for Harrap himself, I did not know, but I feared that his outrageous self-deceit would have acknowledged my complex concept as a self-evident truth. That ultimate self-complacency would have withered whatever love still bound us. But it would have been worse had Harrap, in the total fury of his total obsession, cursed me for my doubts and shut me out of the community of the Quest. Therefore I was quiet. Still the true miracle – the miracle of a faith-intoxicated man's moving the Horse by his will alone – was more splendid than the orthodox miracle of the Gods in the Beast.

We dealt lightly with the people of Gaustana-lezli. They were hardly more civilized than the barbarous nomads, these dwellers on the edge of the inhabited world, as they knew the world. They gave us their submission gladly once they understood that they were not required to put away their own Gods, so like our own, but simply to affirm the supremacy of the Gods in the Horse and to swear fealty to the Great Kings of Kamardol. They had given freely of their meager stores when we were almost too weak to enforce our demands. Even Harrap, who considered all gifts our simple due, spoke with gratitude of their openhandedness. When their stores began to run low on the fifth day after our arrival, he declared, 'We must move on toward the prize the Gods have granted us – bejeweled Gaustana.'

But the Horse was still content with the fresh pastures He had found after the barren desert. Mocking Harrap's impatience, He obdurately frolicked in the long grass beside the watercourses. Although my private revelation was wrenched askew by His failure to respond to Harrap's will, I knew we could but wait upon the flowering of His desire.

On the morning of the sixth day, Anand drew me aside and suggested, 'Let the Bastards ride ahead, Yakir. Perhaps, the Horse will follow them, so accustomed is He to their following Him.'

I gave the order, seeing no desecration in the essay – or,

perhaps, I should better say, suppressing my misgivings by arguing that we could not force the Horse to follow, since He would move only as He listed. But I did not consult with Harrap. Nor did I tell him what I had done when Gorbabordol's courier reported that the Horse was moving and the remaining forty-odd princes following. It griped my tongue to remain still when Harrap, mounting so gaily for the predestined conquest of Gaustana, chided my lack of faith.

'To follow perfectly, Yakir,' he said, 'that is our only care. He moves when He should move – and always toward greater glory.'

I bit down my retort. Of the several replies that quivered on my tongue none would have served a good purpose, and any might have provoked further strife between us. Besides, I was troubled by a matter as grave as the puzzle of the Horse's will. I would have spoken to Harrap of the fealty we had won from the peoples in our road, so lightly given, so light, perhaps, in worth. What was the true value of their ready submission, when we could not remain to enforce it? Was the homage they offered the true Gods more than facile play of hands and lips? Were we extending the realm of Kamardol or were we deluding ourselves with shadow conquests? Harrap should have been as concerned as I with those questions, but I finally judged that it would be purposeless to raise them with him. Instead, I put my fears plainly to the priest, though I had not much hope of pertinent answers.

'Do not,' he counseled, 'concern yourself that the Gods can be cheated. They hold us and direct us to Their ends. Great city or remote hamlet, it does not seem to matter to Them . . .'

'This,' I interrupted, 'is not a question of size, but of men's hearts.'

'The Gods are pleased or They would bid us slay the impious. Yet all They have demanded was the slight chastisement we administered to the Cosmopolítēs . . . As for the rest, here on my chart I have stored up the matter of a thousand claims. We are the first. It is not our task to hold, but to find – and They, later, to take. In my chart and in your notes we carry the seeds of the empire that will be called Great Kamardol.'

I pursued the mystery no further with the priest and not at all with Harrap. I gave myself instead to the delights of the trail, rejoicing in the cool air's caress on my cheeks and the breath in my nostrils that bubbled like new wine. After the barren desert, where the humpbacked dunes crawled under the lash of the cruel wind, it was good to watch an immense fertile fan open beneath the dancing hooves of our horses. The living earth grew wider in extent each day, changing from the withered green of the first oases to the fecund green of the orchards, the vegetables, and, above all, the vines hung with the red, the purple, and the blue gems that were flowers and fruit.

Having learned to read the face of the hidden continent, our men knew that the Horse's black hooves, flashing beneath their silken white fringes, were leading us toward the ultimate mountains. But they rejoiced in the earth's abundance without fear of the new ordeal. They had learned that the mountains, lavishing water upon the lowlands beneath them, bestowed all life upon this secret world. Moreover, the fires of the sands had burnt away their terror of the mountains.

Our easy progress was almost a repetition of the idyllic road of conquest that had brought us to the first passage of the sands before Cosmopolis. The people lived amid fertile fields in settlements too small to offer us resistance. The garrisons of the occasional forts we passed did not dispute our progress, and Harrap was content to pass them by on his road to Gaustana. He was sustained by the Brahmayanas in taking their passivity for submission.

'If they shall oppose the crossing of the Horse over their lands,' the texts directed, 'those princes shall be destroyed. Still, if, through their perception of the will of the Gods, they shall not hinder the Horse upon His chosen way, then they shall be deemed to have acknowledged and accepted the suzerainty of the Supreme King who had sent out the Horse.' We did not test the quality of their submission, for our two thousand spears were pointed at the glowing target – bejeweled Gaustana. All else was but painted rubble to Harrap.

I had marked the growth of this new obsession from the moment when, thirst-racked beside the fresh waters, he had first heard the ringing name Gaustana – and had appeared to dismiss it from his mind as if it were no more than another hamlet of a few hundred half-nomads. The constant tolling of that name in our ears had forced first curiosity and then a concentration that excluded all else. 'Gaustana, bejeweled Gaustana, the greatest city of the world,' as the men of the oases called it, had become to Harrap the essence of all toward which we strived. It was, at once, the ultimate prize and the final test. Failure could blight all the meaning of our Quest. Success would exorcise all error. Gaustana had become at once the prize to crown and sanctify all our suffering and the most formidable obstacle to our triumphant return to Kamardol.

'Yakir, I know now that it is Gaustana toward which we have been led all this time,' Harrap told me beside the fire on the fifth day after our departure from Gaustana-lezli. 'The Gods are stern in Their generosity. We are bidden to take this great fortress-city with but two thousand men. If we succeed, we shall be masters of the heart of the continent – and masters of the continent itself.'

'We shall not fail, Harrap,' I assured him, though I knew he set an absurd value upon a single city, however proud. 'But should we fail?'

'I have thought of that possibility too. I know that in this trial we shall be alone. We could, indeed, fail, but we must not.'

'This is a lonely Quest, Harrap.'

I was surprised when he took the inner meaning in my aimless remark and answered gently, 'It has been lonely, Yakir, has it not? For all of us. When the Gods command, a man can hear only Their voices. The voices of other men are far away.'

'It has been so, Harrap,' I agreed, so softly the words barely sighed over the crackling of the dry boughs in our fire.

'But we shall all be lonelier soon,' he resumed – as if I had not offered to reclaim our comradeship. 'When the Gods have brought us to Gaustana, They will, I know, depart from us for a time. We shall be tested without Their aid . . . each man alone with his courage.'

'Why, Harrap?' My pent exasperation spoke in my stead. 'Why do you create ever greater obstacles? Why do you torment your spirit? We have done well. If I could speak at this moment

to the people of Kamardol, I should say we had done magnificently. The terrors we have conquered . . . the lands we have
won . . . the faith we have held firm . . . all have been so immense
that few men – even now – few men can stand beside us in their
deeds.'

'What you say, Yakir, is perhaps true. But it is not enough.'

'Why?' I asked again. 'Why do you throw back into Their faces
the great treasures the Gods have bestowed on us? Why has this
new city, only half glimpsed through a fog of ignorant tales, why
must this city be the touchstone of our deeds . . . of our lives?'

'Because I know that it is so – and it must be so!' he answered
and would say no more.

I was bound to a man who was driven toward the dark edge of
self-destruction as some men yearn toward forbidden thighs in
beds hedged by divine proscriptions and a thousand sharp
swords. Harrap could no more rest upon his triumphs than the
besotted lecher can give enduring fealty to his most recent
conquest. I was half afraid that only death could confer the glory
he sought, but not this life. Still, I did what I could to prepare for
the encounter we could not avoid.

The men of each oasis laved us with praise of the might and
wealth of Gaustana, but they told us little of value, neither the
strength of its armies nor the number of its inhabitants. Even the
shape of the city was hidden from us – how it lay on the ground,
its gates, walls, moats, and other defensive works. I pounded at
the elders who made submission to us, seeking to extract the
hard metal of fact from the ore heaps of verbiage. Exasperated,
I gave them to the torture of the ruby daggers. The dullards
writhed as their flesh burnt, but merely repeated screaming what
they had already intoned in grave dignity, 'Gaustana is a great
city, the greatest city of the world. The walls are higher than
twenty men, and the towers above them are sheathed with gold.
Its people are many, many tens of thousands, and they are
shielded by four divine protectors whose abode is the Mount of
Spirits.'

Such gabble served only to inflame Harrap's single passion, so
that he relentlessly pressed me to learn more of Gaustana. His
insouciant confidence, which had made light of our earlier trials,

was quite flown as he contemplated the ultimate test. He brushed aside my suggestion that we could do no more than trust to the Gods in the Horse – and the surprise of our attack.

'It's damned unsatisfactory, Yakir, you know that,' he retorted. 'We shall be more surprised than surprising if we attack blind. Besides, I've told you the Gods will not assist us as They have done. They give us Gaustana to win – or lose – by our own powers. I must know precisely what we challenge.'

I could give him no answer – neither the knowledge he craved nor any alternative to its possession. Besides, it soon appeared that we would not surprise Gaustana. The land grew ever more fertile, the cultivated strip ever broader, until only the golden dust glittering in the twilight wind recalled to us brooding danger of the desert beyond. But the fertile land was almost barren of men. The neat villages with their serried orchards and serpentine flower gardens were empty of all but a few old monks who served the shrines. Not our Gods alone had withdrawn from us, as Harrap had warned, but even men. Surprise would not contrive our triumph, since the Gaustanans obviously knew of our coming.

We were, instead, forced to guard ourselves against surprise attack. I strengthened the depleted force of princes by sending up the knights and the archers after Gorbabordol reported that armed men had appeared on his flanks at dusk, galloping across his path in a broad sickle that almost cut off the Horse and withdrawing after loosing a torrent of bolts. The main body, too, was harassed by dim figures. It was always the same – a quick clash, sometimes coming to swords' length, but usually at long range. Those assaults left our men uncertain of the numbers of the enemy or his losses, but always nursing two or three wounded and occasionally sorrowing over a man slain. The dark riders were seeking to frighten us, who could not be frightened, and to learn our strength, as we could not learn theirs.

The Horse cavorted onward like a colt discovering ever new and more succulent pastures. Occasionally He sprinted ahead, straining the Bastards' ponies and waking the hope of imminent battle in our veins. Then, finding a clear pond swaddled in fields of tender green, He sported for a day or more. When we had been nineteen days on the road that should have taken us to

Gaustana in fifteen, Harrap summoned a council. He was, I knew, wrung by yearning for the test and by the strain of delay. I had heard him swear aloud at fate and, just once, mutter that the Gods had perverted the Stallion's will. He had accepted, almost with glee, the temporary isolation from the Gods he felt, but he would not formulate to himself his new fear that the Gods had turned against him. He would certainly not repeat that fear to any other. Nonetheless, he summoned us to council.

Eight hours past the crest of day the sun still laid his horizontal bars above the land as if reluctant to release the world to darkness. We kindled our fires to roast the rabbits the archers had shot and the goats the soldiers had found in the villages. The flames strove, pale yellow, against the pellucid light. The transparent dusk was chill, and we seven were cold though we sat within the shelter of a deep green bowl beside a stream that trickled like an irregular crack across its bottom. We drew close to the fire.

Harrap leaned an elbow on his saddle. His broad face was deliberate, composed, though an irrepressible pulse throbbed within the empurpled cicatrice between his eyes. Beside Harrap, Mirab sat on his heels, his blunt straight nose a bar of light in the pale flames, his upturned mustaches spun-silver filaments. Gorbabordol and Ranbir sat cross-legged side by side on a gaudy square of thick striped cotton. The princeling's long, sallow face shone with an oily sheen. His straggling black beard was cocked combatively above the yellow cloak drawn close around his high, narrow shoulders to set himself away from the squat captain of the Royal Guard. Ranbir's round face, capped with stiff hair pressed down by the weight of the square helmet that lay by his side, acknowledged neither his neighbor's shrinking nor even his presence. Like a stream falling upon a bed of shallow rocks, firelight cascaded over the graven maze of lines that guarded his features. Instead of white foam, it tossed up a curtain of roiled light that shrouded his thoughts.

By the chance of the order in which we had taken our places, we amateurs of warfare, the men of the word, sat opposite the professionals of death, the men of the sword. Opposite Harrap, the priest uncomfortably bestrode an irregular boulder. His cheeks, so firm and florid when we left Kamardol, hung flaccid as empty saddlebags on either side of his loose, bloodless lips. Their cracked gray surface gave no light back to the fire. I sat beside the priest, sharing a coarse woolen saddle blanket with Anand. His skin was drawn so taut that ridges in his fleshy forehead seemed to be baked in red clay and the dark pits of his nostrils gouged by a brutal potter's thumb.

The council by the fire, bringing us together for the first time since we had left Kamardol, displayed the seal our eight months' Quest had stamped upon us all. We glittered with the gold chains and the bright gems we had chosen from the tribute to flaunt our triumphs. But only the two old soldiers, Ranbir and Mirab, wore the same aspects they had at the Consecration of the Horse. Even before we rode out, time and battle had set their features beyond reshaping. We others were transformed, carved by the sand and the snow, baked by the sun, and shrunk by the cold. With our abrupt gestures and suspicious glances, we were more like a band of desperate slaves plotting escape than the captains of an irresistible army. I was glad that I could not look upon myself.

'Gentlemen,' Harrap began abruptly, 'we ride toward certain defeat. The Gods have not deserted us, I believe. They have, however, withdrawn from us, commanding us to strive with only our own skill. That skill, it would appear, is inadequate to our task.'

'The Gods,' the priest offered soothingly, 'may yet show us the way to conquer Gaustana. They can return as suddenly as they departed.'

'We can hardly stake our Quest on that, O Brahman,' said Harrap, shaking his dark hair. 'I propose that we draw back.'

'Retreat? . . . Withdraw? . . . How? . . . Where? . . . The spears of Kamardol flee phantoms?'

The separate words rang clear, though I could not match them to their speakers. But the noise that broke from us six in our astonishment was not like human speech at all, but like the desperate barking that goes up from a herd of mouse deer when arrows fall from unseen bows.

Harrap was at his commanding best, though his words counseled despair. He waited, glowering, until the mindless cries had cried themselves out.

'Gentlemen, our dilemma endures your protest,' he said, his rumbling tones almost a caress, a simulacrum of despair so skillful that, I believe, I was the only one who knew that he was shamming. 'We are sworn to follow the Stallion, and He goes forward. Even if we could abandon Him, where would we go? Who knows the route that will take us to Kamardol? Yet He goes ever forward toward Gaustana.'

'Then we must . . . There is no choice . . . We must attack!' Mirab asserted.

'If we could,' Harrap answered. 'But what shall we attack? Yakir, tell us what you have learned of the defenses of Gaustana.'

I nodded to Anand, preferring to let him speak for me so that I could later press my own idea without appearing to speak as Harrap's voice. In form, of course, I was his voice, as well as his eyes and ears.

'The Colonel-Adjutant has asked me to report, O Prince,' Anand declared. 'We have heard much of the enormous wealth of Gaustana, but we do not know within a million talents what that wealth is. We have heard that Gaustana is a great city of towering walls and myriad soldiers. Of the height of the walls, the number of soldiers, their arms, their tactics, their stores, we know nothing. We do not even know whether the city is built in a valley, on a broad plain, or upon a commanding hill.'

'You see our problem, gentlemen?' Harrap asked.

From the murmur of affirmation, Gorbabordol's voice burst strong: 'Then, General, let us attack. Thus we shall discover all we must.'

'Reconnaissance in force,' muttered Mirab. 'Good old tactic!'

'Even if the Avatar leads elsewhere?' the priest asked himself.

At the same instant, playing to Harrap's apparent wishes, I began to argue: 'We hold the honor of Kamardol in our hands, gentlemen. Picture it – our failure to return because we have been destroyed in a battle we undertook without sanction. Or, worse, our return without the Horse, He having been snatched from us!'

'I had forgotten the Stallion,' said Mirab brusquely.

'He won't let us live, and He won't let us die,' sighed Gorbabordol.

'We must find out what defenses they muster.' Ranbir spoke for the first time. 'A small probing attack, perhaps . . . or, if we could seize a few captives.'

'We are, Ranbir, bidden to exercise artfulness in our courage, not foolhardiness,' Harrap chided. 'If Gaustana is truly strong, we should lose the probe, having learned nothing. If the Gods should give us a captive and he should speak the truth, I should be grateful. But I cannot hazard the honor of Kamardol and two thousand lives upon the unlikely truthfulness of a captive we are not likely to take.'

'Still, we must know . . .' insisted Ranbir.

'That we must. But how?' Harrap prodded us.

'If we could but put two or three men into Gaustana . . .' I mused.

'Under cloaks of invisibility, perhaps?' Harrap mocked. 'They know we are coming. If they are what we have heard, they will not let a mouse approach their walls unless he tells a plausible tale.'

'The city lives by trade, even amid its peril,' Anand murmured.

'Do you propose that we starve them out?' Harrap gibed. 'That we invest a great city for years with two thousand men?'

'No, Harrap, not that,' I interrupted. 'But traders must come and go. You spoke of a plausible story.'

'So I did. What do you propose?'

'A small trading caravan,' I answered eagerly. 'Too small to be a threat. Barniar and myself, two merchants of Hindustan, with ten or twenty porters and camel men. Ranbir's men would serve . . .'

'I'll go myself, instead of you,' Harrap broke in, having brought the council to the goal he sought.

'With your face, General, so well known . . .' Ranbir began.

The priest was already objecting, 'And leave us without the consecrated leader if you should fall?'

'I don't like it,' Harrap grumbled, thwarted when he thought he had won his end. 'Barniar we cannot trust, and you, Yakir, should not go into peril that is not your peril, but mine own.'

'What else can we do, except wander aimless before the gates of Gaustana?' I insisted.

My task was no more difficult than turning a rampaging bull without violating his sanctity, for Harrap was determined to undertake the mission himself. But finally it was done, and agreement was won. Barniar and I would go into the city, offering to trade part of the tribute of Cosmopolis and accompanied by ten of the Royal Guards arrayed as servants and camel men. Harrap added two conditions: a small column would move hidden toward the city a few days after our departure to bring us back to him; if we had not appeared within ten days, he would attack, even if the attack appeared doomed to fail.

Finally reconciled by duress to my going in his stead, Harrap was like a man who has at last seen an encrusted arrowhead work its way out of an old wound. He raised his goblet to each of us, pledging victory. So half the night passed in toasts and oaths repledged. No longer manacled by frustration, we contemplated Gaustana as a prize we might win, rather than a rock on which our Quest must shatter.

I awoke early the next morning and dressed in the robes of a peaceful trader with only a trumpery dagger at my belt. Barniar rejoiced in the opportunity to prove himself to Harrap, who held his life. We agreed to make a great circle in order to come upon Gaustana from the south, rather than the northeast whence advanced the armed threat the city knew.

My foot was in the stirrup when Gorbabordol brought a courier to Anand, who would assume my duties.

'Six mares in season,' the princeling shouted, 'broke away from our herds last night. They are gone into the north, closing the desert, seeking fast. The Stallion follows, bellowing and snorting like a still unsheathed bull of three winters.'

'And your men?' I asked.

'He is moving so fast we are falling behind. I fear we have not the numbers to follow Him in the living chain and guard Him, too. Not even with the knights.'

'We follow Him this instant,' commanded Harrap, who had been drawn to the tumult.

We parted thus beside the trickling stream with no time for

farewells or last thoughts. My little caravan trotted southward, and the parent force streamed in a great crescent to the north.

As he mounted, I called to the priest, 'Command the Gods in your prayers to bring us soon together again!'

In a few moments – it seemed no more – we twelve were alone. The empty land lay all around us.

Twenty-four

We came to Gaustana on the fourth morning after our parting, approaching the city from the south through valleys interlaced and knotted with watercourses as the back of my hand is with veins. The rulers of Gaustana had dug the web of canals to lead the water where they wished. Every field received its share, even when the water level dropped low, as it had in the late summer of our coming.

So much men had done, and the earth had yielded her fruits to their labors. Riding through the green valleys to Gaustana, I remembered the dusty approaches of Cosmopolis with their meager fields. The other city, it was true, lay further from the mountains, which are the ultimate source of moisture that is life in the secret part of the continent. But neither was the realm of Gaustana blessed with the rich soil and abundant water that makes the land south of the mountains bloom with little human effort. For all its startling fertility, it was but an island in the sands. Yet, as we later learned, it gave life to more than fifty thousand. The crude well lines and despairing hedonism of Cosmopolis fed hardly twenty thousand, who lived always under the shadow of famine. The minds and hands of the men of Gaustana had won abundance from a land the Gods made only for the gaudy hardskinned lizard, the spiny, dusty cactus, and the small furry creatures that hide all day in burrows, coming out at dusk to sit all night with heads flung back and mouths agape to catch the droplets of dew that are both their food and their drink.

I wondered what manner of men these were who had created a secret kingdom amid the sands and who appeared content with it, not seeking to extend their sway. I wondered more when we came within sight of the walls of the city, somewhat larger than Kamardol, but smaller by far than the great cities of Hindustan.

Gaustana was perfect of its kind when we first spied the city dark against the swift desert sunrise. We saw walls of sandstone and granite take form as the diffused pinks and violets of the dawn gave way to harsh daylight that painted angles and straight lines. The city capped a rounded hill close to the granite cliffs on the eastern heights of the broad valley that extended almost true north and south. Those cliffs rose above the two tallest towers, which shone square and red against their gray backdrop. A second hill somewhat lower was as well placed for observation or defense just north of the main eminence and was crowned by a small citadel. Its walls were yellow, as were the square boxes of barracks those walls enclosed. The barracks reached in like a massive stairway to a square hall faced with rough-hewn columns. The smaller hill was smooth and treeless, and it was bare of the clusters of brick dwellings divided by broad avenues that spilled down the rump of the greater hill. The yellow citadel with its sweeping glacis was obviously the military strongpoint, while the greater city gave shelter to the civil populace.

Noting how well sited the paired eminences were to support each other against attack, the greater commanding the southern road into the valley, the lesser the northern road, I tied a knot in the fringe of the shawl I wore in my character as a peaceful merchant of Hindustan. Knowing we would be watched all the time we were in the territories of Gaustana, I had decided to use the ancient method of knotting strings to note my observations. Immediately I had tied the knot, I thanked Vishnu that I had not tried to make written notes, for we were challenged within ten minutes of our first distant view of the twin citadels.

Twenty horsemen wearing dark cloaks and round helmets that were flat on top like inverted pots swept down from the grove of junipers on our right hand. Their lances were leveled, and their leader, whose orange cloak was lightly barred with white, held a long curved sword. Like his followers', his face was hidden by a pointed mask of joined steel plates that jutted out from the sloping sides of his helmet to give him the neckless, powerful aspect of a great, blind mole.

'Know you not that the road is closed?' He spoke the Prakrit patois we had first heard from the people of the oasis Gaustana-

279

lezli, his voice rolling hollow from his steel snout. 'Know you not that this land is forbidden?'

As we had agreed, Barniar replied, accentuating the liquid accent of his native place, 'O Captain of Hosts, we bear no evil. Our small numbers, armed only for defense against bandits, would not threaten an oasis of a single well. How much less, then, the realm of Gaustana that is a bejeweled glory at the heart of the continent?'

'You speak like a man of Hindustan,' said the officer, the keen edge of contempt cutting through the booming echo of his voice within his helmet. 'Say who you are?'

'Merchants,' quavered Barniar, 'poor merchants of East Hindustan who have come to peddle some poor trinkets hardly worthy of your attention. Trinkets of ivory and amber . . .'

'I am not interested in your wares,' the officer cut him off. 'I am a sculptor and a farmer, not a merchant. Have you come so far, not knowing this land is forbidden except by invitation?'

Marveling that a captain of the guards should describe himself as a farmer and, if I heard right, a sculptor, I answered, 'As my cousin has said, O Captain of Hosts, we bear no evil. We have heard only that sometimes the great city condescends to buy wares, amusing if hardly of any value. So we have come to bejeweled Gaustana.'

'It is forbidden, merchant,' the officer repeated sternly. He waited a full minute before adding, somewhat less sternly, 'But you have come a long way in your small numbers. We are bidden to succor the wayfarer. I will not turn you back.'

'Praise and honor to your graciousness, towering as your might,' Barniar said hastily. His self-abnegation made my teeth ache, though the officer swelled beneath the flattery as a tight-clenched rose opens to the dewy dawn. 'We are indeed tired and worn after our long ride.'

'I have not said that you may stay and trade. I am empowered only to turn away travelers or bring them in for examination. Ride before us. We shall ride behind.'

I was, once again, startled by the inconsistency between the captain's aspect and his words. Sinister behind his black steel snout, his manner was far sterner than the routine interception of a small caravan demanded. The guards before Kamardol would have been more casual. They would not have prated about forbidden lands as if the Gods had laid a taboo on this pleasant and somewhat arid valley. Still, no officer of Kamardol was 'bidden to succor the wayfarer.' His task was to halt the wayfarer.

Puzzled by those incongruities, I was glad that we had come to Gaustana. This was obviously no Cosmopolis to yield in form, without yielding in substance, to the lightning of two thousand spears, nor was it a party of marauding Huns to be harried into extinction by the exercise of tactical craft. This was, in truth, a city, perhaps the seat of a coherent, powerful civilization. Only through the direct observation we sought could we find the key to conquest – the secret flaws the Gods discerned before commanding us to scourge the city. Already savoring the impressions I would receive when we came into the city, the direct imprint no travelers' tales could stamp upon the eye and ear, I knew we would not fail in our task. I would search out the flaw, and we would take Gaustana. I had already marked two avenues of attack that were impossible, and I knew that I would, in time, find the way destined for our conquest.

I had, from outside, already formed a general impression of high, forbidding towers and high-angled battlements. I could already have drawn a plan of the greater Citadel with its geometric suburbs, its barbicans, guard posts, and ironbound gates, too high and too broad for perfect strength under the ram and far too large for ordinary traffic. They were the only obvious weak point I noted, and we were ourselves too few to lay the protracted siege that could breach them. Still, I was heartened. My own small caravan would soon pass unresisted through those gates to find the inevitable weakness of Gaustana. It might well lie in the people themselves, rather than in their fortifications.

We did not enter those gates. We had come so close without hindrance because we appeared a common trading caravan, but we could come no further because our humble condition demanded no courtesies. Perhaps we might have done better to approach in state as an envoy from the Kings of Kamardol. I put that thought aside. A royal embassy, arriving uninvited, might well have been turned back at the pass – with courtesy or without.

The captain of the guard directed us to a compound set in a hollow on the outer fringe of the dwellings. Looking up at the high walls, I thought at first we were imprisoned. But the captain said we were free to depart under escort whenever we wished to leave the realm. As long as we remained, he added, we might not leave the caravanserai. Merchants would come there to trade with us, if we were, after examination, permitted to trade.

Disgusted, I flung myself on the floor of the bare hall while Barniar saw to the unloading of our goods. I slept long, seeking refuge from my frustration, although the baked clay bricks concentrated the intense heat in which the caravanserai trembled. Late morning in late summer in the desert would have been unpleasant had we been given a windswept garden at the crest of the hill with thick awnings of brush to divert the sun. It was almost beyond enduring in the caravanserai's hollow bowl, which was cut off from the slightest breeze though wholly exposed to the sun. When I awoke several hours past the crest of the day, my tunic was sodden with sweat.

The Gaustanans had given us only a single amphora of water, which they had need to conserve against the dry winter that lay ahead. We had emptied our own skins of their stinking liquid upon first seeing the seeming abundance of water in Gaustana. Allowing myself a double handful to wash the salt sweat off my face, I sourly resolved that I would go on no more journeys in any other character but my own.

Although I had suffered physical discomforts much more onerous, I could not endure our enforced cringing and the Gaustanans' disdain. In our debased position we could not even protest that our quarters must have been abandoned when the city hangman found a better torture chamber or that the water given us was hardly sufficient for an inactive cricket. Had we protested, we would have received no more attention than would the cricket's pleading for water. No more than they could have understood the cricket could our hosts have comprehended that humble merchants, intent only upon profits, might complain of their treatment.

I had despaired when I learned that we were to be confined beyond hope of gathering the information we sought. In my anger I swore that I would somehow find the key to unlock this city to our troops – and break its aloof pride. I was reflecting on the pleasure of watching protracted tortures when a pair of men-at-arms in those damnable snouted helmets entered the hall. One set a small wooden stool precisely in its center.

'Rise, rise for the Lord Examiner!' they commanded with the kindly contempt of a servant addressing a bewildered dog.

The Lord Examiner himself followed them by a few minutes. He did not glance at us until he had settled his flabby bulk on the stool, which it overlapped in all directions. Within his pallid jowls, a smaller face was enclosed, sharp-nosed, hollow-eyed, and avid. His pendulous body, swathed in a fine white-linen overrobe barred with yellow, moved with neither the slow grace nor the ponderousness appropriate to its bulk, but abruptly and angularly. All his gestures spoke of a fanatic against himself as well as the world. With delight I watched round globules of sweat form a puddle in the crease between his second and third chins and trickle down the broad bosom of his green tunic. The taut fabric outlined pendant breasts like a fat old woman's. He dabbed at the spots with a silken kerchief, displaying neither annoyance nor concern, but the abstracted air of a lackey polishing a lamp. He liked his body, it seemed, no more than I did.

'You are merchants of East Hindustan?' The flat voice squeezed between thin, colorless lips neither asked a question nor affirmed a fact. It flung a challenge.

'Yes, My Lord!' Barniar's answer was greasy with the oil of humility. 'We have undertaken a perilous journey over the mountains and across the sands to your glorious city. We have heard that among your people, there may be some who may be amused at our paltry goods.'

'Whence come you?' the Examiner demanded as if his first question had not been answered.

'From the land between the rivers, My Lord,' replied Barniar, 'from the edge of the great salt sea, we have made our way northward. . . .'

I composed my features into a humility as Barniar droned through the tale upon which we had agreed. It was substantially an account of his own travels until his imprisonment by the mountaineers. He told it convincingly, despite constant sharp interruptions from the Examiner. Listening, I half believed myself that we had truly bought our way unhampered through the territories of the rajahs of the eastern mountains. As Barniar spun his tale, sometimes impassioned, sometimes cringing, the imagined journey became a living reality in my mind.

Barniar told the tale so fluently that I wondered how much cunning fantasy had embellished his account of his captivity among the Huns. I hastily suppressed the thought that flawed my concentration. My purpose was not to guard us from Barniar's duplicity, but to convince the Examiner that we were, in truth, but harmless merchants.

While our porters showed our packs, Barniar prattled that we offered choice pieces from the wealth of the heart of the continent, brought earlier from Cosmopolis and other cities of the north. He concluded with the merchant's ritual plea to the official: 'Please choose what you will, My Lord, for yourself!'

'You are Brahmans?' the Examiner challenged, ignoring the offer.

'Yes, My Lord,' Barniar replied. 'In East Hindustan we Brahmans often set up as merchants. We keep but a small part of the proceeds for ourselves, the rest going to support our temples and our schools.'

'I have heard how wholly unselfish you Brahmans are,' he sneered. My heart leaped. If he permitted himself such a personal barb, our tale must be believed.

'In the east,' the Examiner continued, 'it is true. But I have never heard of Brahmans of the west trading as merchants.'

I feared then that this cunning had crept through our disguise.

'We are of the east, My Lord,' Barniar insisted, 'though I too have heard that our haughty brothers of the west consider our trade sacrilege. With their powerful patronage they have no need to sacrifice themselves in support of their academies and their shrines. We, however, count the sacrifice not an abasement, but an ennoblement. We feel . . .'

'I am not interested in your petty, superstitious quarrels,' the Examiner interrupted contemptuously.

My breath coursed once more through my throat. He was not,

284

after all, toying with us, knowing already that we came from the west, which had sent an expedition against Gaustana. He was merely parading his knowledge of the lands south of the mountains.

'Tell me again of your travels!'

'So be it, My Lord,' said Barniar submissively and began again.

'No, not you! You, fellow! Tell me of your travels.'

I endured the probing questions and the exclamations of disbelief. At the end of my tale the Examiner appeared content.

'Know you, merchants,' he declared, 'that you may stay and trade. You will remain within the caravanserai, and our merchants will come to you. I am half satisfied that you are what you say you are. Should it prove otherwise, there is but one punishment. It is death.'

'Thank you, My Lord, thank you,' hymned Barniar. 'We have no fear of that. And now, My Lord, will you not choose some trinkets for yourself?'

Again the Examiner ignored the proffered gifts. He leaned forward as far as his great paunch permitted and smiled. His narrow lips curved over small, even teeth, his pouched eyes came alight, and his aloof manner dropped away. His lean inner face worked with passion, though the great encircling coil of flesh from his forehead to his chin remained unmoving. His true inner face was a small dark animal writhing in a pit of snow. It was not a pleasant passion. I was drawn, nonetheless, to the man's intensity, half in fear that he might still be toying with us and half in fascination at the abrupt transformation. I forgot, for a moment, my overwhelming disappointment that our mission was in vain.

'And, now, do you not wonder why this realm of Gaustana is forbidden? Brahmans that you are, though merchants you be, have you no wonder as to what manner of land you have come upon?'

Barniar answered properly, that is to say without the particular emphasis that might have dammed the Examiner's garrulousness.

'We have of course, My Lord, heard innumerable and magnificent tales of the transcendent glory of Gaustana. But we would, of course, hear much more – whatever, My Lord, it pleases you to bestow upon us out of your wisdom.'

'Know you that even after the death of the blessed Ashoka, the Bodhisattva, the greatest Emperor the world has known, there was peace and joy throughout Hindustan and in the southern marches of the continent. But slowly the old ways – the evil, superstitious ways – began to creep back again. One man was oppressed by another, who asserted that the Gods had set him apart at birth. No – do not interrupt. I have not come to argue with you. I am not foolish enough to believe that I can turn you toward Enlightenment. I hope only to give you some knowledge that, someday, perhaps. . . .'

We were entrapped by a true fanatic, a man possessed by a single obsession. Despite his own disclaimer, I realized, he would strive to bend us to the Buddhist heresy that, struggling south of the mountains, had found new soil among the weeds of the desert.

His monologue rolled on for five hours into the cool of the early evening. He might have been somewhat briefer had Barniar and I not encouraged him with careful questions and judicious objections. When he finally stopped, we possessed a description of Gaustana that would have taken us weeks to amass by other means – if we had been permitted to roam freely through the city and to question the citizens without hindrance.

I was puzzled at the Examiner's readiness – nay, determination – to give us so much information, even though I later learned that it was his practice to harangue all newcomers whom he judged capable of understanding. The desire to confirm their own beliefs by converting others was strong in the Gaustanans, as it is irresistible to all heretics and, indeed, to all who are outcast because of strange practices, sexual, social, or spiritual. Gaustana, I later heard, had within the past decade begun to send out men charged with the mission of bringing the people of the far oases to their belief. Still, the Examiner knew that an armed force threatened the borders of his realm, and he should not have been so careless with information when any intelligence might assist the invader. I believe he must have spoken without guarding his words because of the same arrogance that led him to accept our false identity even at the moment of peril. So complacently certain were the Gaustanans of their perfect security amid their aloofness and superiority that they could not conceive that any power could truly threaten them. Perhaps he hoped to frighten all enemies off by the tales we would spread – all remarkably true in detail. At any rate, the Lord Examiner spoke and we listened.

I must repeat his account in my own words, for I could not possibly reproduce the torrents of words he poured forth with a fanatic's fluency. Besides, my final account came from others as well – from foreign traders who were confined with us in the caravanserai, from the Gaustanan merchants we saw, and from my own brief incursion into the forbidden city. I shall, therefore, set down the report I gave to Harrap, reserving only the technical military data for a later treatise that will be a manual of strategy for the generals of Kamardol. Intent upon conquest, Harrap was impatient with the discussion of history and society he thought irrelevant. I thought them irrelevant neither to our immediate purpose nor to our greater purpose. My report then:

When, perhaps a century after the death of the heretic Emperor Ashoka, the True Religion began to reclaim its proper place, certain baseborn men fled north of the mountains. They went not only in fear of their lives, but in fear of being deprived of the dignity that they had usurped through the pernicious doctrine that holds all men to be born without predestined places. They took with them not only their families and their wealth, but other Pariahs who did not yet profess their heresy and some men born men who had renounced their human status. Chief among the fugitives were the descendents of a concubine of Ashoka. These leaders took to themselves the title of Waysah, which means 'the seed of the Bodhisattva' – or so they came to interpret the term. The Waysah in time became kings of a city they established in the desert. Their realm they called Gaustana after the Buddha.

Hidden between the mountains and the sands so that the world knew it not, the community grew large. The Gaustanans were notably industrious, and they discovered veins of gold and semi-precious gems, which, when the time came, they exchanged for the goods they could not themselves make or grow. Through the centuries the original settlers were joined by others – to the Gaustanans, the oppressed who were vigorous enough and bold enough to flee to a new and fuller life; to me, the dregs of the established societies, criminals who refused to accept the proper order of mankind as ordained by the Gods and who rejected the just orders of their anointed kings.

The Gaustanans welcomed all the fugitives, for they were eager to employ their skills and their energy. The Waysah laid three conditions upon them. They were required to accept and embrace the heresy that the Gaustanans called the Dharma, the Truth, being the doctrines of the Gautama Buddha. The new-comers might amass wealth by their labors – as long as they rendered total obedience to the Waysah. By those two conditions the Gaustanans compelled all men to bow to authority – spiritual and temporal – though they professed to detest compulsion and authority alike. Finally, no one might depart from Gaustana except on the business of the Dharma or the Waysah. Only within the past fifty years had the Waysah permitted outsiders to come to Gaustana to trade. All strangers were received as we had been – that is, they were sequestered within the caravanserai, where they dealt only with designated lower officials and authorized merchants. In form the Gaustanans set no high value on trade, for they asserted that they themselves possessed all material things necessary to a holy life. In practice trade was a pillar of the city's existence.

When we came to it, Gaustana was a settled and powerful community, numbering upward of fifty thousand men, women, and children in some seventy-five hundred families throughout their domains. No more than two thousand were soldiers permanently under arms. They served chiefly to lend pomp to ceremonies and to guard the kings and high officials. Their chief force the Gaustanans called the militia. A fixed number of able-bodied men were, in strict rotation, required to render one week's service in arms each month. The total number of militia, the Examiner claimed, was nearly fifteen thousand. I learned later that in his desire to impress us with their strength, he had included men of great age and boys just beginning their training, indeed everyone who would soon wear or had ever worn the black snouted helmet. They could, in reality, probably muster no more than five thousand fighting militia.

The captain of the patrol that had halted us was such a militiaman, rendering his monthly service to his king. He was, as he had said, a farmer in his normal life. But he was also a sculptor. Every man of Gaustana – and most women as well – freely labored to enhance the glory of the Dharma. Many were sculptors who created the images of the Buddhas, the Bodhisattvas, the Arhats, all the pantheon of Gaustana. Their works varied from intricately worked gold statuettes no bigger than a thumbnail to the enormous stone idols carved into cliffs three hundred feet high. Other Gaustanans were painters who adorned the images or re-created scenes from the life of the Buddha in murals and great scrolls. Dancers, actors, and poets gave of their talents in dramas that at once exalted the Buddha and diverted the populace. Those who lacked particular talents served in other ways. Some directed the constant hymn of praise to the Buddhas that was the heart-beat of the life of Gaustana. Others worked as carpenters, masons, cooks, and plumbers – all the craftsmen who built and maintained the great religious edifices. All such service, they claimed, was given voluntarily, and no man or woman demurred, nor could any demur. These religious labors amounted to a full half of all the labor performed in Gaustana.

Only one group performed no manual or artistic labor for the glory of the Buddha, since they were held to labor without ceasing for His glory. In the realm of more than fifty thousand, at least five thousand males were monks. Splendid in many-colored robes and snug in their palatial monasteries, they spent their days in prayer, divination, and recording the *Sutras*. All things were given to these monks without their being required to pay either in money, which the Gaustanans called dinara, or in labor. They were honored above all others except the Waysah because their constant prayers were, the Gaustanans said, 'as the blast of ten times ten thousand brazen trumpets calling the Heavens to shower their benevolence upon Gaustana.'

The King of Gaustana vigorously asserted his claim to descent from the Emperor Ashoka. Besides his name-title, Waysah, he bore the appellations Son of the Bodhisattva and Lord of the Dharma. In a somewhat bewildering fashion he also claimed to be in the hereditary reincarnation of Anand, who accompanied the Gautama on his search. The Waysah had originally exercised the functions of both king and high priest. Although he still retained the latter title, he had lost most of the powers of that position – and a portion of his temporal power as well – to another 'reincarnation' of another Bodhisattva who bore the title Lord of the Sangha, the monkhood. The validity of his spiritual birth was certified by the ballots of the monks, for he was also Abbot of the Monastery of the Sacred Mount, the smaller hill, that I had first thought the city's chief citadel.

The Monastery preserved the left arm of the Gautama Buddha and the seamless garment He wore when He lay down under the sāl tree in Kusinagara to die. The Gaustanans believed that the four Protecting Deities that guarded their realm kept their abode on the Sacred Mount and that they were nurtured by the constant hum of prayer that rose like incense to the ear from the Monastery. The diviners declared that Gaustana would endure until the relics were stolen, the Monastery sacked, and the Protecting Deities driven away. They did not predict such catastrophe, but merely asserted that the city would endure as long as it did *not* occur.

Despite the monks' essential contribution to the security of the realm, many laymen were angered by their indolence and their arrogance. They complained that the new technique of 'Enlightenment by temptations like the Buddha's' were no more than a pretext for sanctified orgies. Although both sacrifices and temple prostitution were proscribed by their religion, the monks' sacred revels were becoming a scandal.

I heard one fat merchant, thinking himself safe from our ears, mutter to another, 'My daughter is summoned to the Sacred Mount for "instruction," as they say. Pray Buddha for me that she will not return witless and debauched.' Still, the puffed-up Pariahs of Gaustana held in such awe all the aspects of their religion – which was their life – that they talked only secretly of their unease.

The people of Gaustana appeared, by any standard, content in their isolation – aside from the levies upon their labor, to which they did not object; the straitness of their lives, of which they did not speak; and the increasing perversity of the monks, which they abhorred. They did not feel their religion onerous, for laymen were not compelled to the renunciations to which the monks pretended and many, in truth, practiced. They called their Buddhism the Middle Gate in distinction to both the Narrow Gate sects of Hindustan, with their strict rules and circumscribed promises of the future life, and the Wide Gate doctrines, which were springing up within the mountains to promise all men salvation without effort or self-denial, as long only as they believed. Some laymen refused to amass wealth beyond a competence, just as some like the Lord Examiner neither ate meat nor drank strong spirits. But no man was forced to such excesses of renunciation. Persistent and open debauchery they punished severely, executing the miscreant upon his third offense. A few of their elders, curiously enough, maintained that stringent asceticism should be punished with equal severity. The Buddha, they contended, had preached moderation in all things. Since the essence of their doctrine was the Middle Gate, they contended that an excess of extreme virtue was as abhorrent as an excess of open vice. Those fanatics of moderation were, like all men except the monks, restrained by a unique institution.

In Gaustana all hereditary office except, of course, the Waysah's was forbidden as if the very concept were the handiwork of the Devils. The Gaustanans held that prejudice because they were all in reality Pariahs who sought to evade their preordained destiny. Nonetheless, men were qualified for the dignity they called Judgeship only through their fathers' possession thereof – or through the rare special act of creation-in-concert by King and Sangha. Still the College of Judges could exclude candidates it considered unworthy, whether they were qualified by birth or by creation. The Judges, fifty-six in number, presided over the settlement of all disputes among citizens or between citizens and the realm. Even the Waysah did not oppose its decisions for fear that the College would rule that he could not. The judges were tendered great honor and all they could reasonably desire of material things. They were neither permitted to deal for gain nor required to perform the 'quarter labors,' artistic, manual, or military. They lived, it seemed to me, isolated in isolated Gaustana amid their dignity.

Two nights before our departure, when we had sold all our goods and hoped to gather no further information, I was summoned by one such judge. The Keeper of the Caravanserai explained that the judge wished to buy a certain ivory statuette of the Buddha set with rubies. Since he was not an authorized merchant, the judge could no more than any ordinary citizen enter the caravanserai. Since his dignity would not permit him to come to me outside the walls, I was carried in a closed palanquin through the great gates of Gaustana. I had already learned that the gates were broad and high to the detriment of strength in order to give ingress to the towering images of the Buddha and the Bodhisattvas that were conveyed from the Sacred Mount through the streets of the city on their holy days.

I had contrived to work the sealed curtains of the palanquin apart a crack, but I saw no more than a confusion of lights, brightly painted façades, and well-dressed throngs. I stepped out of the palanquin directly into the ante-chamber of the judge's residence and was led through an unlit corridor to a small chamber half lit by a single oil lamp. A slight man of about fifty years was perched upon a high-backed stool. He seemed to be all foreground and no substance, like a painted leather puppet, for the light was too little to give depth or rotundity to his figure. Gaustana's obsessive secrecy had hardly been breached by my entrance.

We discussed the beauty of the statuette for a few minutes, turning it over in our hands. At length he offered me somewhat more than Barniar had said it was worth. I was torn between the cupidity I should display in my character of merchant and the desire to win favor that should also move the merchant. Since I had been warned that the judge was not permitted to accept a gift, I finally halved the difference.

'I can see that you are a merchant who looks to tomorrow,' the judge chirped like a bright-eyed sparrow. 'But I warn you that I can be of no help to you in the future. Tell me, whence come you?'

I repeated the tale we had told the Lord Examiner, the judge from time to time interposing questions. I feared first that our pretense had somehow been discovered. After fifteen minutes I realized that the energetic old man, who was confined by his own great honors, was merely curious. His persistent questions on the strange customs of men and the mischances of nature were such as my father might have asked. I felt at once annoyance at his frightening me with the intrusive questions and a new sense of security.

'It is odd to see a merchant who is a Brahman,' he said sharply, raising the hair on my neck again. 'And it is odder still to see a merchant whose right hand displays not only the callouses of a sword's hilt, but the thickened fingertips of the lute player.'

'We bear swords for our protection through the wild mountains, Excellency,' I replied. 'We must, naturally, exercise with them. But knowing that all men – even strangers – are secure within your realm, we left them before we entered the borders of Gaustana.'

'And how will you defend yourself on your homeward journey?'

'If our cache has been broken, Excellency, we will buy new swords in a certain border village I know,' I replied. I was thankful that we were no longer turning the statuette over between us, for he could not have failed to see the sweat burst out on my palms.

'The village is called?'

I offered him a name. As the intricate syllables left my lips, I realized that it was the home village that Ranbir had so often described, though he had not returned since enrolling in the Royal Guard as a boy of thirteen.

'And the lute?' the judge asked, apparently satisfied as to the village.

'I play the lute, Excellency.'

'Yes, man. But where is your lute?'

'Among our baggage, Excellency,' I replied, blessing my own stubbornness that would not let me leave the lute behind, 'among the unopened bales.'

'Why is it concealed?'

'Because, Excellency,' I stammered, 'it is not fitting in my country for a Brahman to play the lute, no more than it is for a merchant to do so. I concealed my lute, foolishly perhaps, because I feared that Gaustana might know the same taboo. Besides, to play the lute makes a man appear too youthful, perhaps unworthy of grave business.'

'We have no taboos – no *such* taboos, at least – young man,' he smiled. 'I play the lute myself. Would you play a round with me?'

'I am honored, Excellency.' I gave him the reply he demanded.

A servant brought two lutes of no low quality, and we sang against each other for two hours or more. His execution was passable, though he could never have been more than an eager amateur even before his fingers stiffened.

As I departed, the judge said, 'You must come and see me when you come to Gaustana again, young singer. I cannot help your trade, but I would be glad of your company.'

His questions had, after all, risen from the searching curiosity of an enclosed man. Next morning the Lord Examiner demanded to see my lute. He seemed chagrined at his failure to discover my skill, rather than aroused to new suspicions.

The next night but one we were permitted to depart. We rode southward, whence we had come. During the first day's ride a squad of militia accompanied us to ensure that we neither strayed nor halted. I went meekly, for I already had that for which I had come.

Twenty-five

When we finally rejoined him, Harrap was raging like the Sacred Bull that has known freedom unto license and honor unto idolatry – until the moment the gilt chains fetter him for the sacrifice.

We had been a long time returning. To dull the vigilance of the militia patrols, I had for two days led my little caravan south to the edge of the mountains. Only after another three days had we met our scouts ranging the desolate land in search of us. An additional five days had been consumed by our circuitous ride – west, north, and east again – around the domains of Gaustana before we came to our own force.

When Anand rode out to welcome me a few miles from our encampment, he was wan and bitter. He rejoiced equally to see me alive whom he had not thought to see again, and he rejoiced to relinquish the office of adjutant to me. He could not longer endure Harrap's rages and caprices.

Harrap, he told me, had given the order to mount and ride against Gaustana when I failed to return after the ten days he had granted me for my mission. He had willfully cast off the counsels of strategy, defying his ignorance of Gaustana, its troops, its defenses, and its terrain. He had sworn our officers to a sacred oath to storm the city – to free us if we were held captive, to avenge us if we were slain. The Horse, he had directed, might remain with His escort in the twilight land between the watered valleys and the barren sands.

The challenge, he swore, had been hurled, the will of the Gods defied. The Horse had led us to Gaustana, and the Gaustanans had not made submission, but had dispatched patrols to harry us. Yakir the Singer, he wept, was the blood in the veins of his right arm, his brother by the twin swords and before the Gods, and, like himself, breath of the Stallion, which is the breath of the world. Where was Yakir, he demanded, but slain by the false Gaustanans or shackled by them in iron chains?

The Bastards had gone sullenly to their duty, trotting north to guard the Horse while all the rest turned southward to the battle. The squadrons were mounting one by one, their guidons awakening in the breeze, their bright-scoured armor flashing in the morning sun, their bridles jingling cheerily, their freshly oiled reins soft between fingers that hardly felt the suppleness through the cracked carapace of horn sheathing them. Weary of the savorless wandering, the soldiers yearned toward the liberating passion of battle – and toward the loot of conquest. Black fear, too, was mounted at their backs, close behind their rainbow cloaks, and each man muttered his demand for life to his own Divinities. For the first time they rode against a power wholly unknown, a force that might shatter their shining array as the sand beetle's scarlet and black armor cracks between their own playful fingers.

The scouts were already away and the cavalry screen was beginning to move out when Harrap, his hand on his pommel, directed the priest to invoke victory.

Poignantly ridiculous in a faded yellow robe hanging in loose pleats that had once stretched across an amplitude of proud flesh, the priest stepped out of the circle of horses so that the troops could see him plain. 'There can be no invocation!' he declared, his voice clear and high as if he spoke to tens of thousands in the great arena of Kamardol.

'What have you said?' demanded Harrap, striding forward so that he looked down into the priest's slack face. The broad fingers of his right hand drew the rawhide wrist thong of his axe upward until the shaft lay in his palm, the head hanging down beside his leg.

'There can be no invocation, Highness,' repeated the priest to Harrap and two thousand soldiers. 'The Stallion must be purified before we ride upon Gaustana. As you know, He was not with one mare, but perhaps six before we found Him.'

The axe rose six inches toward the horizontal, though still by Harrap's side, and the corded veins of his wrist swelled. The priest did not step back. He had chosen his moment well. A private declaration to Harrap would have meant bitter argument, but this public declaration even Harrap could not defy.

That realization came to Harrap within seconds. The axe hung loose again from its thong, and he asked bitterly, 'How long will the purification take, O Brahman?'

'I do not know, O prince. Perhaps five, perhaps ten days.'

His cheeks and forehead yellow with sick rage, the butterfly cicatrice crimson between his slitted eyes, Harrap ordered Anand to recall the scouts.

Caged by the ceremony, Harrap had sulked in his yurt, riding out once each day to watch the rites of purification, but speaking to no one. The priest, unperturbed, had repeated the complex rites six times, pouring oblations of milk and wheat to Vayu to restore the sacred seed of the Horse. 'Vayu,' the Brahmayanas say, 'is the vital air, and the vital air is the transformer of seeds; by means of seed, he thus puts seed into the Horse.'

When I heard the tale, I wondered if the priest had contrived the northward flight of the ripe mares to draw the Horse away from Gaustana and delay our assault. He later swore to me that he had not done so. I could not disbelieve him, since he acknowledged that he *had* insisted upon the rites to prevent Harrap's hurling our force against the unknown perils of Gaustana, where it might shatter as even the eagle falls broken when he hurtles against a fog-wrapped crag. Had it been necessary, the priest said, he would have forced an omen. Before the priest's candor, I could not doubt his denial that he had loosed the mares. But I wondered again at the flexibility of his belief, so subservient to his own will that it had no fixed shape.

The priest told me he had hoped only to force Harrap to wait for the intelligence I would bring. I wondered, though, if he had also expected me to moderate Harrap's fierce determination to crush Gaustana – even if the city's power were ten times our own. However, I brought no plea for peace to our council, but anger spawned by humiliation to ignite with Harrap's fury of frustration.

Gorbabordol was with the Horse, and I did not invite Anand since I feared he might plead for his co-religionists. Except for those two, the same men were gathered in the sunlight a few hours after my return who had taken counsel by the fire almost a month earlier – Harrap, the priest, Ranbir, Mirab, and myself. I delivered my report, perhaps somewhat longer, but the same in essence as the account I have already given.

I was about to put forward the plan of attack I had worked out during my long ride when Mirab broke in.

'Well,' he said, 'it's a pity. It is a great pity! Though, as the old King used to say, a battle lost does not mean a campaign failed. But I can't see any other course. I'm sure I'm saying what's in everyone's mind, when I can say it. They're too strong for us . . .'

'It is fortunate,' the priest said ingenuously, 'that the Stallion has turned aside. In this case, neither honor nor the divine word requires us to do more than wisdom counsels. He is today again free and again inspired after purification. We must follow Him, reserving our attack on Gaustana for other times.'

'If their patrols were not spread so wide, or if those patrols sometimes slept,' added Ranbir, 'surprise might carry us to our goal. If the inner valley of Gaustana were more open and not sealed by guards at either narrow end . . . if their citadels were not perched so high and the walls were not built so strong . . . Ah, well, it would have been an interesting fight.'

'I'll get us moving again, then, shall I, General?' Mirab asked, leaning on a short pike-staff as he rose. The question was mere courtesy; he assumed the answer.

'Sit down, Mirab,' commanded Harrap almost jovially. 'We are not quite through. There remain matters to discuss.'

'Oh, other details, eh?' said Mirab, subsiding with a grunt. 'That's all right . . . Just don't want the Horse to get too far ahead.'

Harrap waited until Mirab was still before speaking so low we leaned forward to hear him. 'I find it painful, gentlemen – and I speak now from my heart – I find it painful to instruct my elders, who have been my teachers in warcraft and in the ways of the Gods. But, gentlemen, it seems that you have forgotten the purpose of our Quest.'

'I say now, General, that's not fair, you know,' protested Mirab. Ranbir and the priest were silent.

'We are *not* charged to enjoy a pleasant ride across the pleasant countryside, plucking such easy victories as come our way,' Harrap continued. 'We are *not* charged to shun battle because the enemy is, perhaps, stronger than we are. We *are* charged to follow the Perfect Stallion . . . to open the road for Him if He is opposed. He has now led us to Gaustana, and the heretics of Gaustana would deny Him passage. We have no right to talk of whether we shall attack or not. The only question before us is how we shall attack.'

'I say, General, that's a bit rough, when, after all. . . .' Mirab began. Seeing Ranbir look to the priest to reply, he let his voice die in a mumble.

'Highness,' the priest said deliberately, 'these Gaustanans sought to harry us, but they could not bar His progress. The Stallion turned aside Himself – of His own will.'

'Sophistry,' snapped Harrap, 'Brahmanical sophistry. He has led us across the desert to Gaustana. Must He batter His head against the city gates before you accept the manifest will of the Gods? If we pass through the territory of the greatest city in our path, meeting resistance, but not compelling submission, our mission is a mockery. It is not a true Seeking, but an evasion . . . not what you promised, but a fraud like the false Seekings that have gone before.'

'I read the Gods' will more closely than you, O Prince,' insisted the priest. 'That is my vocation. And I tell you there has been no frontal encounter. We are not committed, unless He leads us directly toward the stronghold of Gaustana.'

'Heresy! We are brought to destroy a virulent heresy,' Harrap's normal rumble was becoming an echo of the priest's own prophetic tone. 'If there is a purpose in our quest, a purpose beyond our own glory, it is this – to shatter the heresy and punish these treacherous, disobedient Pariahs. We are the scourge of the Gods.'

This passionate declaration, this saying of what should not have been said, left us stricken and silent for minutes. I too was shocked, though I had for some time sensed the fatal conviction growing within Harrap. He was, beyond question, inspired, but,

I wondered, did his inspiration come from the Gods or from derangement within himself?

Yet Harrap's will was my own will, for I too was determined to attack Gaustana. He had chosen to carry the argument to the mystery of our purpose, rather than the reality of our predicament. Since he spoke not only in the tones of a priest, but in the words of a priest, I could best support him with textual authority.

'Gentlemen,' I said, 'the Brahmayanas warn against interpretations excessively literal. It is written: "Only a Pariah and a foolish Brahman believe that all answers reside in the text." It is also written: "Him who does not acknowledge the Stallion must you slay." But I would suggest that we discuss our purpose rather than the texts.'

'It is the purpose I discuss,' the priest replied hotly. 'We are, of course, charged to follow the Stallion. That is clear. But beyond that, our greater purpose is to bring Him safe to Kamardol when His year has passed . . .'

'It is written, "Without declining the challenge . . ." ' I objected.

'No challenge has been offered,' the priest answered. His anger was spent, and his voice was calm as a staff officer's presenting a plan of campaign. 'There is only a snare to entrap us – if we insist upon thrusting ourselves into it. How much better would it not be to pass by now, with full honor, and later to return with a great army and crush the hive of heretics.'

'Yes,' agreed Mirab, 'that's the answer, the perfect solution. Soldierly and sensible. Send out some probes now, some probes to get an idea of how they fight. Then, next year, when the Seeking's done, we'll return. We'll return and crush Gaustana, occupy it and add it to our Kings' domains.'

'We have not enough men to hold the city,' Ranbir reminded us, 'even if we take it.'

'No!' Harrap's voice cracked across the bland flow of complacent agreement and mutual congratulation. 'We will not sate ourselves with logical justifications for cowardice. I will attack. This prize shall not pass from me.'

The silence swelled palpable in the sunlight, growing to two minutes, three, and five. I was suddenly aware of the sounds of the encampment around us, the horses nickering and jangling their bridles, the men shouting and clanking their equipment. Disgrace lay palpable between us in the sunlight, black dishonor so close and so clear we could feel its slimy skin against our fingertips. I shuddered to behold for the first time in the history of our race officers of Kamardol prepared to defy their general's command.

'Your orders, General?' I asked formally to break the portentous silence.

Harrap did not reply. He sought no victory by default, but preferred to hazard the ultimate disaster, his will against their combined will. The silent minutes passed, and we avoided each other's eyes.

'We follow you, of course,' Ranbir finally said, brusque and blunt. 'I fear it is to death. It is odd, but I taught you to command – as much as you had to be taught. And now you command our deaths. Your orders, General?'

'Of course,' Mirab echoed, 'we follow you. Was there a question? I never knew . . . thought we were just discussing the matter. Can't help it, you know, can't help the way I feel, but we ride when you say we ride. I may be old, but, by Vishnu, I'm still a soldier . . . know how to take orders.'

'I could, I suppose, dissent further,' the priest said wearily. 'You know full well how I read the auguries. But you leave me little choice. I cannot tarnish this perfect Seeking by withholding the invocation to victory. Even if that invocation is but the prelude to our destruction, the Seeking shall have been perfect to its end.'

Harrap leaned back and invited, 'Now, Yakir, I believe you draw some conclusions. Will you tell us how we take Gaustana?'

I paused for a handful of seconds as if to arrange my thoughts, though I had known for days exactly what I would say when this moment was given to me. Did Harrap, I wondered, not know what he had done – or did he not care? Myself indifferent for the moment because I had won my desire, I began to speak: 'Since we in the open are weaker in numbers than the Gaustanans behind their walls, I believe we must use their own weaknesses against them.

'One weakness I found is tactical. They cannot guard all the diverse trails of both the north and the south and still hold together a main force strong enough to best us. The east and west are so well protected by the cliffs that the Gaustanans pay little heed to those approaches.

'The fundamental weakness – the great flaw – is less apparent. The city *is* the religion; they are one. Yet the monks, who embody their Dharma, are divided from the citizens, both in their hearts and in their habitation and defenses. These same monks, who are no fighters, hold the spirit of Gaustana in their separate citadel . . . the relics and the divine presences that protect the city.'

I spoke at length, expanding on details that I shall not repeat here. They will emerge in my account of the assault we mounted.

I had thought Harrap so engrossed in his purpose that he was half unaware of the abyss of discord – mutiny, in truth – to whose edge he had pressed his officers. But I was mistaken. He was compelled to attack Gaustana – regardless of the peril to our unity or our lives. And he was compelled to force our agreement without employing his practiced skill in persuasion. Thereafter, through the long council, he was self-demeaning in his eagerness to draw us all into unforced concurrence. He was as meticulous in his planning as he had been brutal in his insistence upon the assault.

Perversely, the grotesque shapes of misgivings rose above the waves of my own anger when I realized how gravely Harrap approached the actual trial. He could not but attack. Still, his general's eye, free of all illusion, saw how desperate was the enterprise. Drawing upon the cunning learned in a hundred battles, he sought to perfect his preparations for an engagement his reason would have refused. Mirab and Ranbir, those old campaigners, were charmed by Harrap's concern that so closely matched their own. They were fascinated, too, by the nice problems of warcraft presented to them. They argued as avidly as if they themselves had conceived the enterprise and must win the consent of their reluctant general to the manner of its execution. Aloof almost to the verge of withdrawal, but not beyond, the priest advanced on the auguries.

I was exhausted by my long ride and intense confrontation.

Since there was little more I could offer after my intelligence of Gaustana and the general scheme of attack, I lay down to sleep. Anand undertook to provide in my place information on the exact condition of our forces. The priest, still suspicious of Anand, objected, though he was but playing the adjutant's role. Harrap assented when I pointed out that my long absence had disqualified me, leaving only Anand competent to tell them what they must know. I slept through the long hot afternoon, while the three argued over the maps of the valley of Gaustana and the sketches of the fortifications I had drawn. They shaped their tactics, often rejecting them to begin anew, while three and a half days' ride to the south the city prepared for another of those gorgeous, bloodless festivals to the Buddha that were its chief occupation.

The regular drumming of many hooves awoke me, and I saw a troop of cavalry sweeping out of our camp.

'More training – at this time?' I asked Anand.

'No,' he replied, 'they ride first to Gaustana.'

'And sacrifice the little surprise we may still hold? Confirm the fears of the Gaustanans, at the least?'

Harrap himself answered me: 'They go to search out the routes from the north – and to alarm the Gaustanans.'

I must have gawped my incredulity, for he chuckled and explained, 'They are so much more numerous than ourselves that we can only triumph by using their own strength. It is not their weakness that will defeat the Gaustanans, but their strength. We must turn their virtues against them, their vigilance and the quick response of their eager militia. This cavalry raid is the first step. We will draw them into a mass attack against our pikes and arrows, reversing the normal roles of defenders and attackers so that they take the heavy losses. And, in the while, a small force under Ranbir will strike at the citadel of their faith. He will cut out the heart that bids them fight, and the limbs will die.'

As sudden hope contended in my heart with disbelief, the three commanders rocked back on their heels and snorted with glee. Anand grinned broadly, and even the priest smiled. They were tossed in currents of hectic exuberance, their faces shining with delight. I had seen such masks of gleeful anticipation in the past. When Harrap and I were boys, learning first weaponry, then tactics, and finally strategy under Ranbir and Mirab, we had chortled and romped so when our complex deviltries enraged our elders.

'Ho, Yakir,' Ranbir wheezed through his laughter, 'we have need of you again. Come draw us once more plans of the valley and as much as you can of the citadels.'

'They must be as accurate as you can make them,' added Harrap. 'Leave out what you cannot be sure of, rather than hazard toward error.'

The final plan of attack was so ingeniously simple that I too hugged myself in secret glee as I drafted the specific orders for individual units. As cast in writing for clarity, it read thus:

1. The light cavalry will ride a day ahead to draw out the defenses and to discover both favorable routes into the valley and sites where we must guard against ambush. The risk of charging the cavalry to alarm and reconnoiter at the same time is justified. There is no way to reconnoiter without alarming the defenses.

2. The main body, coming up the evening of the second day, will receive the cavalry into its ranks. Together they will attack the fringes of the defense. When the Gaustanans, who will have feared a feint, are convinced that we, in our foolishness, are attacking them head on, they should respond in force to our force. Then, at such a place as is given to us by immediate circumstances, we shall seek to trap them in our ambush. We shall, in any event, put ourselves on the defensive, employing the hedgehog made up of the wall of shields bristling with pikes. The archers shall stand behind in our accustomed fashion.

3. It is expected that the Gaustanans, convinced they can crush us, will throw the greater part of their forces at our hedgehog. Their losses should be severe.

4. Having approached Gaustana from the east over the mountains, the Royal Guard of three hundred, supported by the infantry of the Palace Guard in the number of two hundred, will strike at the Monastery of the Sacred Mount. They will, just before dawn of the third day, let themselves down by ropes from the cliff overhanging the Mount and overcome the timid monks.

5. When the sun shines full, the Sacred Mount should be in our hands.

The Guards will flash a burnished shield thrice in the sun to report their success and shall fix the great war banner of Kamardol to the highest point of the citadel. They shall report difficulties by flashing rapidly and repeatedly.

6. The main body shall immediately move from defense to attack when the citadel is taken. All shall shout: 'Your relics are ours! Your Protecting Spirits are flown!' The fanatics, broken by their losses and this augury, should then fall easily to our swords. The city, unprotected, will be ours.

7. We have planned as best it is given to us to plan. We shall fight with all the strength and courage we hold, knowing that we cannot retreat. The rest will be determined by the Gods, for whose truth we fight. We dedicate the city to Varuna and Pragpati.

'It is not a bad plan, is it?' Harrap asked, warming us with his pleasure. 'Just tight enough so we know what we are doing. Just loose enough so we won't be laying snares for our own feet.'

My own joy was almost as effervescent as Harrap's for I saw in immediate prospect my revenge upon Gaustana and also the ultimate proof of the Seeking. But my joy was smirched minutely, as a single drop of oil will mar the perfect brilliance of a pool, though the water sweeps sparkling underneath and all around. A small part of me, perhaps the detail-ridden adjutant I had become, regretted the deaths we must pay. But when had great enterprises ever been consummated or great truths proved except in blood? I was also disappointed because Harrap had refused to allow me to accompany Ranbir's force, saying he needed me to himself. When I suggested that Anand assist Ranbir in coordinating the attack, Harrap answered, 'Certainly not. Keep him by you – and watch him. I do not wholly trust this transmuted Brahman, converted at once into a soldier and a Buddhist. Remember, we attack his co-religionists.'

During the long ride south, I told Anand of Harrap's distrust. He hesitated when I asked how he could ride so untroubled toward the destruction of a Buddhist realm. 'Yakir,' he finally answered, 'perhaps I should be troubled, but I am not. I have sworn my oath to Kamardol and now to Harrap. I cannot break that oath, it is clear.'

'And that is all? So simple?'

'Not really, I fear. Look you, the doctrines of Gaustana are to you a heresy of the Old Religion. To me they are doubly heretic for they deny the essence of the Dharma. I suppose I hate such heresy even more than you hate these men you consider not men.'

'I do not,' I said, 'quite understand.'

'Look you, Yakir, the way of the Buddha is to open the world to all men, so that the truth can go out. The way of the Buddha is universal, unlike the Old Religion, which divides man from man and realm from realm. The Gaustanans have closed themselves off. They rule prohibitively. They falsely rule in the name of the Buddha. I would see them destroyed lest their aberration prevail, corrupting the essence of our way.'

'And were this a perfect Buddhist city?' I asked.

'I do not know. I fear I might not ride with you. However, I do today!'

Twenty-six

It went from the beginning as if the Gods compelled the defenders to play the roles our strategy assigned them. Our scouts and cavalry drew the Gaustanans' forward defense out of the valley, their provocation so successful that they fled at the gallop from three times their own strength. By afternoon of the second day the valley of Gaustana was in turmoil. Men in black armor and snouted helmets streamed from the gray and red city, frantically forming ranks and riding north like ants streaming from an anthill under a cloud of wasps. Perhaps a quarter of the number rode south to guard against an attack from that direction. Harrap was content with the first phase of our stratagem. The forces deployed to the south, he observed, could not enter the battle during those critical hours when the main force broke themselves against our hedgehog.

We observed the Gaustanans' deployments only during the isolated moments when we climbed a hill and deliberately displayed our strength to the enemy. For most of that hot afternoon we cantered through the network of defiles that pierced the heights north of the valley. A constant wind blew at our backs, raising the powder soil so that we rode under a canopy of golden dust. Occasional gusts tossed the canopy, lifting high the columns of dust stirred by the bundles of long grass and brushwood Harrap had ordered each man to trail behind his horse's crupper on a six-foot rope. We rode in open order, each man at least twelve feet behind his predecessor, and a banner hastily contrived fluttered from every tenth lance head. We must have appeared a great host to the Gaustanans, at least four times our actual strength.

All our hopes of triumph were committed, as was all our force, to the fanatic ardor of the militia, which must carry them raging onto our spears. I trembled in fear that I had misread the character of the Gaustanans. If they held back in caution or, worse, crept slyly round our flanks by devious passes they alone knew, our lives, as well as our mission, would pay the forfeit. As the afternoon rolled toward dusk, the flow of time untrammeled by the passions of men, our screen of scouts reported that the Gaustanans would accept only glancing combat, refusing to close and fight. Toward dusk, I told my fear to Harrap, for I could not contain it longer.

'Look you, Yakir,' he said, 'there was no other way. But the risk is great, far greater than even Ranbir and Mirab have said. If we rode on our own purposes – if the Gods had not ordained our Quest – I would stake you five gold talents to one of yours that we will *not* win, and two talents to one that we would *not* survive. The favor of the Gods makes the stakes even.'

'But,' I persisted, 'if the Gaustanans will not engage in the defile? On the plain they could surround us and chop us to pieces.'

'Not if they believed I held greater force in reserve. This is an exercise of wit against an opponent whose mind I do not really know. If they believe I command but a few thousand, they should let me come onto the plain, where they can destroy me at their leisure.

'If they think I am more powerful than they themselves, they must stop me in the defiles, where my full strength cannot bear. They should put themselves on the defensive within the defile if they think me overwhelmingly powerful. That would not suit my purpose at all. In the defile the defense must triumph unless it is overwhelmed by numbers. They must be lured to attack us in the defile. I have, therefore, contrived to make them believe us stronger than we are, but not too strong.'

'Then,' I said bitterly, 'we almost certainly ride to defeat, as Mirab and Ranbir warned. The plan seemed so simple, so irresistible . . . Do you now await the intervention of the Gods?'

'No. I command Their favor, but I do not expect Their intervention.'

'Then, we die here on the edge of the desert – and Kamardol forgets our fame?'

'Think you I seek death before our mission is done?'

His voice was low, lest the flag-bearer overhear the doubts he would confide only to me. But his eyes were slitted with joy, and his lips curved exulting while his broad fingers held the reins in negligent repose.

'What then, Harrap?' I grinned back at him, borne up by the current of his glee and the confidence that had sprung between us again.

'They must first think I am so strong that they cannot prevent my debouching onto the plain. Then, when perhaps I am harried on the plain and forced to retreat to the defiles, the Gaustanans must conclude that I am but foolhardy in my weakness. Tasting victory, they must pursue me into the defile. And I, always falling back, will appear to be retreating. But all the while I shall be breaking their strength.'

'It is uncertain,' I said.

'Were it certain, it would not be war,' he laughed and commanded a courier to tell the scouts that they must soon begin falling back on us as if hard pressed.

The long desert dusk thickened palpably. The golden dust was overcast with grayness, black where the shadows of the crags fell upon the defiles. From the gloomy depths we saw the sunlight fading on the cliffs as a fish at the bottom of a pool looks up to the dying light on the surface. Our cavalry trickled slowly back toward us, and we opened our ranks to let them in. Their lieutenant was disgusted, though he looked as if he were returning from an arduous leave, rather than a skirmish. He scrubbed the caked sweat and dust from his forehead with his scarf, but he bore no mark of battle. I saw no bound-up wounds, no broken swords, nor dented armor.

'They would not engage,' he said, 'nor take the bait. Instead, they have thrown a barricade of boulders across the defile. And there they sit waiting, about a quarter of a mile before the defile opens onto the plain.'

'Ah, were the plans of men the will of Gods,' Harrap quoted self-derisively. 'This is neither one nor the other. Those amateurs of war cannot make up their minds.'

He plaited his reins round his knuckles, painstakingly undoing the tangle before speaking again: 'Well, it seems I must lose a few infantrymen . . . though I cannot afford them.'

The infantry advanced at the trot, their pikes leveled beside their long shields. Some fifty archers found a path to the heights, where they slew about twenty Gaustanan scouts. A half hour later it was done. It had cost us thirty lives to roll the barricade aside. The green cloaks of the infantry lay crumpled among the boulders, and Harrap shook his head in sadness. 'There was no other way,' he said briskly, more to himself than to me. 'And this only the foretaste.'

I sought an answer to heal him for the battle. Before I could speak, the cavalry had burst through the gap in the barricade, carrying us with them. Hooves drummed on the yielding sand. Curtains of yellow-gray dust and reverberating echoes smothered speech and thought. Insensate as the wind, we did not stop to hew down the double file of horsemen in black snouted helmets drawn up across the defile. We rode over them, feeling only a momentary check to our speed and a slight lifting like the wind's motion when it hurls a haystack down and sweeps over the debris. My horse screamed at the blood stench and hurdled the carcass of a dappled mare. The blood puddled red into black from the javelin in her rounded belly. Sealed within our small realm of dust and tumult, we erupted from the mouth of the defile onto a broad plain that sloped gently down toward the twin citadels of Gaustana.

The shifting light of dusk confounded my eyes, so that my vision was now preternaturally brilliant and clear through the billowing dust, and, a moment later, barred by darkly wavering shadows shaped like no works of man or nature. The militia of Gaustana awaited us, aligned in a crescent formed of squadrons of two hundred, their horses hock-deep in the shorn yellow stubble of the wheat. The random image flashed across my mind again when I saw their black array faceless behind the round helmets' blunt snouts: Was it a host of immense moles that opposed us? Harrap led our first five hundred in a broad sweep across their front, all of us hurling defiance and threats with every javelin. Mirab was swinging the second five hundred in our wake. Still the ranks of Gaustana stood unmoving and silent.

Harrap wheeled at the far point of the crescent. Chargers stumbled and curvetted, shrieking protests against the abrupt reversal at the full gallop, but the thousand followed as if he held them on a single line. The militia had stirred only to put a single black horn from the point of the crescent when it appeared that we might sweep around their flank. As our second run across their front swept closer, they began to move forward slowly. Throwing stubbed javelins and loosing bolts from short bows, the black shapes reared massive through the golden-gray haze. Above the shouts of men and the screams of horses and the clash of metal, I heard the constant obbligato of hooves swishing through the stubble like the incessant murmuring and rustling of dancers' silken skirts.

Our trumpets blared at a sign from Harrap, and we pulled back to re-form perhaps a hundred feet from the ponderous advance of the militia. For nearly a minute, Harrap waited in apparent indecision, while our force turned and twisted in confusion. When his hand came down, the trumpets shrilled the charge, though the fifty feet separating our ranks from the militia were too narrow for us to gather momentum. We came upon them softly, almost gently, recoiling after a few seconds so that there was hardly time for a single thrust at the black figures. Again we pulled back, though hardly bruised, to reform in apparent confusion and indecision.

Twice more, as dusk coagulated into night, Harrap led us in stumbling, ineffective charges. Each time, the Gaustanans, now advancing at a round trot, pushed us further back until we were huddled in a disordered mass at the mouth of the defile. The trumpets cried aloud in shame, and our rear ranks turned to stream into the defile, while men groaned and horses shrieked. The startled militia paused just long enough to permit all but our front rank to join the rout.

When it came our turn, we broke off the travesty of combat and darted into the tunnel-dark defile. The way was clear, and within three minutes the hedgehog opened to admit us. Behind the stolid infantry, the cavalry closed into tight units. The mounted infantry hung their bridles over their horses' muzzles and grasped their heavy pikes.

It was, I suddenly realized, black night. Our laborious drills of the past months kept us from stumbling blindly so that our weapons would become more perilous to ourselves than to the enemy. We had fled as if utterly broken and demoralized. Yet I had seen that our losses were slight, a stove-in helmet or a broken arm, a slashed leg or a crossbow bolt embedded in a shoulder-plate – no more in all than twenty or thirty wounded and four or five lying dead or insensible on the plain outside. Had we, I wondered desperately, conjured up the image we sought? Had we convinced the Gaustanans that we were fleeing with dreadful losses? Had we roused their blood anger to storm into the treacherous defile for the kill?

'They're too timid, their blood too slow to heat,' Harrap said bitterly in my ear. 'They'll not trust themselves in these canyons in this blackness. But Ranbir must attack by dawn. I wonder when . . .'

His head, which had been no more than a dark globe slightly denser than the enveloping darkness, began to show its familiar contours. Sudden light flooded his ravaged face. The arc of an orange moon grew out of the cliff above us, so enormous it seemed I could lay my hand upon it if I stood on the cliff. The flat plain outside must have been dawn bright. In the moment the light came I heard the Gaustanans advance. Their long brass horns keened a mournful battle chant, and the militiamen exhorted each other with staccato cries like a pack of terriers running down a badger.

Expecting to strike the soft rear of an unruly rout, the Gaustanans impaled themselves on our heavy pikes. The infantry of Kamardol was drawn across the defile forty abreast, the first rank kneeling with pikes canted up, the second forty erect with leveled pikes, and the third forty thrusting their pikes between their comrades' shoulders. From the twanging bows behind them a torrent of arrows rose high in the air to fall in a cataract upon the militiamen's heads. Our infantry bent inward like a plate of steel under the smith's hammer. But they did not break.

They were engaged for almost five minutes before Harrap spoke and our trumpets implored: 'Give way! give way!' The infantry fell back slowly, like men too dazed and battered to run.

They opened a gap in their line to entice the militiamen to death within our ranks. In the ruddy-orange light that overflowed the defile I saw Gaustanan cavalry clambering over their own dead to come upon us. When our infantry halted, turning wearily as a mortally wounded badger at bay, the militia charged again.

'Had they not been born warriors, these men of mine should have been great mummers,' Harrap laughed in delight. 'See how stricken they appear, how close to collapse, though hardly a man is scratched.'

Clapped within the throng compressed by the cliffs on either side, I could see no more than the helmets and pikes of our infantry tossing in the moonlight. But I saw clearly the dark and faceless waves of Gaustana beyond, coming on again and again as we drew slowly back. Amateurs or not, Pariahs though they were, the Gaustanans were not loath to die. I marveled at their tenacity and the courage that hurled them time and time again at the impenetrable hedgehog.

Harrap had created a splendid spectacle of deceit. The Gaustanans did not know they were battering themselves to death against an enemy who was barely hurt. Their blood lust and the half-lit confusion concealed their own losses and they knew only that the men behind the long shields were falling back ever faster. It must have seemed to them that each charge would be the last before our rout became a slaughter. Dying in their tens and hundreds, while we withdrew leaving only a few tens on the battleground, the enraged fools truly thought they were prevailing. They charged again, growling in their throats like ravening wolves. We spilled into a broad place in the defile, and the melee became general.

Time, which had marched in measured cadence through the afternoon, was transmuted by men's passions. The minutes passed, now with the lunatic speed of a fakir whirling in the climax of his trance-dance, then with the agonizing slowness of clouds building up foot by foot and week by week for the monsoon that eventually spills the cool rain on the parched earth.

I raised my shield to parry a thrust, and uncountable, interminable hours passed before my own sword point searched out the soft flesh between the black helmet and the breastplate. In

313

the instant it took to whirl my head to spy out a new challenge, I saw an entire section of militia gather itself, lay its lances, charge with fearful impact, draw its swords, realize in panic that it was surrounded, and die to disintegrate like the pinch of spilled powder the courtesan blows from her silken sleeve with a casual breath.

The early dawn began to come on, turning the golden moonlight pale and obscure before granting us the whole light of day. During the false darkness we began to press the enemy back, forcing his maddened units into collisions so that they died by their fellows' swords. Their counter-pressure slowly slackened, then abruptly dissipated, and we rode forward in formation over the Gaustanan dead. Our discipline, so arduously instilled, prevailed still over our weariness. When day's full brilliance broke, we stood once more on the plain where the battle had begun that eternity that was but a moment earlier.

That moment had not passed – or time had reversed its flow. Before us stretched the same dark crescent of ten squadrons, each two hundred strong, we had taunted the night before. We had been decimated, yielding just more than a hundred and fifty dead and wounded. It was no great price to pay for the destruction of two thousand, but the slaughter was not enough. Despair and clarity came to me in the same instant. I realized that the stratagem had denied itself, the straitness of the defile keeping the full strength of the militia from engaging. We had won the battle and lost the campaign.

Harrap ordered the charge. The black ranks undulated backward, awed that we had survived the night almost intact while the canyon had swallowed up their ten squadrons. They broke just before the impact, fleeing our lances. But they re-formed at a distance and slowly advanced upon our weary ranks. Again our trumpets screamed the charge.

Behind me the priest shouted, 'Behold . . . behold, my brothers, the city is ours! Their relics are taken . . . their Protecting Spirits have flown!'

Men around me took up the chant, while I gazed beyond speech upon the twin citadels of Gaustana rising from the dawn. They lay untroubled, the red and gray walls and towers of the city and the yellow steps of the Monastery of the Sacred Mount sustaining each other. From the Sacred Mount a shaft of light flashed thrice, piercing the dusty dawn, then flashed thrice again. The green-and-scarlet war banner of Kamardol broke from the peak of the citadel, taut in the rising wind. Within those serried yellow boxes, serene against the sky as a painted backdrop, many men had died – and Kamardol had triumphed.

'Your relics are taken! Your Guardian Spirits dispersed!' I was shrieking with the rest. My distended throat ached, and my voice was rasping hoarse.

We hurtled upon their ranks in our frenzy. The militia held, though many heads turned in despair toward the alien banner flaunted from their sanctuary. Harrap spoke urgently to his flag-bearer, and the trumpets repeated his command, high and shrill and stern. While we re-formed for the spearhead charge, the Gaustanan line stiffened amid the billowing dust whipped high by the rising wind. I felt their new resolution across the field of the yellow stubble of the scythed wheat. Without hope of victory, bereft of their Protecting Spirits, they would die in good order, though their city was lost.

No troops could hold against the wedge of steel our spearhead charge drove into their ranks. Our heavy cavalrymen were in the point and behind them the weight of a thousand and a half armored men and horses. Breaking through the center of the crescent, they curved around to attack the militia in the rear. The expanding sides of the wedge ripped an ever broader hole in the militia's front. They broke then, but re-formed to fight by squadrons. And that was good, for we slew them piecemeal as they stood. It was charge, break, and re-form for fully half an hour, while the black figures in their snouted helmets grew ever fewer in my sight, except when I glanced down where the yellow stubble was crushed and red and strewn with figures.

I envisioned the brief siege that would wear down the remaining thousand or so troops who held the city itself. Our discipline would crush the despairing militia outside the gates – if they did not simply flee. Gaustana was ours, and the sacred power of the Stallion was proved. I laughed as I hacked at an arm that raised a mace against Harrap's helmet. My laughter was contemptuous of my past unbelief. Gaustana was ours. All that came thereafter would be but repetition, the further proving of truth had already been proved transcendentally.

The wind was still rising. The yellow dust stung our faces and obscured our sight with its sharp grains. I lifted my streaming eyes to gaze upon the twin citadels before they were hidden by the storm. Our battle flag was secured by a single corner. The green-and-scarlet folds writhed and flapped in the wind as if they would soar to the sky. As I watched, our flag broke free and billowed upward for an instant before the wind cast it into the passageways below. In its place, another flag unfurled – the white flag of Gaustana, barred with the five sacred colors of the Creed of the Middle Gate, red, yellow, blue, orange, and green. Hardly seen through the clouds of dust around the summit, quick flickers of light as from a polished shield trembled against the sky. I counted eighteen before they stopped.

Harrap, too, had marked the metamorphosis, and his voice grated low beside me. 'If Ranbir has failed . . .'

He paused, irresolute for the first time, and after a moment ordered the trumpeters to sound the attack. We resumed the slaughter, though all the warriors knew the flags had changed. Our own exultant fury had given way to methodical – almost dispassionate – butchery, and the militia no longer fought with the sullen savagery of men who expect to die. A new viciousness born of hope inspired the sword strokes of those beaten, exhausted men. Their numbers too seemed to increase. I realized that reinforcements were hastening to them, freed from the city's walls by the recapture of the Monastery. We could hardly see them through the solid wall of dust borne by the wind, but they came upon us again and again. We were, this time in earnest, fighting a defensive battle.

I cannot describe the hours that followed, in part because the dust storm rose to its screaming peak. Harrap and I were cut off from all sight of either the enemy or our own men, except when we collided with dim figures tossed about by the flood of battle. The driven dust pursued us into the defile, hammering our backs as we fled. In part I cannot describe the closing action because I will not. No more I will tell of the five days that passed in shame

316

and agony before we found the Horse again. Besides, I still do not know whether the great storm defeated us in the beginning by blinding us or saved us in the end by forcing the Gaustanans to break off the pursuit. I will say no more than we of the main body lost more than one third our men, more than five hundred, in the battle and the storm.

When we found the princes and the Horse, they told us that Ranbir was slain with all his force except for fifty Palace Guards who had come too late to attack the citadel and six mountaineers who swarmed up the ropes to life. The monks we thought so swollen with ease and debauchery had fought savagely. How, the survivors asked, could five hundred men prevail over five thousand – all prepared to die for their sacred relics amid their familiar places after giving way to the first shock?

No man, not even Harrap raging, could reproach the five hundred dead on the Sacred Mount, and no man, not even Harrap, reproached me whose false estimate of the monks had contrived our disaster. No man but myself as I numbly sought to re-form the less than a thousand and two hundred that remained of the more than two and a half thousand who had set out from Kamardol only eight months earlier. Fight again we might, but flee we must, lest the Gaustanans fall upon us in our weakness.

Ranbir, they told me, was dead, pulled down by five sturdy monks. Blood streaming from his torn face and slashed neck, he had fought to his end to keep our banner flying for the few additional minutes that might give us the victory. Ranbir was dead, among the men he had called his snow monkeys and the Palace Guard he had despised. At the end, they had stood on a mound of the slippery corpses of their fellows and the enemy. Each of the mountain mercenaries and each of the infantrymen of Kamardol had slain at least two – and some three or four – of the monks. They had fought more savagely in the end than in the beginning – perhaps believing they could buy victory with their deaths; perhaps each man, alone, in the ultimate aloofness, determined to make a good death before his Gods; perhaps simply because they could not do otherwise.

Ranbir was dead, who had given me my first sword, who had beamed like an uncomprehending but indulgent uncle when I first came to him boasting of my lute and my songs that he called my 'foolishness'. Ranbir was dead, and he was no more to me than a cipher in the long list of the fallen I would take to Kamardol, if I returned to Kamardol. Ranbir was dead, and I did not believe him dead.

It came to me the evening we found the Horse, when we lay on the edge of the desert, not daring to light fires against the sudden cold because they might bring the avengers of Gaustana upon us. For the first time the hard edge of reality thrust between my ribs. All feeling and warmth drained from my breast. I felt only the frozen emptiness of impotence. My viscera were ripped out through the wound, and sharp handfuls of broken ice were packed into the aching hollow.

Ranbir was dead, whom I had called 'Father'. Ranbir, who had been to me more real because more alive than the withdrawn father of my flesh. Not all the weeping of all the women of Kamardol, nor all the prayers of all the priests, nor all the sacrifice of all the cattle, nor even all my own horror and grief would give him the breath to speak one word more.

Pulling my cloak over my face, I whispered the prayer for the dead recited by his mountain tribe, the prayer he had taught me: 'May the mountains be anthills beneath his feet, may the women tremble and open their thighs at his coming, and may all his get be sons! May the rivers never freeze, the fruit trees bear forever, and the mountain goats fly to his lance! He is gone where all these prayers are the everlasting glory of reality!'

It was no good. Not all my prayers and all my songs could alter the reality Ranbir had met on that wind-scoured summit. No power, not the Gods Themselves, would breathe life into the broken body that had lain among the sacred relics of strangers. We had contrived his death, Harrap and I, and oh, if only we could take back those fearful days and that fatal decision. But nothing in this world could draw the terror from my staring eyes.

I had slain by my own hand I knew not how many, perhaps ten or twenty or more in my days. I had watched the deaths of hundreds, men of Kamardol and their alien enemies. But I had never truly looked upon death squarely before that night on the edge of the desert. It was no youthful game we played, no high-spirited sport with men and kingdoms for stakes. Our Quest lay in the hands of the stern Gods, Who neither forgive our mistakes nor correct Their own.

Ranbir was dead, I knew. We had killed him, Harrap and I myself.

Twenty-seven

I do not know whether the forces of Gaustana pursued us and we evaded them by the speed of our flight. It may have been that the sandstorm the Gods had sent and the slaughter we had done kept them from pursuit. It may have been that our movements, wholly obedient to the Horse's northward course, were so guided that the pursuers could not search us out.

We fled into the desert as the driven hare darts into the thorny thicket where the hounds cannot follow. The immense land was itself so varied and the routes across it so many as to confound pursuit. Coming upon Gaustana from the east, we had passed through the empty desert, where the pulse of the world was still except for the monstrous creeping of the dunes. On our northward flight the sand was broken by swamps and rocky outcrops, by dried lakes and patches of twisted shrubs, by creeks that broke the cracked earth to run brackish for a few miles before drying, and by springs and wells within the tight circles of the coarse grasses they nurtured. Though no fertile valleys opened before us, there was always just enough water to sustain us, as it sustained occasional encampments of nomads and the small beasts who were prey to the eagles. Whatever the reason, we saw the Gaustanans no more from the moment the wind hid them behind its moving wall of yellow sand.

The Colt went north, glorious in His swift freedom. He fled as if repenting His adventure with the mares, and the whiteness of His purity was burnished by the sands. He alone was free of the shame that enwrapped us. Isolated by our pain and our shock, we passed through the heart of the continent like a dying king hidden from the world by the thick curtains of his palanquin – and the world already half gone from him. I could not charge the Colt with fault, for He had led us around Gaustana. Our disgrace sprang from the anger that had seared all wisdom from me – and from the obsession that still rode Harrap. I assuaged my anguish by watching the Colt lead His escort across the open ways. His spirit ran forever free and forever true. He had not led us false, for we ourselves had willfully mistaken the plain signs He had given us.

Nor did the soldiers repudiate the Horse, though they might have hated Him as the incarnate force that had maneuvered our debacle. Even in the first shock of the rout, they counted their losses coolly. Our greatest loss, of course, was the Palace Guard, whom the regulars regretted little, and Ranbir's Royal Guard, whom they regretted less. Perhaps they dared not assail the Gods who guided Him, for He embodied the divine grace that might bring them home again. He was, in truth, their only hope of homecoming. Even though He led them away from Kamardol, the soldiers would often ride ahead to renew their courage by looking upon Him.

Harrap's fame and the old love the soldiers bore him still held them fast, and they did not speak against him. All their resentment flew to a single, fixed mark. The Gods, they swore, had punished us for our fratricide upon the Little Kamars because the rites of atonement and propitiation had been skimped. Moreover the Mother Goddess of the Earth Herself, they lamented, still pursued us in Her fury for our destruction of the well lines of Cosmopolis. Though no man called Harrap by name as the instigator of the two great sacrileges, the soldiers pleaded that the priest perform the Rite of Grand Expiation. Harrap denied their pleas, largely because he would not take upon himself the sins of expiation and there could be no Rite if there were no penitent.

I contrived to be almost always beside Harrap during those days to give him whatever comfort I could. But he took no comfort of me, and he spoke to me only when he was compelled to respond to a question or to give an order. For the greater part, he permitted Mirab and me to order the march as we wished. His spirit had withdrawn to a high and cold plateau of grief where he was above all his disgrace. Only once had he spoken of Gaustana. When we learned of Ranbir's death, he had cried, 'O Gods!

What have I done? The risk was great! But I was commanded!'
Thereafter he was silent. Nor did he ride forward to look upon
the Horse, as he had previously in his times of unease.

I was drawn to take counsel with Anand in my perplexity, but
I could not speak to Anand of Harrap's mindless anguish. To
consult Anand would be the final drawing away, the ultimate
acknowledgment that the love that had been between Harrap
and me was wholly passed. Though Harrap would take nothing
of me, my own love was still strong – stronger perhaps than it
had ever been because he so needed the succor he would not
take.

Instead, I went to the priest. He had been with us from the
small beginning of the Quest, and Harrap's sickness of the soul
was a matter for him, both as physician and as priest. I begged
him to find with me the means to restore my old playmate. 'He
has suffered worse defeats,' I said. 'He has taken two and three
times the losses of Gaustana. And always his first concern was to
save his forces – and then, his second, to recoup the battle. He
has never taken defeat gaily. Though he is no fool, defeat has
always made his resolution stronger. Now he is like an old woman
gone to the temple to sit at the God's feet and await death.'

'He has never before this seen his entire purpose destroyed,'
the priest said.

'True,' I answered, forgetting my own guilt in my concern for
Harrap, 'this was his greatest defeat. Never had he longed so
terribly for a victory and never told its treasures and its glory
before its realization. All the more reason we must succor him.
If we could only contrive that he should gaze upon the Horse and
draw strength of will from Him.'

'Hardly that . . . certainly not that.'

'Why not?'

'Because it is between Harrap and the Stallion now. They are,
this moment, enemies,' the priest answered slowly. When he
disdained cant, his words gave form to the fear I had not dared
admit to myself.

'Look you, Yakir, if the Horse led true, the fault is all Harrap's.
If I read His intent truly, we have not merely suffered a dreadful
defeat, but Harrap has betrayed the Seeking by attacking

Gaustana. Harrap *cannot* look upon the Horse! Either Harrap himself has betrayed his fate or the Horse is a false messenger. One formulation or the other must be true. Yet Harrap can accept neither.'

'That is not true . . .' I began to protest, but stopped. Impaled upon the hateful truth of the priest's contention, I asked again, 'What can I do now?'

'There is only one way. And that may not succeed. You have said that you share his guilt . . .'

'Yes!' I cried.

'Then speak to him of your guilt. Confess your own shame, which is real. Ask his succor for yourself. Then, feeling himself not wholly alone, he may speak . . . He must speak or silence will seal him off from man and the Gods.'

I went to Harrap, speaking in shame of my own guilt as the priest had advised. Finally he spoke, and it would have been better had he not spoken. 'No, Yakir,' he answered gently, 'the fault is not yours – any more than it is mine. We did as we were commanded. We read the signs correctly, when all the others would have denied them. The guilt is not ours. Yet we were misled.'

'How were we misled?' I asked, fearing his answer, but fearing to remain silent when he had finally consented to speak with me.

'Do you truly not see how? It is so obvious to me! The Stallion is a vehicle, not a manifestation – a vessel, not an avatar. He was for long the Vehicle of the Gods that wished us well. Now other forces have filled Him.'

There was no reason for me to speak, no words I could say.

'There are in the world other Gods than our own,' he continued. 'Some we may have offended merely by neglect. Others may be in fee to our enemies. And those other Gods, I know, have possessed the Stallion. They have led Him astray from His true road. And those other Gods, I know, contrived our . . . contrived Gaustana!'

Harrap's explanation would absolve us both – him of his heavy burden of guilt and me of my lighter one. But I could not accept it. 'If the Horse were truly possessed,' I contended 'would He not have led us directly to the city and disaster? Would the sign not have been so manifest that we could not even argue – as we did?'

'No, Yakir! The Gods – especially They Who wish us evil – are not so simple or direct. They wished to give us time – to lead us on – until we entrapped ourselves utterly by our own decision.'

'Then you hold the Horse is false?'

'No, the Stallion Himself is neither true nor false. But He has been possessed by Gods who are false to us. He is now *Their* vehicle, *Their* vessel.'

'Then we must command the priest to cast Them out . . . to invite the return of the Gods Who had guided us so well. And we must expiate our error in allowing ourselves to be misled.'

'No, again! There was no error. I could not do otherwise when all the signs . . .'

'Why not, then, eject the malicious Gods before they lead us to new disaster?'

'The time is not yet. We must suffer longer. But the time will come when we can make the proper sacrifices.'

I told the priest merely that his stratagem had worked, for he saw that we had talked at length. Later, Harrap went among the troops again, and praised them for their courage and their skill. But he did not hear them when in their new camaraderie the soldiers pleaded with him to command the Rite of Grand Expiation for fratricide and defertilization. Nor did I tell the priest of Harrap's determination that the Horse must be purged when the season came. It was enough that Harrap had come a little way back. I had no heart to set him and the priest against each other, the one insisting that the auguries had deliberately misled us, the other insisting that the guidance was true but misread.

So we rode north, still aching from the catastrophe. The sullen days ran in featureless train as if the Quest were suspended, though the very lack of incident gave us time to heal. The daylight hours were hot and dry, but the nights grew colder as we went further north, and I smelled snow on the wind. It was already autumn, and the nomads were making their winter camps, crowding their felt yurts into the low places wherever they found a scanty flow of water. These nomads we bowed to

324

the worship of the Horse, their various submissions accomplished at the cost of no more than a few lives, all theirs. We came twice to settlements called cities, presumably because they did not shift from their minor oases. They were, in reality, no more than a few hundred hovels surrounded by ludicrous parched-earth walls that would keep goats from straying but would not stay an attack for more than ten minutes. We had no need to attack, for the elders of these simulacra of cities made submission when they saw our array. We took fresh meat from them, and the little staple food they had.

Despite his belief that our Quest would not run straight again until the malicious Gods had been expelled from the Horse, Harrap grew calmer with these petty victories.

'We are not wholly lost, eh Yakir?' His inherent ebullience was not wholly crushed by the weight of his prevailing melancholy. 'But this is trivia. The season for the proper sacrifices will come. We will reclaim our own true Gods – and ride to our greatest glory before He takes us home.'

Unmindful of Harrap's oscillating feelings, the Horse led us north without pause for thirty-five days, until we came to the foothills of the Mountains of Heaven. I name those mountains thus because the priest's chart showed that we had come far north of the great city from which the Horse had turned aside after Cosmopolis, and we knew that the Mountains of Heaven hedged the heart of the continent to the north. The snows of early winter lay three and four inches deep on the ground and the winds from the end of the world pierced our cloaks with sharp fingers. Their assaults were intermittent, almost playful, as if they wished only to remind us of their fearful power that had harried us without mercy during our passage through the mountains.

Our rough-haired ponies tucked their heads into the wind, and the plodding camels put on their patched and shaggy winter coats, greeting the cold with the same decrepit hauteur they had shown the heat. The men grumbled at moving ever further from Kamardol, but they did not whine like defeated troops. From time to time, Anand reported, they spoke to each other of their yearning for the Grand Expiation. But I heard them turning defeat into victory, boasting that they had survived Gaustana, which would have destroyed any other troops in the world. The tale grew with each telling until it was only the sandstorm that had snatched the triumph from us.

Harrap sat drinking koumiss with the soldiers around their campfires and heard their boasts. Heavy with self-congratulation, they asserted that no other troops could have slaughtered an immensely superior foe – and still have saved themselves when the winds joined the ranks of that foe. No other general, they said, could have conceived so audacious an assault – and still have extricated his force when fate went awry. Harrap did not demur. Viewed in that special light, Gaustana was, after all, a remarkable feat of arms. I hoped his new equanimity would deter him from conflict with the priest, though conflict was inevitable if he insisted that the Horse was possessed. But the obsession endured.

'It was no mean deed, Yakir,' he mused, 'this battle of Gaustana. Had the malicious Gods not possessed the Horse, we should have taken the city. Even then, the enemy needed the great storm's aid to withstand us. But the time of the sacrifice – His purification – will come. Then we shall be liberated for even greater feats.'

The Horse had turned west along a well-traveled route that skirted the foothills. The thread of men and beasts had worn deep ruts in the loose yellow soil that lay under the feathery layers of snow. The soldiers rejoiced that He had taken a course toward Kamardol. But the Horse plodded where He had soared, and He went no more than three or four miles each day. I thought at first that He was tired or that the premonitory voice of instinct made Him reluctant to follow the homeward road. But His coat was dull, where it had shone; His eyes were filmed, which had been lit by His will; and His stomach was distended, that had been a perfect curve of taut muscle.

I was not immediately concerned for the Horse Himself, since He seemed merely to have taken an inflammation of the bowels from eating coarse grass. I feared rather that His illness would confirm Harrap's conviction that He was possessed and that the soldiers too would embrace that delusion. Then would we be compelled to the conflict between Harrap and the priest that might destroy the soul of the Seeking.

I told Harrap of the inflammation when he questioned our slow progress, for he would still not look upon the Horse. He only commanded, 'See to it, then Yakir.'

Our farriers examined the Horse where He lay in the snow, His hoofs cast asplay, His throat heaving with His constricted breath. They laid on poultices of hot herbs and fed Him cathartic oils, but He grew worse by the hour. The priest emptied his saddlebags of his stock of drugs, and we forced them down His throat. Still the swelling grew, stretching the skin of His belly till it pained me to look upon Him.

'There is but one possible remedy,' the priest sighed at last. 'It is at least as dangerous as the illness. A knife, driven into His stomach, will let out the vapors that choke Him. But a misblow would . . .'

'And who will hold the knife?' I asked. 'Who will hold the knife that may destroy the sacred Stallion – and will at least mar His perfection so that His is no longer the flawless purity of the sacred vehicle?'

No man spoke when my eyes ran round the circle of knit faces. Still a Brahman, I could not do the deed, and Gorbabordol and Anand both stood in indecision. Gorbabordol looked away, and fear squeezed his sallow features. At length, Anand put his hand on my hand, and drew his dagger from his belt. 'Where?' he asked.

'You – a Brahman?' I gasped.

'But Brahman no longer,' he smiled.

'And if He dies, your life dies with Him. The soldiers will tear you apart.'

'That I know. But better to die so, trying, than to die slowly amid the rabble we shall become if He dies – without purpose and without discipline. As to the desecration – marring the Horse – I count it little beside the deeds we have done and the deeds we will do.'

They looked to me to give the word, but I temporized, saying, 'I must speak with Harrap. *This* command I cannot give.'

I found Harrap with the leaders of a caravan that had overtaken us as we lay beside the road. They were merchants, hurrying to make home before full winter. They were merchants, but unlike any merchants I had ever met, grave and stately men who called themselves some Jews and some Persians, all of the Kingdom of Bokhara. They could speak a rough-hewn Prakrit, and they seemed to understand my urgency when I broke into their formal courtesies to demand a decision of Harrap.

'A beast . . . valuable . . . that lies sick so,' said one of the Jews, a short, stout man of middle age with a thick black beard that showed only a few white hairs. 'And you have exhausted all your remedies? Perhaps . . . something I have can help. Very valuable, eh?'

'More valuable than you can conceive,' I answered, seizing him by the sleeve in my haste.

When we came to the Horse, where He lay surrounded by the awed princes, His eyes were closed and He shuddered with each breath. His stomach was as distended as the pigs' bladders that children blow up for sport, so that it seemed even the touch of a fingernail would rupture the taut skin. The Jew was unperturbed. He looked first at the eyes and mouth, drawing the lids back gently and pulling the locked jaws apart with surprising strength. He felt the stomach, searching out the shape of the bowels beneath the skin with his fingertips. To conclude his examination, he fastidiously drew on a white glove of thin silk and thrust his hand beyond the wrist into the anus.

'I think something can be done,' he said, delicately peeling off the fouled glove and dropping it into the snow. 'I hope it is not already too late.'

He beckoned his servant to bring his saddlebag and spoke slowly as he knelt in the snow to mix the powders and oils he measured from silk-wrapped packets and small leather flasks, 'An – how do you say it – obstruction of the lower bowel. We shall try.'

While ten men held the Horse, the Jew poured a massive potion down His throat. He was almost struck by the wildly kicking hind legs when he attached a long leather tube to a bladder filled with red liquid and forced it into the Horse's anus.

'It is done,' he said. 'We must now wait. God will decide.'

We waited for ten or fifteen minutes – no longer I know, though it seemed a day and a night. The Horse lay still, exhausted by His struggles. His stomach was so swollen I was sure it would burst.

'The knife!' I finally nodded to Anand.

At that moment, the Horse shuddered greatly, every muscle in spasm as in His death agonies. Slimy yellow fluids burst from His anus, staining His white legs. He shuddered again and lay still. Even the convulsion of breath in His throat was stilled.

My dagger was at the Jew's throat, but he smiled so that I could not strike and said calmly, 'It is working. Watch!'

The Horse was breathing again, and the yellow slime poured from his anus, mixed with hard, twisted knots of grass. His hooves rasped the snow as He struggled to rise. The soldiers supporting Him, He rose painfully, His head hung low. He moved a few tottering steps, His bowels still in flux. When the flow ended, He curved His long neck down to lick at the white snow.

'He will be all right now,' the Jew said. 'But you must not travel for at least four days. Can you wait?'

He looked at me oddly when I swore, 'For four days or forty days.'

I must have babbled in my joyous relief, as I stripped off my gold chain and my rings set with diamonds and rubies and thrust them into his hands. His forehead was astonished, a long line knitted between his heavy eyebrows, but his small blue eyes glittered in amusement. 'I am glad,' he said, 'that you reward your physicians as handsomely for success as you would . . . punish . . . punish them severely for failure. I do not think, though, that I would like the appointment.'

'Take these,' I urged him. 'There is more for you, much more.'

'I will take this,' he anwered, choosing a thumb ring of no great value in the shape of a hooped serpent with small ruby eyes. 'This I will take to remind me how far man has come. But for the rest, I am merchant and no physician.'

Nor would he accept any greater reward, though I pleaded with him as we rode back to our camp. But he asked curiously,

'What is this animal that you would reward me for a simple cure as if I had snatched a great king from death?'

'He is the vehicle of our Gods,' I replied simply.

The Jew looked grave and saddened, if I correctly read his expression behind his thicket of beard. He put no further questions to me.

Harrap demanded the merchants' presence at a great banquet of thanksgiving. At first they pleaded they must move on if they were to make Bokhara before deep winter. But they finally yielded – perhaps the more readily when the cavalry mounted a great tournament of joy, displaying at once our skill and our might.

While we watched, I whispered to Harrap, 'All is well now, is it not?'

'How so?'

'The Horse is cured,' I replied.

'Yes, and we give our thanks. The evil Gods that possess Him failed to destroy Him.'

'It seems to me,' I persisted, 'that the illness and its cure have defeated those Gods.'

'By no means. The illness has but proved the possession. Our victory is not so easily won. The evil Gods must be expelled.'

I was oppressed by vague but heavy foreboding as I made ready for the banquet. Since we carried no tent that could accommodate the fifty who were bidden, twenty-five of our officers and the twenty-five chief men of the caravan, I ordered a great ring of fires lit. We sat in an amphitheater of flickering red and yellow flame amid the scent of burning mountain pines. The moon was a taut bow of pale silver, and the stars glittered far distant in the clear northern sky. To do the merchants all honor, Harrap brought out the golden serving vessels we had taken as tribute, the least of them fit to accompany an emperor into the tomb. We ate from carved, begemmed platters, and we drank from golden goblets engraved with epic scenes instead of the battered tin or white-scoured wood that had served us all our journey. Soldiers bore wine in long-necked ewers through the circle of flame, and no man had to call twice for a drink. We reveled like a company of kings before a battle.

The meat and fowl dishes were lavish, for our hunters had been fortunate. The Persians ate heartily, pressing their own pickled and sugared delicacies on us. The Jews, however, refused our meat, taking only the spice-dried vegetables we served to awaken appetite. Explaining that they lived under a dietary taboo, they offered us slices of their meat, rolled and studded with black peppercorns. It was good of its kind, though too mild for my taste. The priest would not taste their beef, despite the indulgence of the campaign. He sat slightly apart so that he might not have to purify himself after supping with the casteless.

The stocky Jewish merchant who had cured the Horse was on my right. His purple and white robe of fine wool was so full that the stripes ran into each other, constantly altering their outlines in the shifting firelight like the wing feathers of starlings in flight. On my left a lean Persian squatted, his lustrous brown beard twisted into thick curls that fell on the breast of his brown robe. He had put off his conical cap of red silk, but the Jew, removing his fur hat, had revealed a small silken cap that just covered his crown. It was like the white cap the priest always wore, except that it was smaller and black.

The Persian was inquisitive. He questioned me persistently about our realm of Kamardol and our purposes in the heart of the continent. I answered fully, not solely because I was compelled by hospitality, but also because I saw no harm in these peaceful merchants. When I explained that we followed the Horse, Who was guided by the Gods, the Persian fell silent as had the Jews. I asked his own religion.

'We believe,' he answered slowly, as if fearing to offend me who knew that all men followed their own religions, 'that there are but two spirits in the world. One is the Good, which is the more powerful. The other is the Evil, which is only slightly less powerful. Our world is a battleground between those two spirits, between Light and Darkness. Our God is in the sun and in fire.'

'And men?' I asked, fascinated by this extraordinary concept. 'What becomes of men? Are they bound to the wheel of life forever, or do you believe that the soul passes with the body?'

'The soul lives on,' he answered. 'But the soul can be saved only by following the Good.'

331

I was amused by the simple assumption that the Gods could be neatly ordered like chessmen, white and black, good and evil. If good and evil were so clearly delineated in the intricate pattern of the world, if the life of the Gods and the life of men were so clearly divided, how happy would men be.

'And how,' I asked, 'does man follow the Good? It would seem a difficult task.'

'It is not easy. But we are given guidance, just as the day is divided into Light and Dark. And there came to mankind only a century ago Him called Mitra who was a manifestation of the Good. His rules we now follow, for He has lifted us up.'

The Jew, who was called Daobid, snorted, 'It is an old argument between us, Sarkaataris. But I cannot listen to you spooning delusions into this warrior's head. Know you, Colonel, there is only one God, and He transcends good and evil, for He has created all. For us Jews, we need only follow His laws. Evil, as Sarkaataris calls it, comes into being only when His laws are transgressed by men.'

I put to Daobid, the Jew, the same question about the soul I had asked Sarkaataris, the Persian.

'We do not know,' he confessed, 'whether each man's soul continues separate after his body's death. Perhaps each soul goes back to Him, the Creator, to become part of the single, eternal soul. But it does not matter. We are commanded only to obey the Lord God on this earth.'

This Jewish doctrine, at once harsher and more simple than the Persian's, was even less rewarding than the sterile beliefs of the early Buddhists. I was astonished that a man who appeared so learned could believe that which even a ten-year-old boy of Kamardol would reject as excessively artless.

'And man?' I asked again. 'What does your God give to men?'

'The world and the joys of the world, but no more. Sometimes He protects us and nurtures us, but often He sends disaster upon us.'

'Why?'

'That we do not know. We know only that the Lord God, for His own inscrutable purposes, ordains joy and sorrow.'

'Always? Will it be ever so?'

'No,' Daobid answered, 'not always. Our prophets say that in His own full time the Lord God will send Him Who is the Messiah to raise us to joy on earth, joy in the acknowledgment and understanding of His will.'

'When will this Messiah come?'

'No man knows, not even the prophets. This Mitra of Sarkaataris's, he may be a prophet, but he is not the Messiah who is promised to the Jews. That one will bring love and harmony. It is clear that neither love nor harmony now prevails on earth.'

At this, the Persian swore. 'Daobid, you desecrate by your words that which you do not know.'

'Your Gods are yours,' Daobid replied stubbornly. 'They may be fit for you, though they are false. But the Lord God of the Jews has promised a true Messiah to the Jews. We do not dispute your beliefs – for you. No more do we dispute the Colonel's beliefs. No man need believe in the Lord God, Who is the only God, except him who wishes . . .'

To turn our guests' mounting anger, I asked of their travels.

They abandoned their tense postures with evident relief. Within the barbaric ring of fire they spoke of the court of the Emperor of China, where they had bought silk. They told how the Chinese were harrying the Huns from their domains. They spoke of salt seas extending forever beyond the sight and knowledge of men, who journeyed for months upon their faces. And they sighed for the easy life and the great profits of the merchants who carried their goods to China upon the waters of those salt seas.

I was delighted by their fantasies, which made me laugh by their wild improbability. They were, in any event, much more entertaining than the frenzied disputation between Jew and Persian over their equally chimerical Gods. The evening passed with laughter and great drinking of wine. In the morning the caravan departed, laden camels to the number of more than a thousand swaying on their cushioned feet down the long, cold road to Bokhara.

Later that morning, Harrap summoned me from the spring where I was watching the Horse graze and slowly draw back His strength. 'What thought you of our guests?' he demanded.

333

'They are learned in all things, but simple to foolishness about the Gods,' I answered.

'Would they acknowledge the Stallion?'

'I think not,' I replied. 'But, of course, it did not matter. They are merely wayfarers. There was no need to demand submission of them.'

'Still, they cross our territory, the land the Perfect Stallion has given us. Why did we not demand submission of them?'

'It simply did not occur to me,' I answered, puzzled by his vehemence.

'Would you call them Brahmans among their own?' he demanded.

'I suppose you could,' I answered doubtfully. 'They are undeniably learned in their own religions.'

'You are right,' Harrap declared emphatically, spilling much emotion on the trivial question. 'They are Brahmans. Yakir, they are the ones. It is ordained!'

'What is ordained?' I asked, bewildered by his words and his apocalyptic tone.

'The sacrifices ordained to purge the Perfect Stallion. These Jews and Persians are the sacrifices ordained. By sacrificing them, we shall expel the malicious Gods who have possessed Him. Then shall we come home to Kamardol in glory.'

I took the meaning slowly from his words like a convalescent sipping gruel in careful spoonfuls lest he gag by taking too much at once. We stood face to face and toe to toe, but I felt myself shrunk small and set far away, as if we stood on opposing mountain peaks. I looked upon the shrunken Harrap opposite me, seeing all of him at once and at a great distance, and he was a man I had never seen before that moment. The level gaze that had spoken steadfastness now glared total unawareness of the lives of others; the flat planes of the cheeks that had displayed true simplicity were the very shape of barbaric brutality; and the butterfly scar that had been the mark of courage was the mark of malignity. I was choked by horror so dense that I could only stammer out what was, in truth, the least objection. 'But . . . but . . . the laws of hospitality . . . We have drunk wine with them.'

'The demands of the Gods are above the laws of hospitality,' he said. 'Order the pursuit.'

'I cannot, Harrap!' I said. 'I cannot!'

'Why not?' His tone was puzzled. 'Do you not see that they are the men the Brahmayanas – and even your own "Song of the Seeking" – speak of? "Slay even the Brahman who does not know the Horse." So it reads.'

'They are not Brahmans. They are Jews and Persians.'

'But Brahmans among their own, you agreed.'

'It is different,' I protested.

'I do not see that. But, I ask again, would they acknowledge the Stallion?'

'I do not know. Probably not, though we have not asked them.'

'Then let us ask them – and release those who make the proper obeisance. But act now, man . . . Give your orders.'

'But Harrap,' I protested still, 'the True Religion has put aside the sacrifice of humans – even the Pariahs. You would return to barbarism.'

'Barbarism? I return to barbarism?' he flared. 'After the perils I have endured for the True Religion, you speak to *me* . . . to *me* . . . of barbarism?'

'I do so speak!' I heard with surprise my own voice firm and my words defiant. 'And I speak so to *you*. We have all suffered hardships. We have all endured perils beyond any men of our race had ever known. But we have been searching for the future, not striving to re-enter the past. The cult of the Mother Goddess is forbidden – and with that cult, human sacrifice.'

'Look you, Yakir!' he said softly, his anger seemingly swallowed by his eagerness to convince me. 'We have done extraordinary deeds. We have met extraordinary men and learned of their Gods. The soldiers say the Mother Goddess Herself was enraged by our choking the well lines of Cosmopolis. I do not think they are right, but this sacrifice will set their fears at rest.'

'You would kill more than a hundred men who have come to us as guests merely to mollify the soldiers? You were not always so fearful of their muttering.'

'Nor am I now, though I have not abjured the Mother Goddess, as you have. But there is deeper need – a real need. We would not have lost Gaustana if we had not been opposed by the malicious Gods, if They had not possessed the Horse. Can you purge Him of those Gods by any means other than human sacrifice? It is ordained! It has been ordained from the beginning that we must do this!'

The fire of obsession that had fallen briefly within him was rekindled and rising fast. The veils that hide the future opened for an instant, and I saw that I must either give way or, by pressing the quarrel, destroy all that had been between Harrap and myself since we were boys. I knew my course in the next instant, and I was sickened that I could not give way. Still foolishly timid, I sought to avoid that which could not be avoided by giving the softer of the two answers that pressed against my teeth.

'We demanded a miracle at Gaustana, Harrap. I erred – and you too erred. Our estimate was wrong. We demanded a miracle, and the miracle was denied us. The Protecting Spirits of Gaustana triumphed because we gave them every advantage. But that does not mean that our own Gods have deserted the Stallion. It means only that we demanded too much.'

'Too much! Too much you say. I tell you, Yakir, that our entire Quest has been a miracle, a concourse of miracles tumbling after each other. If that particular miracle was denied, there can be only one reason: the Stallion is possessed! He must be purged. All else is Brahmanical sophistry . . . mumbling over dusty texts, instead of accepting the realities that are before our eyes.'

I gazed long at the homunculus opposite me before replying, and I took care, even in my anger, to avoid the ultimate offense. I would not yet charge him with his own contempt of the auguries and with his own bad generalship. 'It is you who are sophistical – in the crudest way. You are turning back to the literal, early texts. We have come beyond them. We know compassion. We know that men are men, not sacrificial beasts – even though they may follow false Gods.'

'Compassion, *you* speak to me of compassion? You, who became a soldier, betraying in a single deed your birth, your scholarship, and the injunction to spare life laid upon you. *You* speak to *me* of compassion? I tell you for the last time – these

336

men . . . are . . . ordained . . . sacrifices. They worship false Gods with childish fervor. The glory of Kamardol is more to me than a word. But you would sell Kamardol itself for ease to a conscience grown suddenly tender. "Beware the Brahman's child when he prates of war," it is truly written. Give the orders, Colonel!'

My anger rose to meet his own, and my hand went to the dagger in my belt. 'I will not!' I cried. 'Give the orders yourself, General. Order the treacherous slaughter of innocent men who have succored us and dined with us. Do it yourself. Do anything – barbarous, filthy, and debased. Do anything, rather than acknowledge your own fault.'

'My fault?' he bellowed, the axe haft in his palm.

'Your fault! That I said. You seek only a pretext. You seek only to hide from yourself the grievous mistakes, the mad errors that ended with the insane attack on Gaustana. You would sacrifice a hundred men more to your implacable vanity. But you too know well. It was not the Gods, but ourselves that betrayed us. Myself – and you, more.'

All was said that could be said. We stood panting as if we had wrestled five hard bouts. The empurpled scar between his eyes writhed with rage of its own. I do not know how long we faced each other, glaring across the abyss of incomprehension. It was time enough to remember a dozen incidents of our childhood, and, in every one, Ranbir guiding us and teaching us. Harrap turned away first, letting the axe haft drop from his fingers in a gesture of utter disgust.

'I will give the orders,' he rumbled, his voice even again. 'It is only by the love I once bore you, Yakir, that you go not first to appease the Gods. We will continue as before, but only because you too are sanctified by the Quest. But henceforth speak to me of nothing other than the necessities of the march.'

'I shall not,' I grated and turned to mount my horse.

I galloped to look upon the Horse, and only after a few miles did I see that Anand rode behind me. I told him sharply to turn back, but he would not. Although I pleaded with him, he stayed beside me. 'You asked me earlier,' he said, 'what might turn me from obedience to the Quest. I could not answer then. But this has turned me. If you cannot order the sacrifice of men, how can I partake of it? I ride with you.'

I gave in, sensing that he would alter his determination no more than Harrap. As we cantered onward, two squadrons of cavalry swept past us. Harrap rode at their head and, beside him, the priest.

Twenty-eight

Even today, when all the conflicting passions of the Seeking are spent, and the unfathomable glory glows in eternal purity, I am glad that I did not take part in the sacrifice of the Persians and the Jews.

The rites, the priest later told me, were performed with the perfect orthodoxy now almost forgotten. Some men were dragged behind horses, and others were whirled on braided ropes. Some were crushed between boulders, and others were flayed alive. Other modes of ritual death perfectly re-enacted the sanctified sacrifices our forebears practiced for two millennia before the prohibition of human offerings. Even the sacred victims' demeanor was wholly archaic and profound. Some died squealing for their lives; others were proudly silent; and many recited prayers to their Gods, who could not succor them. Some among the Jews may have taken comfort from being so swiftly reunited with their Lord God, but I do not know.

Since we have put the simple ways of antiquity behind us, a similar spectacle may never again be seen. I sometimes regret the experience, but I am on the whole glad that I was not there. There is a strange weakness in me. I have come to love the high ardor of death in battle, but I find abhorrent the methodical slaying of either sacrifices or criminals in the gray dawn. Even the sacred instant when the priest raises the shining sacrificial knife to the throat of the ram or the bull makes me cringe within myself. It is odd, but it is so, and I cannot help myself.

Two aspects of that sacrifice I cannot to this day wholly understand. Why did I protest so violently against the sacrifice of men who were, after all, but travelers met by chance? Why did the priest preside without protest, whom I had expected to revile Harrap for his heretical insistence that the Horse was possessed by evil?

The deed did not, as I had feared, rend the fabric of our Quest. Harrap, the sanctified commander, was not divided from the priest, who was the human embodiment of the soul of our Quest. The deed did, however, sunder me from Harrap, who was as much the fiber of my youth as the slow but dazzling growth of my own awareness and my own powers. Our irreconcilable cleavage was a climax more profound than either crossing the cruel mountains into the heart of the continent or the debacle before Gaustana. It followed upon the death of Ranbir, who had been father to us both in much more than the half-jesting courtesy of our calling him 'Father.' The Seeking ended for me that morning, and all that followed was another quest through another world in another time.

I would not have taken back my decision, though the sacrifice effectively quelled the soldiers' dread of further retribution and also dispelled Harrap's terror of the malicious Gods. Whether the Horse was also purged of Spirits Who frustrated our purposes, I cannot say. I still believe that our defeat before Gaustana was in the main contrived by our own errors. It might be avenged, but it could be neither justified nor altered. Nonetheless, the winds of fortune did shift after the Horse's recovery and the sacrifice in the desert. We swept westward across the strip of green that separates the southern fringes of the Mountains of Heaven from the northern marches of the great desert. We were granted both a measure of ease and the quick conquest of cities that were no mean hamlets.

We were no more than a thousand warriors, and our train of followers had shrunk to hardly fifty, at least forty of them eager harlots and the remainder mountebanks skilled in various artifices. Tempered beyond any other troops, the thousand were irresistible except by overwhelming numbers. Such encounters we avoided, entirely by the Horse's guidance, for Harrap would have challenged a force of ten thousand had we met such a force. Nor were we plagued by the knifepoint quarrels over the harlots that I feared. I had ordered that no man might choose a favorite among the women, but must take her who was free when his loins stirred. Only those harlots remained with us who were inspired by a passion of loyalty even greater than their exceeding love of venery. Although it was not properly my concern, I feared that these forty would be injured or even destroyed by the demands of a thousand men in the spring flood of their ardor. But they were spared by our conquests, which ever provided fresh women.

By the Gods' grace, the cities of the northern tier trembled at our approach. The Huns were rolling westward like an immeasurable glacier across the frozen plains north of the Mountains of Heaven. Under the unrelenting pressure of the Chinese, who were, as they phrased it, 'pacifying their borders,' an entire people of many hundred tribes was on the march. Those same Chinese were thrusting their columns like spears toward Ferghana in the west, whence the Horse had come. Only small parties of marauding Huns pierced the Mountains of Heaven to harry the cities on the northern edge of the desert. But the fear of their vicious forays and the greater fear of the implacable Chinese advance rotted the resolution of those cities. Most opened their gates to us, who were neither as cruel as the Huns nor as tenacious as the Chinese. Those who chose to resist us were crippled by their own terror. Their weapons turned in their trembling hands, and we broke them as contemptuously as a mastiff crushes a rat between his fangs. The Gods had contrived matters well for us.

Had I spoken to him, Harrap would have laughed away my belief that the cities yielded to us because they were unmanned by their fear of the Huns and the Chinese. His conviction of omnipotence was fixed in the opalescence of victory after victory that succeeded the mass sacrifice. Had we been as near in mind as we were before the Seeking, I should still not have spoken. His pride insisted that our own fame and our own strength made our ride westward into the winter a broad highroad of conquests. I saw that the Gods had used the Huns and the Chinese to create the terror that served us.

Even today the names of those cities ring joyous in my ears. Yolsol, where the elders capitulated with elaborate ceremony, meeting us twenty-five miles from their gates with tribute of gold, gems and meat – and fifty of their fairest maidens. Arkord, sandstone walls built so cunningly cleft between hills that it could defy a force of ten times our own. The prince would have resisted, but the troops threw open the gates after three hundred of our cavalry swept aside a force of eight hundred they had sent out to test us. Ihlbarghand, which received us with neither ceremony nor defiance, but as dispassionately as it might a caravan of a hundred harmless merchants. But there we all fell sick of a wasting dysentery that passed only after eight days. Each city contributed its treasure, and each gave its homage to the Horse and its submission to the Great Kings of Kamardol. On the priest's chart those cities hung like a chain of diamonds across the white throat of the north.

Greatest of all was Lighfar, which almost purged Gaustana from our memories. A kingdom of twenty-five thousand, its back to the mountains and its face toward the desert, Lighfar was endowed with the gifts of both realms – the water of the mountains and the fecundity of the plains. When we came to Lighfar, the grapes that had been gathered earlier, together with the melons, the pears, and the peaches, overflowed the storehouses of the King. Lighfar sought to resist us with four thousand soldiers, and for a time I feared another Gaustana. But the troops came out unit by unit, instead of striking in mass. The first six hundred, who were mercenaries of the southern mountains, we destroyed with our arrows. The troops of the city ran themselves into our ambushes and battered themselves against the hedgehog. When we marched into the city, having paid ninety-eight lives for its possession, Harrap stabbed the King through the throat with his sword of ceremony, while the princes and the knights slew his ministers and his courtiers. We left a city of no more than ten thousand, its women, spattered with the blood of their men, wailing over their empty coffers amid the ashes of their roofs. Lighfar made true and lasting submission to Kamardol. No one left alive could doubt the supreme power of the Horse.

Swollen by lists of our spoils, the roll of our victories became a thick bulge in the breast of my tunic. Harrap was once more jovial and untroubled. He bore the weight of the Quest so lightly that he appeared wholly unburdened – as he had not been since we brought the Colt home to Kamardol. He spoke with easy good will to every man but me, from the priest and Mirab to the pikemen in the ranks. Only one thing, the priest told me, he would not tolerate, and that was contradiction. Since I would not contradict him again, and the priest could not, he ruled our realm of Kamardol-on-the-march as utterly as the sun dominates the noon sky.

Even toward myself and Anand his manner softened. He could in no event have maintained the silence he had ordained between us, since the enterprise demanded that we take counsel together. Beyond that necessity, the heat of victory seemed to dissipate the fog of his anger against me. We talked with each other like any commander and his trusted adjutant, but the love that had bound two men, Harrap the prince and Yakir the scribe, was vanished. Harrap, I believe, sought to restore that love, wanting my devotion as well as my service. With me alone he was less than imperious. He sought to win my approbation again, as if I withheld that which was essential to him. My recalcitrance perhaps diminished the perfect self-satisfaction his demeanor boasted. But I would not journey again through the green valleys of his love to the bleak wasteland of betrayal.

The mute supplication of his pride was most apparent after the conquest of Lighfar, a perfect battle perfectly fought. Straddling the corpse of the King, he ordered the sack of the city, and then asked me, 'Could I have done otherwise?'

'No, you could not,' I replied. 'The city's resistance demanded this retribution.'

It was true, and I could not say less. But I would not say more, and Harrap had either to slay me too or content himself with the little I gave him. At any rate, he asked no more.

I have sometimes wondered if I should have taken the hand Harrap offered. But I could not. The human sacrifice was wrong, and it offended the Gods. Our duty was to give Them men's lives in battle or in punishment for sins – not in sacrifice. Harrap had warred against the Gods by making the great sacrifice. He had sought to punish Them for Their disfavor by casting Them out of the Horse. Dazzled by pride in his unique prowess, he held the favor of the Gods to be no more than trifling assistance, which was no more than his due and was, at the most, convenient but not essential. I hoped my disapproving withdrawal would keep him from the ultimate folly of setting himself above the Gods. Perhaps I did restrain him from building a shrine to himself in his own heart, where he would reign deified. I fear, however, that my small hindrance was no more effective than binding a snowbank with ropes so that it will not melt in the spring torrents. I fear that he came to think himself as great as – or greater than – the Gods.

The sword that lay always between Harrap and myself after the sacrifice was loose in its scabbard when the Horse led us westward into the mountains from Lighfar. The edge of our enmity was concealed, though still bright and biting. All else was well with our company. We were no more than nine hundred. We had conquered, we had been tried, and we had conquered again. No force in the continent could have resisted us if it mustered less than ten times our number.

Three months only remained before our return to Kamardol for the rites that would crown our Quest. The Horse was leading us homeward, His trail curving slightly southward and westward of our original course, for so the passes ran. If He had taken another course, we might well have chivvied Him. The Seeking required that we return a year after the Consecration, and before that necessity, something of His inviolability dropped away. But there was no need to chivvy Him. He found the long road homeward, leading us through steep valleys among the sullen mountains, where we need fear no human enemy. Harrap congratulated himself anew in his self-devotion. I knew that the favor of the Gods lay over us, and I was content.

The journey of two months through the mountains is a smooth place upon the surface of my memories. My notes are suddenly sparse as if all had already been said. I believe each of us had already found what he sought when we first entered the towering maze of mountains beyond Kamardol.

Harrap had proved himself against man and the malignant Gods. Having tested to the utmost the power that lay within him, he knew that neither man nor Gods could bear down his triumphant will. He knew more: his indestructible name would endure, diamond-hard and diamond-bright; the greater victories he would later win in command of great hosts would never obscure the lonely courage of the true Seeking; nor would his later Imperial grandeur overtop his stature of the Seeking. He had proved himself the greatest hero of his race. Having shown that his powers were without limits – as men measure limits – he had, I felt, already decided to condescend to the Emerald Throne he had earlier spurned.

I had found that I could do whatever was demanded of me – and that it was good to be strong. I had also found that the ways of peoples differ more profoundly than do the deserts and the peaks, but the greatest differences, the wildest variations, live together in the heart of the individual, regardless of the people from which he springs. I too had learned more. The Gods do indeed interest Themselves in the affairs of men, but men seek to beseech – or to direct – Their intervention, not so much in vain as in the blindness of dark ignorance; the Gods will, upon occasion, alter Their will on the pleas of men, but we cannot invoke Their favors except by chance; nor could we hope for sudden enlightenment, there being so many Gods with so many divergent purposes that we know neither to Whom to address ourselves nor in what form to make such address. The perpetual Seeking remained to us, and it was good that so many peoples sought their Gods in so many different manners. Until, in time, we men came to full knowledge by our own striving and Their favor, we must not draw back from the perpetual Seeking.

Anand remained skeptical of the Gods' concern with men. He accepted only the injunction that was self-enjoined to behave toward every other human as if he were oneself – except when the other's desires threatened one's existence or stood in the way of one's duties. Anand smiled wearily when I contended that his belief was sterile because it lacked any generative or enlivening principle. I argued that his belief made man himself the only authority over himself.

At length Anand asked how I could speak so confidently of the favor of the Gods when Harrap's massacre of the Jews and

Persians had won him so much felicity, though we two knew that the deed was evil.

I answered that we men cannot command the Gods by our deeds, be they good or evil. I charged him, in turn, with making men his Gods, as do the Cosmopolítēs; I asked how he could so enshrine the common soldiers who had rejoiced in the human sacrifice.

'We possess only that which is given to us,' he answered gravely. 'But of that which is given to us we can take the best, rather than the worst!'

What Mirab had sought I knew no more than I knew what he had found through the Seeking. Perhaps it was only his own life that he had preserved alike from the petulant anger of Chandra the King and from the perils of the trail. He believed, as far as I could see, as he always had believed, that the Gods were merely another – and particularly capricious – order of generals.

The priest remained the enigma he had been since I first discerned the complexity of motive and deed behind his habitual mask of orthodox simplicity. He had always insisted that he rode only to restore the power and the dignity of the True Religion. What he had sought for himself beyond that clear and simple purpose, I could not penetrate. No more could I discover how he truly believed in the Gods. I knew that his purposes were by far more complex than he avowed, and I knew that his beliefs were by far more subtle than he professed. But I knew no more of their true substance at the end than I had known in the beginning.

However, I wander from my narrative. It should be enough to say that a sense of completion came upon us in those closing days of the Seeking, though the final stages lacked incident only in contrast with what had gone before. Our route was more roundabout than that we had taken to the heart of the continent, and we skirted the highest peaks. Nonetheless, the blizzards of full winter harried us, fiercer than the variable spring storms of our outward journey, though less capricious and sooner done. We clashed twice with small hunting parties of Uighurs, but did not pursue them.

We approached the passes above Kamardol from the west, our route intertwining with the trails Harrap, the priest, and I had taken when we brought the Horse home from Ferghana as two skeins coil about each other on the weaver's floor. The familiar places awoke memories in me, and some regrets for some things we had done and others we had left undone.

But Harrap grunted comfortably, 'We have come a long way since then, have we not?'

The Horse quickened His pace, perhaps drawn by memories of warm stables and abundant fodder. Yet we still lacked a month of the proper time of our return, and Harrap, suddenly reluctant, would not have us pass those remaining days within the borders of Kamardol. He ordered us into camp in a well-watered valley that cleft the foothills of the last range above Kamardol. Beyond the peaks, the gray and white slopes tumbled down a hundred miles to the City. He also sent ten cavalrymen under a sergeant through the passes to Kamardol as if it were a hostile realm they must scout in secret. I do not know whether tactical caution or fear of what we might find in Kamardol counseled Harrap to halt, though he believed no power could stand against his will. Perhaps he wished to hold fast the mystery of the Quest until the exact day fixed for our return, when we should ride in glory into Kamardol.

The Horse was eager to cross the last range. Four times in three days the princes formed a chain across the pass to turn Him back. Thereafter, He accepted the bar to His will, which had previously commanded our will, and He grazed placidly within a few miles of our encampment. The Horse accepted the fundamental alteration in His world with readier comprehension than most men display when their lives are turned.

On the morning of the fifth day after their departure two of our scouts returned at the gallop. Their horses' sides heaved, and their muzzles were foam-flecked. The men's faces were drawn, and their eyes swam with fatigue. They pressed through the throng of soldiers, ignoring their shouted questions, and slid from their saddles beside my campfire to report. Forsaking his dignity, Harrap hurried to us.

'There are many changes, Highness,' the cavalryman blurted, his weathered face pale, for his blood slowed at the horror of his tidings. 'King Gupta is dead, and King Chandra rules alone. The

347

Ladies Tamar and Ambiala approach half a day's ride behind, and . . .'

I did not stay to hear the report out nor to tell Mirab of his daughter's coming, but found myself galloping along the trail to the pass. I do not know how long I rode alone – perhaps fifteen minutes, perhaps half an hour – when Harrap overtook me. We did not speak for several hours amid the silent snows, but pressed our horses up the slopes until we saw a small party winding down toward us, alternately appearing and vanishing among the crags. It was another hour before we drew close enough to discern the flash of helmets above green and scarlet cloaks.

There were but nine riders, completing the party of our scouts, all muffled against the snow-laden wind. There were no women. I checked my horse and half wheeled to return to the encampment without speaking to the cavalrymen whom I hated in that instant because their stolid presence deprived me of my joy. But my hot anger was dispelled in the next instant, and terror chilled my limbs so that I could not feel my fingers within my gloves. Desperate with fear that Tamar had fallen on the trail, I spurred my horse up the slope that lay between us and the cavalrymen.

Floundering through the loose snow, slipping backward on the half-covered rocks, we came to the head of the column. I looked again at the soldiers, and my fears fell away. My hands trembled of their own, and a vast serenity enfolded me though my blood spurted through my veins in joy. Behind the leading cavalrymen I saw Tamar's golden-brown hair, its luster hardly dulled with dust. I saw her grave, glowing face, unique in this world, above the green and scarlet cavalryman's cloak she wore. I hurled myself from my horse, only half seeing that Ambiala rode beside her, and she met me in the snow, and we embraced beside the trail under the peaks.

I pressed her to me, my hands searching under her cloak to prove by all my senses that she was indeed beside me again. I do not know what I said or what she said, but her tone was at first fierce with passionate joy and then soft and crooning as if she were soothing an infant. When our bodies drew apart, though our hands were still linked, I saw that the cavalrymen gazed up at the mountains as if they had never seen snow or rocks. Harrap was talking quietly with Ambiala.

We paused on the slope, sipping from the soldiers' leather bottles the finest wine I have ever tasted, while Ambiala told their tale. Tamar interrupted from time to time with small additions. But chiefly she sat silent, her head on my shoulder and her hand in mine.

'I thought you were dead,' I whispered. 'They told me you were coming, and I saw only nine soldiers.'

'Two were slain by Chandra's men,' she answered. 'I am sorry. We wore their cloaks.'

After the departure of the host of the Seeking – Ambiala said, compounding what she knew at the time with what she later learned – all went well between the Co-Kings Chandra and Gupta for several months. They knew they had failed to stop us at our beginning when they heard of the death of the nags and again when one of the bands of the Little Kamars Gupta had sent out to ambush us did not return. Still the Co-Kings remained complacent. They were certain that we would not survive the unknown perils of the heart of the continent. They, of course, ordered the rites to continue as they were prescribed for the year of our absence. Priests offered continual sacrifices, and the minstrels of different orders sang the sacred cycle of the ten sets of hymns for ten days before repeating the cycle. The parody of piety was meticulously played for the people.

Four months after our departure the Co-Kings, hearing no word of us, gleefully concluded that we had all perished. They could not believe that Harrap truly intended to take us wherever the Horse led, even into the heart of the continent. They were certain that he would have ranged in safety along the borders of Kamardol if he still lived. Had he done so, they must have heard some tidings of our deeds. Receiving no reports, they could only believe that we had been destroyed by men or the mountains, for they could not imagine that we had vanished into the heart of the continent. No more could they restrain themselves from seeking to destroy each other once their common fear of Harrap was dissipated.

Their strife began in small ways, in petty contests for power and prestige. Chandra would issue decrees favoring the Buddhists without Gupta's consent; Gupta would absent himself from the Council, thus negating its decrees. Gupta's power rested upon his fierce fellow tribesmen, the Little Kamars, but they were loath when they saw how Chandra bore him down. Besides, they charged him with the loss of the three hundred we had slain. Still, the contest was roughly equal – Gupta's twisted ruthlessness against Chandra's ponderous pertinacity. Mourning Harrap, the Army disdained the struggle between the elephant-king and the cobra-king. The common people said scornfully that the worm had attacked the sow and asked how the worm could hope to triumph.

The struggle – Tamar interjected – was by no means unremitting. Often Gupta would lay an attack on his brother's power and then fail to press it through. He preferred to retire to the scented gardens of the courtesans where he would lie for weeks, sodden with wine and exhausted by venery. Chandra was beyond those temptations. He was responsive only to the heavy yearning toward total power that stirred in his sluggish veins.

While Gupta – Ambiala resumed – darted hectically against him in sudden, slashing attacks, Chandra built his power in his own ponderous manner. To the Buddhists he gave money and sanction to proselytize among the Pariahs and the Shudras. Those outcastes and the very lowest castes – themselves barely human – were formed into Brotherhoods of the Dispossessed. By accepting the Buddha and swearing fealty to Chandra, they might gain abundant 'new rights and privileges in recompense for past suffering.' Chandra sought by gifts and by intimidation to gain control of the network of spies, *agents provocateurs*, and informers the priesthood of the Old Religion directed. The priests, of course, tried to forestall him since the secret service was a traditional buttress of their power. The furtive rabble of barbers, peddlars, harlots, servants, fakirs, and players was naturally eager to serve him who paid most. Chandra poured treasure without stint into the twisting channels that reach into every household in Kamardol. In return he received much intelligence, by no means all fabricated, and control of a thousand wagging tongues to cry out whatever outrageous slander or sycophantic praises his policy required.

By gifts, threats, and flattery the secret service and the ruffians of his household troops shaped groups of the drifting toughs of the streets into 'assault waves' that would riot in anger or storm in joy as they were commanded. With hypocritical punctiliousness, acting always by the authority of the Co-Kings, his brother as well as himself, Chandra ordered the ancient authority of the village elders 'not encroached upon, but supplemented' by a core of central officials who would 'speedily make the needs of the people known to the Co-Kings and subsequently convey the Kings' benevolent responses.' That core reported directly to Chandra and obeyed only his orders. Among the villages they spoke of 'the new order of all men equal and blessed by the Buddha.' Nonetheless, they took counsel of – and gave authority to – all outstanding men of the old order who would work with them in their way. The officers and soldiers of the standing Army Chandra bribed with promotions and rich gifts, hoping to buy their support – or at least their neutrality – when his household forces clashed with his brother Gupta's.

Those manifold tactics – Tamar added – were subtle and effective, though the recounting is bald and elided. Torrents of gold were expended in all the giving of favors and in the making of new institutions. In the beginning Chandra remitted a quarter of the taxes to buy the people's love as he was buying power by his other expenditures. Still the common people yearned for the days of glory they had lived under the Great King. They still prayed that the Great King would return to restore the certainties and security of the old order – or, if the Great King were dead, that Harrap would reappear to reign over them in the old way. Finding that he could not buy devotion – and, assuredly, not love – Chandra had restored all the old taxes, imposts, and levies. Within a month, he had added half again to their weight, for he believed that his new weapon of associations, spies, officials, and street brawlers was so powerful that he need not concern himself with winning the people's assent. He was content with the surface loyalty he could command when the throngs cried, 'Hail to

Chandra! Hail to the Great King Chandra!' Besides, his new manner of rule was increasingly costly to maintain.

From one deed only – Ambiala took up the tale – Chandra long refrained. He paid all honor to his brother, the Co-King, nor ever struck against Gupta in the open. But his manner had changed abruptly only a month ago. The people whispered that the Great King was dead, though the gates of the Monastery of Ghokrao guarded the fate of the monarch who had abandoned the world. Still the people argued that the Buddhists would not keep their secrets from their protector and chief ally. They believed that Chandra had not dared to strike directly at Gupta until the monks told him his father was dead – whether by the design of the Gods or the hands of men no one knew.

Then Chandra moved with the crashing speed of an elephant aroused. Decrees bore his name alone. The Little Kamars were ordered dispersed to the frontiers on the pretext that they alone could guard the marches and open the new territories Kamardol required. All men vanished who spoke Gupta's name – unless in derogation – or, unthinking, called him King. Gupta's household troops met with heavy losses in sudden brawls against Chandra's men, who were barely disguised as common hooligans.

'When his own troops were slain by street toughs who suddenly flashed cavalry swords and maces,' Ambiala said, 'even Gupta could no longer sink his perception of peril in debauchery. Perhaps that was what Chandra wanted.'

Gupta finally cast off his torpor – she continued – and led his household troops against Chandra when he went out in the morning to pray. Then the massacre began, for the Army stood aside. Gupta was slain that morning among his household forces, and all Chandra's half-brothers that afternoon. That night the Old Queen fell ill in her modest villa. Chandra gave out that it was the decrepitude of age, but the City whispered of poison when she died two days later, calling in vain on Ranbir and Harrap to protect her.

Chandra next discovered that the 'enemies of the people of Kamardol,' though few in number, were a grave danger because of their implacable determination to overthrow the blessed new order. He ordered mass arrests, and no one knew what became of the adherents of Gupta. Anyone who was known to have dealt in any way with Harrap – or to have spoken well of him – was also taken. Chandra explained through all his followers – official and subterranean – that it was not only evil but sacrilegious to yearn for the safe return of the vanished prince. Harrap, he gave out, had plotted to betray Kamardol to his mother's people.

The Army, too, was winnowed, but with more subtlety than brutality. Officers disappeared one by one, and their posts were taken by Chandra's henchmen. The assault was slow in order to avoid arousing alarm, which might have led to resistance. Even the wariest officers could find no occasion sufficiently grave to join with their fellows in mutiny, since each deed appeared a separate matter and each was formally justified. Paralyzed by its sworn fealty to the Crown, the Army was gradually deprived of its power in the realm. Officers and soldiers would have rallied to a determined leader. But they had no leader.

'So it was, only a week ago,' said Tamar, 'when Ambiala and I learned that we were marked for arrest. Chandra has generally spared women, since he is contemptuous of their power to harm him. But we two were too intimate with the "dead traitors, Harrap and Yakir." Chandra seems to fear you, whom he thinks dead, more than he fears the rising anger of the people. Your father and mother, Yakir, have fled south, along with many others. Your father said you would know where he had fled – if you still lived and I should find you.'

I nodded, remembering my father's cousins in Sindhia, five hundred miles to the south, and asked, 'But yourselves, you and Ambiala? How did you flee?'

'We are here, are we not?' she asked gaily. 'Fearing that Chandra would look for us to the south, we came north with a few women attendants, trusting in the Gods to bring us to you.'

'That was mad!' I exclaimed.

'Perhaps it was,' she agreed, unruffled. 'But we are now with you, are we not?'

'You are – by the grace of the Gods alone. How came you to our scouts?'

'We were riding north on our mules, dressed as a peasant woman and her daughters . . .'

'I played the fat old mother – I,' Ambiala glowered.

'We found,' Tamar continued, 'as we had not known, that Chandra had set the troops of his own household to guard the frontiers. They stopped us, at least thirty of them, and they were taking their sport by force of our attendants – we two were reserved for last – when your eleven cavalrymen rode down the road. Your men called haughtily to the ruffians to release us. They were astonished when Chandra's men attacked them.'

'Household troops attacking regular cavalry, Highness,' the sergeant interjected, his voice quivering with incredulous indignation. 'And they not even three to our one. It was unbelievable.'

'Your poor men did not know that Chandra's ruffians now ride over even the Army,' Ambiala smiled. 'But the skirmish was brief.'

'Two dead, Highness. We lost two good men,' the sergeant said.

Since Harrap would not ask, I did, 'And the others, Sergeant, Gupta's men?'

'All dead, of course, Colonel. When they find the carrion, they'll put it down to marauding barbarians,' the sergeant said. 'The ladies we buried.'

'Of course!' Harrap said lightly. 'Why did you ask, Yakir?' He added, 'You have done well, Lieutenant.'

The sergeant glowed, already feeling the white scarf of his lieutenancy on his shoulders.

Harrap's gesture was extravagant. The sergeant had done no more than was customarily demanded of our soldiers. Perhaps Harrap, like myself, still knew awe of Kamardol, alone among the realms of the continent. Perhaps he was grateful for the gift of Ambiala, whom he took into his tent. I do not think he acted in fondness for me to whom the sergeant had brought Tamar over the mountains.

It was only a small part of my mind that pondered Harrap's curious gesture. I gave hardly more attention to our plight. Yet no more than nine hundred men were sworn to return within four weeks to our homeland, where even our names were proscribed and where the King would seek to destroy us, whom he thought already dead. I knew that Harrap sent messages to certain commanders, ordering the couriers to dress as peasants and to confess themselves early deserters who knew not the end of the Seeking if they were found out. Since he did not command my counsel, I did not inquire further.

Extraordinary as my complacency may now appear, I did not even mark it at the time. Not lassitude, but the intoxication of utter contentment possessed me.

Tamar enveloped me as if I had never known her before. Her body was more mysterious for being so well known. Her familiar excitements were renewed and transformed by our long separation, and I knew they would be forever fresh to me. We lay sunken in love within my small dark yurt, so wholly united that the congress of our bodies was almost superfluous to our communion. Her lustrous hair entwined my arm. Her full throat, a breadth too plump by the standards of Kamardol, conquered me by its vulnerability. Her straight nose was at once stern and delicate. Her gray eyes flashed from animal desire to contemplation of eternity in an instant.

All these were lovely to me, yet they were but the husk of her. Her body was a lovely vessel for the utter perfection of her being: the quick leap of compassion and the total understanding that transcends logic; the serenity that welled in her laughter; the joyous comprehension of the world even in moments of sadness that is given only to women – and was given to her beyond all others. These were the true parts of her perfect being, and in her being I found the purpose of my own long quest.

When I told her my thoughts, she smiled and asked, 'Had you to go so far – and stay so long – to find what was always here for you?'

Since that necessity was the single thing her female certainty would not comprehend, I kissed her again and answered, 'Yes!'

Seven days after she had come back to me, we walked, joined by gold-and-white scarves, seven times around the sacred fire while the priest chanted the rites of marriage. I urged the ceremony on her, though she protested that I would break my caste. I had no thought except Tamar and myself, nor did I think of caste again after laughing away her dismay. Caste was less to me than the curl of her eyelash or the whim that took her out to gaze at the crescent moon two hours after the crest of the night.

Therefore, I laughed and asked, 'Would you shame your father?'

Laughing she consented, and the priest bound us. Harrap played the sovereign's role; Anand stood behind me; and Mirab, her father, gave Tamar to me.

Exiles we all were, and exiles we might all remain forever. But we two were exiles in a realm of joy.

Twenty-nine

Spring came again to the mountains, and the first purple flags of heather on the edge of the melting snow signaled that our Quest was nearly ended. The cycle of the Horse was all but completed. Two tangential circles were closed in space and time, but for the minor arcs of a hundred miles and three weeks. Spring past had dedicated us to the Seeking and had tempered us to the road. Spring appearing should have been the season of profound rejoicing that we had survived and triumphed. But spring appearing bore on its scented winds the gravest peril of the sacred year.

Implacable Time would close her circle unless Time forsook us to death – as she had already forsaken to death two of every three of the warriors who had ridden out from Kamardol a year past. Still the full year, rounding from spring to spring, would be no more than the annual miracle of regeneration, its glowing mystery tarnished by infinite repetition, if we did not at its end bring the Horse back to the arena where He had been anointed. Time and human will, which had wrestled mightily with each other from the beginning of our Quest, were locked in an intricate grip. Time would prevail simply by enduring unless we could slip her hold by riding into Kamardol at the appointed hour despite the King's mortal hostility. We ourselves must close the circle of space by returning unscathed to the City – or the inevitable closing of the circle of time would negate all the courage and all the sacrifice of the Seeking.

I knew our dilemma more as a spectator than a participant. The Quest had ended for me with Tamar's coming. Had I been free, I would have brought Tamar and the Horse to Sindhia where my father had already returned to the fields of our ancestors. But I did not command, and I would not betray

Harrap by stealing the Horse – even if I could have done so. When I told Tamar of my fantasy of escape, she heard me through in silence.

'Would the Quest then be truly complete?' she finally asked.

'No, not the formal Quest, as you know,' I answered, casting aside the bearskin we had drawn over us. Within the yurt a thin silk coverlet was warm enough. She lay on her side, her breasts a soft weight on my chest and her legs entwined around mine.

'But my own quest – our own quest – is already ended,' I continued. 'I have found at the end what I abandoned at the beginning. I would now evade the unnecessary peril that confronts us. I would bring us all through to life, you, myself, and the Horse, the Divine Messenger.'

'Do you hold me so cheap, then?'

'I do not understand what you mean,' I answered puzzled.

'Nor do I wholly,' she admitted. 'But it seems to me the Seeking is the price we have paid, and it must be paid in full. There is that within me which warns that the Seeking *must* be brought to its proper close. Our union was shaped by the Quest, and our fate is intertwined with the Quest. If the one is broken, the other too may break.'

'You are become a seer,' I mocked gently.

'Perhaps I am,' she answered, quite composed. 'I do not know how it is that we must return to Kamardol, even unto death. But this I do feel, Yakir, in the heart of me.'

'Then there is nothing more to be said,' I conceded, half amused and half annoyed that she should decide who had remained in ease in Kamardol while I followed the Horse across the heart of the continent in peril and perplexity.

'I know, Yakir,' she said, answering my thought rather than my words, 'that I have no right to judge, for I have not endured the Seeking, as you have. But this I feel as if it were a seal stamped upon my heart. The Seeking must be made whole!'

Perhaps I should have argued that the Seeking had already ended for us with our own fulfillment and that we had paid our obligation in full. Instead, my fingers trailed across the swell of her belly and down to the cleft between her thighs. Her stiffened legs pressed together in rejection of my questing hand, and she said, wholly practical, 'Besides, how could we manage to steal away, even we two alone, even without the Horse?'

'It was but a fantasy,' I answered. 'It seems we are willed to follow Him to death.'

Her thighs opened beneath me, and she cried, 'Come into me, Yakir. Come in now . . . do not wait.'

The remainder of the afternoon was swept away by a tide of repeated ecstasy, such, I have heard, others too have felt just before the curtains of death closed. At dusk a soldier summoned us to Harrap's yurt.

Harrap and Ambiala waited together within the felt hemisphere. It was hardly larger than my own poor yurt, but it was lined with colored silks. Golden plate and jeweled ornaments lay in rich disorder on the painted-hide camel trunks. Hemmed by the yurt's sides, we sat in a tight circle upon striped cushions, our crossed legs almost touching. Ambiala poured chilled wine into goblets of Cosmopolis that were carved with the triumphs of Alexander. My forefinger traced the rampant war elephant of King Porus on my goblet as Harrap spoke. His low voice was the echo of thunder from a distant ravine.

'I have asked you to come so that it would be as it was in the beginning – just the four of us who made the Seeking, Ambiala and Tamar by remaining, Harrap and Yakir by riding out.'

'And the priest?' I asked, reluctant to admit the camaraderie he conjured between us.

'The priest, it is true, has ridden with us from the beginning. But I hold him apart. He has been a messenger, not a maker like you and me, Yakir – or like Ambiala and Tamar, who kept our names and our souls in Kamardol in our absence.'

'We drink to this circle, Prince Harrap!' said Tamar, who would have deprived me of my enmity.

'We drink, Lady Tamar!' Harrap pursued his explanation eagerly. 'No more than the priest would I ask Anand, or Gorbabordol, or even your father, Mirab, Tamar. We four made the Seeking. Ranbir alone among men would sit with us if the circle were unbroken, for he saved the Seeking.'

I felt a quick welling in my eyes, and I clenched my lids to keep the tears within. Still I would not yield to the familiar spell of the past Harrap invoked. 'To Ranbir,' I murmured, 'and to the legions he now commands. We have by their deaths given him many soldiers to lead – and many more foes to fight than followers to command!'

'So we have, Yakir! I drink to Ranbir!' Harrap ignored my taunt. He pressed on as if eager to complete a speech he had by heart before he should forget it. 'All has not been well between us these months, has it, Yakir? Disagreements – even quarrels – are born of such great quests as ours, although ours has, of course, been unique. Men fall out over trivial things, minor disputes that would not keep them apart five minutes in their own city. The Gods have driven us in the same harness for a full year now. It was not to be hoped that the traces would not chafe and cut – cut deep sometimes. I had, however, not thought that you and I, Yakir, would quarrel so fiercely. No more would I expect my right hand to reject my will.'

'It was not wholly my fault, Harrap,' I answered, bemused by his imperious approach to the apology he evidently designed.

'No, I suppose not,' he replied slowly, as if turning the great year over in his memory. 'I may have been short-tempered sometimes, even unreasonable upon occasion. The Gods gave me perfect certainty. They laid a great burden upon me as recompense.'

'We have *all* carried burdens that would crack the spines of other men.'

'That is true, Yakir. But I have commanded. If your burden has been to other men's burdens as a bullock to a mite, mine has been an elephant to a bullock. And, Yakir, I shall always be greatly indebted to you for your support at Gaustana, when even my will wavered for a time.'

'But we were wrong . . . we lost Gaustana. It would have been far better had we not attacked. We would have done better to heed Mirab and Ranbir – and we should then have kept Ranbir from death.'

'Yakir, you still do not wholly comprehend the grandeur of our Seeking,' Harrap said, deliberate forbearance in his tone. 'It was ordained that we attack. This I knew then. This I know now. We were, of course, horribly deceived by the malicious Gods, who possessed the Perfect Stallion until we drove Them out by the sacrifice. I shall not speak of the errors others made at Gaustana, but I know beyond all doubt that our attack was ordained.'

If, as it appeared, I had been invited to a banquet of reconciliation, my judgment was to be the meat and my mistakes the wine. I glared at the man who had supplanted the Harrap I had known all my days. 'Harrap, we waste time and . . .' I began reasonably.

But he was speaking still, his rumble riding over my anger. 'It might, perhaps, have been better to go south into the lands we knew. If the Perfect Stallion had only gone south . . . then we should have laid the basis for a generation of wars and conquest. Now we are turned to the cold north, where men are stubborn and the Gods of the places often hostile. But we shall, in time, conquer wholly. Perhaps it was Their purpose to lead me by such winding roads to the Throne.'

He took his wine in a single great draught and held his goblet out to Ambiala, hardly breaking the rhythm of his speech.

'Or if He had only led us further . . . then we should have sacked Loyang and taken the Emperor's treasure, taken all the wealth of China. We could have done it, Yakir. We will do it when I am Great King.'

'If others can but rise to your splendor of courage and your absolute certainty of vision.'

'No, that is not possible, nor do the Gods demand it,' he replied with equanimity as if my bitter words were but the common coin of flattery paid out by any fawning courtier. 'They need but follow without questioning.'

At that moment I would have taken Tamar's hand and led her from the yurt – to our deaths, perhaps – had Ambiala not urged more wine upon us. The ingrained response to a common courtesy stayed me as the fear of death did not.

'You did not, Harrap, ask Tamar and Yakir here to talk of the past,' Ambiala said in haste. 'There will be much time for such talk during the long evenings in the Great Palace.'

'No, that is true,' he said in surprise, like a man suddenly awakened. 'I must talk with you, Yakir, about what lies before us.'

'Harrap would ask your counsel so that you two are of one mind in the trials before us, Yakir,' Ambiala said gently.

'That is true, Yakir. We must shape our plans together and carry them through with but a single will.'

'I have not,' I answered tartly, 'been advised of what you have newly learned from Kamardol.'

'Harrap,' Ambiala smiled, 'wanted to have all the threads of knowledge in his hand before he came to you. He did not wish to trouble Tamar and yourself in your joy until he knew what awaited us.'

'Of course, Yakir, that was the reason. You were so joyous I could not break it upon you.'

I marveled that Harrap, who scorned even the Gods, calling them malicious, would bend so his will to Ambiala's soft wiles. Certainly, he would never have spared my raptures if his convenience demanded me.

The two women shared a look. Tamar's gray eyes and Ambiala's brown eyes lifted momentarily as their glances brushed. Did compassion for Harrap lie behind their exchange, or were they commiserating with each other like the trainers of two fractious colts? Had they already taken counsel together and conspired to bring Harrap and me together again? Tamar's calm gaze at once answered my questions and instructed me to assist Harrap in the plan he had conceived. I could almost hear her thought: 'Do this if you love me – and want life for us!'

'What have you learned, Harrap?' I asked. 'And what must we do?'

'I have a plan, but first let us drink again to friendship, which endures all strains.'

I raised my goblet, borne away for an instant by the memory of what had been between us. I drank deep, but doubt returned in the next instant. We could never recreate the past far gone after the past just endured.

'Now, Yakir,' he said briskly, 'our peril is great, but no more – in reality, perhaps less – than we have faced before. Chandra, my loving brother, has learned that we live, though not where we hide. He would, of course, slay us. But he must first preside over the Rites of the Returning . . .'

'Else the Seeking will be voided . . . and his royal power a mockery,' I agreed.

'Therefore, he cannot slay you and me before the Rites without blasting his own power. The Rites must be celebrated.'

'That is all well enough . . . except the Horse . . .' the words evaded my vigilance.

'The Stallion?' Harrap asked, obviously puzzled. 'What of the Stallion?'

'My tongue stumbled. I meant not the Horse, the aftermath . . . After the Rites, what will Chandra do?'

'Obviously, we must guard against his plots. My couriers have returned, and the priest has had word from his agents. Their accounts agree. Chandra, newly consecrated by the Rites of Returning, cannot slay us openly. Should he do so, he would enrage both the Army and the people. He would not live an hour after he commanded our deaths. But an accident he could contrive – perhaps fire that consumes us in our sleep.'

'You and I and the others – all apart, but all at once?'

'That is the great obstacle in his way. He could hardly convince the people that we had all been chosen for death by mischance all at once, though the sanctity of the Seeking still wrapped us. The dilemma is worthy of my loving brother's cunning.' He threw back his head and laughed, his throat drawn taut, and I saw again the Harrap I had known and loved. The ruined face, so tragic in repose and so grotesque in rage, was again a joyous gargoyle, distorted by perfect mirth. I laughed in response.

'Chandra must have another scheme,' Tamar said, not sharing our laughter. 'He would make even chance his handmaiden.'

'He must, of course, Tamar. But he is not decided. Our spies cannot be certain. But they believe he will play the same stratagem that destroyed Gupta.'

'He cannot force us to attack him,' I objected.

'I am not so sure that he could not. But he need only make it *appear* that we have attacked him, the Great King, who is anointed by the Seeking to rule empires. The mob would tear us apart – even in our sanctity – if we attacked him.'

'Then,' Tamar observed complacently, 'you need only refrain. If you are scrupulous in refraining, he cannot touch us.'

'It is hardly so simple, Tamar, my wife. As Harrap said, Chandra could contrive the appearance. Nor do I know how long we could endure the humiliation he would certainly contrive for us.'

'I shall not endure Chandra's swinish glee for an instant,' declared Harrap. 'I will destroy him first – before the Rites.'

'How?' I asked.

'Fratricide is the key . . . the soldiers fear and hate fratricide. Chandra has made his own death by allowing the Little Kamar to attack us, though they acted on Gupta's direct command. He has soiled himself so that he is not fit to partake of the Rites. The Army – only a few units are necessary – will slay Chandra before the peak of the Rites of Returning.'

'Then Harrap will be the Great King, himself originator and maker of the Seeking, himself anointed by the Seeking.'

'As you say, Yakir,' he acquiesced.

'We drink!' I cried exalted. In the instant of my setting the goblet down, I knew I should flee south to Sindhia with Tamar and the Horse, rather than dare Chandra's malignity and set in motion a new train of slaughters so that Harrap could be King. But I was committed.

The women drew to the side of the yurt to fondle the ornaments laid out on the camel trunks, and we talked for some time of our dispositions for the morning of the Rites of Returning – where we must place our own men of the Seeking and how we would enjoy the home units. We also talked of Ranbir and of our boyhood, and, for those minutes, we were one again.

The night was thick, and Tamar protested that we must return to our own yurt. As I raised the flap, Harrap charged me, 'Yakir, you must command all this. Therefore have I asked your counsel. I shall, of course, be unarmed and unarmored at the Stallion's head as the Prince of the Quest.'

'Of course, Harrap,' I answered. 'I swear it.'

I could not say otherwise, though my throat and bowels twisted in revulsion. The invitation, the protestations of love – feeble as they were and fouled by his arrogance – all served but one cold purpose. He was determined to bind me once more to himself as we had been bound before the Seeking. No one else could he wholly trust when he stood disarmed and vulnerable for the Rites. I should have preferred him to unveil his purpose from the beginning instead of staging a mock pageant of reconciliation.

'Of course, Harrap, I shall,' I repeated. I could truly say nothing else. Our lives lay in his hand – not mine alone, but Tamar's, too.

'Tell me, Harrap,' I asked after a pause, 'what have you found this year?'

'Why, Yakir, the world . . . the world in my strength . . . and my kingdom . . . my empire that shall be.'

We parted after a few more words. When I swore bitterly at Harrap's pretense, Tamar only answered, 'He is what they have made him . . . and you do not see, Yakir, he truly needs you. He is alone in the world of men except for you. He needs you, but he can ask only in his own way.'

I blessed her compassion and forgot her words.

Strangely inert, Harrap showed no inclination to shift our encampment from the broad valley on the direct route to Kamardol where we lay open to attack. I felt it was folly to put our trust in Chandra's presumed ignorance of our place of refuge. Our deaths before we came within the borders of Kamardol were as essential to him as the breath sighing in his throat and the food churning in his stomach. Only by slaying us and claiming the Horse could he retain the sanction of the Seeking while ridding himself of the threat of Harrap.

Harrap disdained the simple precaution of better concealment. At once fearful of Kamardol and soothed by its familiarity, he felt the Gods would keep us safe.

I should have urged him to move. Despite my own euphoria, I might have done so had I not shrunk from a new contest of wills with him. To protest in vain would have been worse than not protesting at all, since it would have blighted the tender shoot of the new confidence between us.

We put out pickets, of course, but Harrap chose to remain where we were for the ten days before we marched to Kamardol. Besides, the spring blizzards had already loosened the great snowbanks on the encroaching peaks. We were sheltered in our broad valley from both the avalanches and the sudden violence of the winds that hurled mountains of snow into the air like children playing in a bale of goosefeathers.

They came at almost the same instant, the courier from Gorbabordol riding out of the northern mazes where the Bastards guarded the Horse, and the courier from the picket post that guarded the narrow pass leading south through the mountains to Kamardol. On the saddle-bow of Gorbabordol's courier a horned helmet shone in the early morning sun. Seeing that mark of the Little Kamars, I cried to my trumpeter: 'Arm and mount! Arm and mount!'

The trumpets were still shrieking their affrighted alarm while Harrap and I listened to the messengers' quick, confused reports.

'Just before dawn . . .' Gorbabordol's courier forced the words through his racing breath. 'Little Kamars . . . six hundred odd . . . attacked from the north . . . Gorbabordol says he's falling back on encampment . . . The Horse is safe.'

'The mists opened . . . the snow dropped for a minute,' gasped the messenger from the south. 'We saw a force of men, perhaps Little Kamars, more than four hundred riding up the pass.'

'Mirab, take two hundred infantry and hold the southern pass. Do not attack, just hold the pass. Anand, go with Mirab . . .'

Harrap's orders flowed as fast and clear as if he had planned for the attack through the empty days.

'O Brahman,' he directed the priest, 'take the near crippled and the women. You will command those hundred, O Brahman. Hide yourselves in the cleft that reaches out to the northeast just before the northern opening of this valley. Yakir and all the rest will ride with me to the Stallion.'

The shallow valley was a wind-whipped phantasmagoria of flying snow and fog, but its dimensions were drawn clear in my mind. To the south, where Mirab and Anand were commanded, a slow slope rose through cliffs that drew gradually together to the narrow, twisting pass where no more than twenty men could stand abreast. Our valley itself was broad and featureless until one came almost to the northern entrance. There, just within the valley, a jagged cleft burrowed several hundred yards to the northeast until blocked by the face of a cliff. The northern entrance of our valley was a broad opening between gentle hills that gave abruptly on the mazes where twisted defiles spilled onto sudden precipices.

I kissed Tamar, and the swaying curtains of snow enfolded her. Harrap and I moved north through the driven white opacity. We were blind and deaf to all who were more than five yards distant. Though the pace was slow to keep the troops together, only my knowledge of the absolute discipline the long year had ingrained reassured me that more than five hundred men rode behind us. We passed out of the broad northern entrance into winds enfeebled by their hard passage through the maze of defiles. Since the winds no longer bore small snow mountains on their backs, we could see a little further into the dancing mist. The deep and narrow corridor of rock we traversed opened abruptly onto a demi-plateau surrounded by cliffs. Harrap ordered us to halt hard against the cliff wall that rose above a sheer precipice.

'I shall let them come to me,' he explained. 'Gorbabordol and his Bastards, with the Perfect Stallion, will come through to safety among us. Then I shall let the Little Kamars come to me. It matters not which of my loving brothers commands their folly. I shall destroy them under Chandra as I did under Gupta.'

He left it to me to draw up the cavalry facing north. I deployed them between the cliff, which was at our backs, and the precipices before our faces. Our left wing extended east two hundred yards to close the northern defile through which Gorbabordol and the Little Kamars must come. Our right wing rested on the cliff that curved around to the east to half enclose the plateau. We stood on the middle of three great steps formed by the cliffs, the one step above us, the one on which we stood, and the lowest at the foot of the precipice.

'One last battle and we are home,' I shouted to Harrap when my dispositions were complete.

'It has been a long ride, Yakir,' he answered.

The loose wet snow sucked at the horses' hooves, and the men called impatiently to each other. My eyes were fixed on the narrow cleft from which they must debouch, first Gorbabordol with the Horse, then the Little Kamars. I shifted uneasily in my saddle.

A tangle of princes in yellow cloaks and knights in scarlet spilled from the cleft and passed through our front. Flanked by five riders on either side, the Horse appeared among the shifting white mists. His form gradually took on solidity, as if His even whiter purity were being shaped from the mist itself. His escorts guided Him to where Harrap and I waited among our crying trumpets. Gorbabordol and the Horse's lifeguards followed, and I saw that no more than fifty of the hundred princes and knights who were the escort of the Horse had returned with Him.

The Little Kamars hurtled from the defile's mouth in units of ten, and sudden sunlight, striking through the mists, blanched the white horns on their helmets. They charged across the cold wind, their own momentum carrying them upon our lances. A few minutes after their first appearance the full six hundred faced us, drawn up with their backs to the precipice as ours were to the cliffs.

'Fools still,' Harrap grunted, rich with satisfaction.

Loosened by the tumult of the charge and by the trumpets, a torrent of snow fell around us. I could not look at the cliff behind me, for we were full engaged, cut, thrust, and parry. The Little Kamars were fresh despite their long sweep through the minor passes to take us from the north. They were fresh, and we were weary of our long Quest. But we were regulars hardened by the Quest, and they were hardly more than brigands, the only force Chandra could command for his secret treachery. Yet their first charge forced us back. Only after fifteen minutes did we begin to press them toward the precipice. We fought in open order, each man fixed on the single foe before him.

Harrap and I saw it in the same moment. The Horse, unwatched in the turmoil, had bolted through our lines and was galloping southeast toward the sharp corner where the cliff met the precipice. I looked around to draw a handful of men to me. With one mighty heave Harrap shook off the tribesman who clasped him by the neck and galloped after the Horse.

I followed then, with two others and the trumpeter, suddenly aware that the snow was sliding majestically from the lip of the cliff above us, the mass of white death hanging immense as the Great Palace itself. In the next instant, I saw that the Horse had stopped. He stood, sheltered by the overhang, on a minute ledge in the angle where the two cliffs met the precipice. The avalanche would cascade harmless just beyond him as the fiercest waterfall cascades without hurt over a swimmer pressed hard against the rockface.

I screamed to Harrap that the Horse was safe and he himself in the direct path of the avalanche. He pelted forward unhearing and spurred his horse so that the blood ran from its sides onto the trampled snow.

Two tribesmen rose out of the mist on either side of him. I shouted to the trumpeter and catapulted myself after Harrap, riding straight where his path had curved to follow the Horse. The mist blew across my eyes, blinding me for an instant. When it lifted, I saw Harrap, suspended in space beyond the edge of the precipice, a tribesman clasped under each arm. The avalanche enveloped the corner of the plateau before tumbling over the precipice to make a catafalque for Harrap and his foes.

I knew in that instant that I could have turned him from death had I not paused to rally followers. Even as we brought the Horse back within our ranks, I wondered momentarily why I had not done so. I shook off my doubts and turned to my command.

I have little heart to recount the end of that fatal battle. The rage and anguish that clouded my vision then still cloud my memory today. The soldiers had seen Harrap fall, and the enemy too had seen. When even the cavalry of Kamardol faltered in shock, I ordered the trumpeter to blow the withdrawal. My men followed, though they muttered in anger as we retreated through the maze with the triumphant Little Kamars harrying our rear.

We withdrew a long way, passing into the valley of our encampment and then into the mouth of the cleft where the women lay hidden. I had perhaps five minutes before the Little Kamars came through.

'Soldiers, men of Kamardol,' I cried in the sudden quiet. 'Prince Harrap is dead. No one can command as he did. But no tribesman will survive to boast that he saw Harrap die. Attend me!'

I sent a courier to tell Mirab he must, after twenty minutes, draw aside as if he were defeated and let his attackers pass into the valley, himself following behind them.

Hardly had my courier departed before our pursuers streamed in triumph into the valley, their ill-disciplined ranks fragmented by their exulting and by the writhing mist. I let them all come into the valley before throwing my cavalry across the entrance so that they could not escape my attacks.

My troops fought more fiercely than they had ever fought during all the sacred year, Harrap's shade rousing them through my commands to ferocity and endurance such as his bodily presence had never evoked. When the lesser force of Little Kamars came up from the south, I was driving the main body of the tribesmen between the ranks that ground them like a mortar and pestle. The battered reinforcements from the south merely confused the wretched enemy and gave us new targets for our lances. Mirab's arrival completed my victory. The last tribesman died no more than an hour past the crest of the day. Harrap was dead, and Harrap was avenged.

I grow weary with remembering the remainder of that day. I recall, though, that Ambiala heard of Harrap's death with grave composure and rode out with the priest to see where he had died. The priest returned alone, saying that Ambiala had stepped over the precipice as calmly and gracefully as if she were joining Harrap at a banquet. The woman who could never be queen followed the man who would have been king, joining herself to him in death and through eternity as his true wife by her self-immolation.

Before dusk fell Anand had counted our losses, finding only five hundred soldiers fit to ride. They brought Mirab to me on a cloak stretched between the withes of his yurt. His left leg was severed above the knee, and his right arm was crippled, though the priest said he would live.

While Tamar held my hand in one of hers and his in the other and wept, Mirab charged me wearily, 'Yakir, you must command now. It is beyond me.'

'And lead those who still survive to a ritual death?' I asked bitterly.

'If need be,' he answered. 'If we are commanded to death, you must lead us to death.'

Thirty

I had desired neither the dignity nor the power that supreme command confers, though Harrap had made me an unwilling soldier. It had throughout the Seeking been enough for me – and more than enough – when he gave me an independent unit to lead and a fixed mission to fulfill. My desire was only to be a quiet voice at his ear. I aspired only to use my trained logic to guide his flashing intuition, perhaps to restrain him when his ardor would have flung us into disaster – and, when he became King, to play the same role.

That hope had been peeled away, layer after layer, by the successive quarrels between us, for he would finally take no counsel except of his own pride and his own demons. Still, stubbornly, the essence of hope had endured in me. I had somehow continued to believe that the fulfillment of the Seeking would make all things whole between us again, for without Harrap there was no place for me in Kamardol. With Harrap's death, all my hopes of the future died too. Yet I took command of the remnants of our force. No more than five hundred could still fight despite their wounds, and another two hundred or more lay on litters.

Though I wanted neither the state nor the power, I was compelled to accept the command when the priest and Anand joined their urging to Mirab's – and even Gorbabordol concurred. He was surly as always, but positive in his advocacy. All four argued that the soldiers would follow no one except myself, who had been as Harrap's brother since boyhood and who wore the twin of his glittering sword of ceremony. Besides, with Mirab crippled, the task properly fell to me, who had been third in our small hierarchy. Gorbabordol might have disputed my succession and demanded the command by right of his princely rank. But the princeling's arrogance had not won the esteem of the regulars, and there remained no more than fifteen princes to support his claim – if they would have supported him. Gorbabordol therefore added his voice to the others' voices, and I became the General of our battered remnant.

Since men are but men, I might have savored the state Harrap's death gave me if I had any hope of redeeming our Quest in the end. In reality, however, the honor was not merely empty, but bitter too. My course was ordained. No matter how I strove during the eleven days of my tenure, we were all, except the Horse, doomed.

My immediate fear was that Chandra would destroy my enfeebled force by a single new stroke. I did not know then that he could raise no more troops to attack us after we had broken the Little Kamar. Only those half-wild tribesmen, mad with their blood-feud, would dare ride against my sacred remnant. I might have tried to pick up the skein of intrigue Harrap's hands had let fall, though I did not know with whom he had dealt in the regular Army. Ambiala would have known, but Ambiala too was dead, nor was there any purpose in questioning the couriers who had carried his messages for none saw more than a fragment of the design. Since the Army would follow only Harrap, his death had broken all hopes of prevailing over Chandra. I strove, therefore, only to escape a second and fatal attack upon us before the celebration of the Rites of Returning. I knew that we should be slain – by one pretext or another – if we came safe to the Rites. Yet that consummation was my sole purpose. To those Rites I must come with our tattered banners given to the wind in a proud travesty of triumph.

I did not allow myself to dream again of fleeing south to Sindhia with the Horse – in part because Tamar's vision forbade the evasion, but primarily because the mission that Harrap and I had begun together was mine alone to force to fulfillment.

We had made a magnificent Seeking, the greatest ever known. But the Seeking was not yet complete. If I did not bring the Horse back to Kamardol for the Rites of Returning, the Seeking would be no more than a luckless – a pointless – marauding expedition, more costly in men than most and less rewarding in spoils than most. I had learned that our Gods, Who abhorred the sacrifice of unwilling men, gladly accepted the human sacrifice, preferring it to beasts. We had already given Them a great number of lives, but we must offer Them our lives that remained to take if They wished. I knew with sick certainty that Their insatiability would devour our lives too. The soldiers, though, might have been enclosed in wholly different cycles of space and time from those that circumscribed me. Knowing little of Chandra's plots, they were jubilant at mastering – by their destruction of the Little Kamar – the last peril that lay between them and their homes. Their overwhelming jubilation was subdued only by their weariness and by Harrap's death.

I would not lie longer in the open valley where Chandra could not only deprive us of our lives, but could steal the splendor of our deeds already done by slaying us before the Seeking was crowned by the Rites of Returning. Though the soldiers groaned, I shifted our camp to the demi-plateau within the maze where Harrap had fallen. We bore to that plateau all the slain of our last battle, the Little Kamars as well as our own dead.

We heaped up a great cairn of wind-smoothed rocks, and the priest sacrificed sixteen horses, one for each of the sixteen parts of the world where our Quest had run. Our tears running fresh again, we hurled the corpses over the cliff to lie above Harrap in the snow. He would have comrades on his journey, the soldiers of Kamardol, and he would have slaves to serve him, the treacherous Little Kamars. Standing in the blood-sodden snow of the plateau, all broken by the battle and frozen again in jagged pink-stained hillocks, Tamar wept no more. She laid a restraining hand on my arm when I unclasped my sword of ceremony to hurl it after the corpses. 'Nothing else remains to you of him,' she said. 'Will you not keep the sword to avenge him upon Chandra?'

My hands clasped the belt again of their own will. Revenge upon Chandra had not come into my mind, any more than I had plotted revenge upon the hostile mountains or the cruel winds. I thought of the King as no more than another instrument of the will of the Gods. I was wholly given to my intense efforts to read Their intentions. If it were ordained that we must go to death, our banners unfurled through the chanting of hymns and the rising of incense, we should at least make a brilliant sacrifice. I longed to be wholly certain of Their will, and it came to me that I had not thought to consult the priest, whose vocation it was to read the will of the Gods. In that instant, I fully comprehended Harrap's isolation in command. Remembering Harrap with my new understanding, I felt a thrill of fierce pleasure at the prospect of repaying his death in Chandra's blood.

The King would be surrounded by his household troops, but no king can be guarded against the swift stroke of a man who expects to die. I wondered whether I should wield the knife myself or find an assassin who appeared less likely to wish Chandra's death to compass his death. But I saw how it would be for Kamardol with Chandra dead, last of the royal line. If there were no undisputed successor, all the petty princes would struggle with each other to seize the Emerald Throne. The realm would splinter, while the people suffered and died. Reluctantly, I recalled my hasty resolution as I would whistle to a favorite hound who pressed his attack on a tiger to his own mortal peril. I would let Chandra create his own successor – and himself wreak my revenge upon himself – by the coherent and effective opposition his misrule would invoke. I should not see my final revenge, and the people would still suffer, though not so grievously. But there was no other way.

'I shall keep the sword,' I told Tamar. 'And I shall think about a fitting revenge.'

I wanted only four days before departing for Kamardol, so that I might bear my many wounded slowly through the passes. Besides, there was greater safety within the beast's lair. Once we entered the settled fringes, Chandra must permit our sacred procession to pass freely to the sanctified arena.

The Rites of the Returning were all my purpose and all my hope – and beyond them, nothing. Knowing myself doomed, I tried to believe my soldiers might survive Chandra's jealousy. But I knew the King would let no man live who had ridden with Harrap. Behind his jealousy was fear. No man might live to rally the people against Chandra with songs and tales of his brother's valor and his own treachery. I saw how simply Chandra could contrive all our deaths so that the people might mutter, but none would dare to act. The chief among us – myself, Tamar, Anand, Mirab, the priest, and all the princes – he could hold fast under the cloak of royal hospitality until we died by mischance. The soldiers he could herd into a camp to rest from their weariness. Then, a plague might appear, a plague carried unknowing in their blood from the strange lands of the heart of the continent – and every man who remembered Harrap would be silent forever.

Tamar and I were strangely happy during those four days. We were not so much resigned to our doom as determined to meet it fair. Ours was a mood quite different – and stronger – than resignation, though it is difficult to describe. We rejoiced not only in our bodies, but in planning how we would shape the future were the future ours to shape. We were sad, too, not so much because death awaited us across the mountains as because we knew that our love, being without fruit, would never be wholly complete.

'I remember, Yakir,' Tamar sighed in bitter mirth, 'how I used to curse myself. You had, it seemed, only to look at me . . . and there was a baby growing in my belly. Then all the fuss with the abortion. But now . . . if I could only make a son so quickly . . . give him to the light before we die.'

I took joy, too, in the soldiers' ready obedience, which sprang from their belief that I had brought them safely home by breaking the Little Kamar when they had us all between their shields and their spears after Harrap's fall. Anand said the soldiers told each other that I had done as much as Harrap himself to conjure the victories of the year of our Quest. It was, perhaps, fortunate that I had so little time to accustom myself to the pleasure of command. If I had indeed led them through the Quest, I could not save them in the end. Still, as Tamar said, there must be much truth in a conviction held so strongly by so many. It was, in any event, not unpleasant.

I spoke little to Tamar of the manner of Harrap's death, nor did I recall it to myself except when the thought took me unaware. Two opposed currents of thought flowed unbidden in my mind. The one was assurance that my honors were truly won. I believed that I had done everything – even more than our past comradeship demanded – to succor Harrap, throughout our Quest and at the moment of his death. I believed that Harrap, maddened with his own great powers, had died rather than yield the slightest portion of his pride by awaiting my help. The other thought came less frequently to taunt me. I feared that I had, from the beginning of our Quest, sought Harrap's degradation – or his death. I believed that I could have saved him had I put spurs to my horse fifteen seconds earlier. I could not, however, decide which voice spoke in truth – or if either spoke wholly in truth.

When we began our final journey toward the south, I drove both pleasure and regret from my mind. Our ragged and pain-filled order of march so fully commanded my attention that my personal thoughts were as evanescent as the fleeting image of the white dove or a black swan glimpsed in the wind-ruffled waters of a lake as the bird soars overhead. The soldiers were joyous, singing their jubilation and their gratitude for the homecoming they had not truly expected. Tamar, Anand, the priest, and I were calm, though we knew the fate that awaited both the soldiers and ourselves. We had chosen our end, and the uncertainty was done.

The clouds withdrew to let the placid sun shine through and the ponderous snowbanks frozen again by the cold each night hung as if fixed forever amid the flux of spring. We had given much care to the Horse before we set out, and the men groomed Him with love at each pause, praising Him with their hands. He shimmered constantly in the dazzling light of the snow. He was as impeccable as if He had sprung of the union of those two purest elements, the light and the snow. Eighteen months past Harrap, the priest, and I had brought the Colt down the same pass and across the ford into Kamardol. Between the files of princes he shone larger, rounder, more powerful, and, strangest of all, more precisely molded. The journeyman sculptor had shaped a statue that was perfect to his own eye and the beholders'. The master sculptor had taken that image – adding a little here, flicking away a little there, and smoothing it with cunning hands to create a masterwork beyond human perfection.

Thus I brought the Horse home to Kamardol a second time. He was unstained by the blood we had left, and given, in His cause, as He was unmarred by the anguish of spirit and body we had endured in His Seeking.

The soldiers sang my 'Song of the Seeking' when we came down the slope to the ford we four had crossed that night when even the ferryman was gone to the Great King's obsequies. I hardly heard them. The City lay before us in the plain, its iridescent cupolas sparkling above the somber necklace of the towers. But Kamardol itself was less real to me than the memory of Cosmopolis and Gaustana and Lighfar and the squalid oases of the yellow desert.

Across the ford a multitude awaited our coming – peasants in white, nobles in colored silks, soldiers in burnished armor, and priests and monks in red and golden robes. Their incessant cheers prevailed over both the thin lament of our own trumpets and the joyous chords of the City's massed lutes as we bore our wounded through the icy waters on litters lifted high between mounted soldiers. A multitude of colored banners tossed on long staffs flaunted brilliant as the sun, but I saw only the single banner that had so briefly streamed in the high wind above the Sacred Mount of Gaustana.

The great officers of the Court made their formal salutations. Their stilted attitudes faltered for an instant when they saw how few we were and became aware that hardly a man who could still sit in his saddle but had himself wounds bound up. Their faces grew grave, their sleek, home-pampered faces, when I told them Harrap was dead. But exultation at the greatest Seeking of all soon stilled their sorrow. Even the great officers cheered like schoolboys when to their eager offers of assistance I replied that we required only a clear road before us to the City.

There was more than bravado in my reply, though bravado there was in plenty. We were not, I realized, as they who had remained in Kamardol, and we would never again be as they. I felt myself alone among my own people, and in my cold isolation I felt intense revulsion from the fat faces, shining oily with good living, that chattered their mindless congratulations.

Dazed at the ending of our Quest and contemptuous of them that had not ridden with us, I still saw that many faces were absent that should have greeted us – and, further, that many new faces crowned the silken robes of the great officers. I still commanded wit enough to draw aside the old Captain of the Guardians of the Ford and give my wounded into his care. He seemed to understand when I charged him to disperse them throughout the Army so that they could not be found easily. He did not merely promise, but saluted with the stiff formality due a commander-in-chief and rendered the full formula of obedience in archaic words. I was startled when the scarred veteran called me General. But I wore the title more easily for knowing that I had done all I could to save the severely wounded from the death that awaited all the rest of us.

We rode up Alexander's Road toward the encampment beside the great arena we would enter in the morning. The villages that had been deserted when we first brought the Horse to Kamardol saluted our slow progress with the happy din of drums; with showers of petals that, crushed beneath our horses' hooves, released a sweet green fragrance; with the lowing of the cowherds' long horns; and with the crackling of silken banners in the joyous wind. The village called Alexander's Rest had leashed its lean dogs, but the beasts bayed in chorus and strained against their tethers as if they would overwhelm us with caresses whom they had berated as intruders on our last coming.

I fingered the bas-relief image of Alexander on my worn silver coin – and remembered much. I can recall all this now, and the scent of coriander, chilis, and bread baking. At the moment I hardly felt or heard or saw. I had come home to Tamar in the mountains. This mock homecoming was no more than a prelude to be endured before the Rites of the Returning – before death appeared to us at the King's command.

Tamar and I had no need for words, or perhaps no words left for our needs. But passing Alexander's Rest, I spoke low to Anand at my left hand. 'Is it not time for you to leave us? This was never your Quest, not as it has been ours even in the marrow of our souls. Is it not time for you to leave us? Is it not time for you to evade death by going to your fellow Buddhists?'

'It is not the time, Yakir, my General!' he answered, and his tone was fierce, though I had not meant to offend him. 'Each man goes on his own Quest. This has been my Quest, as much as yours or any man's, and I count it the best fortune that we could go on our separate Quests together.' He paused to brush the clinging petals from his face. 'How long do you think I could evade death – even among my fellow Buddhists? I could win life, perhaps, by going to Chandra now and by befouling the Seeking to the people all the rest of my days thereafter. I left Kamardol a lieutenant of cavalry in a great force. I am returned adjutant of the bravest fragment that ever survived a year of unending battle. I too am known, too well known, to evade fate by deceit. It has been my Quest, too.'

I was startled by his vehemence, by the sudden harsh anger in his normally soft and hesitant voice. His words spoke meaning clear to me. All the pageantry rehearsed by those who had remained in Karmardol was less in meaning than a shadow-play of painted donkeyhide figures manipulated by apprentice players.

'Besides,' he added, with quick laughter in his voice, 'you may need an adjutant.'

'Where I am going?'

'Wherever you are going!'

So I parted from Anand, our parting an affirmation of the unknown. Still my unappeased curiosity prowled the small world of the Seeking that was the only reality I knew. I beckoned the priest to take Anand's place beside me as if I wished him too to accept the monotonous cheering.

'Tell me, O Priest, before we die,' I asked, 'has our Seeking truly been the great venture your auguries promised? Are you content with what you have found?'

'That answer, of course, still depends on the Rites of Returning,' he began portentously, but his voice assumed a lighter and yet more earnest tone as he sensed that I asked neither out of vanity nor out of mockery. 'I do not know, Yakir, truly I do not. There are so many things . . . and one or two in particular. Had I the time, it would give me matter for reflection . . . for prayer . . . for a space of years. But this way, I suppose, I can say only that I do not know, but I sense something . . .'

'You can tell me no more?' I interrupted.

'No, not at this moment. Though we shall all have completed our Quest, found our answers, before the week is finished.'

'And that is all? That is all – after *this* year?'

'Yes, I suppose so . . . but perhaps not. Have we not passed beyond the question of success or failure? We have discovered – mapped, in truth – unknown realms . . . on the ground and in the spirit. Unless my brethren of the priesthood are all fools, we have saved the True Religion, indeed . . .'

I did not press him, and at length he resumed of his own will. 'Unless the rulers of Kamardol are fools, we have given them the matter of a hundred conquests. Dominating the heart of the continent, Kamardol could in time command all Hindustan and the south. We have even become rich ourselves – as long as it is given to us to possess the riches of this world. I should not call our Quest a worldly failure.'

'And for yourself,' I insisted, 'what have you found?'

'For myself? A certain, shall we say, a certain confusion?' He would speak no more to the question though I pressed him hard.

We came at dusk to the encampment prepared for us beside the arena, where the priests were droning the prayers that had not ceased since we rode out of the same arena a year earlier. Neither the priests nor the King should we see till the morning.

I ordered Anand to admit the soldiers' women and children, who clamored outside the gates. I only grinned back at him when he, grinning, protested, 'But it is written that the escorts of the Stallion shall go pure into the arena.'

I could do no more for my men, and I went to Tamar in the great silken tent that had been erected for us. We talked that night of many things besides the Seeking. We slept little, and wishing little sleep, we were not disturbed by the raucous din of the encampment – the shouting and singing, the laughter and weeping of children, and the shrill cries of women long deprived of pleasure.

At length we slept. Exhaustion claimed us, though we had no joy and little repose in our sleep. We woke two hours before the dawn, when the constant tumult of the encampment swelled upward to hail the new day. My men rose early to groom the Horse and to burnish their own battered armor. Chandra had sent word that not only the remnants of the anointed four hundred – the princes, knights, archers, and yeoman – might come into the arena, but all who had survived the Seeking. His gesture seemed to me not sprung of grace but the desire to have us all within his hands.

I kissed Tamar once before she rode off among the escort of honor the King had sent, the better, I feared, to keep her from speaking with the courtiers and the better to seize her when he would. We said no more than 'Goodbye' since our hearts were as wrung dry of words as our eyes of tears. I turned my back so that I might not, watching her going from me forever, show my weakness to the troops. But I heard her call, and in my weakness I turned again to her. 'Till this evening, my love!' Her voice floated high and clear above the din of the camp. 'Till this evening!'

'Till this evening!' I cried. 'Wherever we meet again!'

I untied her long scarlet scarf that I had wound around my helmet, and let the ends trail in the morning wind. Her back receded from me, slender in pale-blue silk and curved taut as a fowler's bow above her hips that turned to fit the sidesaddle. The shining curtain of her hair rippled around her slender shoulders.

Beside me Gorbabordol waited with the remaining Bastards, his long, saturnine face a mummer's mask above the plain white robe he wore as a Prince of the Rite. Thirteen princes had survived, and all were dressed in the same white robes. In their midst the Perfect Stallion waited, calm as if he stood among His own herd on a hillside in Ferghana. I instructed Gorbabordol again in his duties, telling him what he already knew, that the Stallion must appear when my trumpet sounded. He grinned at me, his yellow teeth bared in mock patience. 'I shall obey, General!' he entoned.

In my belt pouch I found a brown cone of sugar for the Horse. He took it from my fingers with His lips, nodding His thanks with grave courtesy. I stroked His neck with my palm, caressing Him with the slight circular motion he loved, and tried again to read the mystery of the Godhead in those domed eyes. 'Be proud, Little One,' I whispered into His cocked ear. 'Be proud, my son – and all will be well.'

Turning from the Horse, I mounted to lead my five hundred around the closed curve of the horseshoe arena to its open end. We were tattered and dingy beside the regular soldiers who rimmed the outer curve of the arena. Three thousand at least they numbered in their shimmering mail and their brilliant cloaks that swept over their horses' cruppers – as if Chandra feared the people. The cavalry cheered us, and we took their cheers gladly. Their trumpets blared the 'General's March' and the 'Prince's Salute,' while the flag-bearers made their guidons dance in the morning air.

Since I could not make my protest heard, I bowed to acknowledge the honor I hardly merited. My men sat straighter in their worn saddles, flaunting the dented, rusty armor and the torn, threadbare cloaks they had refused to exchange for the splendid new equipment the King sent us. They wore their grimy bandages as if they were the finest silks of China, and the stains on those bandages the most precious jewels of all the world's royal treasuries.

The arena was an enormous cauldron boiling over an immense fire. The cheering and the music rose up like clouds of fragrant steam. A medley of odors foamed around us: blood and ghee, torn earth and milk, flowers and incense. Sight was overwhelmed by the infinity of flashing colors that shot out their rays to pierce our aching eyes: the yellow-robed priests; the jewels of the naked female dancers; the black-cloaked household troops of the King; the women of the people in their dusky-rose and purple skirts beside the russet-brown tunics of their men; the gorgeous silks of the ladies shimmering beside the gaudy robes of the nobles. All that great throng – except the King and his wives, five colored dolls atop the high golden tower in the far curve of the horseshoe – rose to pay us honor.

The lutes raised their joyous cry, and the strings of my own lute of themselves cried back in joy from my saddle-bow. The trumpets sang their own glad pæan, and a thousand priests raised the chant of Varuna the Victorious. Perhaps the uproar died of itself, perhaps the multitude, sensing an alien sound amid the tumult, signaled, one to the other, to be silent. There was sudden silence and out of the silence my own men singing my 'Song of the Seeking.'

While they sang – and I alone was silent to savor the words – I swept the arena again with my eyes. The twenty-one stakes were all bare around the Great Altar and the single central stake of cedar, which was tiled with gold plates. Each day of the sacred year of the Seeking the prescribed sacrifices had been offered to the Gods and the sanctified carcasses had been taken from the arena to be consumed by fire. Exactly four hundred and forty-one beasts had already gone ahead through the gates opened by the priests' chanting – bullocks and sheep, cocks and dogs, deer and bears. Atop his golden tower, full four stories high, the King sat surrounded by his wives and his chief officers. His black-cloaked bodyguard filled the three lower levels and formed a tight circle around the tower's base. This was no loving King toward whom I led my men to make obeisance, but a King who, ruling the people by fear, had begot upon fear terror that ruled him too.

We halted, and I raised my hands in stiff salute, for I would not bow in my saddle as custom prescribed. Chandra's bloated face, yellow with bile and greasy with self-indulgence, smiled down upon me with stained brown lips. I saw every loathsome feature clear, though his face was no bigger than my thumbnail at the distance between us.

'You have done magnificently,' Chandra declaimed, and I wondered if he had already counted his share of the treasure we had brought back. 'You have brought me the keys to all power! You have been the stones of which I shall build my empire! I grieve for my brother, I grieve deeply, though he gladly gave his life for this day's glory – and for my power. But my private grief must not intrude upon the realm's joy. You have all done well, and you shall all be rewarded beyond your dreams – and particularly you, Yakir, my General.'

The murderer spoke thus of Harrap, his victim. My hand darted toward the empty sling, where my javelin would have lain had we been permitted to wear weapons other than swords into the arena. Although the King was wholly safe atop his golden tower, a ripple ran along the black rank of bodyguards that confronted us. My own men, believing still that the Little Kamars had attacked us only to close their blood-feud with Harrap, cheered the King's confirmation of my rank.

'We are overwhelmed by your praise, Majesty!' I bit off the words, having chosen the shortest acceptable formula. As I led my men to their stations at the side of the arena, I knew that the hatred that lay between Chandra and myself could be dissolved only by death. And I knew that he would certainly not die first.

I nodded to my trumpeter, and for the last time he sounded the Advance of the Seeking. The High Priest, standing on the Great Altar before the golden tower, began the Invocation, his single voice commanding the Gods in high, sweet tones. I saw for the first time that the priest of our Quest stood beside him, where only the Coadjutor might stand. Absently, I reflected that the priest might somehow live, and, absently, I was glad. The High Priest's chant was rising ever higher.

All sound died when the Perfect Stallion trotted into the arena, followed by Gorbabordol and his twelve princes, all in white. A mare neighed a muffled neigh, and the Stallion's ears pricked. Throwing back His broad head on the sinuous column of His throat, He answered her as if He were responding to the High Priest's Invocation.

The tumultuous voice of the throng broke over us again when the Stallion galloped towards the Great Altar, searching for the mare. But she was concealed within the Altar itself, and He submitted bewildered when the priests cast a long rope around His neck. They brought the free end to the great central stake and knotted it to a hook cunningly hidden among the enameled golden plaques. He snorted, and His sharp hooves cut the blood-soaked turf in disgust at the scent He hated. The priests came toward Him, leading the four wives of the King to the ritual that is so shameful that it must in its own course ask forgiveness of the Gods, pleading for purification in the midst of the enormities it commits.

They anointed Him with ghee and with blood, with soma and with wine, with the urine of cows and with whey. All the while, the priests chanted, the lutes wailed, the clowns mimed, and the dancers flitted around the arena.

They called Him by many awesome names: the Thunderbolt and the Sun, the Lightning and Varuna, the Wind and Pragpati, the Breath of the World and the Avatar of All the Gods – and many more names divine and glorious. Still adoring Him while the chorus of priests chanted and the lutes and trumpets shrieked together, they led Him to a cloth of gold spread twice-folded before the altar and laid another cloth of gold over Him so that He was wholly covered. I closed my eyes when the Stallion vanished beneath the shimmering cloth, seeing only in my mind's horrified eye what they would next do to Him.

He would be 'quieted,' as the Brahmayana says, by a single stroke of a mace of steel and gold. Then the King's chief wife would come forward once more, the three lesser wives following with eyes downcast behind her, and all attended by four hundred handmaidens who had waited behind the tower of gold. The chief wife, the Queen they called her, would slip beneath the cloth of gold and grasp the dead Stallion's member, pressing it to her own sex, while the High Priest intoned the Liturgy.

'May the perfect Stallion, God and beast, bestow His seed upon you. Of Him is the universe made, of His blood the rivers, of His eyes the seas, of His bones the mountains, and of His bowels the land. May you, O Queen, grow fruitful with the seed of the universe, as the King, your husband, is now endowed with the supreme power of the universe.'

'O Mother, Mother, no one is taking me,' the Queen would cry, mocking all our great deeds and debasing His bright courage. 'The Beast lies asleep. And I am anointed with scent and clothed in silks for His pleasure.'

The High Priest would urge her to greater efforts, and the Queen would cry as if to the Stallion, 'Let us two entwine our limbs.'

'Come, lay Thy seed in her cleft,' the High Priest would command. 'Lay Thy seed in the channel she has opened to you between her thighs. Make play with the organ that nourishes life in women, dart it back and forth within her sheath.'

The black dialogue would continue while the Queen lay beside the dead Stallion under the shining cloth. At the same time the attendant priests and the attendant ladies would make great sport, calling each other cock and hen and mocking each other's sex, mocking the men who had left their bodies across the heart of the continent, in the snows and in the deserts, for this, the degenerates' febrile, vicious pleasure. When their sport was finally ended, the King and his wives would sit around the poor dismembered carcass, sucking the marrow from His cracked bones. Out of this mummery, the Brahmayanas declared, would spring supreme power for the King and the realm.

I saw those scenes against my eyelids through my tears. Hearing a great cry that was not of the liturgy, I opened my eyes.

The Stallion was dead, the cloth of gold crumpled above Him, and the King's wives approached, trailing their handmaidens. The tower of gold, where the King sat, seethed and writhed with the swarming of astonished courtiers like the witless scurrying of giant black ants when their towering anthill is cracked by an elephant's hoof. An officer of the cavalry in full armor leaned over the balustrade. He was waving a dark object like a ball.

First in horror and then in fearful glee, I saw that he dangled by its long greasy hair the head of King Chandra. The black-cloaked bodyguard stood stricken and irresolute. Some began to climb the tower, but they heard the pounding of hooves behind them and the regular cavalry swept into the arena to ride down the black bodyguards.

Dazed by the surge of the troops, I could not move, and my own men were frozen by shock. I felt Anand pulling at my cloak. 'Listen, Yakir, listen, Yakir, listen!' he cried. 'Hear what they are shouting!'

The soldiers wheeled to face me, bending low in their saddles in obeisance. 'Yakir, Yakir, Yakir shall be King!' they shouted. 'Yakir who wears the sword of Harrap. Yakir-Harrap, King of Kamardol by the Secking!'

I cast my helmet away and spread my cloak wide. Two cavalry officers came forward with the Crown from Chandra's head. The acclamation became total, for the people too, were shouting.

'Yakir! Yakir! Yakir-Harrap, King of Kamardol!'

Afternote

> Here the Chinese scribe, presumably reproducing a note appended by the first translator, remarks: 'The hand in which the following brief finale is written is quite different from that which set down the bulk of the original Sanskrit manuscript, being smaller and more precise and, further, displaying a meticulous predilection for complex diacritical marks, which were archaic even at the presumed time of the original composition and were all but forgotten when the work of translation began.'

I am setting down some few additional facts so that the account of my son's life will be as complete as human knowledge can make it. Although only the Gods can see truth whole, the abrupt ending of his own account pains me. It is necessary that history, which is more than the sum of the lives of individuals, be set down as fully as the chronicler's material permits. I shall place this manuscript among my personal records, for I would not have Yakir's shamefully naked revelations lie in the State Archives of Kamardol which I preserve even here in Sindhia. Perhaps, after the passage of many generations, Yakir's record and my own slight addition may come into the hands of a man of our family who can discern some central meaning, which my son sought, in vain I believe, in the events he described. It may, perhaps, be a man who is not even of our blood to whom the gift of insight is given. It must, however, be a man of a later age.

My wife and I were escorted in honor from our first exile in Sindhia to Kamardol soon after our son was hailed King, and I became, once again, Chronicler to the Court. Though he insisted that I assume the style of Prince-Progenitor and First Minister of the Left, I performed the same duties I had always performed.

Once again I recorded the moraines that the flow of men's passions leave upon the lives of their fellows and upon the structure of the realm.

On the instant the soldiers and the people called him King, my son saw that he and Tamar must partake of those aspects of the Rites of Returning which he considered so abhorrent. He could not avoid them, for the playing and the consuming were the essence of the sacrificial mystery, the act that endowed the King and the realm with supreme power and overflowing fruitfulness. Tamar performed the symbolic copulation with the dead Stallion under the cloth of gold, while the priests and the ladies-in-waiting spoke the words that re-create the joy of generation, mocking and irreverent as they may seem. Yakir and Tamar took the cracked bones from the priests' hands and sucked from their ivory tunnels the smoking marrow that contained the secret strength of the stallion. I do not believe that he performed those acts only because he could not otherwise accept the proffered Crown. I believe that he realized he must ignore his fastidiousness if he were to imbibe the potency the Seeking conferred on the King. So the Horse, the Avatar of all the Gods, was reborn in my son, who consumed the source of His strength.

The splendor of the Seeking that had passed purified the Rites of Returning of their discrepancies. Much that had already been twisted by necessity was put straight by the sanction of the deeds done in the heart of the continent. It did not detract from the total sanctity that the sacrifice of the Stallion came before the crowning of the King or even that Yakir had come fresh from Tamar's bed. Since not even the most naïve novice priest believed that the gross Chandra had prepared himself for the Rites by passing the year in perfect celibacy, there could be no protest against my son's newly married state. Above all, Yakir was enveloped by the glory of the Seeking – an aura of searing flame that purified all. Besides, Kamardol had need of him. His accession alone could bind together the different elements of the realm that Chandra had set against each other and against the Throne. My son has, perhaps inadvertently, demonstrated in his own account why he was on that particular occasion the indispensable man, that creature more often met in poets' fancies than in the sober chronicles of history.

His manuscript, which I gather was written piecemeal and helter-skelter, both during the Quest and after his Enthronement, is one of the most puzzling historical documents I have ever encountered. In general rich in information, it is distressingly reticent on certain essential points. Shockingly candid in parts, it compels me to the belief that he dissembled in other parts. I cannot, for example, quite credit the vicissitudes of his attitude toward the Sacred Rites or his adumbrations upon the validity of the True Religion. Certain of those inconsistencies I am prepared to accept as the vagaries of a spirit tried by a hard pilgrimage, though I do not wholly understand them.

I cannot, however, accept Yakir's implication that he was unaware of the plot to make him King until the chorus of twenty thousand throats demanded that he accept the Crown. Perhaps he had seen so many miracles that he could not admit that his final apotheosis was no miracle, but the culmination of a painstakingly laid scheme. Chandra was, of course, struck down by his military equerry, an officer he had himself elevated so high that even his constantly darting suspicion did not look for treachery in that quarter. To appoint no equerry would have been to confess that he feared his own troops. An equerry he had chosen from among the subalterns and raised him high so that he owed all to the King. Chandra did not appreciate that the terror of ostracism by his fellows, who were his world, could compel his hand-shaped equerry to bow to the solemn order of the Army's senior commanders – and slay the King. Chandra had won no more personal loyalty from his equerry than he had from any other of his servants, great or small.

The Army had, of course, always wanted Harrap to be King. After his death by treachery, the commanders were compelled to find another candidate or submit to Chandra's gradual destruction of their caste and their power. They found Yakir, a Brahman of an old Court family, who was bound by generations of service to the Great Kings of Kamardol and particularly, through myself, to the last Great King. He was also a warrior, whom his soldiers, I am told, had come to love as much for his compassion toward them as for his hardihood and courage. Finally, he was Harrap's other face, the man who had been beside the Supreme Hero from boyhood and throughout the Seeking, the man who wore the twin of Harrap's own sword of ceremony. Since he was all those things, and the surviving General of the Seeking as well, the people would acclaim him.

Whether Yakir was also the man who for long willed Harrap's death and sealed that death by his dilatoriness, I do not know. Since I alone have read his account, and then only long after his Enthronement, no man but Yakir was troubled by that doubt. All needs thus came together, and Yakir became King of Kamardol. He ruled under the style of Yakir-Harrap, and his symbol was a silver stallion. When the people, after his reign had endured a few years, began to call him the Great Horse King, he was not disturbed that both those names, Harrap and Yakir alike, fell into disuse.

He wore always on his right wrist a circlet of twisted hair taken from the tail of the Perfect Stallion, and he took great care to preserve the line pure that the Stallion had begotten on the six errant mares before the attack on Gaustana. Foals that were blemished by even a single spot of color he sent to the cavalry to mount officers who had by their outstanding deeds merited the honor of riding the King's own horses. The pure-white foals he kept for himself, breeding them to each other, sister to brother, to perpetuate the breed he loved. Five times he found colts that were indistinguishable from the Perfect Stallion in their conformation, and those were extraordinary in both speed and stamina. But never did he find one that could wholly match the Perfect Stallion in those qualities, and never was there one that bled after great exertions.

Tamar, his Queen, gave Yakir two sons and a daughter during the first five years of his reign, and it was not until the sixth year that he took the additional three wives that his dignity demanded. Bolela, his Brahman wife who was the daughter of my own younger sister, my wife and I loved best, though my son was indifferent to her. But it was to Harrap, his second son by Tamar, to whom our hearts were given.

My digression to largely personal matters is, perhaps, improper, although these notes are intended to fill out my son's account for our family archives. I shall, therefore, return to the public matter of Yakir-Harrap's reign of nine years and two months.

Supported by Anand, who became his First Minister of the Right, and the priest of the Quest, who became his High Priest, my son sought to shape a new society in old Kamardol. Mirab before his death was his advocate in the Army, and Gorbabordol spoke for him among the nobility. I cannot judge that Yakir succeeded in his grand purpose, though he was, without question, far more visionary and far more daring than any of the Great Kings of Kamardol who had preceded him. Others had vastly extended the boundaries. Some had imposed sweeping changes on men's lives and their positions relative to each other. None before my son had attempted to remake the entire structure of Kamardol itself.

Yakir believed that religion was the source from which all men's lives flowed and that the quality of that source gave each realm its own particular character. In Kamardol, the source was divided, and the realm too was divided. Seeking to heal the rift among the people, Yakir created a New Religion by drawing together into a unity the Old Religion, Buddhism, and even the ancient cults that centered on the Mother Goddess of the Earth. He also added certain new elements he had discovered on his Seeking.

Under the High Priest's inspiration, he taught that all the Gods were one God Almighty, Who showed Himself in different guises to different realms and even to different individuals. He decreed that each man might worship as he pleased, but that no man – or group of men – might through religious practice possess or mulct other men. Caste he strengthened, declaring that its distinctions reflected, however imperfectly, the same distinctions of nature that endow the horse with greater speed than the bullock – and some horses with much greater speed than others. Despite the distinctions of caste, he stressed, all men were truly men, and he ordered that there be no order of men, such as the Pariahs, who were excluded from manhood and from humanity. Under Yakir's rule caste was, therefore, transformed. He compared its distinctions among men, who were all equally men, to the different manifestations of the God Almighty men worship, all flowing equally from the Godhead though they diverge so greatly in their outward forms. He affirmed that caste was divinely ordained, but its purpose, he said, was to distinguish men by their functions, not to separate lesser orders of men from other orders that were greater in their essential quality.

He offered sacrifices each year to the being he called the God Almighty, the One God. He sacrificed only birds, snakes, and other wild creatures, which are set apart from men. He forbade the sacrifice of animals that carried their young in their wombs and nursed their newborn. The Horse became the central being of the New Religion in the people's hearts, though Yakir declared time after time that the Horse was but another emanation of the One God. He himself was worshipped beside the Horse – and he permitted that worship. He said to me often that it was necessary to bind the men and women of Kamardol by such a central and specific belief until their souls grew into unity with the beautiful but abstract precepts of the New Religion.

The reader to whom I speak across the centuries – be he of our blood or of an alien line – may feel that I have permitted my critical judgment to be distorted by paternal feeling in judging Yakir guiltless of self-deification. I have, however, applied to this small account the same rigorous standards by which I have always tested my public chronicles. It would, moreover, be pointless to seek to obscure the apparent truth – as far as I can comprehend the truth – in a document that, I hope, will convey some greater truth to a mind fit to discern it. Besides, *why* should I lie? The one to whom this account comes must finally judge for himself whether I speak the truth when I say that Yakir did not glory in the worship of himself.

What he truly believed in his own heart I do not wholly know, but he appeared obsessed by a search for definition of the Good and the Evil – terms meaningless to me because they imply a great separation among the Gods, instead of a constant interplay of tension among Them. Yakir, moreover, sought to make that definition absolute, above the alternating contention and harmony among men that is its earthly manifestation. Since there are hundreds of tracts* from his own hand and others' hands discussing the principles of the Good and the Evil and expressing his hopes of unmistakable revelation through a human Avatar in his own time, I shall write no more on this matter.

Yakir's temporal ambitions were as sweeping as his spiritual ambitions. The Army he favored because it had created him and also because it seemed to him the one entity in Kamardol that had already attained that integration of divergent forces he sought for the realm. Favoring the Army, he was moved to give the Army employment. Time after time the troops of Kamardol went out into the heart of the continent to extend our realm by subduing the cities that had made symbolic submission to the Seeking. In the fifth year of Yakir's reign he sent a great force under Anand to conquer Gaustana and slay all the monks of the Monastery of the Sacred Mount. He called the city Avalometsera, which means the Glory of the Mountaineers in archaic Sanskrit, but he never visited it.

I shall not dwell long on certain matters because they are set forth at length in the Official Chronicles. As men know well, the Kushans swept out of the northern mountains and conquered Kamardol nine years and two months after the inception of Yakir's reign. They hung the King up as a butt for their arrows, and he died shouting his affirmation that the One God Almighty renders justice to all men. Tamar they strangled first. That horror of destruction I did not see, for I had fled south to Sindhia before the last attack, taking with me Harrap, the King's second son, on the pretext of showing him the graves of his ancestors. Thus ended the reign of Yakir-Harrap, the Great Horse King of Kamardol, and thus ended the separate history of Kamardol. The Kushans made our realm one with their other conquests and used it as a base for their southward conquests.

Though great forces were at work, Yakir, I believe, provoked his own fate. Among the mass who called themselves the Kushan were Uighur and Huns, Sakas and Gaustanans, Greeks and Turkyis – all the peoples of the heart of the continent whom he had tormented with his swift attacks. They were formed into a single body by the implacable advance of the Chinese, that

* None, apparently, has survived. – R.S.E.

394

advance as slow and as permanent as the building of the great walls that are the monuments of the Han. Seeking refuge from the Chinese, the Kushan came down upon us. United, they conquered Kamardol, which had subdued them individually. Yakir first schemed to divide them in order to fight them one by one. Later he sought to treat with an array he could not resist. However, their overwhelming fear of the Chinese had made the Kushan a force indivisible – as irresistible by human agency as an avalanche roaring down from the high mountains.

Historically, Yakir's reign was but an episode, and historically, I suppose, our ends may appear to have been preordained. But it seems to me, touching upon the question that tormented my son, that each man contrived his own fate. Of Yakir's end I have already written. The High Priest, who was the priest of the Quest, found his martyrdom at the hands of the Kushan. Anand survived to serve the new masters of Kamardol – and to turn them aside from oppressing the people of Kamardol. Recognizing their own administrative inexperience and the people's antipathy, the Kushan sought men of Kamardol to administer the realm for them. Yakir's sons – and even his daughters – they slew, but they invited Anand, who had been Yakir's First Minister of the Right, to serve the people of Kamardol by serving its new rulers. Holding that I was not touched by Yakir's subsequent Kingship, they even invited me to join them, who was Yakir's father and his First Minister of the Left. After much thought I turned back their offer, though I felt some guilt toward the people of Kamardol and much sorrow at rejecting the opportunity to carry on the Official Chronicles at first hand. I concluded sadly that my task was to remain in exile in Sindhia and watch over my grandson Harrap, whom the Kushan thought dead because Tamar had dressed a servant boy in his garments on the day the City fell.

Before that day, before his fate finally felled him, Yakir had, I believe, found what he had sought. He had wanted power, just as Harrap had wanted glory beyond his own imagining and Ranbir had wanted only to serve. Anand and I, more simply, wanted to survive.

All men, it seems to me, seek certain ends, though they may

not themselves know their true desires. Each of us found what he sought, attaining the end he truly desired for himself. As I have already said, men contrive their own fates and the Gods are far away. The Gods may be neither commanded nor implored to fulfill specific human desires, except for the slight effect the invocation of the Gods by men may have upon events by turning the minds of men. Men make their own ends by their deeds – or by their inaction. Some men, of course, find their ends in great enterprises like the Seeking, while others find their ends more simply and more directly.

The tale is told. Were this, my account, a portion of the Official Chronicle, I should now close with the sacred formula that ultimately answers all questions: *Thus it happened by the will of the Gods!* Since I have written a personal note to history, I shall allow myself two further brief observations. Both are personal, and each is part question and part portent. They may perhaps inspire the hypothetical reader of the future to insight beyond the matter of these pages. That reader, who may exist only in my own imagining, has become to me as real as the passionate men and women whose lives and deaths I saw.

Since old men regret the past, it is perhaps not unseemly that I regret my failure of complete understanding with my son. I have never fully comprehended one constant impression I derived from both Yakir's conduct and his narrative: He appears to have felt that I invariably disapproved of his behavior. His judgment was not correct, though I often would have acted otherwise in his place, and I grieved to see him rush eagerly into errors and grave predicaments my counsel would have averted. However, I by no means disapproved of all his deeds, since his ends were his own. Perhaps such tension must always lie between father and son, the father feeling his judgment ignored by his son's resentment, the son feeling himself pressed by his father's disapproval. Yakir's attitude was, in any event, more pleasing to me than either hatred or indifference.

I have also been troubled by another matter, which is not as trivial as the first. The people of Kamardol have, quite naturally, reacted to alien oppression by reverting to the ancient beliefs during the past few years of Kushan hegemony. They worship the Mother Goddess with all the ancient and awful rites, and they also worship the Perfect Stallion and the Great Horse King. Were their rites not celebrated in secret, the number of their sacrifices of men and beasts – and the agonies of their victims – would exceed by far the numbers and the agonies of those given to the Mother Goddess in times long gone when Her cult was the only religion. I myself am chiefly troubled by the violation of the precepts of the True Religion, which has been my constant faith since my birth – even when my son was creating his own religion. It is also disquieting that Yakir, who abhorred the sacrifice of both men and the familiar beasts, should be worshipped in the blood of both.

I have, otherwise, passed beyond fears of the future or regrets for the past.

The young Harrap, whom my wife and I have raised as our own child in Sindhia, often plays outside my door. He delights most in sporting across the green fields astride a white colt of the Stallion's line. The boy's treble shouts are answered by the colt's soft nickering, and together they race through the mists of dawn. They are dim to an old man's eyes, and sometimes a curious fancy afflicts me, overpowering all my reason. It appears to me that both the boy and the colt are those that have gone before now reborn in almost identical form and that the Gods do direct the lives of men and that the Seeking will go forth once again into unknown realms, which are farther and stranger than was the heart of the continent in the time of my son Yakir and the Perfect Stallion.

More About Penguins and Pelicans

Penguinews, which appears every month, contains details of all the new books issued by Penguins as they are published. It is supplemented by our stocklist, which includes almost 5,000 titles.

A specimen copy of *Penguinews* will be sent to you free on request. Please write to Dept EP, Penguin Books Ltd, Harmondsworth, Middlesex, for your copy.

In the U.S.A.: For a complete list of books available from Penguins in the United States write to Dept CS, Penguin Books, 625 Madison Avenue, New York, New York 10022.

In Canada: For a complete list of books available from Penguins in Canada write to Penguin Books Canada Ltd, 2801 John Street, Markham, Ontario L3R 1B4.

In Australia: For a complete list of books published by Penguins in Australia write to the Marketing Department, Penguin Books Australia Ltd, P.O. Box 257, Ringwood, Victoria 3134.